HUNGRY HILL

by

Daphne du Maurier

LONDON
VICTOR GOLLANCZ LTD
1985

First published 1943
This edition 1981
Second impression May 1985

ISBN 0 575 03063 1

Printed in Great Britain by
St Edmundsbury Press, Bury St Edmunds, Suffolk

HUNGRY HILL

CONTENTS

BOOK ONE

COPPER JOHN, 1820–1828

I

O N T H E third of March, 1820, John Brodrick set out from Andriff to
Doonhaven, intending to cover the fifteen miles of his journey before
nightfall. It was typical south-westerly weather, the clouds travelling
low, and the soft, blustering wind bringing scattered showers that fell
heavy for five minutes and then passed, leaving a space of blue no larger
than a man's fist in the sky, with a glimpse of a sun that promised nothing.

The road in those days was rough and uneven, and John Brodrick,
swinging from side to side in the chaise, called to the post-boy to have a
care, unless he wished to break the bones of the pair of them and land in
the ditch for the night, with no supper into the bargain.

There was constant talk of a new road being built, but there the matter
ended, like everything else in the country, and never a penny would
come from the Government for the improvement of the roads. The expense in the long run would fall upon himself and the other landlords.
The trouble was that none of the others had energy enough to put their
hands in their pockets, and if they were prevailed upon to do so would
oblige with so ill a grace, and with such a pother of words about the
hardness of the times, the arrears of rent, and the slackness of their
tenants, that it would save time and temper to leave the matter alone,
and let the road become little better than the bogs around Kileen.

However, the elections were pending soon in Slane, and if Hare wished
to hold his seat, which no doubt he did, John Brodrick would put it to
him pretty forcibly that votes were not given for nothing, and certainly
not for Ministers to sit in London twiddling their thumbs and neglecting
their own country.

How few men of enterprise there were, when all was said and done. It
was not a question of conceit, but he could think of no other man but
himself who would have achieved what had just been done that day in
Andriff, and who would have had the vision in the first place to know
that such an undertaking was possible. Too risky, old Robert Lumley
had said in the beginning, shaking his head and bringing up objection
after objection—how they would never get a return for their money, and
would all be beggared, and be forced to sell their land.

"Risk?" John Brodrick had answered him. "Why, no doubt there is a
risk, just as every day in every man's life he risks breaking his neck when

he steps outside his door. I grant you the expense in sinking the mine will not be trifling, machinery will be necessary, much labour will be required, and I admit freely that the land here is a different proposition from that of Cornwall, where they shovel and wheel out ore as fast as they can put it in a barrow, whereas we shall not be able to break an ounce without gunpowder. But the copper is there, ours for the taking. One of the most experienced directors of mines in Cornwall, a Mr Taylor, has been over the ground with me this past week, and his opinion of the place is the same as my own. There is a fortune awaiting us, on my property, Mr Lumley, and on yours. If you are agreeable to forming a private company under my direction—and mark you, according to the conditions I have just shown you, which my agent has drawn up, you can see well for yourself I shall be risking more than you—then I can promise you that within a few years your royalty will be more than a thousand pounds a year. If you would rather not be a party to the agreement, then there is no more to be said."

And he had risen from his seat, gathered his papers together, and made a signal to his agent that there was nothing further to discuss. He had got half-way across the room before Robert Lumley called him back.

"My dear Brodrick, there is no need to be hasty. There are naturally one or two points that require clarifying before I make my final decision."

And then they had sat down once again, and patiently gone over everything that had been gone into twenty times before, with old Lumley quibbling at his already gross percentage. At last the agreement had been signed, the papers sealed, hands shaken, and some refreshment taken in the old library at Castle Andriff, with John Brodrick impatient to be gone now that his object had been achieved, but forced to stay and exchange a few words with his host for common courtesy's sake.

"I shall hope," he said, "to see you at Clonmere whenever business brings you to Doonhaven. My daughters will be delighted to welcome you, and my sons to give you some sport with your gun," and old Lumley, civil enough now he had won his point about his twenty per cent share in the future mine, replied with an invitation to the young Brodricks to shoot the hares and the pheasants at Duncroom whenever they had the wish.

And so John Brodrick called to the post-boy and climbed into the chaise, just as Lumley's son-in-law, Simon Flower, returned from hunting, his face and his boots bespattered with mud, his arm round the waist of his twelve-year-old daughter.

"Well," he asked, smiling all over his handsome, florid face, "and did you get the old gentleman to put his name to your piece of paper?"

"We have formed a company to work the copper mines at Hungry Hill, if that's what you mean," said John Brodrick drily.

"Did you now, and all in the space of a few hours?" returned the other. "And here have I been working away these fifteen years trying to

get him to put a few slates on the roof of the castle, for I swear to you the
rain blows in on my face as I lie in bed, but he won't allow me enough
to get even the mortar mixed."

"There'll be money to spare in a year or two that will give you a new
roof and an additional wing to your house if you want it," said Brodrick.

Simon Flower raised his eyes to heaven in mock humility.

"It's my conscience that will go against me," he declared, "and I tell
you in solemn truth, my dear Brodrick, that if I think the copper is going
to come out of the mountains by the sweated labour of young men and
of children, why, I won't touch a penny of my father-in-law's money; I
would rather the roof of my house fell in upon me."

John Brodrick looked out at the pair of them from his chaise: the smiling, careless Simon Flower, his contemporary, who had never done a
stroke of honest work in his life and lived contentedly upon his wife's
money; and the pretty, flushed child, with her slanting eyes, laughing in
agreement with her father.

"You had better become a director of the company, Flower, "he said.
"It will mean long hours, you know, supervision of the work at the mines,
keeping the fellows in order, taking ship to Bronsea every six months to
the smelting works, keeping a check on accounts, and a dozen other
things beside."

Simon Flower shook his head, and sighed.

"It's a pity," he said, "that the mines should be started at all. We are
peaceful enough as we are. Why do you want to have us all troubled and
excited, and the people sweating, and the poor old hill broken into with
explosives?"

John Brodrick settled himself in the chaise.

"I believe in progress, and giving employment to all the poor devils
who find living next to impossible in this country, and making money
to provide for my children, and my children's children, when I die,"
he said.

"Ah," said Simon Flower, "they won't thank you for it. All right,
Brodrick, go and start your mines and make your fortune, and I'll sit
back and reap some of the benefit." He smiled, and kissed his daughter
on the top of her head. "Think of all the weary miners digging for our
comfort," he laughed, and lifting his hat, he waved it gaily in farewell.

Typical, thought John Brodrick as he looked out across Mundy Bay—
typical of nearly every man in the country. Irresponsible, indifferent,
their heads full of nothing but dogs and horses; half the year spent on the
Continent chasing the sun, and the rest in yawning on their own doorstep. Despised by their tenants, their land a disgrace, and, to crown all,
more than a trifle drunk at two o'clock in the afternoon.

He dismissed Simon Flower from his mind with little trouble, having a
great contempt for people he did not understand, and, watching the long
Atlantic rollers sweeping into Mundy Bay, he began to think about the

ships that would presently bear the ore from the harbour at Doonhaven, round the coast and across the channel to Bronsea. The shipment
would be the hardest part of the business, for the harbour dried out at low
water, which would compel the vessels to take the ground, and in bad
weather they might be weather-bound for several weeks at a time. He
remembered how, when poor Sarah was alive, they had been held up in
Mundy for more than three weeks, on account of the weather, for the
master would not risk his ship in the south-westerly gale even for a short
distance, and the road was not fit to travel, with Sarah in her condition,
just before Jane was born.

No, the vessels would have to make fast time during the summer
months, for the winter would necessarily be a slack period, and he thought
with satisfaction of the two or three fine ships he had noticed lying alongside the wharfs in Slane a few weeks back (one of them newly launched,
the paint on her barely dry), which might be purchased for a compara-
tively low figure if he went about it at the earliest possible moment, before
the story of the new mining company was spread abroad. Owen Williams,
of Bronsea, would keep his eyes open for likely vessels his side of the
water. It was lucky he had already come to such an excellent agreement
with the firm for the future handling of the ore and its distribution to the
smelting companies. He supposed he would be crossing to Bronsea with
increasing frequency during the years to come, and he decided he would
have to look out for some small property within easy reach of the port,
for to stay in Bronsea itself would be impossible. It would make a change
for the girls, too. Clonmere was lonely and cut off from all amenities—
they were beginning to remark upon it now they were grown up,
especially Eliza. It was a different matter for the boys Clonmere was a
vacation to them after Eton and Oxford, but girls could not hunt hares on
Doon Island or paddle the bogs after snipe.

The chaise was passing the little church of Ardmore, strange, lonely
landmark by the sea, the farthest outpost of the scattered Doonhaven
parish, and now the road rose and twisted to the foot of Hungry Hill.
John Brodrick called to the post-boy to stop.

"Wait for me a moment," he ordered. "I shall not delay you long."

He climbed a short way above the road, until the boy and the chaise
were hidden, and after walking for five minutes or so he came upon the
site of the future mine. He stood for a while looking about him, his hands
behind his back. Curious to think that in a few months there would be
shafts sunk, and chimneys built, and all the grim reality of industry, a
road cut here where there was as yet no path, the lean-to-sheds, the huts
of the miners, the hum and whine of machinery.

Now the scrubby grass blew softly in the wind, and the sun, coming for
an instant from behind a cloud, shone upon the lichened stone so soon to
be blasted by gunpowder, and suddenly a snipe rose from the ground in
front of him, twisting and darting in erratic flight.

John Brodrick looked upward, and above him stretched the great mass of Hungry Hill, wild and untrodden, the summit hidden in mist. He knew the hill in every mood, in every season. In winter, when cold and frost left Doonhaven untouched, there would be a cap of snow on the top of Hungry Hill, and the lake near the summit would have a thin sheet of ice upon the surface. He would see the white face of the hill from the grounds down at Clonmere. Then the gales and rain of February would come, hiding the hill in a curtain of driving mist, until one morning in early spring he would wake to a day of unbelievable brilliance and promise, the air full of that spongy softness, so tender and so beguiling, that belonged only to this country of his birth, and there would be Hungry Hill smiling under the blue sky, the mist dissolved, the gales forgotten, a continual temptation to forget the business of the day and the work of a conscientious landlord, an everlasting reminder that there were snipe to shoot, and hares to hunt, and fish hiding in the waters of the lake, and warm, rough grass where a man could fling his body and lie sleeping under the sun.

Yes, the heat of midsummer too, the silence and the peace, the hawks that hovered in the sky, the butterflies that skimmed the lake, and bathing in the lake as he remembered doing when he was a boy, the water cold and clean.

Now the hidden wealth of Hungry Hill would be revealed at last, her strength harnessed, her treasure given to the world, and her silence disturbed in the name of progress. The forces of Nature, thought John Brodrick, must be made to work for Man, and one day, this country, so poor and so long neglected, will take her rightful place amongst the rich nations of the world. Not in his time, nor in his sons' time, but maybe in little more than a hundred years it would be possible.

Another cloud came across the sun, a spot of rain fell upon his head, and John Brodrick turned his back upon Hungry Hill and went down to the road below.

When he reached the post-chaise, he saw a man standing in the road, waiting for him. He was tall and bent, and leant heavily upon a stick, a man of about sixty years of age, whose light blue eyes made a strange contrast to the mahogany of his face. He smiled when he saw John Brodrick, a smile that had little welcome in it and no pleasure, but appeared to be caused by some secret mirth of his own. John Brodrick nodded to him curtly.

"Good afternoon, Donovan," he said. "You seem to be a long way from home with that bad leg of yours."

"Good-day, Mr Brodrick," returned the other. "As to my leg, he's used to tramping the hills and the roads, and serves me well enough. And how did you find the site for the new mine looking?"

"What do you know of a new mine, Donovan?"

"Maybe the fairies told me about it," answered the man, still smiling, and scratching his white hair with the end of his stick.

"Well, there's no harm in anyone knowing now," said Brodrick. "Yes, there is to be a copper mine on Hungry Hill. I signed an agreement with Mr Lumley of Duncroom this very day, and we intend to start proceedings very shortly."

The man named Donovan said nothing. He stared a moment at John Brodrick, and then turned his blue eyes away from him, upward, to the hill.

"You'll be having no great advantage from it," he said at length.

"That we propose to find out," said Brodrick shortly.

"Ah, I'm not talking about the fortune you'll make," said the other, waving his hand in contempt. "The copper will do that for you, aye, and for your sons and your grandsons too, while me and mine grow poorer on the bit of land left to us. I'm thinking of the trouble it will bring you."

"I think we can take good care of that."

"You should have asked permission of the hill first, Mr Brodrick." The old man pointed with his stick to the great mass of hill that towered above them. "Ah, you can laugh," he said, "you, with your Trinity education and your reading and your grand progressive ways, and your sons and your daughters that walk through Doonhaven as though the place was built for their convenience, but I tell you your mine will be in ruins, and your house destroyed, and your children forgotten and fallen maybe into disgrace, but this hill will be standing still to confound you."

John Brodrick ignored this flow of rhetoric, and climbed into the chaise.

"Perhaps," he said, "Mr Morty Donovan would like to take shares in the copper mine, and then perhaps he would not show his dislike quite so plainly? I shall be paying good wages to the men employed in the mine. If your sons feel like doing some honest work for a change I shall be delighted to employ them."

The old man spat on the ground in contempt.

"My sons have never worked for a master," he said, "and never shall do while I live. Doesn't all the land here belong to them by rights, yes, and the copper too, and couldn't we take it all, if we had the mind?"

"My dear Donovan," said Brodrick impatiently, "you live in the past of two hundred years ago, and talk like an imbecile. If you want the copper why don't you form a company, and engage the labour, and erect the machinery?"

"You know well enough I am a poor man, Mr Brodrick; and whose fault is it but that of your grandfather?"

"I'm afraid I have no time to discuss those ancient quarrels, Donovan, which are better forgotten. Good evening to you." And John Brodrick gave a sign to the post-boy to drive on, leaving the old man leaning upon his stick, staring at them, the smile gone from his face.

John Brodrick looked out over the view below them, as the chaise topped the hill. Yonder, across the bay, lay the little harbour of Doon-haven, with Doon Island at the entrance to the bay, and beyond Doon-haven, at the head of the farther creek, stood his own grey castle of Clonmere, like a sentinel guarding the waters.

The chaise rattled down the hill into the town, and past the harbour, scattering the cattle and the geese in the market-place, nearly running over a dog which came barking at the wheels, and avoiding by a miracle a small, barefooted boy who was chasing a hen into a cottage, and so past the Post Office, and Murphy's shop, and up out of the village beyond the few cottages on the hill at Oakmount, to his own gate-house and the park. The gates were open, at which he frowned, for it was by such carelessness that his cattle had strayed last time to the moors, and were caught and kept by one of Morty Donovan's men, and branded with Morty Donovan's mark into the bargain, to add to the usual unpleasant-ness between the families, and he resolved to speak firmly to the widow Creevy at the gate-house on the first occasion, and to remind her that her position was one of trust, and if she neglected it he had other tenants who might fill it to greater advantage.

Across the park they went and through the second gate, past the belt of trees that his grandfather had planted, past the rhododendron bushes that had been the pride of poor Sarah and were now watched so tenderly by her daughters, and down on to the smooth gravel ride beside the creek and the sunk garden, through the archway of stone, and so back to where the sweep on the ride ended before the grey walls of Clonmere Castle.

2

The Brodricks dined at five, and by the time John Brodrick had washed and changed his travelling clothes, dinner was upon the table, with his family assembled round it, ready to welcome him after his week's absence in Slane and Mundy. His wife Sarah had died some years previously, and his eldest daughter Barbara now filled her mother's place at the end of the table. She came forward to kiss him, her example followed by her two sisters, Eliza and Jane. Henry, John Brodrick's eldest son, had already welcomed his father on his arrival, and now stood by the sideboard sharpening the carving-knife in preparation for his father's attack upon the roast pig. Thomas, the serving-man, stood in attendance by his side. Before carving, John Brodrick said grace, and this formality disposed of, he proceeded to slice the meat on to the plates handed him by Thomas.

"Is it true, father," asked Barbara, "that there has been some horrible plot to assassinate the Cabinet Minister during his tour of the country?"

"I fear it is only too certain that there was some such plot," answered her father, "but luckily it was discovered in time, and no harm done. The whole affair must have been inspired by some of the dregs of the people and whoever was responsible will be brought to justice. There was talk of little else in Slane, needless to say. It will have some effect at the elections."

"And is Mr Hare to stand for the County again?" asked Henry.

"I understand so. Which reminds me, Henry, there is something you can do on the occasion. You can tell all my freeholders to hold themselves ready to vote as I wish them, and if any should absent themselves on the day without valid excuse of ill-health, he will find himself without a roof over his head."

"I can vouch for one or two," laughed Henry, "who will find themselves stricken with fever when the time comes, and the priest by the bedside."

"The Reverend Father will keep himself scarce, and out of trouble, if he has any sense," said John Brodrick, and he took his place at the head of the table.

The empty chair by his side caused him to frown.

"John is late again," he said. "Did he not know I was returning?"

"I believe he went across to the island," said Barbara swiftly. "He wanted to arrange a day's shooting with one of the officers in the garrison. Perhaps he has had some difficulty in bringing the boat back."

"I will not stand unpunctuality from anyone, and certainly not from a nineteen-year-old boy," said her father. "Clonmere is not Andriff Castle, and I have not the careless go-as-you-please temperament of Simon Flower. You can all of you remember that. Kindly teach your brother better manners, Henry. I thought civility the least you would learn at Eton and Oxford."

"I'm sorry, sir," said Henry, exchanging a glance with his sister.

"John has never had any idea of time," complained Brodrick's second daughter Eliza, who thought, by seeming to side with her father, to find some favour. "He was still fast asleep at breakfast this morning—Thomas had to call him twice."

The unfortunate John, entering at this moment, found all eyes upon him in sympathy, excluding Eliza's and his father's, and, hastily making his excuses and flushing scarlet as he did so, he took his seat at the table and added to the misery by spilling the gravy on the cloth.

"Curious," observed his father drily, "how a prolonged stay in this country makes a boor of a fellow, so that he dribbles his very food. Your friends at Brasenose College would hardly recognise you. However, let us talk of other things. Thomas, you may leave us. Master Henry and Master John will wait upon the ladies. No, the fact of the matter is," he said deliberately, looking round at his children, when the servant had left the room, "I have something to tell you all, concerning the future."

He laid his knife and fork upon his plate, smiling at Henry as though in confirmation of some previous conversation, while the rest of his family waited for him to continue.

It was a proud moment for John Brodrick. For months now, ever since the possibility of extracting the copper from Hungry Hill had become a certainty in his mind, he had thought and dreamt of little else. He had set himself the task of breaking down the apathy and mistrust of his neighbouring landlord with determination, for he knew that his capital alone would not cover the initial expenses. Besides which, the actual site of the mine was not entirely his possession. Part of the lands of Hungry Hill belonged to the Duncroom estate of Robert Lumley, and without his consent to form the company the mine could not be started. And at last old Robert Lumley had signed the agreement, and the work could begin. It was not, John Brodrick told himself, as he gazed proudly upon his young family, that he wanted a fortune for himself or for them. The money would come, he knew that, he took it for granted. Henry would live in comfort at Clonmere after him, and Henry's children. He would buy more land, plant more trees, build another wing on to the castle, and buy land the other side of the water too, should he have the mind.

No, it was the principle of the thing with which he had most concern. There was wealth in this country of his, ready for the taking, and only the laziness of his fellow-countrymen prevented them from enjoying it. He looked upon it as a duty, something be owed to his country and to the Almighty, to glean the hidden wealth from Hungry Hill and to give it, at a price, to the peoples of the world. He glanced up at the portrait of his grandfather that hung above the mantelpiece in the dining-room, John Brodrick who had built Clonmere, and had been shot in the back in 1754 on his way to church, because he had tried to put down the smuggling along the coast. He knew his grandfather would have approved the starting of the mine. It would have been a matter of principle, just as it was for his grandson. Well, maybe the people would shoot him in the back as they had done the first John Brodrick, and maim his cattle, and set fire to his crops, but they would never frighten him from doing what he believed to be his duty. Smiling, he looked at each of his family in turn.

"This afternoon at Castle Andriff I signed an agreement with Robert Lumley, forming a company to work a copper mine on Hungry Hill," he said.

The young Brodricks stared back at him in silence, and he thought, with mingled pride and amusement, how like they were to one another, and how each one, from tall Henry down to the little Jane, although possessing features and a personality of their own, had the one characteristic in common, the unmistakable Brodrick quality of knowing themselves to have more brains and breeding than the usual run of their fellow-creatures.

He remembered his father Henry, who had broken his back out hunting at Duncroom, and how, when they would have carried him on a hurdle to a neighbouring cottage, to place him on a bed, he cursed them, saying, "God damn you, let me die in the open, in my own time," and they waited there, five hours under the rain, while he stared up at the sky.

And here was his own boy, Henry, twenty-one next year, with that same look of easy confidence in his dark eyes, as he smiled across the table at his father, the only one with whom he had already discussed the mining prospects, and who had shown his usual gay enthusiasm and willingness to help.

There was Barbara, twenty-three, and the eldest of the family, her soft brown hair falling over her forehead, which was wrinkled a little as she thought over the news, for Barbara needed time to consider when any new project was put before her; she was conservative by nature and mistrusted changes. Eliza, her sister, and a year younger than herself, stouter, fairer, and more like her dead mother in appearance, was already speculating upon what the future should bring for herself. Father would make a fortune, of course, and then perhaps they need not live all the year at Clonmere, but could visit Bath during the season, and even the Continent perhaps, as Lord Mundy's daughters had done a year ago.

The Continent passed through Henry's mind too, as he watched his father's face. He loved Clonmere, he loved his family, and he believed that the sinking of the mine would be a sound proposition, workable in every way, and a benefit to the people and the country. If it meant that he would be able to go to France, to Italy, to Germany, to Russia, to see all the pictures and to hear all the music that he had heard discussed in Oxford, why then, the sooner Hungry Hill was open to pick and shovel and machinery the happier he would be.

His brother John stared out of the window, down to the creek below the house. He and his sister Jane were the darkest of the family. There was something almost Spanish about their olive skins and their warm brown eyes, a southern gypsy quality that the others lacked.

Mines upon Hungry Hill, he thought, noise and machinery to drive away the wild birds and the rabbits and the hares, and a crowd of wretched devils working underground day after day, glad of the employment to keep themselves from starving, and cursing the master who gave it to them, all in the same breath. He knew how it would be. He had seen it happen before in Doonhaven, whenever his father talked to the people about progress. They were all smiles and civility to his face, and as soon as his back was turned they muttered amongst themselves, and went and broke down a fence, or stole a cow, or lamed one of his horses, in a strange, impotent resentment.

Oh, well, father would have his mine, and they would all become millionaires, and that was that. As long as he, John, was not asked to supervise the work at the mine, or take up any position of responsibility, he did not care, and if they would leave the summit of Hungry Hill untouched so that he could exercise his dogs there, and lie on his back in the run, and be left alone without feeling all the time that his father was expecting him to do something, then the new company could sink a hundred mines for all he cared. And Jane, who at eight years old was already the beauty of the family, petted but unspoilt, the darling of them all, with her lively imagination and strange fancies—Jane saw a great stream of copper running down the side of Hungry Hill, the colour of blood, and a crowd of miners dabbling in it like little black devils, with her father seated upon a throne like God in the midst of them.

"When do you propose to start the work, sir?" asked Henry.

"Within the course of the next month," replied his father. "The preliminary excavations may begin even sooner. I have someone coming over from Bronsea to supervise matters and he will bring an engineer with him. We ought to be underground before midsummer, and with luck should have three months' trial of the mine before the autumn sets in. We don't want to lose the top prices, if we have anything to sell. But the return for the first two years is bound to be small, while we are paying off expenses."

"What about the labour, father?" said Barbara.

"I have engaged a Cornishman named Nicholson to be head captain of the mine," he answered, "and he will, of course, bring some of his own people over with him. After that—well, we shall see."

There was a pause for a moment, and then Henry, glancing sideways at his father, said gently, "There will be a certain amount of resentment, sir."

John Brodrick rose from the able, and cut himself another slice of pig from the sideboard.

"Naturally there will be resentment," he said shortly. "There was resentment when the Post Office first came to Doonhaven, there was resentment when the Dispensary was opened. I expect nothing else. But when the people here learn about the wage-packets that the Cornishmen put into their pockets every week, then we shall hear another story. It's been a hard winter, hasn't it? Perhaps they will think about the winter to come. I rather believe they will. And I shall get them coming up to Hungry Hill, asking for employment."

His son John frowned, picking at the table-cloth with his fork.

"Well, John, what is your opinion?"

The boy flushed. He was never very articulate in his father's presence.

"Yes, sir," he said slowly, "they will come to you for employment all right. But they will be bitter about it. They will think 'Why should we be obliged to him to keep us from starving?' It will make a twist in their minds, don't you see? And they will do their best to obstruct the work of the mine, even though it feeds them."

"You appear to sympathise with them," said his father.

"No, sir," stammered John; "it's only that, you see, even now, after all this time, we are looked upon as interlopers; there is no denying it."

"That is ridiculous," answered his father impatiently; "we belong to the country as much as they do. Why, your great-grandfather lived here, and your great-uncle before him. There have been Brodricks in the country back into the sixteenth century."

"Why did they shoot my great-grandfather, then?" asked John.

"You know very well why they shot him—because he believed in doing his duty to God and the King, and upholding the law. Smuggling was an offence, and he was determined to put an end to it."

"No, sir," said John; "that was just the excuse given. The Donovans shot my great-grandfather because the land here was theirs, before it was his, because the old Donovan chiefs possessed Clonmere, and Doonhaven, and Doon Island when the Brodricks were copying-house clerks in Slane, and they could not forget it. And they haven't forgotten it, even to this day. That's why Morty Donovan lets his tenants steal your cattle, and that's why your Cornish miners will stay one season on Hungry Hill, and no longer."

There was a silence, John Brodrick did not answer. He stared thoughtfully at his second son, while the rest of the family, astonished at their brother's outburst, sat in trepidation, scarlet and ill at ease.

"Very good, John," he said at length. "Eton and Brasenose have done more for you than I thought. A few years in London, at Lincoln's Inn, and they will make quite a speaker of you. And now, Barbara dear, if you have finished, I suggest we leave the room for Thomas to clear, and perhaps you will pour out tea in the drawing-room."

"Yes, father," said Barbara, and glancing reproachfully at John for the disturbance he had caused, she led the way upstairs to the drawing-room, where the serving-man had already placed the tea-tray in readiness.

"Silly fellow," said Henry, patting his brother on the shoulder, for their father had not yet come upstairs; "what induced you to speak so, at such a time? You know the irritation it causes my father just to mention the Donovans. And to damp his ardour, too, about the mine."

"John dear, it was thoughtless," said Barbara, "especially when you were late for dinner too. Now you will be in his bad books for a week at least."

"Oh, confound everything," said John wearily, throwing himself into a chair. "Why do I never do anything right? And why does everyone, myself included, always dislike hearing the truth? You don't think I like the Donovans, do you? Old Morty Donovan's a scoundrel, I know that."

He held out his arms to Jane, who came and sat on his knee, her arms round his neck.

"What shall we do, sweetheart? Shall we run away together, and build a little cabin on Doon Island?"

"It would be horrid in the winter," said Jane, laughing, and playing with his collar; "you would soon become ill-humoured, and vent it upon your Jane. Henry would endure discomfort better than you."

"Henry endures everything better than I do," sighed John, "don't you, old fellow? You attend all the lectures at Oxford with the greatest equanimity, and are on breakfasting terms with half the dons. He has a visiting list of acquaintances, too, nearly a yard long. The only fellows who visit me in my rooms are tradesmen, or sporting chaps wanting to sell me a dog."

"Do you suppose," broke in Eliza, "that once the copper mine starts paying we shall all be very rich?"

"So rich, Eliza," said Henry, winking at John, "that all the impoverished Earls of the country will come from miles around to court you. You had better start planning your wardrobe soon. Poor Mrs Murphy will have to get in a good stock of needles and thread and material."

"Mrs Murphy," scoffed Eliza; "thank you very much. I shall purchase my dresses in Bath or Cheltenham, I shall never go to Mrs Murphy again."

"That would be rather unkind," said Barbara. "We could always allow her to make some of our things. She tries so hard to do her best, poor woman. You could keep your Bath finery a secret from her."

"Barbara, the peace-maker," said John, "who pleases everybody and vexes none; where should we be without you? Jane, stop playing with my collar, you little plague. Isn't it your bed-time? Do you want me to carry you to bed, or will you wait for Martha to fetch you?"

"I haven't said goodnight to father," said Jane.

"Then you shall say goodnight, and afterwards I will take you to your bed," said her brother.

The child ran downstairs, and, listening at the library door, heard voices coming from within. She saw the wide-brimmed hat on the settle, and she made a face up at John, who was watching her from the stairs.

"It's Ned Brodrick with father," she whispered.

"Never mind, go and kiss him goodnight," said John.

Jane's small shoulders shook with laughter, and then, drawing herself up and composing her face to suitable gravity, she knocked at the library door. Her father was standing before the fireplace, confronting his visitor, whose features, though leaner and more cadaverous, bore a striking resemblance to his own. Ned Brodrick was, in point of fact, his natural brother, and John Brodrick, with a curious sense of family duty, had made him his agent now for a number of years. The mother, an extremely respectable woman who had been dairy-maid at Clonmere when she had caught the roving eye of John Brodrick's father, lived on a small pension in one of the cottages at Oakmount, and Ned dwelt with her. The ten pounds annuity left to him by his father when he died in 1800 was given to him with the pious hope, expressed in old Henry Brodrick's own words, that "the sum would keep him out of the mischief that had brought him into the world". The hope had not been fulfilled, however, for Ned Brodrick, disregarding his father's wishes, had become the parent of no less than four illegitimate children, all by different mothers. He was glad, therefore, to supplement his annuity by what he could earn as agent to his brother, and he was careful never to presume upon his relationship in any way, so that John Brodrick was always "Mr Brodrick", and his nieces "the young ladies". He was, as it happened, as good an agent as John Brodrick could hope to find, and if he made a little extra for his own pocket now and again by falsifying the rent-roll of the tenants, it was no more and no less than any other man would have done in his place.

"Good evening, Miss Jane," he said now, with his customary bow and his usual look of solemnity, so far removed from mischief that it seemed hardly possible he could have ignored Henry's Brodrick's will.

"Good evening, Ned," replied the child, turning swiftly from him and lifting her face to her father.

John Brodrick picked Jane up and kissed her on both cheeks, his hard, rather ruthless expression softening as he did so. This little daughter was very dear to him, dearer almost than Henry, if it were possible, and he looked forward to the time when she should become a companion to him and not merely an enchanting plaything.

"Goodnight," he said gently, "sleep well," and watching her for an instant while she opened the door, he then dismissed her from his mind and turned back again to his brother.

Jane climbed the stairs in search of John, but of course—it was typical of him—he had forgotten his promise, and she had to wander along the passage to his room in the tower, at the end of the house. Jane found him with the window flung open, looking out towards the creek, shining silver under the moon, with the dark hump of Doon Island away in the distance. She knelt on the window-seat beside her brother, and they were silent for a moment.

"John," she said presently, "what will they do to Hungry Hill? Will they spoil it, so that we can never go there again for picnics?"

"They will spoil the part where the mine is to be," said John; "there'll be chimneys, and shafts, and engines. You've seen pictures of mines, haven't you? But they won't touch the wild part at the top, and they won't spoil the lake. We can still go there and enjoy ourselves."

"If I were Hungry Hill I should be angry," said the child. "I should want to slay the human beings who dared interfere with me. You know how the hill looks in winter, John, when the clouds are upon it, and the rain drives down. Like a giant, frowning. If I were my father I would not have sunk my mine there, I would have found another place."

"Yes, but other places don't have the copper, sweetheart."

"Then I would go without the copper."

"Don't you want to be rich, and marry an Earl, like Eliza?"

"Not in the least. I am like Barbara, I only want all of us to be happy."

"I should be happy if I didn't owe money to half the tradesmen in Oxford," sighed John.

"Are you very much in debt? It's a bad thing, I have heard my father say, to owe money, especially to people in a lower station than oneself."

"It isn't bad. It's merely irritating. Don't let's talk about it any more. I'll carry you to bed," said John, who always changed the conversation when he drew near to matters affecting his conscience, and taking the little girl in his arms, he carried her to the room she still shared with the old nurse Martha.

Martha was at supper, and Jane undressed solemnly before her brother, folding up her clothes as she had been taught to do, and she knelt at his knee and said her prayers with a devout intensity and a lack of embarrassment that wrung his heart. When he had kissed her and tucked her up, he went down the corridor to the drawing-room, but paused outside the door without entering. Somehow Eliza's chatter and Henry's good-natured teasing would have jarred upon him this evening, and turning round he went down by the back staircase, and so out of the side-door to the stables across the yard, where his bitch Nellie lay, with her litter of puppies.

Tim the stable-lad was awaiting him with a lantern, and together the two boys knelt in the straw, their shoulders touching, while John held the weakling of the family in his strong but gentle hands.

"Poor pup!" he said. "We'll never make anything of him, with this squashed foot of his."

"Better drown him, Master John," suggested Tim.

"No, Tim, we won't do that. He's healthy enough, it's only that he'll not be winning any prizes for me, but that's no reason why I should take his life. All right, Nellie, I wouldn't hurt your babies."

John always forgot his problems when he was with his dogs. Their devotion and their dependence brought out the best in him, and he would willingly have passed half the night in the stable but for the fact that Tim must have his supper and go to bed.

"Is it true, Master John, what they're saying in Doonhaven?" asked the lad, as he bolted the stable-door and put the empty pail down by the pump.

"What are they saying now, Tim?"

"Why, that Mr Brodrick is going to blast away the whole of Hungry Hill with dynamite that's coming over in a ship from Bronsea, and we are all going to be turned out of our homes to make room for the Cornish miners he'll be bringing."

"No, Tim, that's a fairy-tale, and you're a rogue to repeat it. My father is going to sink a mine in Hungry Hill, true enough, he and Mr. Lumley, but you won't have to move for the miners. The work will give employment in Doonhaven, and bring money to the people who are out of work and have no land."

The lad looked at him doubtfully, and shook his head.

"They say in Doonhaven it doesn't do to interfere with Nature," he said. "If the Saints wished for the copper to be used, why then it would be running down the side of the hill in a stream, where we could find it."

"Who told you that, Tim? Was it Morty Donovan?"

"That is what they say in Doonhaven," said the boy, refusing to be drawn, and he wished his young master goodnight, and took himself off to the kitchen.

John shrugged his shoulders, and thrusting his hands into his pockets he walked round the house, and down the steep grass bank to the drive and the creek beyond.

The moon shone upon the inlet below the castle, and a broad path of silver led to the wide stretch of water around Doon Island, whose dark outline hid Mundy Bay and the open sea.

Away beyond Doonhaven, some seven miles distant from Clonmere, rose the black mass of Hungry Hill, remote and forbidding in the moonlight.

Back in the library John Brodrick spoke impatiently to his agent.

"I myself gave permission to the officers of the garrison to shoot as many snipe and woodcock as they pleased on the island," he said, "as long as they did not destroy a hare or a partridge, and they took it upon themselves to look after the preservation of the game as far as they could. I cannot believe that the officers, most of whom are gentlemen, would have forfeited the pledge. And yet you say they have half the hares destroyed?"

"It's what Baird himself was telling me, Mr Brodrick," said the agent, "that it was one or two of the younger officers he saw out shooting, and Morty Donovan was with them."

"Morty Donovan? Always when I have any annoyance or trouble it is Morty Donovan who is responsible. You can call upon him from me, Ned, and you can tell him that if I hear of my game being destroyed on Doon Island without my express permission, then the persons concerned will be punished with the utmost severity, and have to answer for it at the Mundy Assizes."

"I will, Mr Brodrick. The man should be ashamed; it's what I've said often enough in Doonhaven."

"Morty Donovan doesn't know the meaning of the word, nor do any of his family. So you think they will make trouble when we start work on the mine?"

"I don't say they will make trouble, Mr Broderick, but for myself, I would not care to be one of the Cornish miners you are importing. It may be that they would do better for themselves if they stopped at home."

"You are as bad as the rest of them, Ned. I believe when my back is turned you go and gossip in the cottages like any old woman; yes, and tell your beads too into the bargain."

"It's God's truth, Mr Brodrick, I never consort with the people at all,

except to gather in your rents, which is a sorry business at the best of
times; and as for telling my beads, haven't I handed round the plate at
the Established Church Sunday after Sunday for as many years as you
have sat in the place yourself?"

"That's all right, Ned. I'm not complaining. You've always done your
duty by me, and I won't forget it. But what irritates me beyond measure
is that an ignorant, half-educated fellow like Morty Donovan can so play
upon the superstitions of the people in Doonhaven as to lead them to
believe that what I am doing for the district is some sort of devil's work
or witchcraft, whereas if they had the sense to understand it I am going
to put the bread-and-butter into their mouths for nothing."

"There's no gratitude in the country, Mr Brodrick, that's the fault."

"Gratitude, is it? I don't ask for gratitude, damn it. I only ask for
common sense. Well, that's enough of the matter. You had better walk
home, Ned, while the moon is up. There's nothing further I want to
discuss this evening. Don't forget to tell that woman at the gate-house
to keep the gates closed. I'm tired of seeing my cattle on the moors with
Morty Donovan's mark branded on their backs."

And so alone at last, and the estate book put away, and his papers
neatly filed, and all business done for the day.

Presently he would go upstairs and chat with the girls for an hour or
so, ask them their opinion about a small property across the water to
make a change from Clonmere, from which they could pay visits to
Bath now and again during the season, and when the girls had gone to
bed he would stir the fire with his foot and tell Henry about the mining
methods in Cornwall, the suggestions of the fellow from Bronsea, and
how old Lumley had stuck out for his twenty per cent royalty, and what
a pity it was that Simon Flower was such a good-for-nothing.

But first he would take a turn in the grounds, have a breath of fresh air
from the sea to clear his head. He walked down the bank, as John had
done, and presently, as he looked out across the creek to Doon Island,
he became aware of the figure of his second son, standing aloof and
strangely lonely, in apparent aimless meditation.

"Not with the others, John?" he said abruptly.

The boy started. He had been unaware of his father's approach.

"No, sir."

There was a silence, neither knowing what to say to the other, and both
remembering the incident at dinner. Then the boy, impulsive, stammered
an apology.

"I'm sorry, sir, that I spoke as I did this evening."

"That's all right, John. I had forgotten it."

The father wondered whether he should tell the boy that he understood well enough what he had been trying to express. He was forty-
eight, his son was just nineteen. He knew that the first John Brodrick
had been shot in the back for the same reason given by his son, he knew

too that the Donovans of the present day had not forgotten it. These things he found convenient to forget. It did not do to have long memories in this country. That was the great fault of the people, they remembered too much. He believed in justice, in fair dealing, in scrupulous honesty with those less fortunate than himself, but it was dangerous to go farther than this. Once a man became sympathetic in this country he became soft, he became idle, he allowed his mind to dwell on supposed injuries, on long-dead feuds, on a past that was buried and gone. If John was not handled properly, was not made to understand discipline and service and respect for his elders and betters, he would turn into another useless idler like Simon Flower.

So John Brodrick said no more. He stood by the side of the creek looking out towards his future mine, and his son stood by his side, nervous, irresolute, watching the moonlight shimmer upon the blank, dark face of Hungry Hill.

3

When John Brodrick told Robert Lumley that his royalty in the mine, after a few years, would be near a thousand pounds, he did so in no spirit of foolish optimism, but in firm belief in the accuracy of his statement. Actually the sum paid into the old man's account in the Slane bank at the close of the fourth year exceeded fifteen hundred pounds, all initial expenses having been paid off in the second year.

The price of copper had never been so high, and by purchasing three vessels that were wholly employed in shipping the ore from Doonhaven to Bronsea, John Brodrick managed to keep freights low. Robert Lumley, when he saw how matters were progressing, forgot his former caution and would have had his partner employ double the men he did, so that every ounce of ore might be extracted, but this John Brodrick refused to do.

"We might," he said, "employ more miners, and merely pick out the best of the copper as fast as we want, but my object is that nothing should be lost to our families, or left behind in such a situation that we never could get at it afterwards. If Captain Nicholson goes down too deep we defeat our own object. The force of water is too great to be dealt with, and in a short time whatever ore is there would be lost beyond recovery."

Old Robert Lumley would drive down to Doonhaven once in every six months to inspect the mine, and each time he would find fault with some part of it or other, understanding nothing of the work himself, until John Brodrick, who made a practice of riding over every day, and knew the mine as well as the miners themselves, would lose his patience and his temper.

"You complain that the mine is not properly conducted?" he said. "Perhaps you would like to read this letter from the foremost expert in the country, who visited us last month?"

And the old man would peer at the letter of praise through his spectacles, and lay it aside again, and say that anyway, properly conducted or not, the miners were too well paid, and Captain Nicholson in particular.

"In Cornwall," John Brodrick told him, "they have a custom long established by which the proprietors make a payment to their Captains every year in proportion to the produce, in addition to the fixed salary. I propose to do the same with Captain Nicholson."

"But that will mean another deduction from our profit, Brodrick?"

"It will indeed, but I consider the deduction necessary. Captain Nicholson has worked this mine from the start, in conditions that at times have been extremely unpleasant for him and his men, owing to the opposition of people in the neighbourhood, and he has never once suggested returning to Cornwall."

And so Robert Lumley would argue and protest and finally be won over, and drive away again in his carriage, leaving the Director in high ill-humour, wishing he could buy the old man out of the Company and be rid of him for ever.

The mine was a success, and the profits were high, but there had been many difficulties to overcome, and they were not all over yet. For one thing, the people in Doonhaven had proved even more obstructive than he had anticipated. He had not expected them to welcome the Cornishmen, he had been prepared for a certain amount of animosity, and had provided, as he thought, against it. For instance, he had huts erected, at his own expense, close to the mine on Hungry Hill, and fitted them up with the necessary furniture, bedding, and cooking apparatus Some of the men were married, and brought their wives and children.

It was when they went down into Doonhaven to buy provisions that the trouble started. Murphy's shop would quite unaccountably appear to be bare, without so much as a candle or a bar of soap on the premises, and Murphy himself, with smiles and apologies, declare to the disappointed Cornish housewives that never a candle had he seen for three months, and as for soap, why his own wife had been scouring the beach that morning for a bucket of sand to wash down the floor of the shop. It was the same if they wished to buy eggs, or butter, or even milk from the farms. The chickens would not have laid since Easter, they would have a disease amongst them, and as for the milk, why the sun had turned it sour and it had all been thrown away, not even the pigs would touch the stuff. In fact the unfortunate miners and their families would have starved had not John Brodrick sent one of the ships express to Slane for provisions, and this perforce became a custom, so that the only means of feeding the workers at the mine was by getting provisions once a week from Mundy, for they could get nothing at all in Doonhaven. It spoke highly indeed for Captain Nicholson that he was able to prevent his men returning home.

They became, with the aid of the provision ship, self-supporting, and

by planting vegetables and keeping a few chickens, managed to live in
not too uncomfortable a fashion. But even so the potato plants would be
lifted in the night for no reason, the cabbages would disappear, and
the chickens wander, and if questions were asked in Doonhaven or the
neighbouring cottages, the answer would be a shaking of the head and a
raising of eyes to heaven. John Brodrick would be obliged to send over
sacks of potatoes from his own fields, and cabbage plants, and a brood of
young chickens to make up for the loss sustained by the miners. In winter
there would be losses of firewood, and no turf to be had, and the miners
be forced to go and cut timber or gather the driftwood below Clonmere,
on John Brodrick's estate, to keep themselves and their families warm.
Ned Brodrick went round among the people, and by a deft mixture of
threat and persuasion would inveigle some half-dozen of the younger
men to try their hands at the mine, and at last, at the beginning of the
second year, they began to wander up, in twos and threes, to ask for
employment at Hungry Hill, but even so, the animosity against the mine
remained.

No, it had not been easy, thought John Brodrick, and indeed it was a
relief sometimes to get away from Clonmere and across the water to
Bronsea, and so up to the cheerful, homely farmhouse of Lletharogg that
he had bought for his daughters, where they would spend two or three
months of the winter now, every year. Henry's dream had been realised,
and he had visited Paris, Brussels, and Vienna, while John was still
reading for the Bar in Lincoln's Inn.

It was during the autumn of 1825, when the family had been settled
in Lletharrog since August, that John Brodrick had a letter from an
anonymous correspondent in Doonhaven The writing was smudged and
practically illegible, but the message ran: "You'd do well to come home
if you wish to stop trouble." The letter was addressed to the shipping-
office in Bronsea, and he put it in his pocket and forgot all about it. A
week later, when one of his ships, the "Henrietta", docked at Bronsea
with her shipment of copper, John Brodrick remembered the letter, and
as a matter of curiosity showed the message to the master of the vessel.
The man looked thoughtful, and did not speak for a moment or two.

"You have not heard from Captain Nicholson, then, Mr Brodrick?"
he said at last.

"No, not since the first of the month, when he writes as a matter of
course. Why? Is anything wrong?"

"Maybe he did not wish to cause you anxiety. There's little to go
upon anyway. No, sir, I'm wondering whether the letter you have there
refers to the losses they have had lately at the mine."

"Losses? What losses?"

"I cannot tell you a great deal about it, sir, having only been in Doonhaven for this shipment, and we were loaded and away in four days.
But there's stuff being taken into Slane and Mundy and other places

along the coast, that doesn't find its way into your vessels, and is not handled by Captain Nicholson or by us."

"How do you know this?"

"Two or three of Captain Nicholson's own men were speaking of it, sir. The ore is taken up from the mine right enough, but it's when it is above ground that the mischief starts. I understand that Captain Nicholson is to order some system of watching by night, for it is then that the stuff must be taken away, but whether he has done so or not I cannot say."

"Is the matter discussed at all in Doonhaven?"

"Not directly, sir. But I had the feeling that the people knew about it all the same."

John Brodrick thanked the master of the "Henrietta", and, ordering his carriage, drove back to Lletharrog, resolved to write to Nicholson that evening and demand an immediate explanation. The letter was never posted, for the very next day there arrived a letter from the mining captain himself, written in great haste and obviously in a state of extreme agitation.

"A system of plunder is in progress," he wrote, "that, if it continues, will eventually put a stop to our work. Little by little I have noticed losses of material that was stacked above ground, ready for shipment, but two days ago a large consignment disappeared, over which I had stationed a watch, for I had my suspicions that the theft took place after dark. The man in charge—one of my own people, a Cornishman named Collins—was found in the small hours of the morning with a broken head, and is not likely to recover. It seems he was struck from behind, and saw nothing of his assailant. This attack has so intimidated the rest of his fellows that I am having difficulty in getting men to undertake sentry duty at all, and some of them are even talking of packing their things and returning to Cornwall with their families."

John Brodrick read the letter aloud to his daughters and announced his intention of travelling home to Clonmere immediately.

"I shall send word to London to Henry and John to join me," he said, "if they can see their way to do so. I have little doubt who is at the bottom of the trouble."

"You mean Morty Donovan?" said Barbara, after a moment's hesitation.

"He may not take part in the actual plunder, in fact I think he is too shrewd a man to do so," replied her father, "but if he is not the brains behind it I shall be extremely astonished."

"Who do you suppose wrote the anonymous letter?" asked Eliza.

"I neither know nor care," said John Brodrick. "Possibly one of my tenants who is too scared of Morty Donovan to declare himself. At any rate, the writer of the letter does not matter. What matters is that the men responsible should be tracked and punished, and this I am determined to do, if I risk my own head being broken in consequence."

His daughters looked at each other in distress.

"I implore you," said Barbara, "not to do anything rash. Could you not get assistance from the garrison on the Island?"

"Dear child," returned her father, "if I cannot quell one or two of my own country-people who have fallen into mischief without engaging the military to take up the matter for me, I should never be able to hold up my head in Doonhaven again. Your great-grandfather did not ask for help when he put down the smuggling seventy-five years ago."

"No," said Jane, "but he got shot in the back for doing it."

John Brodrick looked at his youngest daughter with severity.

"I suppose your brother John has been talking to you," he said.

Jane shook her head, her eyes filling with tears, and suddenly she got up from her chair at the breakfast-table and ran round to her father, putting her arms about him.

"If you go home," she said, "please let me come with you. I'm not afraid of the Donovans or anybody, and you will need someone to look after you and see that the house is in order. I'm not a child any longer, I'm nearly fourteen."

John Brodrick smiled at her, and patted her cheek.

"D'you think Copper John cannot take care of himself?" he said. "Don't look embarassed, Eliza, at your end of the table. I know very well what I am called in Doonhaven. So, Jane child, you would look after me, and see that those lazy servants have the water heated, and the dinner served on clean plates, and the linen on my bed not wringing wet? Well, you must ask Barbara her opinion; it is not within my province. But whatever is decided, I leave here tomorrow for Bronsea in order to embark in the ship that sails for Slane in the evening."

A letter was dispatched to London informing Henry and John of their father's return to Doonhaven, and asking them to join him at Clonmere if they could conveniently do so, and the following day John Brodrick and Jane, accompanied by old Martha, embarked on board the steam-packet that plied regularly between Bronsea and Slane. John Brodrick took the opportunity while in Slane, where they were obliged to put up for the night, to see if he could glean any information there about the illegal sale of copper, and if it was known who had the handling of it.

The manager of the shipping office was interested and sympathetic, but hardly helpful. He admitted that he had heard of an underground market in the county and that there were always unscrupulous agents who were prepared to handle the stuff and have it shipped across the water to the smelting companies, but who the agents were, and what shipping firms were concerned, he was not prepared to say.

John Brodrick left the shipping office in a spirit of grim determination. Matters were even worse than he had expected. He had been away exactly three months, and in that space of time a system of plunder had developed that bade fair to put an end to the mining business altogether.

He blamed Captain Nicholson for not having made him aware sooner of what was going on, and Ned Brodrick too.

The latter was awaiting them in Mundy, and on seeing the expression on his employer's face, at once sought to justify himself for not having written.

"I would have taken ship and come over to you at Bronsea," he persisted, "but that Captain Nicholson was so persistent that he could deal with the matter himself. And to tell you the truth, sir, I have been so hard put to it with the business of the estate that I felt I must leave the concerns of the mine to him."

John Brodrick said nothing. He guessed that the truth of the matter was that his brother had passed the three months of his employer's absence in idleness, sitting about in his mother's cottage at Oakmount with his feet in the fireplace, and when the weather was fine enough shooting the woodcock on Doon Island, or courting one of the numerous widows in the neighbourhood, who apparently found his lean form and cadaverous appearance not wanting in attraction.

The carriage covered the distance from Mundy to Doonhaven in half the time it had taken a few years back, for the new road had been completed at last, chiefly owing to John Brodrick's influence with the member of Parliament.

"The only injury it can receive," he observed to Jane, who was leaning from the window of the carriage, "is from the banks that support the road giving way, but I see no prospect of that ever happening. I wonder if Simon Flower has won his bet, and has travelled the distance in two hours, as he boasted he would. Here we are at the mine. You had better drive on to Clonmere with Martha, Jane, and send the carriage back for Ned and myself."

A thin rain was falling now, and the summit of Hungry Hill was hidden in mist. A broad track led from the road to the mine, the surface deeply rutted by the trucks that passed to and from the mine down to the harbour at Doonhaven, and beside this track were built the miners' dwellings, the long row of wooden huts, and finally the sheds and tall chimney of the mine itself. The men who were not below ground, but were employed on the surface, touched their hats when they saw the Director approach, and looked at him with a certain amount of curiosity, there having been no rumour of his return. It was soon known throughout the mine that "Copper John" was home, and the general feeling was one of relief, mingled with apprehension, for stern measures would certainly be taken to deal with the theft of material, and the innocent might suffer with the guilty.

Captain Nicholson received the Director in the counting-house, where they could talk without fear of being overheard. His honest face, usually so full of confidence, was lined with anxiety, and it was plain that he had not slept properly for days. He confirmed that the copper was being smuggled out of the mine and taken into the next county, also to Mundy and to Slane, and there disposed of, but the fellows who were doing it were too cunning to be caught.

"I am convinced," he declared, "that the men I brought with me have no part in the business, and that it is certain of the local men, Mr. Brodrick, who are to blame. Those of the local men who are not responsible shield their companions, from a misguided sense of loyalty and from fear of reprisals."

"Do you search the men when they come off duty?"

"I do, Mr Brodrick. Every man goes to the washing-room when he comes up from below, and is searched, my own people the same as the others. We can find nothing upon a single one of them. And yet the stuff must disappear from the dressing-sheds, before being loaded into the trolleys. No other way would be possible."

"I should like to go down into the mine, Nicholson."

"You shall do so, sir; I will accompany you myself."

The two men donned overalls, and the specially shaped hats, with a lighted candle in front, worn by the miners, and descended the long ladder that led to the various levels below ground, some so narrow that they were only wide enough for each man to go single-file. Copper John inspected every gallery, and spoke to each man he saw.

During the time he spent underground he left no corner of the mine unvisited, he even helped to lay the charge of gunpowder against one portion of the rock that required blasting, and waited for the subsequent explosion and the clearing of the rubble, and when he and Nicholson climbed at last to the surface it was already late in the afternoon. Copper John showed no sign of fatigue, however, and proceeded at once to inspect the dressing and sorting sheds, and even the row of trolleys drawn up in line by the side of the track, until the gathering darkness made further exploration out of the question.

"Well, Nicholson," he admitted, "we have had little success so far, but I am in no way dispirited, and I think you may be certain that before long I shall get to the bottom of this business. Continue as you are doing, and search every man as he comes up from work, also set a watch by night, paying the men who do so double wages. I shall be over here again in the morning."

On the following afternoon Copper John set out from Clonmere westward to the Kileen moors, in company with his agent and brother, Ned Brodrick.

The air was soft and warm for the lateness of the season, and the snipe twisted and dived above Kileen bog, flushed by Ned Brodrick's water spaniel, which ran ahead of his master, his keen nose to the ground. Doonhaven lay beneath them and behind them, hidden by the woods of Clonmere, with the tip of Hungry Hill in the far distance pointing to the sky. The brothers ignored the road that would have taken them westward across country to the Denmare river, and, turning right, struck a path that ran closely beside the bog for about a mile or so, until it was ended abruptly by a fence that enclosed some farm-buildings, while a rough drive wound up the short, steep hill to the house at the top.

It was a drear, desolate spot, with the piece of garden round about bare and uncultivated, and the house itself of a dirty brown stone, with large, staring windows, for the most part curtainless, and as they walked up the strip of garden a mongrel dog, half-greyhound, half-terrier, came snarling from an outhouse, his tail between his legs.

A woman appeared at the door of the house on hearing the disturbance, and, seeing the strangers, made at first to shut the door, then, apparently thinking better of it, opened it wide, and curtseyed.

She must have been good-looking in her youth, and even now there was something fine about her features and her dark eyes, while she held herself with dignity.

"It's not often we have your company, Mr Brodrick," she said. "I'm afraid you must have found it rough walking out to this poor place, with the road the state it is in. Did you wish to see my husband?"

"I do, Mrs Donovan," replied the other. "Is he within?"

"He is, and has not been outside for these last three weeks or more, so troubled he has been with that leg of his, that gives him no peace, day or night. You will find him in the parlour, where he has his bed now, since his illness. Don't trouble to wipe the mud from your shoes, Mr. Brodrick, it can do no damage to my poor carpet that is falling to bits for want of repair."

The note of self-pity was not lost on John Brodrick. Apologising for the darkness of the passage, the woman opened the door of the parlour.

"Here is Mr Brodrick and the agent to see you," she announced, "the gentlemen having walked all the way from Clonmere."

The room was cold, and full of smoke from the turf fire that gave little heat, and lying upon the trestle bed beneath the window was Morty Donovan, propped up by many pillows that were none too clean. His mahogany face was paler, and he had aged considerably since John Brodrick had seen him last. He lifted his head at their entrance, and turned his light blue eyes upon them with a blank expression.

"Sit down, gentlemen," he said, "if you can find a chair that will bear you without breaking. I cannot stand up myself, as you can see, this leg of mine having betrayed me at last. Bring some claret for Mr Brodrick, woman, and three glasses, instead of gaping there. We may be poor, but at least don't let ourselves be wanting in hospitality to the gentry when they call upon us, and I have claret yet in my cellar that would bear comparison with any you may have in Clonmere, Mr. Brodrick."

The agent looked hopefully at the woman. A glass of claret would have been more than welcome to him at the moment, but his employer waved his hand in dissent.

"I did not come to your house to drink your health or my own, Donovan," he said, "nor to pass the time of day as neighbours. I have come to tell you that I am perfectly acquainted with the mischief you are causing on Hungry Hill, and that I intend to put a stop to it. It is for that purpose alone that I have returned to this country. If you do not command the men under you to desist in their system of plunder, I shall have every man at the mine arrested and taken into custody."

A slow smile crept on the face of Morty Donovan.

"And see them all acquitted at the Mundy Assizes," he said. "I have no notion what you are talking about, Mr Brodrick; I have not been near Hungry Hill these many months. As to plunder, I should ask your Cornish workers what they do with the stuff, and Captain Nicholson, who has money enough to buy his wife an embroidered shawl, so they tell me, to parade the street in Doonhaven like a peahen."

"The Cornishmen are innocent, you know that well enough," replied John Brodrick, "and the men of Doonhaven would have worked honestly, and been glad too for the employment, but for the way you have gone behind my back and spread your poison."

"Poison, is it?" cried the old man, pretending to lose his temper. "Is it poison to call down the mercy of the Saints to forgive you for the distress you have caused in Doonhaven with this same mine, where you have the men and the young boys, scarcely more than children, working and sweating to make your fortune? I call on the walls of this house to witness that no word of mine has gone forth to cause you annoyance; rather my speech has been filled with pity for you."

Copper John heard him out without interruption, unmoved by the flow of eloquence.

"You can talk yourself hoarse, Donovan," he said, "you are perfectly aware that none of it will make any impression upon me. Whatever methods you employ to carry away the ore in secret to Mundy, and to Slane, and into the next county, depend upon it I shall discover them, and you and the culprits concerned will be severely dealt with. I suppose you do not wish to end your days in prison, but that you will do, if you persist in robbing me and the members of my company."

Morty Donovan made no answer. His blue eyes had lost their fire, and he leant back in his bed as though weary of the discussion.

"And if the men of Doonhaven do sell your copper unbeknown to you," he said, "it's yourself who is the cause of it, Mr. Brodrick, for starting the mine in the beginning, and putting the poor creatures in the way of temptation."

This last was more than Copper John's patience could stand.

He rose to his feet and curtly bade Morty Donovan good-day.

"Remember," he said, "I came here to warn you, and your sons too if they are acting for you. And I will thank you to leave my tenants alone, and keep your cattle where they belong."

So saying he brushed past Donovan's wife, who stood in the open doorway, and followed by his agent went out of the house into the yard.

"I was a fool to waste my time coming out here," said Copper John,
"but at least I have given him warning, and he knows now what to
expect."

At this moment the cur belonging to the farm fell upon Ned Brodrick's
spaniel, and the two tumbled over one another, snarling and snapping,
and would not let go for all the agent did to separate them. Mrs Donovan called shrilly from the house, and a man appeared from the outhouse across the yard and pulled the mongrel away, cuffing and kicking
it, so that the poor brute ran whining out of the reach of his boot.

Sam Donovan was about thirty years of age, and was an unfortunate
mixture of his father and his mother, having the fine points of neither.
His blue eyes were weak and watery, and the stubble of beard on his
chin concealed a loose, flabby mouth, He had a way of smiling sideways
and looking down at his feet, scratching his ear as he did so.

"Good-day, Sam," said John Brodrick curtly. "Should you want to
know why I entered your father's house, you had best go inside and ask
him, while the memory of my visit is still fresh in his mind."

"If it's Tom Moore's fence that has brought you here, I wasn't at
home when the cows intruded there, I was down in Doonhaven," said
Sam Donovan, glancing from Copper John back to the agent. "The fact
of the matter is that fence of his is too far to the north, it encroaches on
our land, and anyone else would tell you the same. Tom Moore had no
business to put up the fence at all."

"The matter of that fence was brought up for arbitration six months
ago, and you know it perfectly well, Sam Donovan," broke in the agent,
at once in his element, and desirous of showing his authority. "Didn't I
come over myself and measure the ground, and have two unbiassed
parties here to witness the fairness of what was agreed, and you remember
you said yourself at the time . . ."

"That will do, Ned," said John Brodrick impatiently. "The matter is of
no importance, and Sam knows that if his father's cattle broke down the
fence his father must pay for the damage done, and there is no more to be
said. Let us get home before we are both drenched to the skin."

He turned abruptly away, without bidding Sam Donovan good-bye,
and his agent was obliged to follow him, regretting the break in the argument, which might have lasted some considerable time and would have
resulted in going once more into the house and continuing the discussion
over a glass of whisky, had he been on his own and not in company with
his brother and employer.

The weather had changed, as it so often did in the country, to clammy
mist and drizzle, and the rain swept now over the moors as though the
sun had never shone for the day. One thing was certain, thought Copper
John as he stode along beside the bog, always five yards or so ahead of

Bнн

his agent, the time had arrived to make the Donovans understand, finally and for ever, that their influence on the people of Doonhaven must finish. The ridiculous family feud belonged to a past that was dead and buried. If the Donovans had come down in the world it was from their own idleness and feckless way of living; the prosperity of the Brodricks had nothing to do with it. Any fortune that he, John Brodrick, was making came from his own energies and his fortunate ability to march with the times. If the Donovans did not understand this, and continued their policy of obstruction, then the Donovans would be broken. And the sooner they were broken the better it would be for Doonhaven. There were too many families like them in the country, proud, idle, and good-for-nothing, ever ready to raise a protest against the law, a continual menace to the Government and to loyal landlords like himself. Until these people were brought to heel and made to fit in with progress and the general scheme of things, the country would never prosper.

So Copper John decided, coming out on to the road and leaving the wet bog and the brown moors behind him, the rain streaming from his coat. And as he reached his own gate-house, at the entrance to the park, and, dismissing his agent, proceeded to walk down the carriage road, the sky cleared, as suddenly as it had clouded, the grassland shone and glistened under the sun, and down in the wood by the water's edge the herons rose from their nests in the tall trees, and with heavy flapping wings flew slowly down the creek. He turned up from the drive, and stood on the bank of smooth grass before the castle, looking with pride and affection at the strong grey walls of his house, the tower at the end, the mass of trees climbing the hill behind, and thought how he would build on additions to the house, making it stronger still, with bigger windows, other towers, not for his own sake, but for Henry's, and for Henry's children, and in days to come this castle of Clonmere would be a landmark far and wide, and people travelling the road from Mundy to Doonhaven would stop below Hungry Hill and point westward across the water, saying, "There is Clonmere, the home of the Brodricks." And beside it would be the tall chimneys of the mines.

4

Henry and John arrived from London at the end of the week. Meanwhile, there had been no further incident at the mine, and Captain Nicholson gave it as his opinion that the return of the Director of the company had frightened the pilferers, and possibly brought them to some sense of honesty.

This opinion was short-lived, however, for on the day following the young men's arrival, one of the trolleys, which had been fully loaded at the close of the preceding day's work, and which was stationed in the customary track outside the cleansing-shed, where the copper was washed and separated, was found in the morning, when wheeled to the dressing-station, filled not with copper but with iron residue. The men who had been in charge of this particular trolley were summoned at once by Captain Nicholson and closely questioned, but both appeared stupefied at what had happened. Captain Nicholson went down the mine, and, crawling along the narrow gallery, came to the load that had been worked the day before. Gunpowder had been used frequently during the week, and the bitter, pungent smell still clung about the rock-face of the mine, and the rubble had not all been cleared away. The men who were working the seam, and had filled the buckets, were Doonhaven men, not Captain Nicholson's own Cornishmen, but, like the surface men, they professed themselves ignorant as to how the iron residue came to fill the trolley, and in proof of their innocence reminded the Captain how he himself had been present the evening before when their shift came off duty, and had supervised the now customary nightly search, and not a trace of any mineral had been found on their persons.

"Do you think we swallow the stuff?" asked one of them, in high indignation. "And will you be cutting open our stomachs to look for it?"

"It's my belief," said his companion solemnly, "that the spirits in the old hill make away with it, and put a charm on us in the doing of it, so that we cannot see them crouching beside us with their little barrows."

"The only spirits that come into this mine you bring yourself in a bottle from Murphy's shop in Doonhaven," said Captain Nicholson. "Go on, get to work, and remember to hold yourselves in readiness for further questions from Mr Brodrick when he arrives. It's my belief he will have every one of you arrested by the police and taken into Mundy."

The new setback meant a great loss of face for Captain Nicholson, who had been congratulating himself that the trouble was over, and it was with extreme reluctance that he sent a lad over to Clonmere with a note to the Director, explaining what had occurred.

Copper John came within the hour, in company with his two sons, and listened to Nicholson's story in silence, his face hard and expressionless.

"Well, Henry," he said at the conclusion, "your brains are young, and you arrive here fresh to the business. What do you make of it?"

Henry looked thoughtful. He did not reply immediately. Although he was now twenty-five, and his brother a year younger, they were so used to deferring to their father's views and opinions, and keeping their own thoughts in abeyance, that to be appealed to in this way was something of a novelty.

Henry's travels in France and Germany had given him plenty of confidence, however, which his brother still lacked, and he was the lucky possessor too of great natural charm and grace of manner, in addition to a good brain, and, glancing across at Captain Nicholson with a smile, he asked for permission to descend the mine.

"By all means, sir," said the Captain, "and I will come with you myself."

"No, don't trouble to do that," said Henry. "I think it might be better if I went alone, and possibly my brother could come with me. We may strike upon something that will give a clue to the business and solve your troubles."

"I wish you success," said his father, with a short laugh, "but take care not to lose yourselves. John is quite capable of tumbling down the shaft and breaking his neck."

The brothers left the small counting-house and walked past the dressing-sheds and the trolleys to the ladder, close to the shaft head.

"Well," said John, "what's in your mind?"

"Just something," smiled his brother, "but I shan't tell you yet. I want your help, all the same. When we get down to the level where Nicholson told us the men were working yesterday, you must somehow get the fellow there in conversation, while I look about the place without interference. When you see me blow my nose, that will be your signal."

"What am I talk to the man about?" objected John.

"Anything you please. Tell him about your new greyhound. But keep his attention distracted."

"What a tom-fool business it is!" said John. "If I were my father I should let matters alone, and leave the fellows to take the copper. There must be enough to go round. Confound it, Henry, look at the mess they are making of Hungry Hill."

He pointed at the tall, lean chimney, the long row of sheds, the clustered huts where the miners lived.

"And all," laughed his brother, "so that I can amuse myself in Paris and Brussels, and you can race your greyhounds."

They put on mining hats and overalls, and were soon descending the long, steep ladder into the mine. The atmosphere was a curious mixture of chill and oppression, and the candles stuck in brackets at intervals gave a gloomy, fitful light.

They reached the first level, where they could see the figures of two of the miners beside the shaft, engaged in steadying the buckets on the chains before they were raised to the surface by a windlass. Henry enquired where the blasting operations were in progress, and the two brothers were directed to a lower level.

"It's the narrowest level in the whole of the mine," said one of the men. "You will have to go single file, and crawl part of the way."

Henry was obviously enjoying himself, and looked about him the whole time with keen interest, now and again tapping the rock-face, and whistling under his breath, a habit of his when thinking very hard, while John, who with his superior height found the low ceiling highly uncomfortable, followed his elder brother in silence, aware that with every step he took farther into the bowels of the mine he became more and more depressed. He longed to be up and out of it, away in the fresh air on the top of Hungry Hill, and to him there was something

degrading, almost evil, in burrowing like this into the depths, breaking
the age-old rock with gunpowder to extract the hidden mineral.

A low rumble and muffled explosion not very far distant warned them
that they were nearly within reach of the work, and through the gloom
and smoke they edged their way along the gallery close to the miners.

The men's faces looked grey and haggard in the dim light, and once
again John was filled with a sense of oppression. If any harm came to
these fellows through their grim work, it would be the fault of his father
and himself.

Henry was amongst them immediately, chatting easily, asking questions, while John stood aloof, looking at the dripping walls and the
rubble caused by the last explosion, which the men were now clearing
with their picks and shovels. He heard his brother enquire how far the
gallery ran, and where they had been blasting during the previous weeks,
and one of the men, a Cornishman, whose work it was actually to ignite
the train, pointed to the far end of the gallery, where a mass of rubble
appeared to be uncleared and the height of the ceiling little more than
four foot.

"We wasted our time there," he said. "The rock goes chalky, and
there is no mineral deposit. You could blast away for weeks, and you
would only find chalk. It's my belief the hill slopes suddenly here, above
ground, forming a wide hollow, and we are not so very far from the
surface."

"Yes," said Henry, "I have often come upon those hollows while
walking about the hill—almost like natural quarries. I should say there
were earthworks here in days gone by."

"Yes, sir," said the Cornishman, uncertain what was meant by an
earthwork, and then John suddenly perceived that his brother was very
vigorously blowing his nose. He at once moved into the group of men.

"Do you ever have accidents during these explosions?" he asked.

The man turned to him civilly. "No, sir," he said; "it's only a matter
of being careful. Of course it's specialised work."

The Cornishman showed John where holes had been bored in the side
of the rock, for the charge to be inserted. John asked many questions,
showing a keen interest most foreign to his nature, while the other three
men, glad of a respite, leant on their tools and entered into the discussion,
which worked round to when and where gunpowder had first been employed for mining purposes.

No one noticed or cared that Henry did not join in the conversation,
and had disappeared in the gloom to the end of the gallery. When he
finally returned—John having meanwhile re-told the story of the Gunpowder Plot with great eloquence, professing himself firmly on the side
of Guy Fawkes, and thus earning for himself a certain amount of respect
from two of the men, who came from Doonhaven—ten minutes or a
quarter-of-an-hour had passed by, and John, glancing at his brother,

perceived that his clothes were covered in chalk and that there was a look of intense excitement in his eyes.

"Well, John," he said, "if you've had enough of it, we'll leave these fellows to their work and get up to the surface," and with a brief word of thanks to the men he began to edge his way back along the level to the ladder.

They climbed to the surface in silence, John asking no questions, but as soon as they were above ground, and Henry had dusted the chalk from his clothes, he turned to his brother in triumph.

"My instinct was right," he said. "I know how these devils take the stuff away. Wait until we get to the counting-house, and you shall hear the whole story."

Their father, who was beginning to show signs of impatience, was walking up and down the room, his hands behind his back.

"Well," he said, as his sons entered, "no bones broken?"

"Not yet," said Henry, "but there may be before this business is finished. Captain Nicholson, can we be overheard here?"

"No, sir. The clerk has gone to her dinner, and not a soul but ourselves is within earshot."

"Very well then," said Henry. "I am able to tell you that your stuff is being stolen below ground, before it is ever brought to the surface."

"What the devil do you mean, Henry?" asked his father sharply.

"Only this, sir. I have always understood that in prehistoric days Hungry Hill was inhabited by cave-dwellers, who burrowed passages and tunnels underground, a few traces of which remain to this day. I have come across caves and hollows myself, when walking the hill, but never bothered to explore them to any depth. It was only when I heard about the disappearance of material that I remembered them."

"Well?" said his father.

"Just now, down on the second level, I left John to talk to the men who were blasting, and I went to the end of the gallery, where work has ceased, because chalk was struck. I cleared away some of the rubble, and moved one large piece of rock that looked as though it had been placed there with deliberate intention. I crawled in behind it, and found what I suspected. A narrow tunnel, just wide enough for a man to crawl on his hands and knees, sloping upwards, away from the mine. It was worn quite smooth with recent use. I did not explore more than a few yards, for fear of discovery, but I can pretty well guess that it leads out into one of those old hollows in the side of the hill. It would be the simplest thing in the world to have a man crawl along that tunnel and dump the stuff at the end of it, and for someone else to come by night on to the hill by the hollow and load up his donkey and cart. It's easy to see how they work it, too. Two Doonhaven fellows in the business arrange to work the same shift below ground, and one of them goes up the tunnel, while his partner keeps watch. Your Cornishmen are entirely innocent, Captain

Nicholson. I'm sure of that. The fellow who was blasting today had no more idea there was a tunnel behind the chalk than my brother John had, but if he had a little more curiosity he would soon find out. So there you have it, father. And make what you like of the discovery."

He smiled at the two older men, and winked at his brother. His achievement was, after all, something of a triumph.

"Well, Nicholson," said Copper John, "my son seems to have accomplished more in half-an-hour than you have done in weeks. Nor do I seek to make any excuses for myself. Now, my plan is as follows. When the men come off shift this evening, you and my son Henry will go down the mine and explore the tunnel to its outlet in the hillside. We will then post a watch every night until we catch the fellows at work. If there is a scrap, so much the better. John, you are the lawyer of the family. What do you say?"

John, whose dislike of the law was intense, and who had not the moral courage to say so, glanced appealingly at his brother, who took no notice.

"I don't know, sir," he havered. "Would you not perhaps consider telling the men that their game has been discovered, and block up the tunnel, and so end the business? Then there will be no bad blood spilt on either side."

"If that's what they teach you in Lincoln's Inn no wonder nobody briefs you for Counsel," said his father scornfully. "I fear my second son knows more about his dogs than he does about his profession, Captain Nicholson. Very well, John, you can stay at home and mind Jane. We don't want any faint-hearts amongst us. I suppose we can depend upon your Cornishmen, Nicholson? Meanwhile, I will find one or two neighbours to give us some assistance. I don't want to appeal to the military in this affair. Simon Flower from Andriff might be prevailed upon to help us; he is hefty enough, whatever else he lacks."

John Brodrick returned to Clonmere in high good-humour. They would soon have the whip-hand of the pilferers, and give them such a lesson that no one would try to interfere with his mine again in a hurry. The whole story was related to Jane, whose pleasure at Henry's cleverness was only tempered by the sight of John's gloomy face, which she knew at once to be caused by his own sense of inferiority.

"Let Henry crawl about the confounded tunnel on his hands and knees," he said to Jane afterwards, sprawling on his father's chair in the drawing-room. "I don't give a tinker's curse what he discovers. I'm sick of the whole affair."

"Why did you come over here, dear, if you did not want to help father?"

"Did you ever know me refuse the chance of a holiday? And the woodcock waiting to be destroyed on Doon Island? Come along to the pantry, and help me clean my gun. The fellows can take every bit of copper out of Hungry Hill for all I care."

It was decided that the following night a watch should be set on the hillside, and that during the day Copper John should sound one or two neighbours as to their willingness to help, while Henry and John rode over to Castle Andriff to see Simon Flower. Old Robert Lumley was in Cheltenham, where he usually spent the winter, and even had he been in the country his presence would not have been much help.

The day was fine, and the sky cloudless, and the two young Brodricks rode over to Andriff in good spirits, bearing a present of woodcock to Mrs Flower. She was a large, rather formidable woman, with a great sense of her own importance, and she never could forget that her husband Simon was brother to the Earl of Mundy, a fact which Simon Flower himself found it convenient to ignore. Castle Andriff, therefore, was a perplexing house to visit, for the drawing-room, which on first inspection appeared to be of a grandeur only equalled by that of a royal palace, with marble floor, and gilt chairs, and Mrs Flower rising like a queen from her throne to receive the caller, would, on looking a little closer, reveal the fact the many of the legs of the gilt chairs were broken, making them unsafe to sit upon, while the marble floor was so muddied and be-grimed by Simon Flower's setters that it would bear comparison with a kennel. A powdered footman, in livery, received the two Brodricks, and escorted them to the drawing-room, his fine appearance spoilt by the darns in his white stockings and the odour of manure about his person, suggesting that his morning had been spent in the stables, while heated voices overhead sounded as though a domestic dispute of some magnitude was taking place. The altercation was not improved by the discordant notes proceeding from a pianoforte, which on entering the drawing-room the Brodricks discovered to their surprise were being produced by Simon Flower himself, who, with a hat on the back of his head, eyes closed, and a pipe of great length between his lips, was swaying backwards and forwards to some strange melody of his own composition.

Mrs Flower, dressed as for a London reception, was mending a tear in her brocaded bedroom curtains, nor did the entrance of the two visitors embarrass her at all.

"I am delighted to see you both," she said, extending a gracious hand, which Henry wondered whether he was expected to kiss. "You find us as usual in a state of disorganisation. Pray take a chair and tell me the news. Not that one, Mr Brodrick, the leg is unsafe. . . . How kind of your father to send us a present of game! It so happens that my husband's brother, the Earl of Mundy, is not at the moment in residence in this country—he generally keeps us very plentifully supplied with game, as you can imagine. . . . Are your sisters still picnicking in the little farm-house? Miss Brodrick must fancy herself Marie-Antoinette at the Petit Trianon. Quite a change after Clonmere. . . ."

She rattled on, hardly pausing to draw breath and never waiting for an answer, and as she talked loudly to make herself heard above the piano, so did her husband increase the volume of sound, until one of the setters, which had been crouching between his legs, crawled from his lair and added a mournful howl to his master's strains.

"Poor Boris cannot abide the pianoforte," shouted Mrs Flower. "Sometimes he will continue howling for an hour on end, but it never puts my husband out of countenance. When are you both coming over to hunt with my father's hounds at Duncroom?"

The strain of conversing under such conditions proved too much for Henry, for all his charm of manner, and he could do little else but smile and bow and gesture with his hands, while John remained steadily mute, as he invariably did when secretly entertained.

At length the concert came to an end, there was a superb flourish of chords and a loud hammering in the bass that drew forth a final moan of protest from the setter, and Simon Flower rose to his feet, slamming the lid of the piano.

"They say it's a sign of intelligence when a dog sings to music," he said, waving his pipe at the brothers. "Did you hear that hound of mine trying to accompany me? I declare he puts his very soul into his voice; it wrings my heart to hear him."

"Don't be absurd, Simon; the animal dislikes it."

"Dislikes it? I tell you the dog will sit by my side like a leech, with his eyes fixed on the notes, so devoted he is to the instrument. But never mind about that; these lads want refreshment after their journey. Come down to the cellar, both of you; we shall do better that way than if we allow my wife to make tea."

He led the way down a narrow, twisting stair to the labyrinths of his castle, and after poking about with a stump of candle he discovered a bottle of old Madeira, which he proceeded to decant on the spot into an ancient carafe hidden in a cranny of the cellar along with some half-dozen glasses.

"When there's frost on the ground in winter and I can't hunt," he said gravely, "I bring my friends down here, and it would astonish you to see how well we pass the time. My wife imagines us to be playing billiards, and to deceive her I get my servant to click the balls about. She never knows but what we are there, the dear trusting soul. Fill up your glasses, my boys, and make yourselves comfortable. There's a beer barrel apiece for you to sit upon."

The two young men and their host did indeed do so much better than if their hostess had made tea for them in the drawing-room, that when they finally emerged from the cellar and blinked their way into the upper regions once more Henry had forgotten his mission, John was in a state of bland benevolence, and their host was singing "O! Mistress mine, where are you roaming?" which song, in John's opinion, could hardly be directed at the formidable Mrs Flower. Tea, however, was being served in the drawing-room, and Henry recovered himself sufficiently to broach, in a somewhat lame fashion, the reason for the visit. The story he told certainly sounded a little muddled, and Simon Flower, in spite of the interlude in the cellar, could hardly be blamed for shaking his head at the end of it.

"I'll not go crawling around in a rabbit burrow for your father or for any man on earth," he said, yawning, the potency of the old Madeira beginning to show in his sleepy blue eyes. "Why, it might be that I'd lose my way, and never a soul would have sight of me again. Do you remember it was in such fashion we lost poor Trouncer, Maria? She got poking into an old badger's earth and that was the end of her, the best bitch I ever bread."

"You mistake me, sir," said Henry; "there was never a question oi your descending the mine and going into the tunnel. My father's plan is for you and the rest of us to mount guard at the outlet of the tunnel on the hillside, and to waylay any of these beggars who may appear."

"Is it foxes or men you are after?"

"Men, Mr Flower. I have just explained to you. The fellows who are stealing the copper from the mine. My father wishes to arrest them and make an example of them. He thinks Morty Donovan is at the back of it."

"Ah, I'll not do a thing against Morty Donovan. Didn't he sell me the father of that same Trouncer I was just telling you of? A wonderful dog, John; you would have appreciated the pair of them. No, why should I lie all night on a hillside to pick a quarrel with Morty Donovan? I don't see what your father wants to meddle in the business for at all."

"But, surely, Mr Flower, you believe in upholding the law? Are you not a magistrate yourself?"

"Shame on you, Simon," said his wife; "there is poor Mr Brodrick over at Doonhaven working all alone to save the property belonging to him and to my father, and you don't raise a hand to help him. I only wish my brother-in-law were at home, Mr Brodrick. The Early of Mundy would never sit by and see such injustice done, and I dare say if I used my influence and perhaps got word to him over the water . . ."

"Very good of you, madam, but you see the matter is urgent. I rather think my father hoped that Mr Flower would accompany us home tonight."

"Tonight? Impossible. I shall not stir from Castle Andriff this night for all the thieves in Europe," said Simon Flower dramatically. "Let Morty Donovan run away with the copper, and may it bring him better fortune than it has to my house."

And clamping his hat more firmly on his head, Simon Flower sat himself down once more to the piano.

Henry looked across at John and shrugged his shoulders, and at this moment the door of the drawing-room flew open and Simon's daughter rushed into the room, her face flushed, her eyes bright with anger, and her mass of chestnut hair in a tangle down her back.

"It's a shame," she shouted, "a wicked shame, and I told her I would not stand it, and no more I will. And I've scratched her face, and locked her up in the linen-press, and I hope she dies."

So saying, she slammed down the lid of the piano, forcing her father to silence, and stood with heaving breast, her eyes upon her mother.

The vision that had so suddenly descended upon them was too much for the young Brodricks. They rose to their feet, abashed and speechless, and indeed Fanny-Rosa Flower, at seventeen, would have reduced any man with a sense of beauty to the same state of silence.

Her present anger only added to her loveliness, the flush on her cheek brought new depth to her slanting green eyes, and the untidy curling hair made her look like a Bacchante from the wild woods. The fact that she was stockingless seemed in perfect keeping with the character. She now noticed, for the first time, that her parents had visitors.

"How do you do?" she said, with something of her mother's regal manner, but with her father's smile. "I am sorry to cause such a disturbance, but I have just had a fight with my governess, and I trust it is the last one."

"Fanny-Rosa," said her mother, "I am pained and surprised. What will Mr Brodrick and his brother think of you? Miss Harris will be smothered in the linen-press."

She left the drawing-room in great agitation, while Simon Flower regarded his daughter with indulgence from the piano.

"I never cared for that Miss Harris," he said; "she had a mean, snivelling manner with her that did not suit our ways. I think it is high time that you did without a governess."

Fanny-Rosa, recovered from her burst of temper, looked out of the corner of her eyes at the two Brodricks, and sat herself down in her mother's chair.

"I thought you were both in London," she said softly. "You do not generally come to Clonmere till after Christmas, do you?"

Henry found himself telling once again the story of the mine, and this time he had a more receptive audience. Fanny-Rosa clasped her bare legs, and never took her eyes off his face.

"I wish I could come with you both," she said, "instead of my father. I would dearly love to wait out on the hillside in the middle of the night. And if you had a fight with your miners I would not be afraid."

"I tell you what it is," said Simon Flower; "your bout with Miss Harris has put you in trim for a scrap. I have little doubt these lads would let you ride pillion behind one of them, and you would give a good account of yourself in the bargain. But you never told us what was the trouble with Miss Harris?"

"She told Tilly and me it was time we learnt to fold up our clothes, and

I said I would not. All young ladies, she said, should do so from habit, and not have them strewn about the floor like girls from the kitchen. 'What would your uncle, the Earl of Mundy, say to your slovenly ways?' she said. 'Maybe he would forgive me if I sat by his side and pulled his whiskers and told him how handsome he was,' I answered her. And with that she looked down her long nose and said I must learn a page of French verbs, so I scratched her face for her, as I told you before, and had her shut in the linen-press, and I can tell from your eyes that you would have served her the same, Mr Brodrick."

She looked slyly across at John, who blushed to the roots of his hair and laughed under his breath. Fanny-Rosa then helped herself to a large piece of cake, and poured herself some tea, while the eyes of the two Brodricks were drawn irresistibly to the fascination of the slim bare feet.

"You have been on the Continent, have you not?" she said to Henry, with her mouth full of cake. "Ah, I know all about you, our footman is cousin to your cook. We were in Paris ourselves last winter, because my grandfather let my father have some money to spend, and we went to Paris instead of buying new curtains for my mother's bedroom."

"Yes, you baggage," said Simon Flower, "and whenever we visited a picture-gallery what should we find in every room but a trail of young Frenchmen behind us? So in the end the people were bowing to us, thinking we were a royal procession."

"It was a Miss Wilson who was our governess then," said Fanny-Rosa, "and I slipped away from her twice when she was conducting me through the streets, so that she thought I had been abducted, and went in tears to the policemen, but they, being French, did not understand her. She was forced to go to a quiet place in the country when we returned, as she had developed nervous trouble. Would you believe it, but I have had a dozen governesses since I was fourteen, and I had my seventeenth birthday last month, so this is the end of it all."

"You will be the end of your parents too," said Mrs Flower severely, entering the room at this moment, after a vain attempt to mollify the unfortunate Miss Harris. "You may think yourselves lucky, Mr Brodrick, that your own sisters do not behave in similar fashion, and I trust you will not give an account of this daughter of mine to Miss Brodrick when you return."

"I tell you what," cried Simon Flower. "Why do you two boys go back home at all? Let your father go down the old burrows after the miners if it pleases him. You shall stay and dine with us, and we will pay another visit to the cellar, and Fanny-Rosa shall come with us."

But Henry shook his head and moved towards the door, much to his brother's mortification.

"You are very kind, sir," he said, "but we have already delayed far too long as it is. My father will be in some anxiety concerning us."

Simon Flower waved a careless hand, and sat himself down to the piano.

"I'll shoot with your father any day he fancies, on Doon Island," he said. "I'd never refuse an invitation of that sort. But to go crawling on my stomach after Morty Donovan in the middle of the night, no, I will not do it, and ye can tell him so to his face."

And with that he burst once more into song, joined by the faithful setter, and the two Brodricks left Castle Andriff to the confused sound of clashing chords, a rich baritone voice, and the barking of at least half-a-dozen dogs, while the elder daughter of the house, an enchanting bare-footed figure, waved to them from the stone steps.

Dazed, bewildered, and still slightly intoxicated, the two brothers rode home at a pace that would have infuriated Copper John could he have seen them. It was not until they were within sight of Doonhaven that they drew rein, and Henry pulled himself to his senses.

"You know, John," he said, "my father is perfectly right. This country will never prosper while it continues to breed people like the Flowers."

John did not answer. The prosperity of the country meant nothing to him. Henry could continue his observations in his critical fashion and abuse Simon Flower if he wished. The only thing that mattered to John was this: that never in his life had he set eyes on anything quite so lovely as Simon Flower's daughter Fanny-Rosa.

5

On the following Saturday evening the Brodricks were seated round the fire in the library, having dined early, as was their custom. Jane had been gathering cones from the woods during the day, and these she now scattered on the smoking turf, making the fire hiss and crackle, the better to shut out the sound of the wind as it moaned in the trees behind Clonmere. There was a full gale blowing outside in Mundy Bay, but the long Atlantic rollers swept past the entrance to Doonhaven, while the straggling length of Doon Island acted as a natural breakwater.

The tide ebbed swiftly in the creek below the castle, making a strong ripple against the wind, but so sheltered was Clonmere from the full force of the gale that only the sudden tremor of the woods above the house gave warning that the still weather had broken at last.

Henry was seated at his father's desk, writing a letter to Barbara at Lletharrog, while John sprawled as usual in the most comfortable chair, one hand fondling the ear of his favourite greyhound, the other propping up a book he did not read. He was watching the cones as they burst in the fire, and Jane, glancing up at his half-closed eyes, wondered what he was thinking.

The week had been quiet. No further pilfering had been discovered at the mine, and though a watch had been stationed on the hillside every night no one had come upon the hill save the watchers themselves. Yet there was a strange feeling of unrest in the air, a brooding sense of disquiet. And the miners, watching one another in suspicion, went about their work sullenly and in silence.

It was not only at the mine that this amosphere prevailed. Down in Doonhaven, when Jane, accompanied by old Martha, went to make a purchase at Murphy's shop, and would have chatted as usual in her happy way to Murphy, whom she had known from babyhood, the man avoided her eye, looking uncomfortable, and muttering some excuse, disappeared into the back of his shop, leaving a young ignorant lad to serve her. It seemed to her too that the people in the market square stared at her with hostility, and when she smiled and said good-morning they turned their backs and pretended not to see. Doonhaven had suddenly become a place of whispers, of figures peering round doorways and then withdrawing, and Jane, who had a place in her heart for all comers and loved the people of Doonhaven, returned home with a heavy feeling of foreboding.

"I don't like it," she said to Henry. "I believe my father takes this business of the mine not seriously enough. All he thinks about is to catch the few miners and to punish them for taking the copper. He does not realise that his mine is hated by every one of the people in Doonhaven."

"The trouble is that they are jealous," said Henry. "They would like all the benefits of the copper, and none of the trouble in getting it. Father knows what he is talking about. If you were not firm with the people in the country nothing would ever be done, and no progress would be made."

"We were happy enough without progress."

"That is just sentimentality, and you have been listening to John."

Jane threw another cone on to the fire. It spat and hissed, and became still. Soon there was no sound but the scratching of Henry's nib at the desk, and the occasional rustle of a page as John turned the leaves of his book. Suddenly the dog pricked his ears and looked towards the door, and the door itself opened, and their father, Copper John, stood upon the threshold. His coat was buttoned to his chin, his hat was pulled low over his brow, so that little of him could be seen but the long nose and the thin lips above the square jaw, while in his hand he carried his favourite stick, short and nobbled, with a head on it like a club. Behind him, in the hall, stood the agent, Ned Brodrick, his lean, mournful face a contrast to the forceful determination of his more fortunate brother.

"I want you two boys to accompany me immediately," said Copper John. "We are starting for the mine in five minutes. Outside in the drive I have some dozen of the tenants waiting, also Parsons, the customs officer, Sullivan from the Post Office, Doctor Beamish, and one or two others that have mustered. There is no time to lose."

The three young Brodricks had risen to their feet, Henry tense and alert, John a little bewildered, awoken too rudely from his dream, and Jane pale and anxious, clasping her hands in front of her.

"Is anything wrong, sir?" asked Henry.

Copper John smiled grimly.

"Word has come that there are some thirty men or more marching out from Doonhaven to Hungry Hill, and leading them are the half-dozen miners suspected by Captain Nicholson. They are out to do mischief, of course, and I propose to stop them."

Jane followed her father and uncle into the hall, where her two brothers were fastening their coats, their faces pale and excited in the dim candle-light. The door was open on to the drive, and she could see the small huddled group of men waiting for her father, shuffling their feet on the gravel, talking amongst themselves in whispers. One or two of them swung lanterns in their hands, and all carried heavy sticks.

There was still no rain, but the wind came in gusts, and the clouds raced one another across the sky. It was about half-past eight, and the night was dark. No moon shone, and the stars were mere pin-pricks of light that came and vanished.

Copper John and his two sons joined the others on the drive, and Jane, standing by the open door, watched them disappear, heard the stolid clump-clump of their boots as they crunched the gravel, while round the corner from the stable came Casey and Tim with the horses, and in a moment the whole party were hidden by the bend in the drive, and so up through the park and away to Hungry Hill.

Doonhaven was quiet and still, a village asleep. The doors were closed, and the windows showed no light. No person walked the street or lingered in the square, and the only sound to be heard was the sea breaking on the beach below the harbour wall.

Once clear of the village, Copper John called a halt, and the party divided. One half, led by Copper John and Henry, continued up the road towards the mine; the rest, with John amongst them, struck across country to the outlet in the hill. Here on the high ground they were exposed to the full force of the wind, which drove them onward blindly, causing them to stumble amongst the loose stones and the heather, and the younger Brodrick, now that he was alone, without either his father or his brother, was aware of a new sense of excitement, almost of exultation, not connected in any way with the mine or the angry men of Doonhaven, but because this was something that he loved and understood, this fighting with the wind on Hungry Hill. Away below him was the sea, sweeping the long length of Mundy Bay, rolling on towards Castle Andriff, where maybe Fanny-Rosa could hear it from her window, and the sound of the sea came to him now, borne on the wind, not a sullen, angry sound, but loud and insistent, a chant of triumph. The men behind him were cursing at the rough ground, their coats bellying around them in the tearing wind. John looked up, and watched the black clouds racing across the sky, felt the first stinging drop of rain upon his cheek, heralding the storm that was to come, and, laughing, climbed yet faster than before, gaining a foothold amongst the stones and the wet, clinging moss, while the wild, sweet scent of heather filled the air. They came at last to the outlet in the hill, so well concealed by the tangle of gorse that in the darkness and the spitting rain it was well-nigh impossible to find, and there they waited, gaining what shelter they could from the weather by the shoulder of the hill, and the wind went on blowing and the night grew darker yet. Ned Brodrick was of the company; he crouched beside his nephew in the heather, his face lugubrious and long, and now and again he would bite his fingers to restore the circulation.

"Your father should have come to terms with Morty Donovan, Master John," he said. "Many is the time I have come to arbitration with the family myself, in a friendly fashion, over a glass of whisky maybe. But your father is a proud man, and high-handed, and Morty Donovan is proud too. I tell you no good will come of this night, and had I my way I would be sitting now in my cottage in Oakmount, with the curtains drawn, knowing nothing of the business."

"I have no doubt you would, Ned," said John, "but here we are on Hungry Hill, with no choice in the matter, and must make the best of it."

"It's a spice of discretion that is needed, Master John," continued Ned. "I have made it a practice this long while, since acting as agent to your father, to agree with him when in his company, and to agree with the tenants when in theirs. Therefore I have pleased both parties and offended none. Never in my life have I held a quarrel with any man."

"And how do you manage, Ned, when the tenants are in arrears with their rent, and you have to drive them for the money?"

"Why, between you and me, Master John, I so work the figures on the rent-roll as to have the appearance that the money is paid, when oftentimes I have not seen a penny of it. But will you take a small drop of something, to keep up your spirits?" And glancing furtively over his shoulder, the agent produced a bottle from the deep pocket of his coat, and, kneeling, with hunched shoulders, in the heather, tipped it to his mouth with a sigh of satisfaction. "I tell you, Master John," he said, wiping his lips with the sleeve of his coat, "but I am devoted to your family, and Morty Donovan would have to walk across my dead body rather than harm should come to any of them. As for yourself, you're the best of the bunch, and that's meaning no disrepect to Master Henry."

John laughed, knowing full well that the agent would have said exactly the same thing to his brother had he been there instead, and when he had taken his "small drop", which must have been some hellbrew of Ned Brodrick's own creation, for it tasted of liquid fire, he handed the bottle back, only just in time, for one of the men, who had been watching a little distance away, came running through the heather towards them.

"There's a glow in the sky to the eastward, Mr John," he shouted. "It's my belief the miners are not coming this way at all tonight, but have set fire to the mine."

The other men were stumbling now down the hill, all of them calling and gesticulating, and John could see an angry tongue of flame leap into the sky from beneath the shoulder of the farther hill.

"He's right, Master John," cried the agent, "there'll be no crawling in the burrows this night, but whatever mischief goes on will be above ground, and in the sheds and buildings. May God curse the creatures for their treachery and devilry."

"Why, look yonder," called one of the tenants; "here's someone coming this way with a donkey and cart. Watch how the cart rocks in the heather—he'll be over for sure."

"You'd say the animal knows every inch of the ground, or the driver has him bewitched," said another. "He's down—no, he's not—he has him guided in the little bit of track, and he's driving the brute with a stick like a madman."

The donkey and cart advanced towards the party, rocking and lurching over the rough ground in wild, crazy fashion, and the man who was seated in the cart waved his whip at the party in derision, shouting and laughing, while his great black cloak bellied about him in the wind, making him a giant fantastic figure.

"It's the Devil himself," cried someone, "it's the Devil come out of Hell to destroy us," and for a moment the party hesitated, uncertain whether to fly or to fling themselves upon their faces and ask for mercy. And then one of the men, less superstitious than his fellows, gave a shout of recognition, and turned to his companions.

"It's Morty Donovan," he cried. "Look at his face, look at his eyes! Mr John, it's my belief he has gone stark staring mad."

The old man was balancing on the side of the cart, his bad leg propped up in front of him; in one hand he held the reins that guided the donkey, and in the other his whip, which he flourished round his head. As he drew near to the party he pulled the donkey to a standstill, and peering down through the darkness, he recognised John, and once more fell to laughing and shouting, shaking from side to side in a wild extravagance of mirth.

"So you thought to entrap them, did you," he cried, "and bind them here on the hillside, and bear them away to prison? Well, I can tell you that you're wasting your time, every one of you. The boys have a big fire lit at your father's mine, Mr John, and not a stick or stone of it will be left by morning. So go join him and your brother, and roast yourselves to cinders, and be damned to the lot of you, I say."

Once more the old man cracked his whip, cursing the donkey to go forward.

"Stop him," shouted someone, "stop him; get hold of the animal; he'll do himself some damage."

One of the men hurled himself at the donkey's head, which, bewildered
and frightened, stumbled in the heather, causing the man to fall, while
John, climbing on to the step of the cart, endeavoured to wrench the
whip from Morty Donovan's hand. The old man was too quick for him.
He turned with an oath, and cut the boy over the head with a stinging
lash, blinding him for the instant, while a torrent of curses poured from
his lips, the wild, extravagant laughter turning in a moment to senseless
rage.

"I have cursed your father tonight, and your brother, and now I curse
you, John Brodrick," he cried, "and not only you, but your sons after
you, and your grandsons, and may your wealth bring them nothing
but despair and desolation and evil, until the last of them stands humble
and ashamed amongst the ruins of it, with the Donovans back again in
Clonmere on the land that belongs to them."

John reeled back from the cart, his face cut and bleeding from the
whip, and his senses dazed from the force of the blow, while the group
of men, shocked and frightened momentarily by the old man's passion,
stood aside from the track. Only Ned Brodrick, with a shaky smile
and outstretched hand seemed undismayed.

"Come now, Mr Donovan," he said; "why now, not a man here, not
Master John himself, wishes you any harm, and that's God's truth. I will
see Mr Brodrick myself and ask him as a personal matter to give his true
impartial judgement . . ."

But Morty Donovan cut him short, laughing scornfully.

"Will you shut your mouth, you fool," he said, "and go and hide your
face amongst the petticoats? Haven't you the same tainted blood in
your veins? Let me go, blast ye!"

Once more the donkey stumbled forward as Morty Donovan cracked
his whip, and the little cart, swaying from side to side, travelled onward
into the darkness, until it was lost to sight round the bend of the hill.

"Are you much hurt, Master John?" asked his uncle, peering into the
young man's face. "Should you not go home and let the women bathe
it? I think we have done all we can for this night."

"All right, Ned, it will soon mend; and as for going home, that is out
of the question. You heard what that old lunatic said? the fellows have
set the place on fire. We must get the shortest way to the mine, there's
nothing else for it."

The blood was running freely down his face, and his head throbbed
painfully, and somehow the exultation of the evening was no more, but
turning once more into the wind and the rain, that was coming now
faster than before, John led the way across the hill in the direction of the
mine. In some twenty minutes the party found their way through
the darkness to the track leading to the mine, and at the far end of it they
could see the tall chimney, lit up by the glow of the fire, and could
hear the roar of voices, shouting and calling directions. The scene was

one of incredible confusion, men dashing against one another in the darkness, some calling orders, some jeering, the whole body of men so mingled
together that no one knew for certain who was friend or foe.

"It's the huts of the Cornishmen that are alight," said a man of John's
party. "Look, sir, down the road there; they have every one of them in
flames."

Such proved to be the case, the wooden buildings lending themselves
only too readily to fire, and in the little strips of gardens that they had
cultivated for themselves stood the women with their children, dismayed
and terrified and weeping, while their men-folk endeavoured to quench
the fires with buckets of water passed from one to the other.

No part of the mine proper had yet been touched, and this was because John Brodrick and his party, with the aid of Captain Nicholson,
had so stationed themselves before the sheds and buildings that the rebel
miners dared not advance without fighting, which they were by no means
fully prepared to do. They contented themselves, therefore, with des-
troying the little dwellings of the Cornishmen, pilfering what they could
find, and terrorising the women and children. When John and his party
arrived on the scene, some half-dozen of the miners, the leaders amongst
them, had succeeded in penetrating into the cleansing-shed, and, en-
couraged by their more timid companions, were engaged in overturning
the trolleys and scattering the contents through the open doors, with
whoops of triumph and satisfaction.

Suddenly John's arm was seized by Henry, who darted forward from
the doorway of the counting-house and dragged him under cover of the
building.

"Keep still—lie down," whispered his brother; "father is going to give
these fellows the shock of their lives."

He was trembling with excitement, and pointed to two figures—that
of his father and Captain Nicholson—who were standing slightly apart
from the building, holding something in their hands. Copper John was
hatless, and his coat too had been thrown aside, showing his square,
powerful frame, while his thick grey hair was tossed and matted from the
wind. He glanced up and saw his second son, and grinned, pointing
to the instrument in Captain Nicholson's hands.

At once John saw what he was about, and his heart went cold.

"Good God, Henry," he whispered, "it's murder."

His brother did not answer, but kept his eyes fixed on his father and
Captain Nicholson. The miners were too intent on their work of destruction to notice the two figures that advanced so steadily and so quietly
to the rear of the cleansing-sheds, and, bending for a moment, were busy
at the ledge of wall. The figures waited a moment, and then retreated
rapidly, returning to the counting-house where John and Henry waited,
and, like them, they threw themselves to the floor.

"Now we have them," said Copper John, and his second son, glancing at him, saw the look of triumph in his eyes, and the hard line of his mouth.

For a minute there was silence, then a shattering explosion rent the air, followed by the crashing sound of falling rubble, of flying sticks and stones, and the screams of men.

Copper John rose to his feet, and looked at Captain Nicholson without a word. Then he led the way out of the counting-house, and stood for a few moments watching the scene in front of him.

The cleansing-shed, fired so swiftly by the train of gunpowder, was nothing more than a heap of rubble and stones, with only the far end of it still standing, and this, ignited in some fashion, was now burning fiercely, while staggering from the ruins came the sole survivor of the team of six who not three minutes previously had been calling and shouting in triumph from within the shed.

A great cry of fear and distress had gone up from the crowd of watchers, and fearing that the explosion was but the first of a series, which would destroy them all, they began to run in panic, screaming and yelling, falling over one another in their haste to get away, and in a moment the broad track to the mine was a mass of struggling, fighting figures, the scene weirdly and horribly lit by the crackling flames of the burning shed.

"After them," shouted Copper John, "let none of them escape," and thrusting his way amongst the crowd, he hit out to left and right with his great nobbled stick, followed by Captain Nicholson and others of his party, while John, standing sick and suddenly exhausted on the steps of the counting-house, with the bitter smell of the gunpowder in his nostrils, could see nothing but this square figure of his father, his stick beating down on the heads of the frightened miners, who scattered before him, bewildered and desperate, all fight in them vanquished by the terrible death of their leaders. And now came the screams of the women and children, for some of them were being trampled upon by the miners in their panic, and the flames of the cottages, lessening in strength because they had spent their full force, were now quenched by the sudden burst of rain from the black sky, rain which fell in torrents, drenching all who were present. In this darkness and sudden downpour the confusion became worse, friend hitting friend, enemy clutching enemy, and above it all the strong voice of Copper John, giving orders, calling directions, shouting advice to Captain Nicholson and the rest of his friends, calling to Henry for assistance, and still John stood on the steps of the counting-house staring at the heap of rubble that had been the cleansing-shed. . . .

It was nearly half-past two in the morning by the time order had been restored to the mine. Some dozen men had been put into custody and locked in the counting-house, the rest had taken to their heels and fled, either to hide in the hills, or else to return to their homes in Doonhaven, trusting that in the darkness they had been unrecognised. The rain, which had now turned to a thin, steady drizzle, with a lessening wind, had put out the last of the fires, and only the wet, smouldering embers showed traces of the Cornishmen's dwellings The families had been gathered, for the remainder of the night, into the mine buildings themselves, until provision could be made for them in the morning. Nothing more could be done until daylight, but already, seated at the table in the counting-house, with a glass of hot rum at his elbow, Copper John was dictating his orders to Captain Nicholson.

"I think I can say with a reasonable amount of confidence that we shall have no more trouble with the men from Doonhaven. They will return to work, those who have not taken to the hills, and it is even possible that we shall have new men coming up, asking for employment. The tunnel, incidentally, that leads from the mine into the hill we will deal with in somewhat the same fashion as we dealt to-night with the cleansing-shed. Remember, Captain Nicholson, to have the rubble of the shed cleared as early as possible within the next forty-eight hours, to enable us to get forward with the construction of the new building to take its place. Also the fellows lying there must have burial—that is, what remains of them, which will be considerably little. . . . Well, gentlemen, I must thank you one and all for your assistance in this night's work. You will not find me ungrateful. Will those of you who are not too exhausted care to return with me and my sons to Clonmere, where my daughter will be very pleased to offer you refreshment?"

One by one the members of the party, wet and haggard, and drooping from fatigue, made their excuses, and so, in the falling rain, in the heavy, intense darkness that comes before the day, Copper John mounted his horse and rode through the silent streets of Doonhaven back to Clonmere, followed by his sons. Jane and Martha and the other servants, tense and anxious, were awaiting them in the hall, and at the sight of them safely returned old Martha burst into tears, shaking her head and reproving her master, clicking her tongue in distress at John's swollen face.

"That will do, Martha, that will do," said Copper John, dismissing the servants with a wave of his hand. "None of us has come to harm and we have no bones broken. Master John will survive his cut, I have little doubt. What we need now is food and drink, and a warm by the fire, and very shortly to bed for what remains of the night, for we all of us have work to do in the morning."

They stood in the library, the four of them—the father with a glass in one hand and the other behind his back, his stern features relaxed for the moment while he smiled at his daughter, who tried to smile back at him, but was still so pale, so anxious, that the smile was a ghostly thing, a shadow of no substance; John leaning against the fireplace, his head resting in his hands, his face swollen and discoloured; while Henry, soaked to the skin, his clothes clinging to his slim body, his teeth chattering, lifted his glass and clinked it against his father's.

"Anyway," he said, "whatever happens, we have beaten them, haven't we, father?"

"Yes," said Copper John, "we have beaten them, Henry."

They drank together, watching one another over the rim of their glasses, and smiling.

The mine, thought Jane, has not been destroyed, the mine will continue to be worked on Hungry Hill, and Morty Donovan has lost. Her father and her brothers were safe. John had a swollen face, but that was all. It was a picture she remembered always, the father and son pledging one another across the table, and she remembered too how John, looking up from the fire at the shivering, white-faced Henry, said suddenly, in anger:

"For God's sake go and change, Henry; you'll catch your death from this night's work."

She remembered how the rain pattered against the windows, and the wind sighed softly, and how, although they were safe, she was still afraid.

They slept deeply that night, the young Brodricks, and only once did their father, Copper John, stir in his sleep and frown and mutter as though at some passing dream. The wind moaned a little, and was silent. The rain whispered, and pattered, and ceased. And away on the heather, five miles distant, a small donkey stood shivering beside an overturned cart, with Morty Donovan lying beneath it, his neck broken, clutching in his dead hands the stones and moss of Hungry Hill.

6

On the first of every month, no matter where he should be, or engaged on what business, John Brodrick of Clonmere would write to his partner, Robert Lumley of Duncroom, and tender him a report on the condition of their mine in Hungry Hill, Doonhaven. It was one of those strict rules that he had laid down for himself at the beginning of the partnership, and although he had no great friendship for Robert Lumley, and saw him perhaps but twice in a whole year, yet month by month the letters would go forth, from Clonmere, from London, from Bath, from Lletharrog, from Bronsea, each letter written in his careful, pointed handwriting signed with the Brodrick seal, a mailed fist holding a dagger, and the paper folded and crossed in the manner of the day. "It is a pleasure for me to acquaint you, my dear Mr Lumley," he would say, "that your royalty for the current year has exceeded that of last, and I have this day, the fourteenth of February, paid into your account in your bank at Slane the sum of Two Thousand pounds."

It was typical of John Brodrick that this interesting piece of information should be followed by a slightly bitter pill.

"I am sorry to say," he would continue, "that our expenses for the year have been equally heavy, and I have been obliged to erect yet another Steam Engine, the cost of which will have to be deducted from your

royalty for the forthcoming year. As copper is now at a high price, I
think it would be worth while to risk a considerable sum in a further trial
of a place some quarter of a mile distant from the present mine, on the
northern part of the hill, above the road. It will be an expensive trial,
but the advantages to the country in works of this kind are so great that I
would risk a good deal for the chance of establishing a further mine, even
though it should not be very profitable."

And the shaft would be sunk, and the new mine worked, and more men
employed and more ships bought for the purpose of shipping the ore
from Doonhaven to Bronsea to be smelted, and so little by little, and then
faster and faster, the Brodrick fortune mounted, and Copper John would
add to his property at Clonmere, twenty greeves here, and twenty greeves
there, land along the coast beyond Doon Island, land beyond Kileen,
on the way to Denmare.

Then there would be the question of appointments in Doonhaven, the
arranging of which the owner of Clonmere would consider to be his
right, and not Robert Lumley's.

"I am sorry we are likely to lose the services of Doctor Beamish in
Doonhaven. It would be a matter of great moment to establish a medical
man of some skill in the county, who would attend to the complaints of
the poor people and in whom we ourselves could place confidence if his
attendance was required. It has been hinted to me that Doctor Armstrong, who has been attached to the garrison on Doon Island, is inclined
to retire from the army and is not averse to settling in the country, and
especially in this district. Colonel Leslie speaks in the highest terms of
his skill, and I believe Doctor Beamish knows him very well. As you are
aware, the method of choosing a Dispenser in the county is by election,
each subscriber to the Dispensary having votes according to the amount
of his subscription. As my subscription is double or even treble that of all
the other persons in the district, I put it to you that I am the only person
entitled to vote, and that if I so desire it, and he is agreeable, then Doctor
Armstrong shall fill the place. . . ."

Needless to say, Doctor Armstrong did, much to the gratification of
the young Brodricks, whose friend and companion he had become.

"As the matter of your tenants," Copper John would add, "on whose
subject you asked my advice in your last communication, I may say that
I consider it a very bad plan to forgive arrears of rent. Those few who
are inclined to pay well find they are not a bit better off than those who
do not, and of course have no encouragement to pay better in future.
My own system is to give the grounds of those who do not pay to those
who do, and thus encourage the latter to pay even better than they did
before."

And John Brodrick, the expression in his eyes a little harder, and the
lines of his mouth a little firmer as the months went by, would close his
letter with remarks about his family.

"We intend to cross the water early in September, and spend the winter as usual at Lletharrog. Henry, I regret to say, is still in very poor health, and we are in a state of great anxiety about him. He does not seem to get rid of his cough, and the doctor he saw in Brighton has recommended a warmer climate for him. He intends to start for the Barbadoes at the same time, or a little earlier, than we leave for Lletharrog. John is well, and has some greyhounds that he declares will be ruined unless they have some courses before next season, and he intends to bring them over to Duncroom when you are next at home. My daughters, I am glad to say, are also in very good health, and they unite with me, my dear Mr Lumley, in sending best wishes. . . ."

And so the line beneath the signature, and the letter folded and sealed and given to Thomas to take down to Doonhaven, and one more duty had been accomplished and the act dismissed from his mind.

Leaving the house, and finding a stick, Copper John would take a turn or two about the grounds. He would walk down to the creek, and examine the state of the tide, observe John's boat as she lay at her moorings, have a glance at Jane's water-garden beside the boat-house, look upwards to the herons in the tall trees beyond, and then across the creek to the smoke from the garrison on Doon Island, and away over the harbour waters of Doonhaven to the rise of Hungry Hill. Then up behind the house to the kitchen garden, where he would find Barbara, in earnest consultation with old Baird as to the best method of treating the new vine in the hot-house, and through the woods that his grandfather had planted, the wind singing in the pines like surf upon the shore, and along the narrow, twisting paths that were Barbara's pride, to the summer-house they had built that spring for Henry. He was lying there now, stretched out on his long chair, with Jane beside him, and she was reading to him.

Henry would look up, smiling gaily, his eyes unnaturally bright, a spot of colour on each cheek, so that his father, ignoring the thin body under the coverlet, would think to himself, he is certainly better.

"You observe me, sir," laughed Henry, "taking my ease as usual, and being most confoundedly lazy. I even have to confess that I fell asleep during the early part of the afternoon, and I believe I would be sleeping still had not Jane crept in to read verses to me."

"No, Henry, you are unfair," reproved Jane. "I came at your special request, and you were not sleeping, you were lying with your hands behind your head and an expression of great weariness upon your face. I only wish you had been sleeping. Doctor Armstrong told John you could not have too much rest."

"Willie Armstrong is an old maid," said Henry; "he fusses over me as though I were a child, instead of a hearty fellow with a rude health temporarily at a low ebb because I was fool enough to catch a bad chill last winter. You wait till I come back from the Barbadoes. I think I shall have myself tattooed and grow a curly beard. Were you going for a stroll, sir? Let me come with you, I have lain here long enough."

And to show how he despised his weakness, Henry threw aside his coverlet and rose to his feet, humming a little tune gaily under his breath, and at once began to discuss some business of the estate with his father, who, taking his arm, walked with him through the woods towards the home farm in the park.

"They will go too far, and father will be so occupied in talking that he will not remember," thought Jane, "and then this evening Henry will be so exhausted that he will eat no dinner, and Barbara will be anxious, and when I look out from my room, some time after midnight, I shall see the light under Henry's door, and I shall know he is not sleeping again."

She went on sitting in the little summer-house, by her brother's vacant chair, and wondered what his thoughts had been, this spring and summer, lying up here day after day, when he had first risen from his bed after this illness. Henry, who so enjoyed activity, discussion, people, and travelling, to be obliged to do without them, and without even the strength to help his father with the business of the mine. Anyone but Henry would have become morbid, restless, irritable, but if he felt any of these things he did not show them. He had always a smile for each member of his family, some jest to make, some amusing observation, and would be full of plans of what they would all do when he was well again, the parties and the picnics they would have.

"We will have one more picnic, anyway," he had said, that very afternoon, "before I sail for the Barbadoes. We will take the horses, and go to the lake on Hungry Hill, as we used to do when we were children, and Willie Armstrong shall come, and young Dickie Fox from the garrison—ah, don't blush, Jane—and Fanny-Rosa Flower, if Mrs White will let her, and her brother Bob, if he is still on leave from his regiment, and we will all enjoy ourselves immensely, and no one will be sick, or sad, or sorry."

And in his excitement and delight at the project he had brought on an attack of coughing, and vividly, horribly, she would remember the night of the trouble at the mine, and Henry standing in the library, shivering in his wet clothes. Well, that was all over, anyway. No more thieving, no more fighting, and Morty Donovan was dead. Sam Donovan had sold the farm, and was keeping a shop in Doonhaven. How angry the proud old man would have been—he would have considered it a disgrace for a Donovan to keep a shop. The other brother lived in a poor way on the road to Denmare. He kept a few pigs, and a cow, and sold whisky without a permit. No, the Donovans would never trouble any of the Brodricks again. The old mine was flourishing, and a new one had been started, and more men than ever were employed. Everything was going smoothly. They would all be so happy, but for the anxiety about Henry. And a little shiver came over Jane. The summer-house felt lonely sud-

denly without Henry, queer and deserted, as though he had already left
for the Barbadoes and the sun was no longer shining through the trees.
They should be thinned, she thought; one day they will enclose the summer-house, and the sun will not come to it at all, and she picked up her
book of poetry, and the cushions, and the coverlet, and went away down
through the flower-garden to the house.

As she stood on the slope above Clonmere she could see John and Doctor Armstrong mooring the boat in the creek. They had been over to
Doon Island to exercise John's greyhounds. John was looking up and
laughing, his lock of dark hair falling over his face, and he saw her, and
waved his hand. The dogs were coupled together, and stood shivering in the bows of the boat, eager to spring ashore, straining at the leash
that held them. The great silver cup they had won last season was now
John's proudest possession, and graced the sideboard in the dining-room.
He had shown it to Fanny-Rosa Flower, when she had driven over with
her father and brother to enquire after Henry, and Jane had been
secretly amused when Fanny-Rosa told him, with great seriousness, that
he should have his family crest put upon the cup, to give it greater
majesty, and that he should also have the Brodrick coat of arms stamped
upon the dogs' blankets.

Poor John, he had sat quite abashed and silent, while Fanny-Rosa
drank her tea, watching him out of the corner of her eyes; and Jane had
wondered how much of what she had said she really believed and was a
little unconscious snobbery inherited from her mother, and how much
was deliberate teasing, done to amuse herself and to provoke John.

How lovely she was, though, thought Jane, and how amusing a companion, and how extraordinary it was that Doctor Armstrong, who had
been at Clonmere at the time of the visit, should have said so firmly, after
the Flowers had departed, that Fanny-Rosa was too flamboyant and
restless for his taste, and had a careless streak to her nature that was not
due merely to youth but was part of her blood. "What type do you admire, then?" Jane had enquired, in all innocence, and he had looked
back at her very earnestly, as though he longed to say something, but had
not done so, and instead he observed that doctors were forbidden by their
profession to admire anyone, in case they became patients, and he left it
to Dickie Fox and the young officers on Doon Island to do all the admiring for him.

All this passed through Jane's head as she watched her brother and the
doctor climb from the boat with the dogs, and she wondered what Doctor
Armstrong would say if he knew that the book of poems in her hand had
been sent across to her from the garrison by Lieut. Fox, with one page in
particular marked with a cross—a love poem, by an Elizabethan poet,
entitled "On Entering My Lady's Chamber". Perhaps he would find it
shocking.

And now Eliza was leaning from her bedroom window, calling that

Thomas had rung the dressing-bell, and it wanted but a quarter of an hour to dinner, and if John and Doctor Armstrong were going to walk the dogs to the kennels they would be late, and father would be put out.

Father was coming down through the woods at this moment, with Henry leaning on his arm, and Barbara had joined them from the walled garden, a basket of nectarines on her arm, the fruit still warm from the sun, and Jane was aware of a strong feeling of happiness, of security. We are all here, she thought, the whole family, smiling and chatting and at ease with one another, dinner will soon be on the table, Thomas is walking through from the kitchen with his tray, the doors and the windows of the castle are flung open, catching the last gold rays of the sun before it sinks westward behind the trees. If only these moments would linger, would stay forever, and there would be no packing up and departing, no covering of the furniture with dust-sheets and closing of shutters and taking the steam-packet from Slane one chilly autumn morning, and a winter ahead that might bring uncertainty and change.

So the long days of August passed, and September came too early and too fast, with the preparations for Henry's journey to the Barbadoes. It was arranged that he should leave Doonhaven by his father's ship, the "Henrietta", which was sailing with her cargoes to Bronsea, and from there Henry would go to Liverpool and embark for the West Indies.

Already he seemed better, stronger, and less troubled by his cough, and on the very day of his depature the long-promised picnic was held on Hungry Hill. The day was fine and clear from the start, with the soft brilliance that late summer brings, and as the little cavalcade set forth on horseback from Clonmere, with Henry driven in state by Tim the stableboy, the tip of Hungry Hill, shimmering under the sun, held a promise of warm grass and scented heather, of gay dragon-flies skimming the still lake, of great rocks and stones, rusty with lichen, lying hot and bare beneath the sky.

They climbed the western face of the hill, away from the mine, and then, when the track became broken and lost, and the carriage could go no farther, John dismounted from his horse and helped his brother into the saddle, while Tim, weighed down by the picnic baskets, stumbled in the rear. What a party they were! Barbara—carrying a monstrous sunshade to keep off the flies—and Eliza, with sketching materials and stool and easel (for she fancied her water-colours), and Jane, with two volumes of poetry and escorted on either side by two young officers from the garrison, Lieut. Fox and Lieut. Davies, the latter having been asked for Eliza but appearing unaware of his duties, and Doctor Armstrong leading Henry's horse, with Henry himself in the saddle directing one way and John directing another, and Bob Flower, who was a Captain in the Dragoons and thought himself a little superior to the young officers from the garrison, and lastly Fanny-Rosa, who kept the whole party, and John in particular, in a frenzy of anxiety, because she would ride her horse at a distance, over the most uneven part of the ground, and when called to in warning shook her head and would not listen.

At last they came to the lake, with shouts of relief from the young men and cries of delight from the ladies, and Barbara at once busied herself with the unpacking of the food and the setting down of rugs, in case the ground was damp—which of course it was not—and see that Henry was not fatigued, while Henry himself lay on his back and closed his eyes and felt the warm grass with his hands and was still and happy.

Fanny-Rosa was climbing a rock to have a better view of the bay, and pulling her petticoats above her knees to give her more freedom, and John, who wanted to be with her, watched her moodily, thinking that if he joined her the others would notice and imagine that he did so because she was showing her legs in this barefaced fashion, which would be perfectly true in a sense and yet not the whole truth. Because he could not make up his mind, he went on standing uncertainly by the side of the lake, wishing he had not come on the picnic, yet knowing that if he had stayed at home he would have been miserable, so his day was doomed anyway.

Jane had disappeared with both her young officers, and Doctor Armstrong, sighing for some reason or other, asked Barbara whether he should help her with the setting out of the food.

"Please do," she said gratefully, hoping he was not feeling unwell (for it was unlike him to sigh), and wondering in the same breath what had happened to the dozen meat patties she herself had packed in the basket. If they were lost there would not be enough chicken to go round, and she must somehow manage to warn the family to take a drumstick apiece and leave the white meat to the guests.

Now Eliza, rather red in the face and frowning, was pulling at her arm.

"I wish you would speak to Jane," she whispered fiercely "She has gone behind a rock with those two young men. It looks so improper. I hardly know what Captain Flower will think of her."

And Barbara, still frantically searching for the meat patties, answered back rather impatiently that "Captain Flower would do well to look after his own sister, and no doubt Jane and the officers were hunting for butterflies."

Eliza sniffed, and said there were plenty of butterflies about without looking for them behind rocks, and as for that Lieut. Davies, she could not for the life of her imagine why he had been asked to the picnic at all; he was quite odious, and his laugh was too loud; she certainly was not going to have him looking over her shoulder while she sketched, he would be dreadfully in the way.

"Perhaps he won't want to, dear," said Barbara absently, and oh, what a relief! there were the meat patties after all—she remembered now she had put them in a napkin to retain the heat better.

"Would you tell everyone that luncheon is ready?" she asked Doctor Armstrong, and he went off at once to hunt up Jane and the officers, and they all returned almost immediately, Doctor Armstrong and the young officers watching one another like suspicious terriers, and Jane herself very quiet and demure, her large brown eyes turned upon each in turn.

"How delightful this is, and how well I feel, and what nonsense that the foolish fellows of your profession, Willie, should send me to the Barbadoes," said Henry gaily, sitting up and looking at the food placed so temptingly in front of him. "Barbara, I starve; two meat patties, please."

And soon the whole party were assembled and tucking in to the chicken and the patties, and the cold bacon, and the jellies, as though they had never eaten before.

Fanny-Rosa sat cross-legged, like a tailor, and John wondered whether he was the only one to notice that her feet were bare beneath her dress— he could see the toes peeping out from under her. She had sat herself down by Henry and was telling him he was the sultan of the feast, and she was a slave-girl ministering to him.

"How extremely amusing it would be if it were really so," said Henry, making her a mock bow. "Shall I bring you back gold bangles from the West Indies, and ear-rings? Slave-girls always wear those things, you know, as a sign of submission."

"Please," begged Fanny-Rosa, "and a tambourine also, and then I will dance for you."

John wished he could talk in that easy, gay fashion. He supposed Henry had learnt how to do it on the Continent, and Fanny-Rosa too.

"If the Barbadoes prove disappointing," Fanny-Rosa was saying, "then you must come back and join us in Naples. I am quite determined to go to Naples for the winter."

"Father and mother have said nothing about Italy to me," objected her brother. "I should think such a project extremely unlikely."

"You will be with your regiment, and have nothing to do with it," said Fanny-Rosa. "If I make up my mind father and mother will obey. We will go to Naples and gaze at Vesuvius, and listen to music, which will delight father, who will become sentimental and drink more than is good for him, and I shall buy a heap of gowns and dress like a Neapolitan, and wear a flower behind my ear, and throw kisses to you, Henry, from a balcony."

"Take no notice of her," said Captain Flower. "I regret to say that both my sisters are quite mad. Matilda, the young one, is even worse than Fanny-Rosa. She spends all her time in the stables, now we have no governess in the house. Castle Andriff is like an asylum."

"Poor Mrs Flower!" said Barbara. "You ought to try and help her, Fanny-Rosa, and set Matilda a good example. Jane is a great help to me, and she is nearly three years younger than you."

"Ah, but Jane thinks always of other people, Miss Brodrick," said Fanny-Rosa, "and I think only of myself. 'Enjoy yourself while you can,' said father to me only yesterday; 'we may all be dead before the year is out.' "

"That is certainly true," said Henry, "but before it happens let us meet in Naples, as you suggest, and I will claim that kiss from the balcony."

And so they continued through lunch, laughing, and teasing, and making plans, while John filled his mouth savagely with cold fat bacon, thinking of Lincoln's Inn, and his gloomy chambers, and the grey, damp fogs of December, that had nothing in common with sunny Naples and balconies.

After lunch there was more conversation, and then sighs, and yawns, and a feeling that everyone must do as they please. Henry rested in the shade of a boulder, with Barbara beside him, under her large sunshade, and Jane and the young officers read poetry behind a clump of heather. Eliza had planted herself down in front of a stunted gorse-bush, through which she could peer from time to time at Lieut. Davies and tell herself how very plain he was, and look from him back to her easel, upon which a sketch of the distant harbour of Doonhaven was taking slow shape. Bob Flower was asleep and snoring loudly, which, thought Eliza, was very ill-mannered of him, and he ought to be looking after his sister, who had disappeared.

John was throwing stones aimlessly into the lake. He had been a fool not to bring his rod, a trout was rising now in the middle, he could see the sudden ripple and the plop of the water, and he began to stroll along the edge towards the farther end of the lake, out of sight of the picnic party. How warm it was on Hungry Hill, how silent and how still. No one would know that only three miles or so to the eastward were the tall, ugly chimneys of his father's mine. The soft moss squelched under his feet, and there came to him the sour, boggy smell of the cold lake-water, and the scent of the heather as well. Poor Henry, he thought; this is what he would like, standing here with the little soft wind in his face, not lying down under a rug with his head on his arm.

A louder splash than usual caught his ear—there must be some big trout in the lake, after all—and he climbed over a boulder to have a sight of the fish, and oh, God! it was no fish jumping at all, but Fanny-Rosa, naked, with her hair falling on her shoulders, wading out into the lake, throwing the water aside with her hands.

She turned and saw him, and instead of shrieking in distress and shame, as his sisters would have done, she looked up at him, and smiled, and said, "Why do you not come in too? It is cool and lovely."

He felt himself go scarlet, and the sweat broke out on his forehead. Saying nothing, he turned away and began to walk rapidly in the opposite direction until his foot caught in a rabbit-hole and overturned him, and he slipped sideways into the heather, cursing and blaspheming, and sat for a while nursing his injured ankle, while a lark rose from in front of him and hovered in the air, singing his song of freedom.

Presently—hours must have passed, he thought; he did not care—he heard someone come and sit beside him, and turning he saw Fanny-Rosa, dressed once more, her face glowing with her swim, her hair wet on her shoulders.

"You think me shameful," she said softly, "you have a great disgust at me."

"Ah, no," he said swiftly, sweeping her with his eyes, "you don't understand. I came away because you were so lovely. . . ."

And he stammered, and could say no more, because she was smiling at him, and the smile was too much.

"You won't tell Miss Brodrick, will you?" she pleaded. "She would never ask me to Clonmere again, and maybe she would write and tell my mother."

"I won't tell anyone, ever," said John.

They were silent, and she began to pluck at the grass with her hands, which were small and slim. She laid them beside his a moment in contrast and then, when he still said nothing, she put her hands on top of his, and in a low, quiet voice she said:

"I think you are angry with me."

"Angry?" he said. "Fanny-Rosa, how could anyone be angry with you?"

And suddenly he had his arms round her, and she was lying on her back in the heather, with her eyes closed, and he was kissing her.

After a while she opened her eyes, but she did not look at him. She watched the lark flying overhead, and then she put up her hand and touched his cheek, and his mouth, and his eyes, and his dark hair, and she said:

"You've wanted to kiss me for a long time, have you not?"

"For nearly ten months," he told her, "I have thought of nothing else."

"Is it a disappointment to you," she said, "now that you have?"

"No," he said, and he wished he could tell her something of the fullness in his heart, something of the tenderness he felt for her, something of the longing that swept his whole body. But words were things of such difficulty, he could not juggle with them, he could only look down at her lying there in the heather, and suffer and worship.

"I thought," she said, "that it was only your old greyhounds you cared for," and she held up her hands for him to kiss the fingers one by one. "That day you came to Andriff," she told him, "in the winter—do you remember?—it was you who seemed light-hearted then, and your brother who was serious. But now that I know you both better I think it is the other way round. Henry is gay, and you are solemn."

When she spoke of Henry he was aware instantly of a pang of jealousy, and he remembered how she had laughed and flirted with his brother all through lunch, and had not looked at him. The memory made a twist in his mind, and he sat up, and gazed out across the hill, and the lark that had been singing overhead came down to earth and was hidden.

"You like Henry, don't you?" he said. "Everyone does."

"I like you both," she said.

In the distance they could hear the sound of voices calling, and Fanny-Rosa made a face.

"They are wondering what can have happened to us," she said. "Perhaps we should be going back."

She got up and brushed her dress, humming to herself, and John, watching her, a pain in his heart, thought how little she guessed the feeling that possessed him, and how foolish she would think him did she know. He had held her and kissed her, and this was to him a thing of so great a magnitude that he knew in all certainty his life from henceforward would be coloured by what had happened that afternoon. Never would he forget the sight of her naked body in the water, never would he lose the touch of her hands and her lips, as she lay in the heather.

But for Fanny-Rosa it had been an interlude, a moment of enjoyment after her bathe, and he wondered, loving her, whether she would have done likewise with his brother, or Willie Armstrong, or the young officers from Doon Island She gave him her hand now, like a child, as Jane used to do, and led him across the hill back to the lake, and as they walked she told him some nonsensical story about Simon Flower and his tenants—how he had given them all whisky one Christmas and sent every man home drunk—and he looked at her profile and the cloud of chestnut hair, and the happiness he had was sharp, and bitter-sweet.

She dropped his hand when they came within sight of the others. That is the end of it, he thought, now the day is finished, there will not be anything more, and he went silently to see to his horse, and saddle him, and help Tim with the rest of the horses; for to have laughed and chatted and made conversation, as Fanny-Rosa was doing, would have been beyond his power. They were alien to him now, the group of people; he would rather be alone or in the company of stolid Tim.

"What a day it has been, and how I have enjoyed it!" Henry was saying, "and you are all to come and see me embark on the 'Henrietta', and wave farewell."

Down they went through the stones and the heather to the track where the carriage had been left, Fanny-Rosa starting the lilting chorus of a song, and the others joining in, the young officers loudest of all. The brilliant blue of the sky had faded now to the still white of a September evening, and little mackerel clouds had gathered about the sun. The first shadows fell upon Hungry Hill. The lovely day, thought Jane, is coming to its close, and behind us we leave the lake, and the rocks, and the heather, and our voices will not trouble the stillness again. Already the day belongs to the past, something we shall look back upon and say to one another, "Do you remember this? Do you remember how Henry laughed, and sang a song with Fanny-Rosa Flower?"

So the party descended to the road, and clattered down the hill into Doonhaven. And there, in the square, were Casey, and another man, and the groom from Castle Andriff, waiting to hold the horses, and everyone dismounted and walked with Henry to the harbour, where the "Henrietta" lay at anchor, the men casting the sails from the yards preparatory to departure. Captain Nicholson was on the quay-side, having superintended the final stowing of the cargo, and Copper John stood beside him, with the master of the vessel. He smiled as he saw his son approach, and, with a word to the others, came to meet him.

"Not too tired, boy?"

"No, sir. I have had one of the happiest days of my life," said Henry.

"Good. That is what all of us wished for you. You have cut it rather fine, though. No time for prolonged farewells, or anything of that sort. The master wishes to weigh anchor as soon as you go on board. The wind is fair, and if it holds you should have a speedy passage to Bronsea."

Henry kissed his sisters, shook hands with his brother and his friends, and the usual forced words of jollity came to the lips of each in turn. "Bring us all back a shawl, Harry, from the Barbadoes," said Eliza, and "Do remember your cough medicine, dear," from Barbara, while there were injunctions from the young officers not to lose his heart to the native ladies. "Get well quickly, my boy, that is the only thing that concerns me," said his father, and then Henry turned and went down the steps to the waiting boat, and the boat pulled out across the harbour to the "Henrietta". He stood up in the stern, waving his hat, and smiling.

"We will meet in Naples," he called to Fanny-Rosa. "That's a promise, isn't it?"

She nodded, and smiled in return.

"I shall be waiting on the balcony."

They watched the boat draw alongside the vessel, and Henry and the master climbed aboard. Almost immediately there was activity, and noise, and bustle, the mate shouting orders from the foc'sle, and the creaking of the windlass.

"Don't let us wait any longer," said Jane suddenly. "I hate to see a ship sail out of harbour. There is so much of finality about it."

"There is your brother," said Fanny-Rosa. "Look, he is turning this way; he is shouting something to us."

"No use," said Copper John, "the wind carries away his voice, and the sound of the windlass. . . . Come, Jane is right. There is little reason in waiting here any longer. We shall see the ship just as well from Clonmere, if we walk to the end of the creek."

A dog ran across his legs as he turned, nearly throwing him on to the cobbles. He swore angrily, and hit out at it with his stick, catching it severely over the back, so that the dog howled, and ran limping to the doorway of the shop where it belonged.

"Keep your animal under control, can't you?" shouted Copper John to the owner, who appeared at the door of the shop, flushed and scowling, and ready to give quarrel. When Copper John saw who it was he turned his back, and walked away from the quay to the market square, his son and his daughters following. The man watched them, sullen resentment in his face, and then bent down to his injured dog, muttering to himself while from nowhere a crowd collected about him, asking questions and giving shrill advice.

"How unfortunate!" whispered Barbara, flushing. "Did you see?"

"Yes," said Jane slowly, "yes . . . it was Sam Donovan."

Looking over her shoulder, she saw the "Henrietta" gathering way through the water, as the boats towed her into mid-channel, and the sails broke out upon the yards.

Their father made no allusion to the incident. He helped Fanny-Rosa to mount her horse, and then exchanged a word or two with Bob Flower, giving him some message to take to Robert Lumley, their grandfather, on the next visit to Duncroom. Doctor Armstrong and the officers shook hands and departed, the Flowers rode away up the hill on the road to Andriff, and the Brodricks, climbing into their father's carriage, drove home to Clonmere. The sun had gone down behind the trees, and the castle and the creek were in shadow. They stood out on the drive for a moment or two, watching the "Henrietta" in the distance, and then she disappeared behind Doon Island and they saw her no more.

Copper John went slowly into the house, his hands clasped behind his back. Barbara and Eliza followed. Only John and Jane walked down to the far end of the grounds, where the last fir tree spread his bent branches above the sea, and they looked out over the wide harbour water to the last gleam of sunshine that played on Hungry Hill.

"I wish it had not happened," said Jane.

"What do you mean?" asked John.

"I wish that father had not hit Sam Donovan's dog."

"Oh, that. . . . Yes, it leaves a sort of sourness to the day. I would have had a look at the dog, but it would have been no use. My father would have been angry, and Sam Donovan taken it the wrong way."

"You could have done nothing. I only wish it had not happened. . . . Do you really think the Barbadoes will make Harry better?"

"I am sure of it. He will be in Naples in the spring. You must have heard him arrange a meeting with Fanny-Rosa."

John turned, and began to stroll back towards the house. Jane took his arm. Both were silent, both were thinking about Henry. Jane remembered his gay smile, his laugh, his wave of the hand from the little boat as it drew away from the quay-side to the "Henrietta", and she wondered how much of it was spontaneous, natural, and how much might be assumed, a mask hiding his illness from his family and from himself. John saw only a balcony in Naples, and on that balcony a girl who was Fanny-Rosa, with a flower behind her ear that she threw to Henry. Perhaps there were lakes in the hills behind Naples, like the lake on Hungry Hill. Perhaps Fanny-Rosa would bathe there too, and show her nakedness to Henry. Perhaps she would walk with him, hand in hand, and then lie down and let him kiss her. Henry, who was so much worthier than himself, who was clever, who was charming, who was finer in every way. Henry, who was ill. . . . The jealousy that possessed him was so shameful and despicable a thing that he was filled with hatred for himself and for his thoughts. Loving his brother, he yet grudged him one glance, one smile, one touch from Fanny-Rosa, even though that glance and that smile brought a few weeks of gaiety, of forgetfulness, to a sick, perhaps a dying, man. Not only grudged, but hated. And for Henry to think even of Fanny-Rosa in an idle moment was a thing so monstrous and so damnable that Jane, seeing John's white face and burning eyes, was startled and afraid, and said:

"What is it? Are you ill?"

"No," he said, "no, it's nothing."

She hesitated a moment, and then went indoors, and John, looking up at the windows of Clonmere, saw that the candles were being lighted, and the curtains drawn, and the evening had come, and it seemed to him that nothing mattered in the world, or would ever matter, but the longing he had for Fanny-Rosa, and he would perjure himself, commit murder, and go to the devil, to have her waiting for him above there, in his room in the tower; waiting for him, John Brodrick, and not for Henry.

7

The autumn of 1827 was exceptionally trying to Copper John. The weather was wild and stormy, so that shipments of ore from Doonhaven to Bronsea were quite impossible during November, and the new mine that had been sunk was proving less profitable than had been expected. For one thing, Captain Nicholson had gone down too deep, and had reached a level where the amount of water made work quite impracticable, in spite of the new pump, erected at a cost of several hundred pounds. It was therefore decided to abandon the spot, and to take soundings a little farther east, and here, though results at once justified the trial, the ground was so rocky that there was not an inch of it that could be worked without the use of gunpowder. Here again expense was considerable. An Order in Council was obligatory for every ounce of powder imported into the country, and Copper John had to keep his barrels stored in the magazine at the garrison on Doon Island, and sign a form every time a fresh barrel was taken across the harbour. Then the price of copper, which had been exceptionally high, dropped considerably. The large smelting companies at Bronsea could pretty well dictate their own terms, and Copper John was of the opinion that he would do well to get rid of some of his produce by private contract.

A hard frost succeeded the wet winds of November, and this brought fresh difficulties to the owner of Clonmere, for the potato crop had largely failed, and many of his tenants were in a fair way to starvation. Under the circumstances he was obliged to tell Ned Brodrick to be lenient with the half-yearly rent roll, and those tenants who were rather better off than their neighbours seized advantage of this, and kept back their payments. The inevitable disputes between one tenant and another, which appeared rooted in the character of the people, broke out, and after a long day's consultation at the mine Copper John would return to Clonmere to be faced with some ridiculous tale by his agent which had neither rhyme nor reason to it, and on which he would be expected to give judgement.

It was a little hard, he reflected, that he was the only man in the neighbourhood to take strong measures, and that he received no thanks and no assistance from the adjoining landlords. Robert Lumley was seldom at Duncroom, and when he was there it was only to drive down to Doonhaven and go through the mining accounts, complaining of his percentage. The Earl of Denmare was never in the country, except to fish for salmon, and Lord Mundy was very much an invalid these days, and hardly well enough to bestir himself in local affairs. As for Simon Flower, it was quite useless to appeal to him on any question at all. A man who drank in the stables with his own grooms, and even sat carousing with them in the drawing-room when his wife was a-bed, so the story ran, was no use as an upholder of truth and justice. Besides, the Flowers were abroad, in Italy—Henry had come across them in Florence, and had some idea of joining them in Naples, which his father felt was a waste of time. The voyage to the Barbadoes had done him a world of good, so he wrote to his family. He was certainly coughing less, and his father was on no account to worry about him. He had no doubt that a few months in Italy would perfectly restore him to health.

It was in the middle of April that Copper John, while spending Easter with his daughters in Lletharrog, decided to abandon his plan of returning to Doonhaven at the end of the month, where the new mine was giving excellent results, and travel out to Italy instead. The decision was taken after Barbara had received a letter at breakfast from a friend of hers, a Miss Lucy Mallet, written from Paris, where she and her mother were renting an apartment. "We have just come on here from Italy," she said, "having been in Rome, and also Naples, where we had the pleasure of meeting your brother, in company with some friends of yours, a Mr and Mrs Flower, and their daughter. My mother and myself were much distressed to hear how ill your brother had been, indeed he looked very poorly when we saw him, and had been in bed all the week, so Mrs Flower informed us. . . ." The letter continued with a description of the sights in Italy, which Copper John did not bother to read. He stared in front of him, tapping with his fingers on the breakfast table, and his daughters sat beside him, white-faced and serious.

"I shall go out to Italy myself," he said at length. "I have been a little uneasy in my mind about Henry all the winter, and now this news decides me."

"Could we not come with you?" urged Barbara.

"No, my dear, I would prefer to go alone. It is rather extraordinary that we have not had an account of Henry's health from the Flowers themselves, if he is so much with them. Simon Flower would not write, but Mrs Flower is not altogether lacking in sense."

"No doubt Henry did not wish any of us to be anxious," said Barbara, "and perhaps made light of his illness, even to them."

"It is quite possible," said Eliza, "that Lucy Mallet has exaggerated. She cannot have seen Henry for two or three years, and anyone would be shocked at his appearance these days, compared to what he used to be. His letters always seem cheerful enough, and indeed in his letter to Jane before Easter he talked of taking part in some carnival."

"And probably overtaxed his strength in the doing of it," said her father. "No, I am quite resolved to go to Italy, and shall in all probability set forth towards the end of the coming week. I had hoped to see Robert Lumley in Cheltenham, but that must go by the board, and I will see him on my return."

He consulted with Barbara as to whether Henry should be informed or not of the proposed journey, and finally decided, rather against her advice, that nothing should be said, and he would arrive in Naples as a complete surprise to his son. It so happened that business matters once more obliged him to delay the date of departure, and it was not until May that Copper John finally set out for the Continent. He avoided the long sea route, and travelled by easy stages through France and Italy, spending most of his journey in writing out, from memory, the profits and expenses of the mine on Hungry Hill, from its beginning in 1820 until the present month of the current year. He ignored the scenery entirely, found the heat excessive, the flies troublesome, the people robbers, and wondered why anyone should waste time and money in travelling for pleasure.

When he alighted from the coach at Naples in the third week in May, hot, dusty, and irritable, the first person to meet his gaze was Simon Flower, seated in a café on the square, smoking an immense cigar, and being entertained by an Italian lady of doubtful respectability. Simon Flower seemed quite unperturbed by the sudden appearance of a neighbour from home amongst the cosmopolitan crowd of Naples, and, holding his hat above his head, waved John Brodrick to a seat.

"My dear fellow, what a delightful encounter," he said. "This little lady speaks no English, so it does not matter what you say before her. I am very glad to see you. What in the world are you doing here?"

Copper John, who found Simon Flower a poor companion at the best of times, and even more so at the end of a long journey, replied shortly that he had not time to sit down, that he was on his way at once to Henry's hotel, and perhaps Simon Flower could direct him.

"Henry?" said the other, his mouth falling open. "But Henry has been gone from Naples for a fortnight."

Copper John stared at him a moment without speaking. Then he sat down at the table, his composure shaken, his plans all fallen to pieces at the news he had just received. He accepted the drink offered him without a word, nor did he protest when Simon Flower pressed a further one upon him.

"You had better tell me," he said at length, "what has happened."

"Nothing has happened," said Simon Flower, "except that you have had a long journey for nothing. No doubt you passed Henry on the road. He was not very well, poor fellow, and decided to go home before this heat grew too much for him. The best thing you can do is to take the next coach and follow him back along the route you came. But stay a night or two in Naples first. I can promise you an amusing forty-eight hours. If this little lady will bring a friend—I know one or two places that . . ."

"Was Henry in a very bad state of health?" interrupted Copper John. "Please understand that I, and my whole family, are extremely anxious about him."

"Well, now, I hardly think so. Have another drink, will you not? It's the only thing to do in this climate, I assure you. My daughter would really know more about Henry's health than I do. She trotted him round, you know, and had him esquire her about the town. You had better ask my daughter."

"Would I be likely to find Mrs Flower and Miss Flower at your hotel?"

"You would, I have no doubt. They are generally resting at this time of the day. That is why I take the opportunity of coming here. This little lady has not the pleasure of my wife's acquaintance."

"I hardly supposed she had," said Copper John, and rising to his feet he bade his neighbour good-afternoon, ignoring his companion, and leaving the pair in a state of benign and delightful intoxication.

He threaded his way through the busy streets, a tall, purposeful figure, the strong shoulders and the square jaw causing many of the idling people he jostled to turn and stare at him, until finally he came to the hotel he sought, and sent his card up to the apartment of Mrs Flower.

She received him with a wealth of apology and fuss—the rooms were most insignificant, there had been the usual misunderstanding with the manager, and really she felt quite ashamed, Simon was so forgetful in money matters, and her dress was not suitable for callers, Mr Brodrick must excuse her. Yes, indeed, Henry had been gone quite two weeks; they had seen such a lot of him, Fanny-Rosa had been so glad of his company, and then really, she hardly knew how it was, but the poor boy must have done rather too much, he seemed sadly pulled down, and one morning he told them he was going home, Fanny-Rosa had been most upset, and said he was jealous of an Italian count—you know the nonsense girls talk—no truth in it at all of course, just some little folly between them, but anyway, yes, Henry did seem to be coughing, and he had left Naples on such a very hot day, dust everywhere, she did so hope it would be better and cooler in France, Mr Brodrick would no doubt catch up with him, she understood Henry was not going to rush the journey. . . .

The door opened, and Fanny-Rosa came into the room. She had a lace shawl thrown over her chestnut hair, in the fashion of the country, and even Copper John, who had little time for admiration, was struck by the vivid colouring, the slanting green eyes, and the real beauty of Simon Flower's daughter. She looked startled when she saw her mother's visitor, and went white.

"What is the matter? Has anything happened?" she asked.

"I've come on a fruitless errand," replied Copper John. "I came to see Henry, and I am told he has left, and is on his way home. We had a letter from some friends of ours, the Mallets, who met Henry here and gave a very poor account of his health, so I threw up my plan for returning to Clonmere and came here instead. I might have saved myself the trouble."

Fanny-Rosa seemed relieved. She sat down beside her mother, and played with the fringe of her dress.

"I think possibly the carnival festivities were a little too much for Henry," she said. "He looked rather unwell afterwards. He was in bed two or three days."

"Such a charming young man, Mr Brodrick," said Mrs Flower; "we were all quite delighted with him. It must have been the last evening of the carnival that exhausted him; he and Fanny-Rosa went to see some procession or other—did you not, my dear?—and returned very late. I know I had gone to bed, and was asleep when you came in. Heaven knows what happened to your father, he never came back for the night, but it was the next day that Henry kept to his room, was it not, Fanny-Rosa?"

"I'm afraid I've forgotten," said her daughter.

She made a little curtsey to Copper John, asked to be remembered to Henry when he met with him, hesitated a moment, and then left the room. Soon after John Brodrick also made his excuses, and departed. He found he had time to dine, rest for a few hours, and then catch the coach for the homeward route. The Flowers had not been very helpful, he considered. Their whole attitude to the business was typical of them— they were as careless and as improvident here in Italy as they were at home at Castle Andriff. It was disgraceful to see a man of middle-age like himself, with a grown family, sitting in a Neapolitan cafe and drinking with some woman of the town, in the middle of the afternoon, as he had seen Simon Flower, and to reflect that the money he did it on, which the luckless proprietor of the hotel had apparently not yet seen, was no doubt a gift from Simon Flower's father-in-law, Robert Lumley, as a result of last summer's profit from the mine on Hungry Hill. He, John Brodrick, the director, worked ten hours a day to obtain the greatest efficiency from the mine, so that it was probably the best-conducted mine in the kingdom, and an idle good-for-nothing toper like Simon Flower sat on his backside in the sun and reaped the benefit.

He left Naples weary and low in spirits, and the tedious homeward journey, with no certainty of coming up with his son, loomed as a nightmare before him. Stage after stage was passed, and town after town, and all along the route he made enquiries after a young man of fair complexion and slight build, who would seem fatigued and possibly unwell. Once or twice he met with success. Yes, the people of the hotel in question had seen a young man answering to the description. He had stayed a night under their roof a week or ten days ago. The young gentleman seemed much tired, and coughed a great deal. He had given a letter to be posted. No, they did not recollect to whom. Not to England. To an address in Naples, they thought. No doubt the present gentleman would soon catch up with his son. . . . And at the next town there would be a blank stare to his question, a shrug of the shoulders, an expression of regret. The young gentleman described had not been seen. . . .

It was strange, thought Copper John, that the Flowers had made no mention of hearing from Henry. He would hardly have written to anyone else in Naples. Possibly the letter, or letters, had miscarried. And on he went, day after day, in France now, the heat somewhat less oppressive, but the route dusty and exhausting and the sun staring down from a glazed blue sky. On the evening of the fourth of June the coach rattled into the little old town of Sens, some seventy miles south-east of Paris, and drew up at the hotel de l'Ecu. Tomorrow, thought Copper John, as he descended stiffly from the vehicle, I shall be in the capital, where I am more than certain to have news of Henry. He would no doubt have called upon the Mallets, and might even be staying in their apartment. What a relief it would be to have the journey three-parts done, and to return home together.

He made his way into the hotel, a dark, stuffy, old-fashioned sort of building, and asked for the proprietor. He came at once, a large man with a cheerful round face, wiping his mouth with the back of his hand, for he was in the middle of supper. Copper John, in his poor, careful French, asked him the inevitable question. Had he met with a young man, of slight build and fair complexion, who might seem fatigued or unwell? At his words the expression on the landlord's face changed in-

stantly. He put his hand on John Brodrick's shoulder, and burst into a
torrent of French that the other could not follow, and then turned, and
disappeared a moment, returning with a woman, his wife, and one or two
other persons. They all began to question Copper John, each one talking
above the other, and finally the traveller, in desperation, said:

"I am the father of the young man. In God's name, does anyone here
speak English?"

There was immediate silence. The woman said softly:

"*C'est le père. Quelle tristesse! Faut lui montrer la chambre. . . .*"

There was another consultation, in low tones, and then the landlord,
his face very grave, asked Copper John to have the goodness to wait a few
minutes; he would send for Monsieur Getif, the doctor, who would explain everything, and knew a few words of English. Copper John was
now greatly alarmed. The people at the hotel had obviously seen Henry,
and this doctor they spoke of had attended him. The woman offered him
refreshment, which he refused, and he sat down to wait, while they stood
respectfully at a distance, watching him, and now and again exchanging
whispered words the sense of which he could not catch. The suspense of
waiting was well-nigh intolerable, but in about twenty minutes the landlord returned, accompanied by a tall, thin man, bearded, and spectacled,
who at the sight of Copper John came forward and bowed, removing his
spectacles and polishing them, as a little instinctive sign of nervousness.

"You are the father, monsieur?" he said, in a hushed tone.

"I am," replied Copper John. "I beg you to tell me immediately, is
there anything amiss with my son?"

Monsieur Getif swallowed, and made a gesture with his hands.

"I regret very much," he said, "you have to prepare yourself for a great
shock, monsieur. Your son has been gravely ill, with a *congestion pulmon-
aire.* I did what I could, but the disease was too advanced."

"What exactly are you trying to tell me?" asked Copper John steadily.

"Monsieur, you must have courage. . . . Your son died yesterday, at
five o'clock in the morning. . . . His body lies in the room above."

Copper John did not answer. He stared past the doctor and the
sympathetic, curious faces of the landlord and his wife, out of the window
to the dusty, cobbled street. A cart rumbled past, and a boy driving
called loudly to the horse, cracking his whip. The bells on the cart
tinkled. The clock on the old church across the square chimed out the
hour. He loosened his cravat, and then tightened his hold on his stick.

"Would you take me upstairs to my son?" he said.

The doctor led the way, the landlord and his wife following in the rear.
They went to a room on the first floor, overlooking the street. The curtains were drawn against the light. Two candles were burning at the
head of the bed, and two at the foot. Henry lay between them. There
was only a white sheet over him, and his face was uncovered. He looked
very young, and peaceful, and still. His clothes were folded neatly on the

chair against the wall. His wallet, and keys, and books were on the mantelpiece. A whisper from the wife of the landlord broke the silence.

"She says nothing has been touched," said the doctor, "it is just as he arranged his things."

"How long had he been here?" asked Copper John.

"Six days. He was taken ill the night of his arrival. He would not permit us to send word to England. It would give anxiety, he said."

"Did he speak of his family at all, of me?"

"No, monsieur, he was too weak. He just lay there, on his bed. He was very patient. It was madame here who heard him cough yesterday morning, and she came in and found him—dying—monsieur, and she sent for me, but it was too late. . . . We are all so very sorry, Monsieur."

"Thank you. I am grateful for what you have done."

One by one they withdrew from the room, leaving him alone with his son. He took a chair and sat beside the bed. Outside the hotel de l'Ecu he could hear the carts as they rattled over the cobbled stones, and the jangling bells of the horses. There were the voices of people too, calling to one another. A woman was singing in the house across the way.

There were things that he should do, and arrangements to be made. He would have Henry embalmed and buried in Paris. Later on they would try to have him removed to England. He would not like to think of Henry lying here, alone, in foreign soil. He must write to Barbara, to Robert Lumley, to the Flowers; there were so many letters he must write. Henry was twenty-eight. He had been twenty-eight three months. He looked younger, much younger, as he lay there on the bed. It made him think of those days when he and Sarah had gone down to visit the boys at Eton. Henry was always so delighted to see them. And at Oxford later. So many friends to introduce. He could not remember ever having to beat Henry as a lad, or find fault with him. Such a companion too, these last years, ever since the start of the mine. He would have married soon, doubtless, and settled down at Clonmere with his bride. Now Clonmere would go to John. . . . He went on sitting in the chair, staring at the body of his son, and the candles burnt lower, forming spots of grease upon the floor beside the bed.

After an hour there came a light tap at the door, and the woman of the hotel asked him whether he would come down and have a bite or two to eat; he must keep his strength, she said, he must not give way.

He remembered that the business of living must be continued, that eating and drinking, and planning and sleeping, were part of existence, that Henry's death would alter none of this. He went downstairs and had his dinner alone in the little coffee-room of the hotel, and after dinner the doctor called and accompanied him to the house of the Maire, Monsieur Jacques-Theodore Leroux, where there were papers to be signed and certain formalities to be gone through. The doctor and the Maire both signed the certificate of death, and another paper which would permit the father to have the body of his son embalmed and taken to Paris within the next few days. This necessary business gave Copper John some measure of comfort. It made something to do. He did not have leisure to be alone with his thoughts. When he had left the Maire and the doctor, he walked a while in the town of Sens until it was dark, and then he returned to the hotel de l'Ecu and went upstairs once more to Henry's room. It was as though he expected there to be some change, that Henry might perhaps have moved, or the things be disturbed upon the chair. But Henry lay still and quiet, as he had been before. Only the candles had sunk lower, and now burnt dim and fitful in their sockets. His father extinguished them, one by one, and as he did so it seemed to him an act of finality. It was his farewell to Henry.

He left the room, and shut the door behind him. He asked the landlord for paper, and pen, and ink. He had recollected, when he had signed the death certificate, that the fourth of the month was the day when he always wrote to Robert Lumley and gave him an account of the work at the mine. He had omitted to do so in May, because he had been about to set forth on his journey, and had only sent his partner a short note, explaining that he was leaving for the Continent. Robert Lumley would consider him very remiss if he left him without word for two months. It was a good thing he had thought to bring with him the details of the mining accounts for the last six months. It would be as well, perhaps, if Robert Lumley had a copy for reference. He dipped his pen in the ink and began his letter.

"*At the hotel de l'Ecu, Sens, Dept. de l'Yonne, France.*
"My dear Mr. Lumley,
"You will, I am sure, learn with regret that the journey to Italy for the recovery of poor Henry's health has proved fruitless. He was unable on his return to proceed further than Sens in France, where he expired yesterday, the third of the month. It is a heavy blow to me, and will be so to the rest of my family, but we must pray to the Almighty to enable us to bear it with fortitude. I take it for granted that you have received the £1499, the whole of your royalty for last year, but I have nothing as yet to remit from the new mine, though I have great expectations that it will prove even more profitable than the first. . . ."

BOOK TWO

GREYHOUND JOHN, 1828–1837

I

T HE SUMMER of 1828 passed slowly, and the days seemed endless to John in Lincoln's Inn, when, standing at the window of his rooms and looking out upon the narrow, stuffy court, he would think of the sea breaking on the shores of Doon Island, and the tide running swiftly up the creek below Clonmere. His work, as usual, held no interest for him, and he would loll in his chair, biting the end of his pen-holder, a heap of untidy papers before him on his desk, while now and again a clerk would appear and ask for some note or other from his file, which it would take an eternity to find. He longed for home more than he had ever done in his life before, and now that Henry was dead it would have been easy enough to give up this farce of the law in London, with the natural and true excuse that his presence was necessary at Clonmere. But something prevented him from doing so, a queer twist that had come into his mind with his brother's death. It seemed to him, during those long weeks in London, that he was in some way to blame for being alive and well, when Henry, who was so much better than himself, lay cold and dead in a gloomy French cemetery. It would not have mattered had it been the other way round. The family would have soon forgotten him. But Henry, so gay, so clever, adored by his sisters and well-nigh worshipped by his father, how could he ever be replaced? They would never get over the loss. They would discuss the circumstances of his illness over and over again, just as they had done at Lletharrog when his father returned from France, and always there would be a sigh, and a harking back to that evening in the mine the winter before.

"It was that night that he caught the chill," Barbara would say. "Don't you remember how he came back to Bronsea the following week with a high fever, and was in bed here all during Christmas?"

"And yet," Eliza would answer, "Henry had often been wet to the skin before and taken no harm from it. John was probably wet too that night, were you not, John, and you suffered no ill consequence?"

"Henry worked gallantly that night; I shall always remember it," said his father. "He did not spare himself. He was an example to all."

And John, listening, standing with his hands in his pockets looking out of the farm-house window at Barbara's trim little garden, would feel an unconscious reproach in his father's words. If John had worked harder that night possibly Henry would not have had so much put upon him. He was aware of being no help to the family. He was the one brother now to whom they would all turn, and yet he failed them. He knew that he should have made some effort to try to take Henry's place, not in his father's affections but in his esteem, by offering to go to Bronsea and to take some sort of responsibility upon his shoulders. Shyness prevented him, a feeling of inferiority, and a fear that if he spoke or moved, his father would think, "How hopeless a fellow he is compared to Henry!" It was better, therefore, to do nothing. He would just sink into himself and be silent. And so, instead of accompanying his father into Bronsea, he would take his rod and go fishing in the stream below the farm-house, thinking all the while about his dead brother out in France, wondering what his thoughts had been that last week, lying ill and lonely in the hotel. And his sisters, in the parlour at Lletharrog, would say to one another, "John is really very selfish. He seems quite unmoved by Henry's death." The only one who guessed the true turmoil of his mind was Jane, and she would come to him sometimes, and put her arm around his neck, but he knew that even Jane, with her intelligence and intuition, could not understand the fierce thoughts that troubled him. At the end of the fortnight he returned to London, and when his father wrote from Clonmere during the hot, dreary month of August, asking him whether he would be joining them as usual, he answered that pressure of work forbade it, indeed that it was unlikely that he would cross the water at all while they were there. His father made no answer to this palpable untruth, but a long letter came from Barbara, full of reproaches, saying that none of them could understand what had come over him; it was as though he had no affection for his home at all. And John, biting his pen-holder in his stuffy London office, tried to tell his sister that the very reason why he did not come was because he loved his home too well. He saw himself, in all the pride of possession, walking round the grounds with his father, discussing some alteration, looking up at the windows and the grey stone walls, and how the momentary delight would suddenly be shattered by the feeling that all this was coming to him through tragedy and mischance, that in reality he would have no right to any of it—Clonmere belonged to Henry, lying in his grave, and his father knew it too, his father would be thinking the very same thought as they walked before the castle together. No, it was useless. Barbara would not know what he meant. John tore the letter into shreds, and did not write again. The family must think what they liked of him. And instead of going home John went up to Norfolk to stay with an old Oxford friend who bred greyhounds for coursing, and most of the early autumn and winter when he could make an excuse to leave London he would be in Norfolk, thinking and talking greyhounds, for, as he told his friends, "Dogs are the only things I understand, and the only things that understand me." To John, a greyhound was a thing of beauty and of moods, sensitive and delicate. And when highly bred, the more

temperamental, the more inclined to brilliancy if rightly handled, or to
hopeless failure if indifferently trained. He would study each dog indi-
vidually, know which one could be expected to do well on different days,
how one would sulk in the rain and wind and lose interest at a trifle, how
another would work with a staunch heart whatever the weather. John
would have great tenderness for them, touching them gently with his
strong, square hands. Then the training would begin, and finally would
come the reward for his skill and patience, the excitement of the course
itself, the betting, the shouts of the spectators, and Lightfoot, the greyhound that had seemed so fragile and nervous a creature when he first
had her, would prove her breeding and her worth in a few minutes before
the crowd, doubling and twisting with the frightened hare, making escape
impossible. Once more John would be clapped on the back and congratulated, with another great silver cup to his name, and Lightfoot,
shivering in excitement and ecstasy, crouching at his knee.

In March the coursing season came to an end, and John, who had
thought of little else for the past six months but his greyhounds, was faced
with the prospect of another long summer in London, making up his
arrears in work, or giving up finally and for ever the farce of Lincoln's
Inn and settling down with his father and his sisters at Clonmere. If he
threw up his work in London he would be able to idle pleasantly through
the summer at Clonmere, race his dogs in the neighbourhood during the
autumn, and bring them back to Norfolk again for the three months after
Christmas, when the family was at Lletharrog. The prospect was too
good to be laid aside, and he wondered to himself if he had been a very
great fool the year before in taking his brother's death in the way he did.
The thing had been a tragedy, but tragedies become less poignant as the
months pass, and no one in the world would have grudged the possession
of Clonmere to John less than Henry.

So in May John said goodbye to the files of paper, the ink, and the dust
of Lincoln's Inn, and with a feeling of freedom he had never known before
he embarked on the steam-packet to Slane, and travelled down by road
to Doonhaven, his greyhounds and his kennel-man accompanying him.
When he came to the rise of the road past the mine on Hungry Hill, and
looked out across Doonhaven to Clonmere, standing grey and solid at the
head of the creek, a strange feeling of pride and delight swept over him
that he had never sensed before. Clonmere had suddenly become more
personal, more significant, the thing of beauty he would one day possess.

His homecoming was a happy affair. His father and his sisters had
walked out along the drive to meet him, and there was no question of
coolness, no shadow of restraint. His father shook hands with him
warmly, remarked how well he was looking, and then proceeded to enquire after the greyhounds. The dogs at once descended from the box
and were exhibited with pride, and then the whole family walked back
to the castle along the path by the creek, chatting and laughing, a sister

on either side clinging to John's arm. The little path beneath the fir trees felt hard and springy under John's feet, and there was the lively scent of young summer in the air, a happy blend of pine, and primrose, and rhododendron, and the salty, pungent, muddy smell of a bubbling ebb-tide.

They came out of the woods by Jane's water-garden, at the head of the creek, and here there were new plants to be admired, and a new flagged path to criticise, Jane, flushed and excited, holding on to his hand, and so on to the boat-house, where one of the men was busily engaged in painting John's sailing-boat, the gig being already in the water. Everyone smiled, everyone was happy, and John himself felt something warm and new stirring in his heart which he could not express. He ran up to his room in the tower. There were his guns, and his rods, and all his old schoolboy books, worn and familiar, and the painting of the chapel at Eton, and the quad of his college at Oxford. There was the case of butter-flies, passionate hobby of one summer holiday only, and the collection of birds' eggs, and on the mantelpiece the random objects that he had gathered from time to time in his boyhood: a piece of flint from Hungry Hill, a queer-shaped stone like an egg he had found once on Doon Island, a patch of dried moss from the bogs around Kileen.

"Tomorrow," he said to Jane, "tomorrow we will go fishing for killigs in the creek," and holding her at arm's length, and cocking his head on one side, he observed, "You know you are becoming very pretty."

Jane blushed, and told him not to be absurd.

"She is having her portrait painted," said Barbara. "We all think it a most excellent likeness, although Willie Armstrong says it does not do her justice."

And there in the drawing-room, standing upon its easel, the paint still wet on the canvas, was the replica of the Jane who stood beside him, wearing the new cream gown which had been purchased in Bath that winter, her pearl necklace round her throat, her warm brown eyes full of the expression he knew so well, wistful and a little unsure of herself.

"And what does Dick Fox say to the portrait?" asked John.

"Oh, he is delighted, of course," said Eliza, tossing her head. "He used to come to every sitting, and talk to Jane to relieve the monotony. No doubt that is why Jane has such a simpering look about her in the portrait."

John, glancing at his youngest sister, saw that she seemed distressed at Eliza's words, and that tears, even, were not far distant. He smiled across at her and shook his head.

"Take no notice of Eliza," he said, "the grapes are very sour," and with quick understanding he changed the subject from the portrait.

So Jane is growing up, he thought at dinner, and is falling in love with Dick Fox on Doon Island, and only yesterday it seemed she was a little girl reading fairy stories before the fire in the old nursery. Dick Fox was

a good sort of fellow, no doubt, but for a moment there was a flickering
jealousy in John's heart that his pet Jane, who had been such a dear companion, should look kindly upon any man but himself, and the thought of
her being kissed and perhaps fondled by a scruffy young officer from the
garrison was distasteful, and did not bear thinking about.

". . . and so I should like your opinion on the lease before I finally
sign it," his father was saying, laying down his knife and fork and looking
across the table at his son.

John started, and "Yes, sir, of course, I shall be delighted," he said,
without a notion of what his father had been talking about.

Barbara gave him a warning nudge with her knee.

"I entered into an agreement," continued Copper John, "to take one-
half of the arrears and let him hold the ground at £130 a year. Needless
to say I have not received a penny, and gave him notice to quit last
March, which he has not yet done. The position is intolerable, as you see."

"Oh, quite, sir. Most intolerable."

"I mean to make every exertion in my power to get the communications opened by a good road between Doonhaven and Denmare, which,
you will agree, will be of incalculable advantage to Robert Lumley's and
Lord Mundy's estates, and if we can once open up the route from the
lakes by Denmare and Doonhaven and Mundy to Slane, I think that visitors to the west would prefer it to returning the same way. Then we
might safely build an inn in Doonhaven. Indeed, it might induce gentlemen to reside in the neighbourhood. What do you think, John?"

"I am of your opinion undoubtedly, sir."

"I don't know whether the Government have money at their disposal
for the purpose, but I shall get all the information I can. They might do
it all at their own risk. It would be a great matter to open up communications with the west part of the country, and ships of war could be supplied with provisions in the event of another war. I only hope our Ministers will not kick up some row unexpectedly, and get us all into a scrape."

"I hope not, sir," said John.

Very little of what his father was saying made any interest to him,
but he hoped that his voice rang with some conviction and that his
father would be satisfied.

"The Flowers are at Castle Andriff, by the way," said Barbara. "They
were abroad as usual, until just recently. I am glad to say that Fanny-
Rosa is not such a harum-scarum, wild thing as she was. Wintering
abroad has given her poise and good manners. But I believe she does
exactly as she pleases. And poor Mrs Flower has no control over the
younger girl at all."

"They say some Italian was desperately in love with Fanny-Rosa,"
said Eliza—"a titled man too, who had a wife already."

"Never listen to scandal, Eliza," said her father. "It does no good to
the hearer, and less to the speaker. If you come into the library, John, I

can show you the exact spot on the plan of Hungry Hill where I think of making a further trial. There is copper there, and at no very great depth either, so that our expenses would be inconsiderable."

John followed his father into the library, and pretended an interest in figures and mining calculations, but all the while his thoughts strayed to Fanny-Rosa. He had not seen her for eighteen months, not since that un-forgettable day on Hungry Hill when she had lain in his arms in the heather beside the lake and Henry had sailed for the Barbadoes. Last year, during the hot summer in London, John had wondered how much she had seen of Henry in Naples. Had she been sorry when he died? His thoughts then had added to the turmoil in his mind, and Fanny-Rosa be-came a symbol to him of something rare, and beautiful, and unobtain-able, a ghost girl in a foreign land he would never see again. She would marry some Italian, and perhaps years later come to Castle Andriff with a brood of babies and a flashy husband, herself coarse and heavy, her charm vanished with the years.

Deliberately he had painted this picture in his mind so that he should not be hurt by the thought of her, and the idea of her marriage to her foreigner, and out of his reach for ever, gave him a peculiar, rather warped, satisfaction. His Fanny-Rosa would be a memory, a phantom thing born out of the loveliness of Hungry Hill, while she who continued living was someone with whom he had no concern. And now all the care-ful locking of his memory was to be broken by the real Fanny-Rosa, no ghost at all, but alive, and unmarried, and even if every Italian in Naples had made love to her she would be more beautiful than ever, and she was coming to Clonmere next week, Barbara had said. She might want to see the greyhounds, and Jim was given special orders to have the dogs groomed and ready on the day the Flowers were expected, and their coats upon their backs in spite of the warm weather, for the scarlet and grey trimmings were really rather fine, and the large J. L. B. looked well against the background.

About two hours before the Flowers were due to come he became fearful and sick of heart, and going to the far end of the grounds, by the last fir tree, he sat out of sight of the castle and stared across at Doon Island, wondering whether it would not be wiser to get his boat and disappear all day, and not come in to the house and meet the Flowers at all. He felt suddenly that he did not want to see Fanny-Rosa, or talk to her, and if he did, nothing would happen as he had planned; she would hate the greyhounds, scorn his cups, talk all the while about the Italians she had met, and the day would be disastrous, a failure from beginning to end. He was still sitting by the creek when he heard the carriage bowl along the drive, pass under the arch of rhododendrons, and sweep round again to the house, and then in the distance came the sound of Barbara's voice, and Eliza's rather irritating, high-pitched laugh. Barbara called "John . . . John . . .", and he crouched behind the tree, determined not to

join them, wondering whether he could return to the house in some way
without being seen, and go and shut himself up in his room in the tower.
The voices were silent, they must have gone indoors, and he heard Casey
come round for the carriage and drive the horses to the stable. Some impulse stronger than himself made him rise to his feet and walk slowly back
across the grass to the house. His hands were trembling, and he thrust
them into his pockets. He was aware of someone looking down at him
from the drawing-room window.

"How do you do, John?"

And glancing up he smiled, for there was Fanny-Rosa, the ghost of
Hungry Hill, and the eighteen months since he had seen her were as
though they had never been, were as yesterday, and fresh and vivid in his
memory were the touch of her hands and the warmth of her lips as she lay
on her back in the heather with his arms beneath her.

Then he was in the drawing-room, he was standing beside her, Bob
Flower was saying something in his ear, everyone was talking, and laughing, and eating cake. He heard himself offering Bob a glass of Madeira.

"Father is at the mine," Barbara was saying, "but he will be home to
dine with us at five, as usual. You men had better get off to your fishing
while the weather holds."

"I should like to come," said Fanny-Rosa. "Does John not permit
ladies in his boat?"

"Why, yes," said John, "why, yes . . . of course. I never dreamt you
would want to come."

And delightfully, joyfully, the whole day had to be planned afresh, for
now that Fanny-Rosa would be of the party Jane would accompany her,
and the Bule Rock being too far and the sea perhaps too rough for them,
they must sail by the island instead, and more food must be put in the
basket, and one of Barbara's shawls for Fanny-Rosa in case the wind
freshened. What happiness in walking down to the creek, and bringing
the boat to the steps, so that Jane and Fanny-Rosa might climb aboard,
and then rolling his sleeves above his elbow, and shaking his hair back,
and singing out to Bob to cast off from the moorings when the sail had
been hoisted and the tiller shipped into place. Down the creek into the
open waters of Doonhaven, with the long, straggling island ahead of him
and the open sea beyond, and away on the left the great mass of Hungry
Hill, green and shining under the sun.

How good to be no longer sullen and wretched and shy, hating himself
for his moods, but instead to be doing the thing that he liked, to be sailing
his boat, with the wind in his hair, and Fanny-Rosa in the stern beside
him. She had not changed, unless to be more lovely, and there was a
grace about her that had not been before. The shawl Barbara had lent
her was green, matching her eyes. She had flung it carelessly about her
shoulders, and she looked up at John and smiled, and the smile held a
promise, and the promise breathed a hope.

"I hear that you know more about greyhound coursing than any man in the country," she said. "Tell me all you have been doing since I saw you last."

He began to tell her about the greyhounds, at first with diffidence, thinking she would not listen, and then with increasing confidence, making her laugh with his account of the racing crowds, the owners with their petty jealousies and frequent dishonesty.

Bob showed interest too, and asked many questions. It was agreeable, thought John, to speak for once in a way as an authority, and to know that his opinion on the one subject in the world that he knew anything about was listened to with respect.

They anchored for a cold luncheon of meat patties and cress sandwiches on the westward side of Doon Island, and then Bob Flower, looking across at the garrison, bethought him of a friend of his, lately gone as Adjutant to the battalion quartered there, and suddenly there was a suggestion that the party should go ashore, and walk up to the Mess, and enquire after him. John glanced at his sister's innocent little face and wondered if Dick Fox was at this moment watching her through his telescope from the windows of the Mess.

When they came to the anchorage Fanny-Rosa declared that she preferred to stay in the boat; she had come to enjoy the water, not the doubtful claret at the garrison, and surely Jane was not like to come to any harm with Bob as a companion, for Bob was known to be the soul of decorum. So Jane stepped ashore, looking very pretty and demure, on the stolid arm of Bob Flower, and it was quite a coincidence that Lieut. Fox should at that moment be coming down the path to meet them.

John put the boat about and sailed eastwards, towards Hungry Hill, and now that he was alone with Fanny-Rosa a queer feeling of restraint came over him. He felt he could not speak, or whatever he said would sound foolish and forced. He kept his eye on the sail, and did not look at her. There, across the water, lay the land, and the great hill rising to the sky. It seemed remote and intangible, the summit golden in the sun, and he thought of the lake, how still it would be, and cold.

"Do you remember the picnic we had there, last September year?" said Fanny-Rosa.

John did not answer at once. He wanted to look at her but dared not. He hauled in the sheet a little closer.

"I think of it very often," he said.

She moved slightly in the boat, arranging the cushion at her back, and now her arm rested against his knee, making a torment and a strange delight.

"We were very merry," she said, "very gay."

She spoke softly, almost sadly, as though reflecting upon a past that could never come again, and John wondered whether it was his love-making in the heather that she remembered, or Henry's laughter and

Henry's smile. The old jealousy swept upon him once more, the old anguish, and doubt, and indecision, and putting the boat suddenly about he bore away from Hungry Hill, towards the open sea. The boat rocked slightly in the swell, and some water splashed in over the bows, trickling down towards her feet. Fanny-Rosa took off her shoes without a word, and leant closer to John's knee.

"You saw much of Henry, did you not, those few months before he died?"

The words were out at last. He could hardly believe that he had said them. This time he forced himself to look at her, thinking he should see some trace of sorrow in her face to add to his pain, but her unconscious profile was turned towards the sea. She shook the spray from her hair, and tucked her slim, bare feet under her gown.

"Yes," she said; "he seemed to enjoy Naples. It was so unfortunate that he left when he did, tired and unwell. We all felt it very much."

Her voice was calm, conventional. Surely if she had cared for him or he for her she would not have spoken thus?

"Henry always liked people, and new places. That is where we differed," said John.

"You are not the slightest bit like him," said Fanny-Rosa. "You are much darker and broader. Henry was more like Barbara."

None of this matters, thought John, as the boat heeled in the freshening breeze, whether I am dark or Harry was fair, or who resembles whom. The only thing I would know is what they really felt for one another in Naples, and why Henry left so suddenly, and his health became worse. Had they loved, and had they quarrelled, and was the last person that his brother thought of lying there in that hotel bedroom in Sens the Fanny-Rosa who sat beside him now? The boat dipped in the swell, and the sea sparkled in the sun, and Fanny-Rosa, laughing, knelt up against him and held on to his shoulder.

"Would you drown me?" she asked, pushing his hair back from his eyes.

"I would not," he answered, putting the boat into the wind and leaving the tiller, with both arms around her while she kissed him on the mouth.

He understood then that he would never know what Henry had been to her in Naples, no one would know. If there was a story to tell of a man who went away from Italy bitter and disillusioned to die all alone in a little French hotel, the mystery would never be told. The secret lay locked for all time in her heart. John would wonder, and John would doubt, he would conjure pictures in his mind to the end of his days of those few months in Naples, and the senseless, futile jealousy would come to him again and again, but it would not be healed.

Henry was dead, Henry with his charm and his gaiety belonged no more to the things that were, and here was Fanny-Rosa alive in John's arms. Such sweet happiness could not turn to poison.

"Will you marry me, Fanny-Rosa?" he said.

She smiled, she pushed away his hands, and settled herself once more on the bottom boards of the boat.

"You will be swamping the boat if you do not look after it," she said.

He seized the tiller and the sheet, and headed the boat again towards Doon Island.

"Will you not answer my question?" he asked her.

"I'm only twenty-one," she said. "I hardly think I want to marry yet awhile and settle down. There are still so many things that are amusing to do."

"What sort of things do you mean?"

"I like to travel. I like to go on the Continent. I like to do as I please."

"All those things you could do as my wife."

"No, it would not be the same. On the Continent I should just be Mrs Brodrick, and the men I met would think 'Oh, she is a bride', and take no further notice of me. I would have to wear a cap in the house like my mother, and talk about preserves, and needlework, and servants. I care for none of those things."

"I should not expect you to discuss any such matters. If you expressed a desire to travel, why, we would travel. If you wanted to sail in a boat, we would sail in a boat. If you wished to drive to Slane in frost and snow, the carriage would be summoned, and we would drive to Slane, even if the horses died on their feet. You see, I would be a most accommodating husband."

Fanny-Rosa laughed. She glanced at John out of the corners of her eyes.

"I think maybe you would," she said, "but what would you get out of the bargain?"

"I should get you," he said. "Is not that enough for any man?"

He looked down at her, and even as he said the words the thought came to him that of course he was wrong, she would never belong to him or to anyone, because whoever married her would only have part of her, a smile, or a caress, or whatever she chose to give from momentary impulse. The real Fanny-Rosa would elude capture, would escape.

They had come abreast the garrison again, and there were Bob Flower and Jane, and the Adjutant, and Dick Fox, all waiting for them on the causeway. People once more, and conversation, the intimacy between them shattered and put aside for another moment, perhaps another day.

"We are bringing Lieut. Fox and Captain Martin back with us to dine," said Jane, and they all climbed into the boat—and there was the damned fellow Martin looking with admiration at Fanny-Rosa. So back up the creek to the moorings below Clonmere, and he landed the party ashore, and moored the boat, and made fast for the evening. He watched them wander up the bank towards the house. Barbara and Eliza had come down to meet them, Eliza bridling at the sight of a strange officer, and he straightened himself a moment and waited while Fanny-Rosa returned the shawl to Barbara, thanking her, and then hung back to admire the water-garden at the head of the creek.

She was pointing to the young iris, calling over her shoulder to Barbara, and as she stood there an instant, the sun playing in her hair, her face grave and thoughtful as she considered the flower, he knew that no picture he had ever made for himself in the lonely hours could equal the loveliness of this one in reality. The ghost-girl of his dreams had come alive again, to fill his waking moments with happiness and pain.

"And you are not too tired?" asked Barbara, as they climbed the bank and stood on the drive before the castle.

"No," said Fanny-Rosa, "I am never tired, there is always so much to see, so much to know."

She looked a moment at John, still busy with the boat, and then up at the grey, solid walls, the open windows, the tower, and the tall trees behind the castle.

"How lovely it is!" she said, and then carelessly, pushing back her curls, "I suppose all of this will come to John, now Henry is dead?"

"Yes," said Barbara, "the property is entailed, of course, and everything besides. Poor Henry! and yet, of the two, I think John had always been fonder of Clonmere."

Fanny-Rosa did not answer; she seemed to have forgotten her question. She was bending and patting the terrier that had come down the steps to greet them.

How improved she is, thought Barbara, how really charming and cultured, with no trace now of that foolish wild frivolity bequeathed by Simon Flower. Even Doctor Armstrong, sternest of critics, could not fault her beauty now, or find a hidden streak behind that perfect face.

2

One morning at breakfast time a groom rode over from Duncroom with the news that Robert Lumley had been seized with a stroke the night before, and was not likely to live. Copper John at once ordered the carriage and set out for his partner's residence. He arrived to find Robert Lumley unconscious, and Doctor Armstrong, who had been summoned earlier, gave it as his opinion that he would only last a few hours. Robert Lumley's son, Richard Lumley, who was not in the country, was immediately written to, but he would hardly reach home in time to see his father alive. He had never been on good terms with his sister, Mrs Flower, and thoroughly disapproved of his brother-in-law Simon, so that Mrs Flower, when she arrived at Duncroom shortly after Copper John, was in a great fluster and agitation that there would be a general family unpleasantness, and seemed more concerned with the prospect of facing her brother, when he should make his appearance, than the fact that her father was lying on his death-bed.

"You will see," said Copper John to his family the following day, when word came from Doctor Armstrong that the old man had died in the night, "that Simon Flower will get what he deserves, and that is what is vulgarly known as 'a kick in the pants'. I shall be very much surprised if he or his wife has a share in the will."

"It will be rather hard on Mrs Flower and the girls," said Barbara. "After all, Mr Lumley professed himself fond of them, and when he was in the country spent much of his time at Andriff, more so than at Duncroom. He will surely leave them something, and if he does not, then Mr Richard Lumley will make some provision."

"Richard Lumley is likely to prove as difficult and cantankerous a man as his father," replied Copper John, "and it affords me small satisfaction to have him as partner in the Company. I only wish I could buy him out of the business altogether, and have the concern entirely in my own hands. However, we shall see what happens."

He was away at Duncroom for two days to attend the funeral and afterwards the reading of the will, and on his return the family could see that he was in high good humour.

He took the crepe from his hat and threw it aside in the hall, and sat down immediately to a large dinner of roast lamb and potatoes, saying little until the first edge of appetite had been turned.

"Well," he said at length, leaning back in his chair, and surveying his son and his daughters, "I have this day done a very ingenious stroke of business. I have persuaded Richard Lumley that it would be to his advantage to sell me his share in the mine."

He smiled in retrospect, and crumbled a piece of bread.

"It is quite true," he continued, "that the second mining speculation was a failure. He pointed it out to me himself and I could not deny it. We went down too great a depth. The Company has lately been obliged to pay upwards of three thousand pounds for the erection of an additional steam engine, and no immediate likelihood of profit. There is nothing, I told him frankly, so hazardous as mining, from the point of view of the proprietors, and it is possible that we have now reached the limit in depth to which we can go in safety. I am, I said, prepared to make further trials, in other parts of the hill, but with what success I cannot foretell. If you would rather I gave you a good price now for your share, say so, and it may mean the saving to you of a considerable loss. It may, and it may not. It is for you to decide."

Copper John took up his knife and fork again, and went on eating.

"And Mr Richard Lumley decided to sell?" asked Eliza.

"He did," replied her father, "and I can say in all sincerity that I do not think he will regret his decision. I paid a very large sum for his share, and I have a lease of the ground for a further seventy years. If you ever have any sons, John, they will be elderly men by then, and can renew the lease or not, as they think fit."

He laughed, and looked at his daughters.

"I imagine," he said, "that by that time there will be little copper left in the heart of Hungry Hill."

"Seventy years," thought Jane, "eighteen hundred and ninety-nine. We shall every one of us sitting at this table be dead."

Copper John filled his glass, and pushed the decanter towards his son.

"And what was the result of the will?" asked Barbara.

"Oh, that," said her father, waving a hand in derision. "Just what I said it would be. Richard Lumley has entire possession. I believe Mrs Flower has a legacy of a few hundreds a year, and some pictures. She took it well, I will say that for her. And I hope she has the sense to keep the money from her husband. The most disgraceful thing I have ever witnessed was the conduct of Simon Flower after the funeral. He could not be found when the moment arrived for the reading of the will, and was finally discovered sitting in the pantry with the manservant, a fellow I have always mistrusted, and the pair of them drinking poor Robert Lumley's port. Needless to say he was in no condition to listen to his father-in-law's will, and went to sleep in the middle of it. Richard Lumley is not likely to have him under his roof again. He had recovered somewhat by the time we all came away—more's the pity, because instead of keeping silent and looking ashamed of himself, he insisted on driving the horses himself, and the last I saw of them was poor Mrs Flower holding on to her bonnet, the carriage rattling down the drive at an excessive pace, and Simon Flower singing at the top of his voice. One of these days the fellow will break his neck, and it will be no more than he deserves."

"I am afraid Castle Andriff will fall to bits entirely now for want of repair," sighed Barbara. "Poor Mrs Flower and Fanny-Rosa! I feel very sorry for both of them."

"We need not worry about Fanny-Rosa," said Eliza. "Bob Flower told me she has so many men anxious to marry her that it is just a matter of making up her mind whom to choose. Her last fancy is some relative of her uncle's, the Earl, and I believe he has a title too."

"One thing is certain," said her father, "that regretting as I do Robert Lumley's death, in spite of the fact that he was an old man, the Brodrick family has come very well out of the whole affair."

And, rising from the table, he went into the library to attend to his letters, as was his custom, pausing a moment before entering, in the hope that John might accompany him and ask for further details of the day's transactions. His son made no attempt to take the hint. He was staring moodily out of the dining-room window, and Copper John, his eyes narrowing and his mouth a little grim, entered the room alone.

So that was the reason, John was thinking, why Fanny-Rosa was so elusive the last time he rode over to Castle Andriff. There had been some talk of a cousin, he remembered. No doubt she would marry him and leave the country, and that would put a stop to it all. Perhaps it would be just as well, for if many months passed like the present, he would end by blowing his brains out. The boating party had been in May, and it was now August, and Fanny-Rosa was no nearer giving him an answer than she had been that afternoon. She had so many moods, so many humours, and a day in her company would be one of wild uncertainty. She would receive him with indifference perhaps, bored and yawning, and accompany him with an ill grace to the hill where he proposed to try his dogs, would find fault with everything he said and did, criticising the way the greyhounds ran, calling it a poor sport and only fit for yokels, so that he would be near to throwing up the whole thing, selling the dogs, and returning home and never going to Andriff again; and then suddenly, like a change of wind bringing fair weather that had been foul a moment since, she would come to him and take his hand, lean her cheek against his shoulder, and ask forgiveness for her temper.

"If you would marry me, Fanny-Rosa," he would say, touching her hair, "then I would be always near, to comfort you when you felt the need of it."

She would say nothing, standing close to him, her hands about his shoulders, looking out from the hills behind Andriff to Mundy Bay below, and she would smile at him and laugh, so that he would be stirred beyond all reason and long only to lose himself in loving her.

Then "Make the dogs race again," she would say, pushing him away. "I want to see them race. I think that Hotspur will be the best, as you say."

And in a moment she would be discussing the points of the greyhounds, with eagerness, with excitement, asking questions about the approaching autumn season, and he would be happy and yet bewildered, wondering what was in her mind and whether she cared for him at all, and if all this play and provocation were simply to pass the time that might otherwise hang heavy on her hands.

The next time he saw her she would be different again, full of some entertainment or other there had been at Mundy House, her uncle's home, where he had guests staying, and where, no doubt, she had met with this cousin that Eliza had heard about, and she would have scarcely a word to say to John, making him feel an outsider, a boor, whose only topic of conversation was dogs and racing. Then he would disappear to his room, or go aboard his boat and sail around Doon Island, forgetting to return to dinner in all probability, even as he had done so often in his boyhood, and, when he did come in, make some indifferent apology, and immediately throw himself into a chair and take up a sporting paper.

Jane, and Barbara too, guessed what was the matter and let him alone, but day by day, throughout the summer, their father became a little more impatient with this son of his, who never discussed the mines, never bothered about the estate, who spent all his time, it seemed, chasing his greyhounds over the unprofitable hills of Andriff, and when he did choose to be home for dinner at five o'clock would sit glum and silent through the meal, or else take too much port and talk arrant nonsense about the politics of the country, of which he knew less than nothing.

"It is extremely fortunate for you, my dear John," he said one evening, when his son had appeared even more absent-minded than usual, and had not showed a sign of interest when his father had mentioned that the new mine, above the Mundy road, was likely to prove the most profitable of the three, "that my endeavours these last nine years have been so successful that, instead of being the luckless surviving son of a beggarly landlord, you find yourself, at twenty-eight, heir to a considerable property and considerable wealth, for which you have not needed to make the slightest exertion yourself, and apparently never will."

There was silence at the dinner-table. Jane gazed steadfastly at her plate, and Barbara and Eliza swallowed nervously. John flushed. He knew he had been remiss, but the port had gone to his head, and he did not care what he said.

"You are right, sir," he said, "I am damned fortunate. Long may the copper flow in the bowels of Hungry Hill. I drink your health, sir, and that of old Morty Donovan, whose death made everything so much easier for all of us."

He bowed to his father, and drank his glass at a sitting.

There was a little gasp from Eliza. Copper John rose to his feet.

"I am sorry," he said, "that you seem to have left what manners you had in the kennels with your greyhounds. Goodnight."

And he strode from the dining-room, slamming the door behind him. The sisters looked at one another in horror.

"John, how could you!" exclaimed Barbara. "Father will never forgive you. What in the world has come over you?"

"Fancy bringing up Morty Donovan," said Eliza, "the one topic in the world we have always avoided. Well, you have done for yourself now, and no mistake. I should think it would be better if you went back to London. You've spilt your wine on the cloth too—it will leave a stain."

Jane had turned pale, and was very near to tears.

"I wish you would not nag, Eliza," she said. "Can't you see that John is miserable?"

"Miserable?" scoffed Eliza. "What has John got to be miserable about, I should like to know? Of course you would take his part, you have always done so. He winks an eye at your ridiculous infatuation for Lieut. Fox, and no doubt acts as go-between."

"What has Lieut. Fox got to do with what has just happened?" said Jane.

"Please, please," said Barbara; "there is no sense in you two making a quarrel on top of everything else. John dear, I know you are not yourself at the moment, and will feel differently perhaps in the morning."

She kissed him quietly, and left the room, closely followed by Eliza.

Jane went and sat beside her brother He put out his hand for the decanter, but she placed it just out of his reach.

"What is it?" she asked. And then, when he did not answer, she said gently, "Is it Fanny-Rosa?" She took one of his hands, and played with his fingers. "You see," she said, "I do understand what it must be like for you, because I am going through the same thing myself. I am not infatuated with Dick Fox—infatuation is such an ugly, stupid word—but I am very fond of him, I do believe, and though I know he admires me, and has an affection for me too, he says he may go abroad at any time, and it is not fair to marry young, in the army."

John took her on his knee.

"My poor little Jane!" he said. "What a selfish brute I am, thinking only of my own confounded feelings, and nothing of yours. How dare this young fool play about with your affections? I have a good mind to thrash him."

Jane laughed, in spite of her tears.

"There you are," she said, "you will not stand the same conduct in my Dick that you bear yourself from Fanny-Rosa. Neither is really to blame. Why should a boy of his age, who will see service abroad, saddle himself with a wife? And why should Fanny-Rosa settle down to domestic life if she does not want to?"

"You have more patience than I have, little one," said John. "I believe you would wait contentedly for young Fox for years, and be no whit the worse for it. But I shall become a criminal and probably a murderer if I have to wait for Fanny-Rosa."

"I am sure she is fond of you," said Jane, "I have seen her looking at you. But she is so lovely, you see, and rather spoilt by that absurd father and all the young men she has met abroad, that she must have time to make up her mind about you. Marriage is a serious thing for a woman."

For a moment John wondered whether he should tell her his doubts about Fanny-Rosa and Henry, and the old misgivings he had tried to bury in his mind, and then he decided that he could not, even to Jane. The subject was too personal and intimate, too deeply painful to be probed and pondered at this late hour, with poor Jane distressed, and himself rather drunk.

"You know," said Jane softly, her large brown eyes full of wisdom, "what I am going to say is very improper, and I hardly know how to say it, but I do think that Fanny-Rosa has a very warm, passionate nature, and that if you were possibly a little bolder towards her perhaps she would—would do what you want, and be obliged to marry you."

John felt himself grow hot under his collar. Good heavens, that Jane, his demure, youthful sister, should have the same thought that had so often entered his own head.

"And you," he murmured, watching her under half-closed lids, "not eighteen for three more weeks."

"I have not shocked you, have I?" she asked, doubtfully.

"Shocked me? No, my Jane, you have not. I was just thinking how ignorant a brother and sister can be of each other, and how many years we have wasted when we might have talked of these things. Bless you. I should not forget your advice, but I doubt if it would be any good."

Jane rose from his knee, and smoothed back his hair.

"Don't worry any more," she said. "I think everything will come all right. I have a premonition that it will, and you know my premonitions are generally true."

Then she slipped out of the room and ran upstairs to join her sisters. John helped himself to the rest of the port, and tried to prepare for his interview with his father. He knew that he must apologise, and the sooner it was done the better. The only possible way to do it was to be well fortified first, stammer a few words, promise to make amends in future, and then leave the library as quickly as possible. Thomas had already looked twice into the room, wishing to clear—he would not be able to delay much longer. And he wondered what he should say to his father, and how he should frame his apology without sounding stiff and awkward and altogether an incredible fool. He got up from his chair and walked carefully from the dining-room across the hall to the library. The door, of course, was closed. He knocked upon it, feeling as Thomas must do when he brought in the letters, and on hearing his father's curt reply to enter, opened the door and went into the room. His father was seated at his desk, engaged in correspondence, and John was reminded of the old schoolboy days when he had committed some fault and must expect a beating. His father did not even look up as he entered.

"Well, what is it?" he said shortly, intent upon some file or other and turning the pages in search of a document.

"I'm afraid I spoke rather hastily at dinner, sir," said John. "I very much regret if I have said anything to offend you."

Copper John did not answer for a moment. Then he pushed aside his papers, and turning in his chair stared up at his son, in much the same way, it struck John, that his house-master used to do at Eton.

"You have not offended me, John," he said, "you have disappointed me. Somehow, after Henry died, I had hoped that you and I would draw closer together. We have not done so, and I do not think the fault lies with me."

He paused, and John realised that he was expected to make an answer.

"I am sorry, sir," he said.

"Your brother showed a keen interest in everything connected with the mines," continued Copper John, "and before his serious illness would accompany me very often to Nicholson's office, where the three of us would discuss matters, and he would now and again make suggestions that both Nicholson and myself found helpful. I think I am right in saying that not once since you returned home have you offered to ride up to the mine with me. Here, at Clonmere, you show much the same spirit of lassitude. There is plenty to be done on the estate, Ned Brodrick would be glad of your assistance, but he tells me he has seen little or nothing of you. It is a source of bewilderment to me, who has every minute of the day filled with work of some sort, to know how you manage to get through your long and, if I may say so, incorrigibly idle day."

The house-master over again, thought John. How many times at Eton, had he heard those same words. And the old feeling of stubborn exasperation came upon him, as it used to do whenever mention was made of his idleness.

"Even when you were in Lincoln's Inn," went on his father, "the work you got through in six months I could have done in six days, at your age."

"We are very different, sir," said John. "You have a natural capacity for work. I have not. Since we are speaking plainly I may as well confess that I dislike intensely doing anything for which I have no ability."

Copper John stared at him without comprehension. Then he shrugged his shoulders, as though further discussion was useless.

"You are now twenty-eight, John," he said, "and your character is formed, and I can say no more. Eton, Oxford, and Lincoln's Inn have done very little for you. I cannot but be disappointed when I see my only surviving son throw to the winds the fine education and the wide opportunities he has had for becoming a responsible member of the community and take upon himself, instead, all the faults and failings that are so marked a national characteristic of this unfortunate country of ours. I can only hope that you never sink so low as our neighbour Simon Flower."

If only, thought John, you would have something of Simon Flower's tolerance, something of his natural charm of manner and generosity, something of his understanding that young men like to be left alone to their own devices, we should be getting on rather better than we are doing now.

"This country," said Copper John, "could be a great one, and a fine one, if the people in it had initiative and a sense of responsibility. They unfortunately lack both these qualities, and so, I fear, do you."

"Perhaps," said John, "they have no desire to see their country either great or fine."

"Well, then, what, in God's name, do they want?" cried Copper John in sudden anger. "Since you are one of them, perhaps you can enlighten me? I have been trying to find out for nearly forty years."

John was filled with sudden pity for this father of his, with whom he had so little in common, and whom he saw now, for the first time, not as a great success, not as the director of the rich copper mines and landlord of a fine estate, but as a lonely widower, who had lost his favourite son and was deeply disappointed in his second, and who, in spite of all his hard work and toil and concentration, had failed to understand or to please his fellow-countrymen.

"Speaking for myself, sir," said John, "I would say that I desire nothing so much as to be left alone. Whether the people of the country feel this too I cannot say."

Once again his father shrugged his shoulders. It was obvious that the two of them would never talk the same language.

"Tell me," he said, "do you ever think of anything else in life but your greyhounds?"

And supposing, thought his son, that I told him the truth, supposing that I made a confession of all the thoughts that fill my waking hours: how I hate the mines for the ugliness they have brought upon Doonhaven, because they stand for progress and prosperity, and how I cannot walk about the estate while he still lives and owns it, because I take no interest in a thing that I do not possess, and which is not mine alone, and how I am at present ill-tempered, ill-mannered, and more than a little drunk because my mind and my body have need of Fanny-Rosa, the daughter of a man he despises, and the only thing that concerns me at this moment is whether she will belong to me or not, and, if she should, whether she also belonged to my brother who is dead; supposing I make confession of all these things, what would he do but stare at me aghast and bid me leave the room, and possibly the house also? It was better to keep silence.

"Occasionally, sir," he said, "I think of the killigs in the creek and the hares on Hungry Hill, but mostly I concern myself with my greyhounds."

Copper John turned back to his desk.

"I regret," he said drily, "that I have not the time and leisure to join you in your pursuits. As there seems little sense in prolonging this interview any further, I will wish you a very good night."

"Good night, sir."

And John left the library, and went slowly upstairs to his room in the tower. He had made his apology—but he knew that the breach between his father and himself was wider now than ever.

3

Jane's eighteenth birthday fell in the third week of August, and it was decided to have a celebration because of it. The portrait was finished, and hung in the dining-room, and Barbara thought that invitations might be sent out to their various friends in the neighbourhood to come and view the portrait on the birthday itself. The dozen people first invited swelled rapidly to thirty, as is the manner with invitations, and then Copper John wondered, since they had gone so far, whether it might not be extended to embrace all the tenants of Clonmere, for whom refreshments might be set out on the grass before the castle, for of course they could hardly mix with the guests in the house. Something of the sort had been done when Henry had come of age, and, as Ned Brodrick agreed, it might induce those who were in arrears with their rent to feel it incumbent upon them to pay something.

"It is a relief," said Eliza to Barbara, "that we are able to be out of mourning for poor Henry, otherwise we should have looked like crows, wandering about in our black gowns."

"If we had still been in mourning," replied Barbara gently, "I should never have considered sending out invitations at all, and I am sure Jane would not have wished me to."

"The gown I had the Christmas before Henry died has not been seen by anyone in this country," continued Eliza, with satisfaction, "although I wore it once or twice last winter in Bronsea, and at Cheltenham, when we went for the week."

"I hope it is not white," said John, who had been listening with some amusement to the plans and preparations. "Both you and Barbara are too sallow for white. Jane has a cream complexion, and can stand it."

"I am sure I am not sallow," retorted Eliza. "It has always been understood that I am the fairest of the family. At any rate I do not have freckles on my nose, like Fanny-Rosa Flower."

"Fanny-Rosa's freckles are very becoming," said Jane. "I would like to have a few myself. Now, do not let any of us become angry or irritable at the prospect of my birthday. I am determined to enjoy myself, and I want everyone else to do the same. I shall wear the dress that I have in the portrait, and the same pearl necklace, and if Barbara can really persuade Dan Sullivan to come and fiddle for us, then I shall lead the quadrille myself, with you, John, for a partner. I doubt if I can persuade father to take my hand, even on my eighteenth birthday."

"I shall be honoured, madam," said John, bowing, "but you will be so hemmed about by the entire garrison of Doon Island that your fond brother will be unable to reach you."

The weather was happily fine on the big occasion, and there was a general stir of excitement as the day wore on to afternoon, and one by one the tenants began to arrive, at a slightly earlier hour than the guests to the castle, and most of them somewhat suspicious of the invitation, a suspicion which they took immense care to disguise with smiles, and bows, and curtseys, and compliments of gross exaggeration upon the fineness of the day, the honour that their landlord did to them, and the very great beauty and outstanding accomplishments of all three Miss Brodricks. Barbara had taken care that the refreshments provided for those "outside" were of as substantial a nature as possible, without inviting to excess, and it was not long before every man, woman, and child on the Clonmere estate was plunging an eager hand into the eatables. Ned Brodrick the agent moved amongst them, wearing an old blue velvet coat that had belonged to his and John Brodrick's father. This coat he wore only on great occasions, such as weddings or funerals, and with it an enormous broad-brimmed beaver hat, which, malice whispered, he wore when he begot his numerous offspring. The present festivity was much to his liking, for he enjoyed moving amongst the tenants, agreeing or commiserating with each in turn, whichever should please most, and keeping his ears well open to any piece of gossip which he might spread with advantage and so cause further gossip.

"Master John, if I may say so," he said, in his quavering, sing-song voice, "you are looking better than I have ever seen you in my life, and that's the solemn truth. And what a great piece of sport you are making with these greyhounds of yours. The whole country is ringing with it, so they were saying in Mundy."

"I have to do something with my days, don't I, Ned?" said John, remembering that only a week or so previously the agent had been grumbling to his father that "Master John gave him no help with the estate."

"You have indeed," answered the old hypocrite. "I only wish my legs were younger, so that I could join you. And what a beautiful man Mr Simon Flower is, to allow you to keep your hounds in his kennels. And his daughter just such another as himself."

"Miss Flower will be here directly," said John; "maybe you had better pay your compliments in person."

"Ah, now you are jesting with me, Master John," said the agent, with jovial false familiarity. "What would Miss Flower have to say to an old man like meself? Look at Miss Jane now—you would say she was her dear poor mother over again, and that's what they all say here today," and he moved towards the youngest of his nieces, forgetting that two minutes before he had sworn, to a rather overheated tenant, that Miss Jane had always been, and always would be, the dead spit of her father.

John laughed, and walked down the bank to the drive, for that was the way the carriages would come, and he thought what a wise philosophy was this of his uncle Ned, to frame his conversation and his mood to suit that of whoever crossed his path, so that no offence was ever given and, whatever false utterances he gave tongue to, at least he did it with a smile on his long, thin face, and with a true endeavour to please rather than to antagonise.

The guests to the castle were now beginning to arrive. Three boatloads were landing at the creek, and from them poured the young officers from the garrison, each smart as paint in his regimentals, and John could see a flutter from Jane's parasol as she stood with her father on the grass before the castle.

Soon she was surrounded, and poor Doctor Armstrong, who had been snatching a few minutes with her before the crowd arrived, found himself outside the circle, and was obliged to go into the house and gaze upon her portrait instead. Barbara was here, there, and everywhere, seeing that no one was without a sandwich, a piece of cake, or a glass of cowslip wine, while Eliza, not too comfortable in the dress she had worn at

Cheltenham, for which she had grown too stout, contented herself with the plainer and less interesting of the officers, who could not get close enough to Jane.

John had walked as far as the park before he saw coming down the drive the horses for which he had been waiting—Fanny-Rosa a little ahead of the groom who attended her. Her habit was green, and matched her eyes, and she wore a ridiculous little straw bonnet that did not cover her chestnut hair.

"Mother begged to be excused," she said, holding out her hand to John. "She said she could not go out so soon after my grandfather's death. As to my father, I left him and Matilda playing cards in the stables with the coachman and your kennel-boy. That is why I have only the groom to attend me this afternoon. I suggested that they all came and brought the cards with them, but they preferred to stay at home. Besides, Matilda has no gown."

"From what I have seen of Matilda," said John, "she would hardly know what to do with a gown if she had one. And I may remind you that the first time I set eyes on you you were stockingless, and your hair was down your back."

"Yes, John, and since then you have seen me with nothing on at all," replied Fanny-Rosa. "Oh, don't blush and frown, and jerk your head in that manner. Poor Nobby is as deaf as an owl. Now tell me, pray, what are we going to do besides admire Jane's portrait and drink Barbara's cowslip wine?"

"We are going to dance the quadrille while Danny Sullivan plays the fiddle."

"I don't know that I care for the quadrille. I would rather dance with my petticoats above my knees, like the country girls in the market-square at Andriff."

"Then you shall do so. But to me alone. Not in front of the officers of the garrison."

"I think the officers of the garrison would be highly entertained."

"I have no doubt they would. But if you show them your petticoats then I shall fetch my gun from my room and shoot you."

John walked beside the horse until they came to the trees behind the house, where the drive divided, one part leading to the back of the stables, and they took the horses to the yard, leaving them with the groom, and Fanny-Rosa dismounted, and slipped in at the back door of the castle to go upstairs and change her habit. She came down again within five minutes, looking more enchanting than ever, and, her arm linked in John's with a possessive air that delighted him, they wandered into the dining-room to inspect the portrait. The room was filled with people, eating, and drinking, and admiring Jane's likeness, and it amused John to see how Fanny-Rosa's manners in public differed from those when she was alone with him or amongst her own family in Andriff. For there, at home, she would be careless, impatient, the wild and wayward Fanny-Rosa who was so close to his heart, but here she was courteous, gracious, with even a hint of the great lady in her bearing.

"Clonmere looks very fine under these conditions," she said to John. "I like to see the people about the grounds, and the house full. It makes for life, and gaiety. Why does your manservant not wear livery? Ours always does. It would look so much better than that black coat."

"We are too far from civilisation here to entertain much," answered John, with a smile. "Listen, there is Dan Sullivan striking up on his fiddle. Let us go and watch the fun."

The drawing-room had been cleared, and Barbara, seated at the spinet, with Dan Sullivan beside her, was launching forth into the opening bars of the quadrille. Her partner, more used to the merry strains of a country jig than the stately measure demanded of him, strove to keep in slow time with Miss Brodrick and the result, though hardly worthy of the Assembly Rooms in Bath, had a certain liveliness that was not unpleasant to the ear. Jane, flushed and happy, had forgotten her invitation to John, and stood at the top of the room facing the irrepressible Lieut. Fox, and John, laughing, held out his hand to Fanny-Rosa. The sight of the youth and beauty displayed before him, the fine dresses of the ladies and the scarlet coats of the young officers from the garrison, proved too much for Dan Sullivan. His fiddle ran away with him entirely. The quadrille, after the first figure, was forgotten, and the strains of a lilting dancing jig soon hummed upon the air, so infectious in its call to caper that quickly decorum and propriety were flung to the winds, the young officers seized their partners by the waists, and there was a general stampede upon the floor, with whistles, and song, and laughter, "for all the world", as old Martha said, watching from the open doorway, "like the boys and girls at Kileen fair." The older generation, shaking their heads, retired downstairs to the dining-room. Copper John, feeling that nothing positively disgraceful could occur while Barbara remained at the spinet, retired to the library with one or two friends, and closed his door upon the sounds of revelry.

The shadows of the summer evening crept upon the castle walls, and a great moon came up behind Hungry Hill and shone upon the creek, and still Dan Sullivan played like one possessed, the sound of his merry music coming from the open drawing-room windows to the grounds below. The madness spread to the tenants outside, already well-primed with food and liquor, and before long the girls had thrown aside their shawls and their shoes, the young men had discarded their coats, and one and all were dancing in the moonlight before the grey walls of the castle.

One of the officers observed them first from the window. "Come here," he cried to his partner, "look what our example has done," and in a moment the window was crowded with laughing faces and waving hands, and Fanny-Rosa, flushed, and with the wicked look in her eyes that John had seen before, turned to him and said, "Let us go down and join them, let us all dance barefoot upon the grass." Doctor Armstrong murmured that perhaps everyone had danced enough for the evening, and to go and caper in the moonlight would hardy be the thing. "Bother 'the thing'," said Fanny-Rosa, dragging at John's hand, "it plagues the existence of every one of us. Come on, follow me, everyone." And they ran down the stairs and through the hall into the open, party dresses crushed against uniforms, mittened hands held in white-gloved palms, and so mingled with the excited tenants on the grass, that shone like a silver carpet, magic and mysterious, under the white moon. They danced, guest and tenant, man and maiden, stiff young officers and haughty young ladies, like wild things from beyond the mountains, as though the moon had cast a spell upon every one of them, and it was not until the moon itself was high in the heavens, shining down upon Doon Island, that Dan Sullivan, the sweat pouring from his face, laid down his fiddle and rested his head upon his drooping arms, and the fairy people he had conjured with his wand became mortal once more, with weary backs, and aching feet, dishevelled hair, and scarlet faces.

One by one the tenants disappeared, laughing, scolding, sighing, with the memory of "Miss Jane's coming of age" to be fuel for gossip for many a long day to come. The carriages were ordered for the guests, the boats were summoned for the officers of the garrison, and John Brodrick of Clonmere, who had seen his castle for the space of a few hours revert to barbarism, stood at his front door bidding his friends God-speed with more sincerity than cordiality.

"Never again," he said firmly, "never again."

And Barbara and Eliza, chastened and drooping, pulled themselves together sufficiently to bow and smile to those who were departing, while Jane, a rebel still, vanished over the grass to say goodnight to Lieut. Fox.

In the stable-yard John and Fanny-Rosa bent over the sleeping figure of the Castle Andriff groom. He was quite drunk, and equally helpless.

"He will never be able to ride back with me tonight," laughed Fanny-Rosa, who, dressed once more in her green habit, trailed her bonnet by its strings.

"I shall ride home with you instead," said John, "and the moon will light us all the way."

She looked up at him and smiled.

"I shall be home," she said, "before you are even in the saddle."

And leading her horse to the block she mounted and seized the reins, and flourishing the little whip in John's face, she rode out of the stable yard, looking back at him, and laughing over her shoulder. John shouted to Tim to saddle his horse, and in a few minutes he was after her, leading the groom's animal beside him, and Fanny-Rosa, when she saw she was pursued, set her horse to a canter and laughed the louder. He chased her up the drive, past the gate-house, down the road and through Doonhaven, and it was not until she slackened rein beneath Hungry Hill that he was able to come up with her.

"You might have broken your neck," he said, "riding at that devil's pace."

"The devil looks after his own," she said, "he would not let me go astray. Oh, John, the moon. . . ."

Mundy Bay lay beneath them like a sheet of silver, and Hungry Hill itself loomed mysterious and white above the road.

"Let's take the horses up there in the heather," said John.

They left the road, and wandered upon the track they had followed once before, nearly two years ago, on the day of the picnic. Then the sun had burnt the grass of Hungry Hill, and the warmth of the day had clung about the rocks and the heather. Tonight all was silent and still in the soft moonlight. John climbed from his horse, and put up his arms to lift Fanny-Rosa to the ground. She laid her cheek against his, and put her arms about his neck. He carried her to the heather and lay beside her, watching the silver in her hair.

"Have you been happy today?" he said to her.

She did not answer. She touched his face with her hand and smiled.

"Will you love me one day?" he asked her.

She pulled him down close to her, and her hand's pressed against his shoulders.

"I want to love you now," she said.

He kissed her closed eyes, and her hair, and the corner of her mouth, and as she sighed and clung to him the thought of Henry came to him once again, ghostly, and unbidden, and even as he held her there against him in the moonlight he said to her:

"Did you kiss Henry thus before he left Naples and went to die in Sens?"

She opened her eyes and stared at him, and he read passion there, and wanting, and strange bewilderment.

"Why should you ask me that?" she said. "What has your brother Henry got to do with you and with me? He is dead, and we are alive."

She hid her face against his shoulder, and all the doubt and jealousy that possessed him were swept aside in the great love and tenderness he felt for her, so that nothing mattered, he thought, but the longing that was theirs alone upon this night under the moon on Hungry Hill. The past should be something buried and forgotten, the future a thing of hope and blessed certainty, and the present that held them now was a joy so vivid and so lovely that the very force of it would destroy the phantoms of his dark and questing mind.

.   .   .   .   .

Letter from John to his sister Barbara, from Castle Andriff, dated Sept. 29th, 1829.

"MY DEAR BARBARA,

"I mentioned to Mrs Flower my father's being obliged to go to
Bronsea immediately, or rather that it was absolutely necessary for him to be
there on the 1st of November, and she has fixed on the 25th of next month
to complete the business, and Fanny-Rosa and I are to proceed to
Clonmere that same day. As she did not say anything about your staying,
I did not like to start the question, particularly as Fanny-Rosa talks of
crossing the water in the course of the month after we are married. I am
glad she has fixed on Clonmere at first, for many reasons. She hopes you
will be a bridesmaid on the occasion. We are to be married in Mundy by
the Rev. Sadler and go off at once. Would Martha stay with us for a
month? She would be a great comfort, and you might be able to do
without her for that time. Find out from her all about it, and also ask
Thomas if he would stay as indoor servant, and if he is inclined to stay I
shall put him into livery at once. Mrs Flower has agreed to let her maid
go with us for a month. I am sorry she did not propose your staying, but
my regret is counterbalanced by the thought of seeing you all at
Lletharrog. The necessity of my father's being in Bronsea by the first of
November has saved me at least three weeks. I hope and trust he will not
object to remain so long, particularly as his changing and going sooner
would throw the business out again. Next Monday three weeks will soon
arrive.

"Find out whether the woman from the Island can cook, and whether
she would come for a month. If she says 'Yes', then we might have her
over for a day and try her ragouts. You must write at once to Miss
Grazely for a dress. Don't let it be white! But it must be very handsome.
You won't, I am sure, refuse to accept it from one who, whatever may be
his charges through life, cannot at least accuse himself of want of affection
for you and the rest of his family. I wish my father would lose no time in
ordering the Landaulet painted and lined like the carriage, with arms on
it, and crimson blinds, and to be finished as soon as possible. I wish we
could have it to take us back to Clonmere—I don't like to take Fanny-
Rosa back in a chaise, and we could easily send it on to Lletharrog. Don't
write unless you have something particular to say, as letters are often lost
here, and make no remark upon my father's being over by the first of
November. We shall have time to arrange everything by Sunday next.
I shall certainly be home by then.

"Your affectionate brother,
"JOHN L. BRODRICK."

4

John and Fanny-Rosa spent the whole of the first autumn and winter
after their marriage at Clonmere, and did not cross the water at all, as
they had originally proposed. The family was at Lletharrog, and John
and Fanny-Rosa had the place to themselves. It was a time of such

peace and happiness to John that he could hardly believe the truth of it, and he would sometimes wonder whether it was not yet another of the secret day-dreams of the past, and he would awake again to black moods and bitter loneliness. Then he would look about his room in the tower and see how in the short time he had been married it had been graced and changed by the touch of Fanny-Rosa. The birds' eggs and the butterflies remained, and the pictures of Eton and Oxford, but there was a dressing-table now against the wall, with little silver brushes upon it, and a mirror, and in his wardrobe there were gowns that hung beside his coats, and beneath a chair a pair of velvet slippers. Her personality clung about the room, and if he stood alone in it, knowing that she was downstairs in the drawing-room or in the garden, he would touch her things with a feeling of strange warmth and tenderness, because they were now so much part of his life, and personal to herself and the love he had for her. She was all that he had dared to hope, and more than that beside. The former indifference and casual coolness she had shown to him were gone, and in their place came a wealth of affection and ardour that he had not believed possible. She was no longer wayward or capricious. She was his own Fanny-Rosa, loving and true, content to spend her days alone with him and no one else for company, and no fine talk now of Paris and Italy and London, and the people she might meet.

"Are you not weary of me yet?" he would ask, when a wet day would keep them indoors.

And she, holding out her arms to him, would say:

"How could I ever be weary of you? I love you too well."

And he would think to himself that all the talk of similar tastes and occupations, of liking the same books or poems, of sharing a common desire to travel—things which were considered important to the success of marriage—was so much nonsense, and no doubt trumped up by jealous people to prevent a man and a woman belonging to each other, for the only thing that mattered, as was being day by day proven by Fanny-Rosa, was that a husband should have understanding of his wife and know how to make her happy and content. It was a great satisfaction too to have Clonmere to himself, and to know that his father was across the water. It made for ease and comfort to feel that the hour of dining was a thing of not much importance, that it could be six or even seven of an evening, and that when they came in from walking in the grounds, or from shooting the hares and the woodcock on Doon Island, they could fling themselves wearily into the chairs in the drawing-room, and not be obliged to file at once into the dining-room for grace and the carving of the roast. He could give his own orders to Thomas and not wait for his father to do so, he could fill his glass after dinner with an easy conscience, and not be aware of his father's eye upon the decanter. It was freedom at last, freedom in his own home that he loved so well, and when old Ned Brodrick called upon some business of the estate John would pat him on the back, and welcome him in, and discuss anything but the matter in hand, to the agent's perfect agreement.

The servants all relaxed under the change of master. When Baird the keeper came every Saturday morning to present the weekly accounts of the outdoor staff he would find "Master John" sitting at his ease in an arm-chair with his feet on the mantelpiece, instead of writing at the desk briskly as Copper John was wont to do. Master John would greet Baird with a cheerful smile, and, barely glancing at the list given him, reach for a key to the desk and take out the money given in the total, at which Baird would make a mental note to increase the sum by half the following week. And if "Mrs John" did wander up to the vinery and take the best grapes before they were fit to pick, and finger all the apples so that they were bruised, which would have distressed Miss Barbara greatly, why, what did it matter when Miss Barbara was not there to see, and "Mrs John" had such enjoyment from the fruit?

Thomas was proud of his livery too, and he would rather wear a tight coat and be told that the kitchen girl thought him handsome, and bring in the dinner an hour late, and finish up what was left in the decanter, than be dressed in his old sober black, and have the table laid by the stroke of five in the afternoon, and be obliged to ask Copper John for the key every time a bottle was needed to be brought up from the cellar.

Each day, during the early winter of 1830, John would say to himself, "Now this morning I positively must ride up to the mines and have a word or two with Captain Nicholson, if only to save my face," and every morning something would come to prevent it. He would rise late, perhaps, Fanny-Rosa taking breakfast in bed and demanding that he should give it to her, and by the time he was up and dressed the best part of the morning would be gone. Or else the day would be crisp and fine, a day for walking the Kileen bog for snipe, and, Kileen being in the opposite direction, why then the visit to the mine must be postponed. On a wet morning he would bethink him of the little brown trout rising in Glenbegh; surely it would be a pity to leave them there, and the mine could very well wait another day. There was always an excuse, and the same held good for business about the estate. Had there been another dispute about the divided ground between Jack Mahoney and the Widow Connor? Why, then, he would say to Ned Brodrick, settle it some way or other that you think best. I know nothing of such matters. Give them a sack of potatoes apiece from our own ground. And the driving to Slane for the coursing would be the only times that he and Fanny-Rosa would venture far from home.

It was a great pleasure to John to have his wife beside him and to see the looks of admiration bestowed upon her, and a pleasure, too, to watch her interest in the greyhounds.

"What has happened," he would smile, "to the wild one who rode her horse across Hungry Hill and would not let me catch her?"

"She has vanished," said Fanny-Rosa, "and a placid, humdrum creature has taken her place. You know, John, I think I am very much like your greyhound Fancy, before she had her puppies. Maybe women are like dogs, after all, and that is why you understand us both so well."

"I think maybe they are," said John, laughing. "They need petting and coaxing in much the same way before they will let themselves be handled. But don't forget that Fancy produced poor Hasty, who is my one failure, and has never won a prize yet."

"That was not Fancy's fault," said Fanny-Rosa; "she had a very dull dog for a husband. . . . Now our son, dearest, will certainly grow up to be the most handsome and the most brilliant man in the country. I dare say he will become the Lord Lieutenant, and might even marry a princess of the blood royal."

"I think, on the contrary," said John, "that he will be even more incorrigibly idle than myself."

"I have great ambitions for him," said Fanny-Rosa seriously. "I tell you I think about him very often, lying in bed in the mornings, while you are downstairs having your breakfast. We will call him John Simon, after you and my father, and he will be the prop and mainstay of our old age. We shall have other children too, no doubt, but he will be the pick of the bunch. I hope the next few months will pass as pleasantly as the first have done. Having a baby is very little trouble, it seems to me."

"I want the months to pass slowly," said John, touching her hair. "Don't forget that at the end of March the family will be returning, and my father will be home."

"I can manage your father," said Fanny-Rosa, "I am not at all afraid of him."

"I am sure you can," laughed John, "but it will not be the same. We shall have to be punctual to our meals, and have no dogs inside the house, and I must feign an interest in the mines, and even go with him in the mornings when he rides to Hungry Hill."

"Yes, but I shall be waiting for you when you come back, which will make all the difference. And if you become exasperated we will creep up to our room and console ourselves. I shall not let him bully you, I promise you that. He will find there are two to fight against, and soon there will be three."

"Fighting is to be avoided at all costs," said her husband. "I would rather spend my days underground with the miners than have ten minutes above in disagreeable and exhausting argument with my father or anyone else."

So January and February passed, and March came in with soft winds and warm sunshine, melting the snow from the tip of Hungry Hill, and the young green shoots began to thrust themselves from the brown earth, and the tall trees in the woods behind the castle lost their dark nakedness. The gorse started to flower on the moors towards Kileen, and the bog itself lost the black sogginess of winter, while the honey scent of the gorse and the warm wind from the sea seemed to draw the full peaty flavour from the earth, and the blend of colour, and warmth, and smell made a richness upon the land. Sometimes John would take Fanny-Rosa in his boat, and pull gently about the creek and the waters of Doonhaven in search of the little killigs which the woman from the island would cook for their breakfast, but more often than not they would lie in idleness in the sunken garden that Jane had made at the head of the creek, John doing nothing, as was his happy custom, and Fanny-Rosa intent upon the rich embroidered gown she was making for John Simon Brodrick. The end of March came all too quickly, and on the 31st old Casey the coachman and Tim the groom set off for Mundy to bring the family back by road, as the steamer was not yet plying to Doonhaven, and John and Fanny-Rosa spent the morning in a desperate attempt to set the house to rights, to clear the dogs from the dining-room, where they had grown into the habit of feeding from the table, to remove fishing-tackle and an evil-smelling jar of bait from the drawing-room, and to hide away the innumerable lace caps of miniature size that might draw attention rather sooner than need be to Copper John's future as a grandfather, though, as Fanny-Rosa said, if the business was supposed to be concealed she would have to hide herself.

John stood on the steps of the castle with his arm about his wife, listening for the sound of the carriage wheels, and in a few minutes now, he thought, Clonmere will be mine no longer, the master will return. It will be my father who will walk into the dining-room and summon Thomas, it will be he who will pay the men's wages on Saturday morning, and I shall be no one once again, the idle, good-for-nothing second son, who was supposed to make a living for himself in Lincoln's Inn and failed.

The dogs began to bark outside on the drive, old Baird came through from the stables and stood expectantly and round the sweep of the drive beside the creek came the carriage, the waving hands of his sisters, their chatter and laughter, and John, holding Fanny-Rosa tightly for one brief moment, said a silent farewell to the Clonmere that was his.

At dinner John resumed his old place on the right hand of Barbara, who, with the kindly grace natural to her, wished Fanny-Rosa to sit at the end of the table. But Fanny-Rosa declined, saying she had always heard that the correct place for a bride was on the right of her host. She said this with a sly glance at Copper John, who, knowing very little as yet of his daughter-in-law except that Simon Flower was her father, was inclined to be suspicious, and looked at her somewhat askance. She sat herself down beside him, therefore, and closed her eyes meekly and folded her hands when grace was said, so that John, watching her, thought what a confounded hoax she was, and what a play she would make of all this when she was upstairs in the tower room alone with him. Dinner passed pleasantly, and Fanny-Rosa made herself so charming and winning to her father-in-law that before the meal was finished he was in high good humour, and even jesting with her about the politics of the country, a matter which usually called forth little humour from him and much anger.

"Fanny-Rosa has done it again," thought John; "another conquest to her credit."

And he saw himself sheltering behind her petticoats for the remainder of his life, putting her in the forefront of any trouble which he himself wished to avoid.

"You see," Fanny-Rosa whispered to him that night, "I will make the old man eat out of my hand before I have finished with him."

"I think you will not," said John. "I think you concentrate on one Brodrick at a time."

If the arrival of the family and the resumption once more of the ordinary routine of home life made a small ache and a clouding of the skies for John, it appeared to have no effect upon Fanny-Rosa. She prattled away to his father, helped Barbara arrange the flowers, read poems with Jane, and discussed water-colours with Eliza, as though all this was just as agreeable to her as when she had sat alone with John, and though he was grateful to her for the ease which this brought upon the household, he wondered that she never said a word of regret for the time that they had spent together. She was a person who would glow and come to life in the company of people, whereas he would withdraw into himself, and he began to see how in their future life together he would sit back, as it were, a little apart from her, watching her move, and talk, and smile, basking in the reflected light of her presence. He would be content to do this as long as she never slipped away from him altogether, and allowed him to love her, and would love him in return.

"Do you know," said Jane to him one day, when Fanny-Rosa had left them and was walking towards the house, "that you look at Fanny-Rosa as though you worshipped her?"

"I do," said John.

"It must make her very happy that you love her in such a way."

"I think she will never know," said John, "or if she does know she would laugh; she would not understand."

"It will be nice to have a baby in the house. He will be sadly spoilt though, by all the aunts. . . . Ah me, your Fanny-Rosa is a lucky girl."

"What is it? You are not your bright self these days, little one. I noticed it as soon as you returned."

"I am only a foolish sentimental creature, John. You know Dick Fox is leaving the garrison, and going to the East?"

"No, I did not."

"He is very excited about it. It will mean promotion you know. He will be away a number of years—quite six or seven, I dare say."

"And does he not want to marry you before he goes?"

"What would be the use, John? He could not take me with him. He is twenty-one, I am just eighteen. By the time he is twenty-seven or eight he may have met someone else he cares for more than me."

"So you will let him go, and say good-bye, perhaps never to set eyes on him again?"

"I have no choice. He will be sad for a few days, and remember the girl of the picture, and then the excitement of the journey and the new sights he will see will put the girl out of his mind."

"And you?"

"Ah, never mind about me. I will be godmother to your baby, John, the fairy godmother who waves her magic wand and brings him good presents, and keeps the ugly witch away."

She blew him a kiss, and wandered off in search of Fanny-Rosa, and as he watched her go he cursed in his mind the young careless idiot, with his damned military ambitions, who could prefer the blood and dust of imaginary Eastern battles to life with Jane, who would give a man so much love and tenderness.

There were other things, though, to occupy his mind, besides poor Jane and her romance that had gone awry. For now his father had returned he had to give an account of his stewardship during the winter, and to explain why the bills had mounted. Ned Brodrick had been questioned, and Ned Brodrick always gave the same answer: "Master John had said it did not matter."

There was a stormy scene in the library when these matters were discussed, a month after his father had come back.

"It would have been better for the men I employ," said Copper John to his son, "that you had spent the winter across the water. As a general rule matters do not become slack in my absence, even for so long as five months at a time, but they have taken advantage of your presence here to do any number of things that I have never permitted. Even Baird, whom I thought I could trust, presents a bill a foot long and tells me he has your authority for doing so."

"I had not realised it was necessary to be so close, sir," answered John.

"Close? No one can accuse me of being anything but liberal with my servants. But I object to being robbed. Some of the items on Baird's account were not only needless but I very much doubt if they were ever purchased. Too late to check up on it now, of course. At the time you could have demanded to see the stuff he claims to have bought, but I suppose you did nothing of the sort. Here are several new farm implements, asked for, he says, by the cowman, of which Ned Brodrick denies all knowledge."

"Perhaps they will last a long time, sir, and then you will not need to buy later."

"You are making fun of me, I suppose, but I find the jest in poor taste. What happens to a man when he lives in this country, that he allows himself to become soft and useless, and lacking in all authority?"

Copper John looked at his son in exasperation.

"I thought marriage might stiffen you, John," he said, "but I believe it has made you more of an idler than you were before. Your wife is worth two of you, and I am glad to see she has such a mind of her own. One other thing that has rather astounded me, is that I hear from Captain Nicholson that you did not make one single visit to the mines in the whole course of the winter."

John had been waiting for this. And he had no excuse to give. To say that he preferred spending his mornings in bed with Fanny-Rosa would have sounded flippant, but it happened to be the truth.

"I meant to ride over several times," he said. "It was very remiss of me. The fact is Fanny-Rosa being unable to ride just now made it difficult, and I did not like to leave her."

"Yet you took her over to Mundy in the carriage several times to attend your coursing meetings?"

John was silent. There was really nothing that he could invent to defend himself.

"I am sorry, sir," he said. "I have been idle, I admit it."

"You are therefore, of course, quite unaware of the trouble they have been having with the new mine, above the road? The pump that I installed there has not proved man enough for the job, and what with the winter rains and the springs bursting there has been considerable flooding. The new pump that I have ordered from over the water cannot possibly be here for a few weeks. Meanwhile we are losing the stuff, by being unable to bring it to the surface. It is a source of considerable annoyance to me and to Captain Nicholson. Here is the summer coming on, and the ore wasting underground."

It was, John thought, the usual story. He had failed in his duties as his father's son. To make his apologies now, to offer to accompany his father every morning, and to sit like a dummy while he and Captain Nicholson discussed technical details of what should or should not be done to the offending pump, was a matter of obligation, no doubt, but he could not bring himself to do it. He felt a wave of irritation sweep over him for the whole business. Baird and his bills, the cowman and the rakes, Nicholson and his ridiculous pump. Why did his father have to take all these things so seriously? John left the library, in an ill-temper with his father and everyone else which was not improved by hearing that Fanny-Rosa and Jane had departed in the small pony carriage for Andriff, intending to spend the day there and return before dark. Fanny-Rosa had said nothing to him of the visit, and the reason was, of course, that he would have forbidden her to go. She was appallingly careless about herself, and because she felt so well was inclined to drive about the country with no thought of her condition. No one but Fanny-Rosa and himself knew how near she was to the time of her confinement, and even they were a little hazy about the actual date. His sisters believed, or pretended to believe, that it would be the early part of July; he himself suspected that it must be somewhere near the middle of May, and already they had reached the last days of April. If Fanny-Rosa was going to have her baby in three weeks time it was an act of madness to go driving the fifteen odd miles or so to Andriff, in a jolting pony-cart, and return the same day, making thirty miles in all, with only Jane for company.

"You must have been mad to let her go," he said to Barbara. "I cannot understand what you were about."

"But John, dear, they went without my knowledge. Fanny-Rosa told Eliza she was certain you had decided to go with father to the mine this afternoon, and she felt restless, she said, and a drive would do her good, but I had no idea they proposed to go farther than a few miles or so. It was Tim who overheard them making plans for Andriff."

"Jane should have shown more sense. She lets Fanny-Rosa do as she likes with her, just as I do, and every other damned fool."

"John!" said Barbara in reproof.

"I've a good mind to go down and see Willie Armstrong and have a talk with him. He has promised to attend Fanny-Rosa when the time comes, and would know whether it is folly or not. I know that I have never let any of my bitches travel a jolting road when they are so near to the business, and here I am, having apparently allowed my wife to do something that I would have spared my dogs."

"You forget, John," said Barbara, hoping to soothe her brother, "that Fanny-Rosa's health is excellent, and nothing seems to tire her. Besides the event is not for some little time yet, after all."

"Nonsense!" said John. "You know very well that it is within a few weeks. Why we all have to pretend to one another, I do not know. At any rate, I shall go down now and see if Willie Armstrong is at home, and if necessary I shall ride over to Andriff and insist upon Fanny-Rosa remaining there for the night."

He went round to the stables and had Tim saddle his horse.

"You are quite sure, Tim, that Mrs Brodrick and Miss Jane proposed to drive as far as Castle Andriff?" he enquired.

"I am, Master John," replied the man. "It was Mrs. Brodrick herself who said that they would be there soon after one o'clock, and would have time to offer some refreshment to the lieutenant before he went to catch the steamer from Mundy."

"What are you talking about, Tim?"

"Why, doesn't Lieutenant Fox leave this day for the East, Master John, and the young ladies arranging to say good-bye to him, him likely enough to be murdered by the savages out there, and Miss Jane crying her eyes out because of it?"

"I see . . ." said John. "No, Tim, I did not know."

So that was the reason Fanny-Rosa and Jane had gone off for the day.

Poor Jane wished to bid farewell to Dick Fox, out of sight of the family, and Fanny-Rosa had offered to go with her.

John rode into Doonhaven, and found the doctor in his house, preparing to sit down to cold meat and potatoes, which he suggested John should share.

"You had better come with me afterwards," said the prospective father falling upon the cold luncheon with a hearty appetite, "and bring back those two madcaps from Andriff. Or you can bring home Jane. I shall stay at the castle with my wife."

"I think Jane will not be in much of a state to return with me," said Doctor Armstrong quietly. "This departure of Dick Fox must have been a great shock to her."

"I would have given a good deal for it not to have happened," said John. "To have a broken heart at eighteen is not much of a start in life. Confound that fellow for trifling with her at all."

"He is only twenty-one himself; they are both no more than children," said the doctor. "I often think what an elderly dullard I must seem to Jane at thirty-five."

"To tell you the truth," John said, "I am more concerned about my wife than about Jane. Fanny-Rosa's baby is due within a few weeks, as you have probably guessed, and a drive of thirty miles is surely an act of madness?"

"Mrs Brodrick's constitution is not likely to suffer," said Doctor Armstrong shortly, and he rose from the table to answer the summons at the front-door, for the house bell was ringing loudly. He was always a little gruff where Fanny-Rosa was concerned. Anyway, he had promised to bring the child into the world, and be godfather into the bargain. He returned now with a note in his hand for John.

"Your servant is outside," he said. "I gather there is some trouble or other at the mine, and your father has sent for you."

John frowned, and tore open the letter.

"Please come up to the new mine without delay," ran the message. "The flooding has become serious, and we need every man available to save the mine from total ruin."

John threw the note across to the doctor.

"There's an end to my ride to Andriff," he said. "You had better come with me, Willie. I'm afraid the business is serious. My father was telling me about the trouble only this morning. I rather gather they have gone too deep, and the engine they have has broken down and is useless. We shall find no end of a mess, I have no doubt."

The two men, with the servant, were up at the new mine within twenty minutes. As they came up the track they had to dismount and leave their horses with the servant, and push their way through the great crowd of miners, two hundred or more, who were gathered about the entrance to the shaft.

"The water's rising all the time," said a man, touching his hat on recognising John and the doctor. "There's one poor chap down there drowned. They've just brought the body to the surface, and two others are missing. Mr Brodrick has been down to the first level himself, but Captain Nicholson persuaded him to return. There he is, sir, at the head of the shaft there."

John saw his father, his head bare, his coat stripped and his sleeves rolled up above the elbows, throw aside the great bucket he had been helping to handle, and shake his head.

"We shall never do any good like this," he said. "The water comes up a foot or more all the time. . . . Is that you, John? Goodday to you, Armstrong. I'm afraid we shall have work for you before we're finished with this. There's nothing you can do to the poor fellow over there."

Every few minutes the buckets came to the surface, on the groaning creaking chains, and the water was splashed to the ground, making a wide stream beside the track, becoming deeper and flowing faster down the side of the hill. The great buckets, usually employed for bringing the copper above ground, were now bringing away the water; and a chain of men, from the flooded level to the surface, were handing smaller buckets from one to the other, each man standing upon a rung of the long ladder that descended to the shaft and passing his bucket to his fellow immediately above. As one or other of the men became exhausted, so a fresh man took his place, and in a moment John himself had thrown aside his coat, even as his father had done, and was taking his turn in the long line. He descended almost as far as the first level, which by this time the flood had reached, and the men who were working there, up to their waists in water, peered up at him through the darkness, their eyes hollow with exhaustion, their faces and bodies pouring with sweat.

"Tell the Captain and Mr Brodrick 'tis no mortal use," said one of them, a great burly Cornishman, who had stripped entirely. "The water is gaining on us all the time, faster than we can bring it away. There's another poor chap must have been caught by it, along the galley, before we came down. I saw his hand just now, floating yonder, but he's washed out of sight. . . . It's the finish of this mine; we can't do any more."

John peered into the great black gulf. There was no sound, apart from the creaking of the chains and the laboured breathing of the exhausted men, except the steady lap-lap of the water as it splashed against the rock-face. The galley path was covered, and was now no more than a dark, narrow channel, disappearing into the gloom. Somewhere down this channel washed the body of a man. The flood-water smelt brackish, sour. John turned, and climbed his way back up the long ladder to the surface, pressing against the miners as they lifted their useless buckets. Copper John was waiting by the entrance to the shaft, his face set in the expression of grim determination that his son knew so well.

"The water is gaining every few minutes," said John, "the men cannot possibly work there longer than another quarter-of-an-hour. You will have to order them to the surface."

"I was afraid of it," said Captain Nicholson. "Mr John is right, sir, we had better get the men above ground before more lives are lost."

"I refuse to be conquered by flood-water," said Copper John. "If we can get it away from the galleys that level will be workable again. There is one way by which we might save the mine, and I propose to do it. By blasting away the rock-face on the level, we can force a passage for the water out on to the hill, and the flood will escape. If there's a chance of saving the mine, I am going to do it."

"Very well then, sir," said the mining captain. "If we are successful, the explosion will break the rock above the level of the road, and the banks will go with the force of the water."

"Damn the road," said Copper John. "Roads can be built again, with the Government's money into the bargain. The Government will not advance me the money for a new mine."

John turned aside, shrugging his shoulders. If his father cared to risk death playing about with gunpowder on that doomed level, it was his affair. Somewhere a woman was crying—the widow, he supposed, of the drowned man who had been brought to the surface. There was a little crowd gathered about the body. Willie Armstrong was with them. The faces of the miners were white and strained, and all the while there was the ceaseless clanking of the chains as the windlass brought the buckets above ground, splashing the water into the ever-widening stream. Why could not his father close down the mine, order the men to return home, and put a finish upon the business? There was something appalling in this grim fight to save a few hundred tons of copper, for which already two or three men had lost their lives. Captain Nicholson was shouting out orders now, and the barrel of gunpowder was being brought along in one of the trolleys. The miners were pressing forward in excitement. Copper John was calling for volunteers. "If Henry had been alive," thought John, "he would have descended the mine with my father and the others," and vividly the memory of three or four years back returned to him. Once again he saw Henry, tense, excited, shivering with the rain, watching his father set fire to the train of gunpowder. Five men had been killed that fatal night because of the copper. Six, if he counted Henry, who had caught the chill that led eventually to his death eighteen months later. How many would have lost their lives today? John moved away from the group of miners, sickened, hating the scene about him. Once again he was oppressed with his own uselessness. He could not even help the widow of the drowned man, as Willie Armstrong was doing. He could only stand on the fringe of the crowd and wait. . . . This time there was no fighting, no shouting and yelling, and the explosions when they came were low and muffled, a series of rumbles underground that sounded like distant thunder. The men gathered about the opening of the shaft talked in low voices, and now and again word would be passed amongst the crowd, from one to the other, that a channel was being blasted successfully through the rock-face to carry away the flood, and that for the first time in four hours the water had not risen. John found himself drawn once more to the ladder beside the shaft. The men moved aside, making way for him. He began to climb down the ladder, and this time a new smell filled the shaft, for with the sour flood-water came the bitter pungent tang of powder and smoke. As he drew near to the level there came to his ears a confused murmur of voices, echoing strange and hollow against the bare, empty rock-face, and beside the voices was a new sound, the full, pressing flow of rushing water, as the flood was sucked down into the new channel blasted in the hillside. Even as John descended now, with Doctor Armstrong close behind him on the ladder, there came the deafening roar of a further explosion, and the crumbling of rock and stones along the galley. Faces loomed up at him from the darkness, eyes, and teeth, and hands, and there was his father himself, his own face blackened by the powder, a great scratch at the corner of his eye from which the blood was running.

"We have done it," he shouted; "the water has dropped three feet already; look at the mark there on the wall beside you . . . see the channel there, in the rock-face, carrying the flood with it. . . ."

The water gurgled and hissed like a live thing, and as it poured in a great black stream into the passage blasted for it the men on the level hacked and tore at the crumbling rock with iron crow-bars and picks, making a passage larger yet, so that the tumbling waters should escape. Copper John seized a bar from the man nearest to him.

"Harder than that, young fellow," he cried, and lifting the crowbar he drove it fast into the rock, bringing down a shower of stones and rubble.

There was a great burst of laughter from the miners, and one after the other they smote at the rocks and stones, plunging along the galley with no fear now that the flood-water had found its outlet, and John and Doctor Armstrong were caught with the same excitement, the same fury. They too seized crowbars and joined in the confusion of sound, breaking away the crumbling rock, while the black, slimy water sank from their knees to their ankles, evil-smelling, frothing, sucking its way in one black stream down the gully in the rock-face.

"Your father is unbeatable," said Captain Nicholson. "I would never have attempted this if he had not been here."

And Copper John, hearing his words, turned and laughed shortly.

"Would you stand by, then, and see some thousands of pounds lost beyond recovery? Come on, man, and put your back into this business."

It was getting on for seven in the evening when the little party returned above ground, weary, begrimed, but triumphant, with the news that the

water had now sunk below the level, and, because of the channels blasted
in the hillside, would not rise again.

"Once we have the new engine erected," declared Copper John, when
he made his short speech to the miners assembled at the entrance to
the shaft, "we shall be able to keep the water down permanently, and
any further flooding will be out of the question. I want to thank every
one of you for your work and loyalty this day, and I can promise you that
I shall not forget it."

He looked round upon the great crowd of men, and something striking
and undaunted in his bearing, the keen eyes in the smoke-blackened face,
the grizzled hair, the square, determined jaw, and the bleeding scratch at
the corner of his eye, drew forth a shout of appreciation from the weary
men before him. "Three cheers for Copper John," shouted someone, and
a roar went up from the crowd about him, a roar half hysterical in its
sudden release from fear, and they began to press forward to shake hands
with him, forgetting their fear in him as a master because he had proved
himself a leader, and Copper John, laughing and protesting, found
himself borne on the shoulders of the miners to see the havoc he had
created on the hill.

"Your father is a very lucky man," said Doctor Armstrong. "He has
won popularity for himself, and has saved his copper into the bargain.
Shall we go and look at the damage?"

The sun was setting over Mundy Bay, and John, blinking his eyes after
the darkness of underground, saw the first cloud of evening forming in
the western sky It was later than he thought.

The servant, who had been waiting all the afternoon with the horses,
came towards him now, with a grin on his face.

"You ought to see the road, sir," he said; "there's a cataract falling
down over it, and they tell me it's destroyed entirely. The banks have
given way in all directions, and the whole road is falling into the sea. It's
a good thing Doonhaven lies in the other direction."

Suddenly John saw Doctor Armstrong's face stiffen, and even as he
watched it the same fear clutched at his heart and he felt the blood drain
from his face.

"Good God, Fanny-Rosa . . ." he cried.

He began to run down the side of the hill towards the road, but even as
he did so he knew it was useless—the flood-water was pouring out of the
side of the hill in a great bubbling cascade, and the torrent of water, let
loose, was crashing down on to the road beneath, bearing with it earth,
and rocks, and stones. Already wide, ugly cracks were appearing in the
ground not far from him, and the crowd of miners, pointing and laughing, were throwing stones and sticks into the cauldron, making game of
the disaster, betting one another how long the road itself would stand the
strain.

"Call my father," shouted John to Doctor Armstrong; "tell him that the pony and trap are out on the road, returning from Andriff . . ." and without waiting for a reply, he began to plunge waist-deep across the stream, to gain the road the other side of the fall, that might as yet have escaped the worst of the flood. Before his eyes rose the ghastly picture of what might be. The pony and trap coming along the road, the two girls chatting, with no knowledge of what lay before them, and then round the bend of Hungry Hill the sudden avalanche of earth and stones from the breaking banks of the road, and the mighty crash of the released flood-waters.

He stumbled down the side of the hill, his breath sobbing, and his mind black with fear. Once he looked over his shoulder, and saw his father and the doctor following him, and some of the miners, Captain Nicholson amongst them, aware suddenly of what might be. As John ran he prayed, who had said no prayer since childhood, and he kept calling her by name: "Fanny-Rosa . . . Fanny-Rosa."

He came now to the edge of the hill, and there was the road, littered with great rocks and boulders and loose earth, more devastated even than he had feared, and a channel of water seeping through it all from the torrent beyond, and God in Heaven!—was that an overturned trap lying there amongst the rocks, and a horse kicking feebly, and someone standing in the midst of the road calling and crying for help . . .?

"Fanny-Rosa . . . Fanny-Rosa . . ." And he was leaping down from the crumbling hillside on to the road beneath, and she was sobbing and trembling in his arms, pointing to the kicking, struggling horse, to the wheels of the trap up-turned, and all the while the sound of the water rushing in his ears, the sound of the water falling upon the road, and his father and Willie Armstrong looking with anguish and horror in their eyes, towards the rubble, towards the stones. . . .

"Fanny-Rosa . . . Fanny-Rosa . . ."

He held her against his heart, he lifted her in his arms, he carried her away from the water and the rocks to the side of the road, to the banks as yet untouched, to the soft, wet grass, kissing her hands, and her lips, and her hair, as she clung to him, weeping.

"I am safe," she cried, "no harm has come to me, I am safe, but Jane, tell them to find Jane, where is Jane . . .?"

And down upon the road came the earth, and the stones, and the angry flood-waters of the mine on Hungry Hill.

That night at Clonmere John Simon Brodrick was born, he who was to be known in the family as "Wild Johnnie", but there was no fairy god-mother to wish blessings upon his dark head and to wave a magic wand; she had forsaken him, and stolen away into the shadows after her brother Henry.

5

When the baby was three months old Fanny-Rosa said that a change of air would be good for him. He was not putting on the weight that he should, and although Doctor Armstrong insisted that he had seldom seen a more robust infant or one with greater lung-power, Fanny-Rosa retorted that doctors knew very little about babies, and anyway the instinct of a mother was the strongest thing in the world. So John and his wife and son and all the greyhounds took themselves across the water, and settled down in Lletharrog for several months.

There was a calm, happy atmosphere about the farmhouse, and at night-time, with the boy safely asleep upstairs in charge of old Martha, the nursery-parlour would have something of peace and quiet about it, the curtains drawn, the candles lit, a small fire burning in the grate, and Fanny-Rosa sitting in the arm-chair next to the fire, bending over the new gowns she was making for the fast-growing Johnnie, looking up at her husband now and again with her vivid smile, generally to make some remark upon the precocity of their son.

It was, John thought, a good idea of Fanny-Rosa's to come across the water to Lletharrog. In the sheltered valley here, with the animals about the farm, and the little village close at hand, the placid stream winding below the house, the disaster of the early summer seemed more distant, and could be forgotten for many hours of the day. The shock and tragedy of Jane's death became blurred, and, in retrospect, a conclusion perhaps more fitting than the many long years of spinsterhood there might have been. John knew his sister too well. Not for her the quick parting and the soon forgetting, the marriage a year or so later with somebody else. Jane would have sighed, and wilted, a flower with a drooping head. It was better to have gone as she had, suddenly, and bravely, at the foot of Hungry Hill, leaving behind her no bitter memories, only the portrait of a girl of eighteen years, the brown eyes warm and hopeful, the small slim hand touching the pearls at her throat. John would miss her, there would be a great emptiness in his heart because of her, but here, at Lletharrog, he believed it best that she had gone.

The first weeks after her death had been very hard to bear. His father, stunned and suddenly aged, had shut himself up in the library and would have speech with no one, nor even Barbara. What agony he endured alone in his dark, cheerless room they none of them knew. But when he emerged, and they feared to find him broken, a shadow of his former self, he was little changed from the man he had been before, only the lines were deeper in his face, the eyes were harder.

John, whose loathing of the mine since the flood had increased tenfold, found it more impossible than ever to discuss business with his father, and he would watch him ride off every morning after breakfast, on his daily visit to the mine, with a feeling of bewilderment, almost of revulsion.

When his father announced in tones of great satisfaction, barely three weeks after Jane had gone from them, that the new steam engine had arrived and been erected, and would pump all the water from the new mine without the slightest difficulty, and they would be shipping ore to Bronsea within a month, John had risen to his feet and left the room. It was not long afterwards that Fanny-Rosa had suggested the move to Lletharrog, and John, for the first time in his life, had been glad to leave Clonmere.

He reflected that now he had a wife and a son, and there was every likelihood of more children to come, he could not continue to live in his father's house with any great pleasure. For six brief months, after his marriage, he had known the pride of possession, but with the arrival of the family Clonmere had ceased to belong to him. One day, years hence perhaps, he would possess it again, but until that day it was better to visit it at intervals, as a guest, and in the meantime find somewhere for himself and Fanny-Rosa and young Johnnie.

"The trouble is," Fanny-Rosa said, "that you make no attempt to stand up to your father. You and the girls are all frightened of him. A good quarrel and a lot of shouting would clear the air."

"I detest quarrelling, and shouting even more," said John. "Clonmere belongs to my father, and until he dies it is better that we do not try to divide it. Therefore, dearest, we have our own house this side o the water, where no one can interfere with us, I can race my greyhounds and you can have your babies."

"I think maybe you have the devil's pride in you, John. You want Clonmere so much that you do not wish to share it with anyone else."

"Maybe I have the devil's pride, and maybe you are right, and maybe too I do not wish to share my Fanny-Rosa with my own black-headed, screaming devil of a son, who has got all the faults of his father, and the wickedness of his mother, and no good in him at all. So the sooner you have another baby the better, to put young Johnnie's nose a little out of joint."

Fanny-Rosa put her arms about her husband, and smiled the way she did, telling him he was jealous, and a bear, and she did not love him at all and then she was gone in a flash, laughing over her shoulder, the old elusive Fanny-Rosa that had won him first on Hungry Hill.

The problem was made easier for them during the winter by his father suddenly buying a house some thirty miles from Lletharrog at the new fashionable watering-place of Saunby, which was within an hour or so's steaming distance from Bronsea, and more accessible in winter than the long drive backwards and forwards made Lletharrog. It was therefore suggested that John and Fanny-Rosa should remain on at the farmhouse and make it their headquarters for the future, while Copper John and his daughters passed the winter at the new house in Saunby, which was promptly named Brodrick House and became their permanent address while living that side of the water. The arrangement suited everyone, and John did not have the bother of finding a house for himself. He was content with Lletharrog, and so was Fanny-Rosa, and so apparently was Johnnie, whose nose remained entirely in place when his sister Fanny was born the following April, and did not shift in the slightest at the appearance of small Henry a year or so later. Johnnie was in fact the tyrant of the household, and no one, except his mother, was allowed to gainsay him in any way whatever. He was a handsome child, with his father's dark hair and eyes, but, as old Martha said, with his mother's ways and his mother's quick temper into the bargain. If he wanted a thing he shouted for it, and when he had it soon tired of it, and shouted for something else.

"The boy never seems content," John would say, staring in perplexity at his small son, who had thrown a fine toy into the fire because he had not liked the colour. "Why does he not sit quietly, like Fanny?"

"He has so much spirit," said Fanny-Rosa, "haven't you, my darling?"

Her darling scowled, and began drumming with his heels on the floor.

"I have never beaten a puppy I reared, and I don't propose to beat my own son," said John, "but I wish to heaven I knew the right way to handle the little fellow, so that he would keep quiet at least. Look at him, now, pulling at Fanny's hair. I don't remember that I ever pulled Barbara's."

"No doubt you did, and you have forgotten," said Fanny-Rosa, lifting her boy and giving him a lolly-pop. "Call Martha, and tell her to take Fanny upstairs; she is being silly, and upsetting Johnnie. . . ."

"I should have said it was the other way round," said John.

"Nonsense! Fanny always whines when her hair is pulled, and the whining excites Johnnie. It is most irritating for him. You shall walk with me to the village, my darling, and we will see what old Mrs Evans has in her shop for you. And if you are a very good boy you shall have dinner with father and mother, and drink ale out of your New Year mug as a special treat."

Why Johnnie should suddenly deserve a special treat, after throwing his toy in the fire and pulling his sister's hair, his father was at a loss to understand, but at least the promise had the desired effect, the scowl vanished, a radiant smile came over the boy's face, transforming him immediately from an ugly imp into a small object of great charm and attraction, and he trotted off hand in hand with his mother, a model of good behaviour.

John shook his head and shrugged his shoulders, and went off whistling to visit the greyhounds in their kennels. The upbringing of children was beyond him. No doubt women knew what they were about, although he had an uneasy feeling that Copper John would have leathered him as a youngster had he behaved to his sisters as young Johnnie behaved to poor Fanny, but to take down the little chap's breeches and lay hands on him

was something he could not bring himself to do. When there was noise
and confusion in the house because of Johnnie, his father would go into
the garden, or down to the river, and come back again when it was all
over. Somehow, it seemed to him the easiest thing to do. And little by
little this policy of avoiding trouble would creep into everything. Fanny-
Rosa ran Lletharrog, and Fanny-Rosa could deal with the servants. If
one of them was idle or rude, well, Fanny-Rosa must dismiss him. If old
Martha did not understand Johnnie and had words with Fanny-Rosa,
well, let old Martha be pensioned off, but for heaven's sake let there be no
scene about it which he would have to face.

"You are as bad as my father," said Fanny-Rosa, "escaping from your
responsibilities. What a good thing for you that I am not a timid, frightened little woman, dependent upon you for everything."

"You are dependent upon me for the only things that matter," said
John, putting his arm round her waist.

"Ah, you great useless one," laughed his wife, "would you forget I am
the mother of three children, and maybe a fourth before we know where
we are? And all you do is to sit about all day and look at me, and yawn,
and smile, and wander down to the kennels to pat your greyhounds, and
even they are becoming as lazy and contented as yourself."

It was true that John had no longer the same interest in coursing.
The season would come along before he realised how the months had
slipped by, and his dogs, having become slack and spoilt during the summer months, with too rich a diet and too little exercise, would need
several weeks' hard training before entering into competition. This required considerable energy and concentration from their master, which
he found himself unable to give.

"It's no use, Fanny-Rosa," he said one day, after returning from a
meeting where his dogs had failed to win more than a few points from the
critical judges, "my coursing days are over. The excitement I had from
it once has gone, I don't know why. It seemed to me, watching this day,
that the dogs were running loose, here and there over the course, for no
very great purpose, and all to destroy a hare, which maybe had a family
somewhere. No, I think in future I'll take my rod and go down to the
river, and even if I should catch a very small fish, why, I could put him
back again, and he'd be none the wiser."

And John would throw himself into his chair, in an untidy living-room
of Lletharrog, no longer recognisable as the neat, trim parlour of Barbara's days, and pulling tiny Henry on his knee, and with Fanny looking
over one shoulder, and Johnnie over the other, he would proceed to show
them the precious case of flies, the gaudy feathers proving an irresistible
attraction to the children. There would be a dog on the opposite chair,
and a cat on the hearth-rug, nuzzling a brood of young kittens, while
toys, needlework, and books lay strewn about the floor, and Fanny-Rosa,
seized with a sudden passion for dressmaking, leant over the table with a

large pair of scissors, preparing to cut wastefully into the folds of an evening gown to make herself a jacket which might hide something of her once
more widening figure.

The coming of the babies made little difference to Fanny-Rosa's looks.
She was, so her husband thought, as lovely as the day he married her;
she was still wayward, careless and capricious, the true daughter of
Simon Flower. Her servants never knew where they were with her. One
day she would be generous, indulgent, giving them roast for dinner and
suggesting a holiday for the lot of them, and the day after a scolding
whirlwind would burst into the kitchen, with a packet of sugar in her
hand which she swore had been stolen from her untidy store-cupboard,
and a flow of language would escape from their flaming mistress that the
servants would declare afterwards could only have been learnt from the
lads in her father's stables. John, hearing the tirade of wrath from the
living-room, would laugh quietly to himself and go out into the garden.
Fanny-Rosa would have her scene, and enjoy herself hugely, storm
upstairs to the children's bedroom afterwards and probably beat the
frightened girl from the village who had replaced old Martha, and then,
like a burst of sunshine after rain, come singing after her husband, with
small Henry tucked under her arm and Johnnie capering at her heels.

"Visiting Lletharrog," Eliza would say, on returning to sedate Brodrick House, Saunby, after a stay of a week with her brother and his
family, "is like visiting a bear-house. There is nowhere to sit, because
the chairs are full of dogs or kittens or babies' napkins. The cooking is
atrocious. I can swear my bed was damp when I arrived, but I did not
like to say anything, as Fanny-Rosa had embroidered me a nightgown fit
for a queen, which was laid out upon the sheets. The first morning she
put the whole household to making jam. I am sure none of it will set, for
the shocking waste of sugar—the children all upon the table eating it up
as fast as it was put into the pan."

"And yet dear John seems very well content?" asked Barbara, her
forehead wrinkling in anxiety.

"Oh, he's as happy as the day is long, in all the confusion. He does
nothing whatever but sit in his chair and laugh. He has grown side-
whiskers, to save himself the trouble of shaving, he told me."

"And the children?"

"The children are all very pretty and quite uncontrollable, and as for
darling Johnnie, he may be wild and quick-tempered, but he is the most
affectionate of them all, and quite attached himself to me, calling me his
'most dear aunt Eliza', and would I marry him when he became a man!"

Poor Eliza, who would soon be forty, was proud of any proposal these
days, even if it came from her six-year-old nephew.

Once a year John and Fanny-Rosa and the children would be invited
to Clonmere for a period of three months, and as Copper John spent most
of his day at the mines, and his evening in the library, the invasion of the

young family caused little disturbance to his routine. Fanny-Rosa, with her usual artfulness, made herself particularly charming, and young Johnnie, grasping instinctively that bad behaviour might very well result in discomfort to himself, was quiet and subdued in his grandfather's presence, and only let his spirits soar when the sound of horse's hoofs had died away along the drive. Then there would be a shout, and a whoop of delight, and flourishing of bows and arrows, and woe betide young Fanny playing with her dolls outside on the grass, or Henry struggling with his top, or baby Edward sucking his comforter when their eldest brother was about, for the doll would be in the rhododendrons in three minutes, and the top flung into the creek, and the baby with his petticoats tossed above his head, and Johnnie himself doing a war-dance with a cock's feather stuck in his dark curls, aiming an arrow at his protesting aunt Barbara, who defended herself behind a parasol. "Johnnie darling, you must be careful, you will do some damage," and Johnnie darling, caring not at all, launched his arrow with a war-cry into the parasol, and then took to the woods to torment old Baird, pulling his peaches off the walls, digging up the lettuce plants, and puncturing the old man in the behind with an arrow when his back was turned.

"Why should Johnnie be so wild?" asked Barbara of her brother, removing the nest of young mice from her work-box. "We never played such pranks as children? He is so intelligent and affectionate in other ways, but he appears to lack a sense of proportion."

"He has the faults of all of us, and none of the virtues," said John. "I cannot beat him, because I see him do all the things that I have always longed to do myself, and never dared."

"I cannot believe you ever wished to pour a basin of slops over poor old Mrs Casey, when she was peeling the potatoes, or tie a cracker round a cow's udders, as Johnnie did yesterday, so Mahony told me," protested Barbara. "The last was a most dangerous thing to do."

"It certainly shows a rather warped sense of the ridiculous," said Johnnie's father, "but I would dearly love to do such a thing myself."

"I don't believe it. You just say that to defend Johnnie."

"The boy will be ruined, you know, unless someone takes him in hand," said Doctor Armstrong seriously, who was Johnnie's godfather. "If he were mine I should beat him regularly, once a week, until he learnt manners. What is the use of his having intelligence unless he knows how to use it? Besides he is not all that clever. Young Henry there will have a far better brain, you wait and see, and no nonsense about him."

"I don't believe beating Johnnie would do any good," said his father. "I've seen more high-spirited dogs ruined by a whipping than were ever made by one. Upbringing has little to do with forming character, that is my opinion. Johnnie was born wild, and he will stay wild, and nothing you or I or Fanny-Rosa can do will ever change him."

And John, at thirty-six, with one or two grey hairs already in his dark head, thrust his hands into his pockets and strolled off across the grass in search of his first-born, thinking with a smile and a pain in his heart of his son's begetting, and how he was created out of love, and passion, and doubt, and tenderness, under the white moonlight on Hungry Hill.

"The truth of the matter is," said Doctor Armstrong to Barbara, "that the boy is not enough of a Brodrick, and rather too much of a Flower. When I think of what goes on at Castle Andriff, I find myself shaking my head over the future of Clonmere."

For to good, sober Willie Armstrong, born and bred in Buckingham-shire, and with fifteen years in the service of his king, life over here was something he found difficult to understand, especially as led by Simon Flower of Andriff. A man of fifty-eight who spent most of his time in the cellar or playing cards with his groom, while his roof crumbled above his head and his tenants mocked him to his face, was, so Doctor Armstrong considered, a figure more to be pitied than despised, but when he allowed his young daughter Matilda to elope with a cobbler from the village, a fellow already married, and invited her to live with her lover in the lodge of Castle Andriff and have one baby after another, then, Doctor Armstrong considered, a man such as Simon Flower was a menace to the country that had bred him. He could not understand how the old fellow could hold up his head in society, but then society was very different here from what it was the other side of the water.

The scandal of Matilda and her cobbler caused little concern, and even Mrs. Flower, who might have been expected to die of shame, merely heaved a sigh and declared that "poor Tilly" had never been quite the same after she fell off a horse at the age of fourteen, and really poor Sulli-van was quite a good sort of fellow, and so obliging the way he came to do odd jobs about the Castle for nothing.

"The person who takes it hardest is Bob," said Fanny-Rosa, putting away one of Edward's small gowns to send to her sister, "and it really must be rather trying to come home on leave, with one of your friends, and have your brother-in-law touch his hat to you at the gate, and Tilly scream 'How are you, Bob?' from the window of the lodge. It is incon-venient that both Tilly and I are expecting at the same time. This gown of Edward's would have come in for our baby, but, poor girl, I cannot very well grudge it to her."

Yes, it was a strange country, thought Doctor Armstrong, and he won-dered sometimes why he continued to live in it, for his original reason for retiring from the army and taking up the practice in Doonhaven was there no longer. All that remained was a picture on the wall of the dining-room at Clonmere to remind him of a dream that could never be. He attached himself to the family for the sake of her who had gone, and it seemed to him that there was a quality each one shared in common with her, a smile, a gesture, a turn of speech, a softness of the voice, from Cop-per John with his dry humour, seldom shown these days, down to the

infant Edward, with his warm brown eyes and slow baby chuckle. Clonmere might become like Castle Andriff, and indeed when Fanny-Rosa
and her children were in residence there seemed every likelihood of its
doing so, with the dogs, and the toys, and the sewing that littered the
rooms, and John might become another Simon Flower, now he was putting on weight and taking no exercise, but the charm they brought upon
the place was greater than the disturbance they created, the castle itself
seemed the warmer and the brighter for their presence.

"The fact is," thought the doctor, "John, and Fanny-Rosa, and that
tumbling godson of mine belong to the country, belong to Clonmere;
they are part of the air and the soil, and they thrive here, like the pigs
and the geese and the cattle. The Brodricks are Doonhaven, and Doonhaven is this country."

Two days afterwards he stood by the bedside of the oldest representa-
tive of the family, Ned Brodrick, the agent, seized by a stroke while
riding round the estate, like his father before him, and as the old fellow
breathed his last he winked solemnly at the doctor, fumbling with his
hand under the bed-clothes, and produced a bag of coins he had hidden
there for years, part of the rent-roll of Clonmere, which he should have
handed long since to the brother who employed him.

The whole family attended his funeral, Copper John and his daughters
standing with bowed heads beside the agent's grave, and it seemed to the
people of Doonhaven, who wailed aloud as was their custom, the most
natural thing in the world that the coffin should be borne upon the
shoulders of Ned's four illegitimate sons.

6

It was in September 1837 that Thomas Dowding, the Clerk to the
Doonhaven Mining Company, returning from the mine in the late afternoon with the sum of £300 upon him, to be banked in the Post Office in
Doonhaven until the following day, when the money would be taken to
Slane, had his unfortunate encounter in the market-square with Sam
Donovan, Sam Donovan's sister Mary Kelly, and James Kelly, his sister's
husband. Mary Kelly, a foolish, excitable woman, was selling vegetables
at her stall hard by the Post Office, as was her weekly custom, and,
according to accounts given later by people standing by, a cabbage rolled
from the stall at the feet of Dowding's horse, causing the animal to rear
on his hind legs and throw the rider. The Clerk, irritated by the circumstance of his fall, rose to his feet from the dust, and accused Mary
Kelly of deliberately rolling the cabbage in the hope of an accident.
Whereupon Sam Donovan and James Kelly, who emerged at that
moment from the public-house opposite, proceeded to set upon the Clerk,
and one of them, whether it was Kelly or Donovan no one seemed to
know, seized his purse and scattered the contents on the ground. Bank-
notes and coins flew about the market-square, and the Clerk, alarmed at

the turn of events, reached for his blunderbuss, with which he had been armed by Copper John for fear of robbers, and discharged it into the air, with the idea of subduing the people, who were by this time grubbing on hands and knees in search of the scattered notes. Unfortunately the shot struck James Kelly in the eye, wounding him mortally, and in a few moments the whole of Doonhaven was in an uproar. The Clerk, terrified for his life, took refuge in the Post Office, where the postmaster, with considerable wisdom, had the sense to bar his doors and windows and send a lad, by a back entrance, for the police, and also for the director of the mines, Copper John himself. Before very long order was restored, the body of the luckless James Kelly was removed to the house of his brother-in-law, Sam Donovan, where his widow had already preceded him in a state of hysteria, and Thomas Dowding, the Clerk to the Company, was taken in a closed carriage to the county jail in Mundy. He came up for trial at the next Assizes, where he was acquitted, after a great deal of contradictory evidence had been heard, and dispatched from court with no more than a severe reprimand to the effect that he must in future be more careful in his use of firearms. The Clerk, considerably shaken by the whole event, was glad enough to relinquish his post to the Company and take himself to another part of the country, where it was hoped that time, and the change of scenery, would banish all memory of the affair from his troubled mind. That was not the case, however, in Doonhaven. The old hatred of the mines, which had sunk into abeyance now for ten years, flared up again, and the Brodricks were looked upon askance in the village of Doonhaven or as they rode about the countryside. Once again the Clonmere tenants had their fences broken, their crops burned, and their cattle maimed. It could not be forgotten that the blunderbuss carried by the Clerk had come from the walls of Clonmere Castle itself, which fact according to the supporters of the Donovans, made Copper John no more nor less than a murderer. James Kelly, who in his lifetime had been a slow-witted fellow, with a partiality to strong ale, became in his death a martyr, the very paragon among men. He was, or so his widow declared, made in the likeness of the Saints, and never an angry word had she received from him in the fifteen years of their married life.

"He was too good for the world and for me, God help him," she said; "and as for those same Brodricks who set themselves to destroy his sweet life, the good God will see fit to punish them in His own time."

It so happened that John, who with Fanny-Rosa and the children was spending the summer at Clonmere, became involved in the affair through chance, since it was he who had given the blunderbuss to the Clerk a few weeks previous to the accident. John found himself summoned as a witness, and was obliged to attend the Assizes with his father. The whole proceeding seemed to him fantastic and absurd, and it was only when he discovered two of his favourite greyhounds, which he had left in great health and spirits the night before, dead by poison that he realised he now had incurred the hatred of the Donovans in place of his father. It appeared to him the basest sort of revenge, to strike at a man through the torture of dumb animals, which were guiltless of any crime whatever.

"What the devil am I to do?" asked John of Fanny-Rosa, when they had buried poor Lightfoot and his brother under the old walnut tree in the walled garden. "I can't go down to Sam Donovan's shop and ask him if he poisoned my dogs. The fellow would smile in that sickening sly way of his, and tell me he did not know I owned a dog."

"But Tim saw that son of his climb through the fence last night, coming from the direction of the kennels," said Fanny-Rosa. "It is obvious that he did it. Why don't you take a stick and thrash the lout within an inch of his life?"

"Yes, and be summoned by Sam for assault," said John wearily. "Oh, confound it, what's the use? Poor Lightfoot will never run again, or Dauntless either. They gave me the happiest moments of my life, after you, Fanny-Rosa. Maybe it's foolish of me, but this business has saddened me more than anything that has happened for years."

He went away by himself, and sat in the little summer-house up in the woods, where Henry used to lie ten years previously, and he thought about Lightfoot and Dauntless, how he had trained them both from puppyhood to be the champions of their year, and now they lay stiff and motionless, having died in agony, without their master near them. He wondered if they had cried for him in the night, and felt themselves lost and deserted when he had not answered them. The fun of those old coursing days, that first season in Norfolk, when Lightfoot had won all the points and all the cups, and then later, in this country, travelling over to Mundy with Fanny-Rosa beside him, the shouts of the crowds, the smile of the judge, Lightfoot slim and eager, waiting upon his master's word, his master's hand. There had been beauty in that dog, and a soul too, he could swear. They had understood one another as human beings rarely did. He had neglected the dogs these last years, allowed them to grow idle and fat like himself. Well, there was an end of it all now. Nothing remained of his coursing days but the silver cups on the sideboard in the dining-room. . . . It seemed such a useless finish. Poisoned by the Donovans. He had never in his whole life harmed one of that family, but he remembered old Morty Donovan cursing him that night in the rain on Hungry Hill. So perhaps the curse was taking effect now. He wished that it could have spared the greyhounds. As John sat alone in the summer-house he began to think about the Donovans, and tried to put himself in their place. Clonmere had been theirs, he reminded himself, before a Brodrick had set foot in the place. And then, of course, like so many other families, the land had been taken away from them after the rebellion in '41 and given to some peer or other, and so to the first Henry Brodrick. It was natural enough that they should show resentment, and natural enough that they should detest the duty-loving, law-abiding John Brod-

rick, who stopped them smuggling, and took away the only chance they
had of making a bit of money on the sly. Small wonder that one of them
took a shot at him when he was riding to church, and small blame if he
was glad when the shot succeeded. They said the blood still welled up in
the creek beside the drive on the anniversary of the day he died. John
and Henry used to go and look for it as boys, but never a drop of blood
did they see, unless it was chicken's blood thrown in the water by
the woman at the gate-house hard by. Anyway, the Donovan who fired
the fatal shot was killed for his work by Brodrick's friends and his house
destroyed. Little wonder there was enmity between the two families.

"If I had the energy," thought John, "I would go down to Doonhaven
and have it out with Sam, and tell him to make an end to the business.
Otherwise the ridiculous feud will never finish. Johnnie and that son of
his will start scrapping about something, though I dare say Johnnie
would hold his own without help from me or anyone."

He left the summer-house in better spirits than he had gone into it.
Poor Lightfoot and Dauntless were dead, but their lives had been happy,
and maybe it was better that they should go suddenly, in their prime,
even if their end had been painful, than live to an old age of rheumatism
and bad teeth, unable to chase a hare when they saw one.

He came down from the woods to the bank above the house. The
hydrangeas were in flower, and Barbara, in her shady hat, was moving
amongst them with her scissors. She did not look well these days, sometimes he feared that cough of hers sounded too much like Henry's. No
use saying anything, though. The children came running towards him,
Johnnie turning somersaults, laying small Edward flat on his face as he
cart-wheeled in the air. Fanny-Rosa came out of the house with the
baby Herbert in her arms. Five children in eight years; they had not
done badly. . . . She handed the little fellow to his aunt, and came up
the bank to meet her husband. Something touched his heart as she did
so. Would she always have the power to move him thus, with her smile,
with her eyes, with the feel of her hand on his arm?

"It's our wedding day on the twenty-ninth," he told her. "We shall
have been together nine years. Did you know that?"

"I'm not likely to forget it, am I?" she said, pointing to the children.
"Maybe it's time I wore a cap in the house, and gave up running about
the grounds the way I do. They say that the tenth year of married life is
the most difficult."

"Do they now? And in what way would it be difficult?"

"Why, the husband becomes weary of seeing the same face every night
on his pillow, and he looks around him to see if he might do better."

"How do you know I have not done so already, and cannot find
one?"

"Because you are too lazy, dearest one, and with the side-whiskers on
your face there's not a woman would look at you."

"I am not so lazy as you suppose. In fact, I propose taking a step one day this week that will astonish you when you hear of it."

"And what would that be?"

"I'll not tell you. You shall plague me as you will, but I shall keep my secret."

The truth was that John was determined after all to go down to the village to see Sam Donovan, and make an attempt to bury the hatchet of nearly two hundred years. It mattered little for himself, but for his children's sake he felt that it must be done. Why should Johnnie, and Henry, and Edward, and Herbert, and Fanny, be landed with ridiculous squabbles in the years to come? So a week after the poisoning of the greyhounds John set off one afternoon on foot for Doonhaven, having reluctantly refused to accompany Fanny-Rosa and the children on a picnic.

"There'll be picnics a-plenty in the days to come," he told them. "For once in my life I am going to do a piece of work."

"Don't let it kill you," laughed Fanny-Rosa.

"It certainly shan't do that," said her husband.

It was pleasant walking in the October sunshine. The path through the woods was crisp with fallen leaves, and the old herons rose from their nests in the trees and flapped away at his approach. The tide was making in the creek. Some of the men were burning leaves up in the park. The good bitter wood smell came floating down to him on the wind. Soon the cock would be in, and he would persuade his father to take a day off from the mines with his gun. They might get a few snipe up in the bog at Kileen, and have another day with the hares on Doon Island. He would suggest to Fanny-Rosa that they stayed on at Clonmere until Christmas. Five small children seemed like ten at Lletharrog. If they went on as they were doing at present he would have to give the farmhouse back to his father and take something larger. It was close and sultry down in Doonhaven, more like summer than autumn in the market-square, and the place seemed deserted, as it always did in the afternoon. He went down to the quay, and along to Sam Donovan's shop. It was closed, and the shutter was up at the window. He knocked on the door, and presently it was opened by Sam's wife, a thin, tired-looking woman, who was wiping her hands on a dirty apron. A girl of ten or eleven, with a mop of fair hair and light blue eyes like all the Donovans, peered over her mother's shoulder.

"Is Sam at home?" asked John, aware that his voice sounded a shade too hearty to be natural.

"He is not," said the woman, gazing at him suspiciously.

"Oh, I am sorry for that," said John. "I came down to speak to him most particularly."

The woman made no reply, and after waiting a moment, John turned away. Perhaps he had bungled the business after all. He heard the child whisper to her mother, and then she ran out on to the quay.

"My father is staying with my uncle Denny, on account of the sickness," she said. "If you want to speak to him you will find him there. Mother and I have not seen him these two weeks."

John thanked the child, and went back along the quay. Having come down to Doonhaven for the purpose, it was something of an anti-climax to find Sam was not at home, and his good effort made for nothing. The church clock struck four. It was too late to join the others for their picnic. No, he had set himself to the task, and the task might as well be done. He would walk over to Denny Donovan's, and see both brothers at the same time. There was nothing like doing the business thoroughly, now he had made up his mind to it. It was an ideal day for a walk too, the air up on the road to Denmare would be grand after the village.

Once again he left Doonhaven behind him, and the gate-house, and the park, and struck up westward on the road across the moors. His father had won his way, and the road had been widened in places, and now ran straight through to the Denmare river, but John did not notice that much good had been done by it, only that more people came down from the country to Doonhaven on market days and Saints' days. Denny Donovan's public-house—it was hardly more than a shack—was some three miles along the road, a dirty, tumbled-down place, with a few bedraggled hens scratching in the yard behind. Denny's cart was put up in the shed beside the house, and his pony was turned loose on the moor beside the road.

"At any rate," thought John, "he is at home, if Sam is not."

He saw the figure of a woman looking down at him from behind a blind in the upstairs bedroom, and believed that he recognised Mary Kelly, the widow of the unfortunate man who had been shot. His courage began to fail him. Perhaps it was nothing but quixotic foolishness after all that had led him here. The door of the public entrance was shut, with a bar across it, and John went round the yard to the back. It was odd of Denny Donovan to close his door against possible customers. More likely than not he had run out of liquor, and had been unable to go into Mundy to replenish his store.

John knocked on the door, and, gaining no response, boldly lifted the latch and walked in. There was nobody below, but he could hear sounds of movement overhead in the bedroom. The public bar had a grey, neglected air about it. There was dust everywhere, and on the bar itself two or three unwashed glasses that looked as if they had stood there for days. He thumped on the bar with his fist, and after a moment or two he heard footsteps coming down the rickety stairs, and Sam Donovan stood before him. He was wearing a night-shirt stuffed into a pair of breeches, and was unshaven. He stood staring at his visitor, and began scratching his ear and half-smiling in the old fawning way that was his mannerism.

"Good-day, Sam," said John, holding out his hand, which the other took, after a moment's hesitation. "I've thought for some time I should like a talk with you, and so I went down to your shop this afternoon, but your wife sent me on here. I gathered you had not been well."

"Ah, it's nothing much that ails me, Mr Brodrick, it's Denny that has had the sickness, and Mary and I came out here to nurse him. They say he caught it from drinking bad water up at Mundy, when we were witnessing there at the Assizes."

"I'm sorry for that."

"Would you come up and speak to him? Sure, he's in bed, but that's no matter, and he can speak now the fever has left him."

John followed Sam Donovan upstairs, and was shown into a small, stuffy bedroom, the same at which Mary Kelly had been standing when he arrived. The windows were tightly closed, and the air was appalling. Sam's brother Denny was lying in bed, and his widowed sister was sitting beside him. She had a black lace cap on her head, which John could swear she was not wearing when he saw her at the window. Denny Donovan looked thin and wretched. Whatever was the truth of the story about the bad water of Mundy, at least he had drunk something that had not agreed with him.

"You're in a poor way, I hear, Denny," said John.

"I'm easier now than I was, Mr John," said the man, watching him over the bedclothes, "but the fever had me racked for days and it's a surprise to me that I am here at all, after what I have suffered. And poor Mary here, having just put her dear husband in the grave, thinks nothing of the infection, nor Sam either, but both of them come out here to tend me. There is affection for you, between brother and brother."

"Yes, indeed," said John, remembering how some few years ago he had seen Sam belabouring Denny on New Year's day, calling him a rogue and a devil, both brothers having celebrated too freely the passing of the year. "And since we are on the subject of affection, I must tell you what I have come to see you about. First of all, I am sorry for that wretched accident where your husband was killed, Mrs Kelly, and I want you to believe it."

"He was a fine man," said the widow. "You would not see another the same, not this side of Paradise."

"It was a sad business," said Sam. "Here's poor Mary likely to starve, and she with no sons to support her. It's little Denny or I can do for her either, being poor men, with families of our own. It's what we were saying only this afternoon, that it would be a saintly act if some kind gentleman should befriend her, but where is one to be found in the country?"

"I would never have given the blunderbuss to Thomas Dowding to carry had I thought he would use it," said John.

"It was for ornamental purposes," said Denny. "He liked to parade it before people. That's what I said to you at the time, Sam."

"If Mrs Kelly is really in need of help, I will willingly give it," said John. "And don't you think the time has come when we might forget the old quarrel between our families, and make it up? I am the first to admit that much of the provocation has been on our side. We have been lucky, through one circumstance or another, and you have been unfortunate. Shall we say no more about it, and all four of us shake hands?"

There was a moment's silence. The widow sighed deeply, and Sam Donovan scratched his ear.

"How much would you be willing to allow my sister?" he said.

"It depends what she's worth to both of you," John replied, and getting up he went and stood by the window and opened it, breathing in the scented moorland air

He had been an idiot to come after all. They had not understood his gesture. They thought that he wanted to buy them off from making further disturbances. It served him right. How his father would scorn him if he knew what he had done. A fool and his money are soon parted. . . . Meanwhile the brothers had been conferring with their sister.

"Mary thinks she could manage on five shillings a week," said Sam.

"Very well," said John, "I will see that she gets it." He put his hand in his pocket, and drew out some coins. "This is the first instalment," he said. "You had better open an account at the Post Office; the money will be safer there."

"Fetch Mr John a drink, Sam," said the sick brother, "to celebrate the occasion. There's a bottle of whisky in the cupboard, and here is a glass for him. I'd join you but this fever; when the spirit goes down me you would say it was molten lead, so swollen is my throat."

This is, thought John, the most senseless moment of my very senseless life, to be drinking whisky with the Donovans, and preparing to keep Mary Kelly for life. I don't think I shall have the courage even to tell Fanny-Rosa.

The widow appeared to have recovered her spirits, and, joining John in his glass of whisky, asked after the children.

"Handsomer boys than yours, Mr Brodrick," she said, "it has seldom fallen to my lot to see. They are like the blessed angels in heaven."

"You would not think so, Mrs Kelly, if you lived with them," said John.

The lunacy of the whole proceeding struck him so forcibly that he could hardly restrain himself from laughing out loud. Here he was, being flattered and patted on the back by the very people who had poisoned his dogs, and giving them money into the bargain.

"Well, good-day to you, Denny," he said, setting down his glass. "I hope you will soon be better and about once more. Let it be a lesson to you never to drink water again."

He went down the stairs, followed by Sam and the widow, who escorted him to the door with smiles and fine speeches.

"Good afternoon, Mr John," said Sam. "Sure, if there is anything I can do for you at any time, down in the shop, you have only to pass me the word."

"Right, Sam, I will remember," said John, and he set off along the road back to Clonmere, shaking with laughter at the fool he had made of himself. At any rate, it might have the result of keeping the Donovans quiet for another ten years.

He arrived home to find the family returned from their picnic, and sitting down to dinner. The children had enjoyed themselves, and Johnnie had lost a front tooth. Fanny-Rosa was flushed, and freckled, and adorable. Everyone was in high good humour, perhaps because Copper John was passing a few days in Slane, and the atmosphere in the house was the lighter for his absence.

Willie Armstrong joined them for dessert, and the curtains were drawn early, and the candles lit, and they all sat round the fire to roast chestnuts.

"By the way," said the doctor, "you will be glad to hear, Barbara, that there is not the slightest likelihood of an epidemic after all. The cases were isolated, and have come into no contact with other people. This diphtheria, as they call it, is a very dangerous disease."

"How thankful I am," said Barbara. "I could not bear to think of fever in the district with the children about."

"Dennis Donovan is an extremely lucky man to have got over it so quickly," said Doctor Armstrong; "but they are all alike, that family, they have the strength of twenty oxen."

John threw his uneaten chestnut into the fire and stared across at his friend. "Did you say Denny Donovan had diphtheria?" he said quietly.

"Yes," answered the doctor. "Why, what's the matter?"

John rose to his feet, and went over to the window. He stood for a moment thinking rapidly, and then turned about and faced his family.

"I'm afraid I have to tell you all," he said, "that I did not know of this, and I have been with Denny Donovan this afternoon."

His friend, his sisters, and his wife stared at him aghast. In a few words he told them his story. His voice was quiet and low. When he had finished he looked across at Fanny-Rosa, as though asking for her love and understanding. She stood very still, terror in her eyes that he had never seen before.

"If you have brought the infection home to Johnnie, I shall never forgive you," she said.

．　　　．　　　．　　　．　　　．　　　．

So much of the room was dark. He could not even see the pictures of Eton on the wall. Nor the cases that held the butterflies. Nor the birds' eggs. And it made a loneliness lying there, because he loved the things that belonged to him, and when he could not see them he felt shut out, a stranger, someone who tossed and turned upon a bed that was not his own. He kept falling too, into a bottomless pit, the sides of which were clammy cold like the rock-face of the mine, and his father, peering at him from above, would shake his head and turn away, saying that he was not worth the saving. he would never make anything of his life. Then his father would change into his tutor at Eton, looking at him over his gold-rimmed glasses, fingering his report. "Brodrick minor lacks initiative. . . ." That was the trouble. He had always lacked initiative. He had never wanted to serve his country, or practise at the Bar, or help his father run the mine at Doonhaven, or do any of the things that people expected him to do. He only wanted to be left alone. The greyhounds had understood him best; they stood beside him shivering and expectant, their long, slim bodies quivering in excitement, their eyes, keen and intelligent, waiting upon his word. He liked to take their muzzles in his hands, shake them slowly from side to side, and whisper absurdities under his breath. Lightfoot, proud and disdainful, not even straining at the leash that held him, and the sudden spring and dive, the twist and turn, and there would be one hare the less on Doon Island.

The room was too hot, it was like a furnace closing in upon him, and when he asked for a window to be opened someone with a voice he did not recognise bade him be quiet, bade him rest, as though he were a child and old Martha was in charge again.

If only he could leave his bed and go out once more, and smell the heather and the grass on Hungry Hill. Bathe in the little lake and feel the soft wind upon his naked body. Fanny-Rosa would come too, she would not be afraid of the infection in the open air. . . . It was queer, he thought, that although his life lacked all purpose, and he had achieved nothing, had disappointed his father, and failed at everything he had undertaken, yet he had made happiness for Fanny-Rosa. Nothing else, then, mattered. It was worth lying here in the darkness to remember that. No one in the world could be more lovely than she had been standing beside the lake on Hungry Hill. Was it ten, eleven, twelve years ago? Was it yesterday? She had been angry with him one day because he had gone to see Denny Donovan, and might bring the fever into the house, and give it to Johnnie. She had shut herself up with the children at the end of the house and would not come near him. And now he had got the fever, and the children were safe; they would not catch it, nor Fanny-Rosa either. The loveliness of Fanny-Rosa. . . . God, what a damn-fool thing to do! To go and sit on Denny Donovan's bed, and drink his whisky, and keep his sister for life. He began to laugh, and wonder who in the world would appreciate the exquisite humour of the whole proceeding. There was no one. Except perhaps Johnnie. One day Johnnie might be told the story, and his funny, handsome, obstinate face would be engulfed suddenly in helpless laughter, and through the mist and cloud of years they would understand one another.

> "The man recovered from his bite,
> The dog it was that died."

He remembered reading that to the children one evening by the fire in the living-room at Lletharrog. Somehow it suited the present occasion very well. In two days' time it would be the twenty-ninth of October, and his and Fanny-Rosa's wedding day. Maybe she would just venture to the end of the corridor and look in upon him, lying here in the room in the tower. She would wave her hand, and blow a kiss to him.

The darkness was upon him once again, and whether it was day or night he did not know, but in a moment of strange lucidity he suddenly saw the whole chain of incidents that had brought him to his bed, and how, but for the lending of the blunderbuss to the Clerk, he would be out in the garden now with Fanny-Rosa and the children. The Clerk riding down from the mines, with three hundred pounds in his purse.

"Jane always said the mines brought ill-luck upon the family," he thought, "but my father will not believe it. He will still be selling copper twenty years hence, when all that remains of me is the silver cup I won for coursing in 1829."

He must have slept a long while, because when he woke he could see a chink of daylight coming through the drawn curtains, and he could hear the pigeons in the woods behind the castle, and the familiar clanking of pails in the stable yard. He felt very tired, and peaceful, and content.

"At least," he thought, "if I have been the dullest of the Brodricks, I have also been the happiest."

BOOK THREE

"WILD JOHNNIE," 1837-1858

I

WHEN JOHNNIE looked back on his childhood it appeared to be one long series of escapades after another, all with the sole object of provoking grown-up people to wrath. It had always seemed to him that there were two worlds, the world of fantasy that he created for himself, where he was master of a lawless band of children who did exactly as they pleased, and the true world of authority, symbolised by his grandfather Copper John, a figure of such power and might that he had only to move about the grounds or enter the front door of Clonmere to rouse in Johnnie a strange fury of rebellion. That grave, set face, that square jaw, those hard eyes, meant that young children must curb their spirits, quieten their voices, and take themselves to the attics if they wished to shout and laugh. And Johnnie, used to sprawling about the untidy living-room at Lletharrog, tumbling his mother's cushions, kicking his muddied heels on the furniture, found banishment to the attics of his grandfather's house a degradation and an insult.

Copper John was therefore an ogre, one of the giants in fairy-stories who lived in a fortress, and Johnnie the gallant young prisoner who ultimately would cut off his head and stand in triumph over his dead body. Family prayers were a time to bait the ogre. This would be accomplished by setting a trap for one of the servants. Sometimes he would fasten a piece of cord round a hassock and lay in underneath the carpet, and, taking himself to the other end of the dining-room and kneeling beside his chair, he would jerk the cord from time to time, shaking the luckless minion upon the hassock, to the great discomfiture of everyone present. Or he would bring in one of his tame mice, and set it free about the floor. Sooner or later the animal would find its way beneath the petticoats of one of the kitchen girls, and he would peep between his fingers and watch the wretched creature struggle with her feminine terror of mice and finally be overcome, uttering a shriek, and thereby incurring the severe displeasure of the ogre. The curious thing was that none of the servants betrayed him to his grandfather. In a sense they seemed to be in league with him, and later in the day Johnnie would go round to the kitchen and sit on the table, where Mrs Casey would be making pastry, and he would call her his love, and his queen, and tickle the old woman under the chin, so that she would find it impossible to be angry with him, and give him some of the pastry into the bargain. "Master Johnnie is too forward," would be the verdict below stairs, but even so none complained of him to the master. He had "a way with him", so they declared, and so for that matter had all the children, even down to young Herbert with his twinkling brown eyes, and for poor Mrs Brodrick to be left a widow after barely nine years of married life, and bring up this lively brood alone, was a sadness the servants could not forget. In fact Mrs Brodrick herself seemed to forget it sooner than they did.

For three months or so Fanny-Rosa had shown every wild extravagance of grief. She had threatened suicide, she had stayed in bed and been nursed tenderly by Barbara and Eliza, she had vowed that she would never be able to continue living, and then, shortly before Christmas, the sisters-in-law had prevailed upon her to accompany them to Saunby for the winter, and the change of scene, the visits of friends, the high spirits of the children, all combined to make her throw off the first transport of grief, and when she returned to Clonmere in the spring she was almost the same Fanny-Rosa as before. Almost, not quite. Something indefinable had gone out of her, never to return. The light, joyous quality, the glow of loveliness that John had awoken in her with his love and tenderness, flickered and died, finally and for ever. Her appearance, her dress, the care of her hair, suddenly these things ceased to matter. Once it had been amusing to buy gowns and hats, because of John, because he would look at her with that light in his eyes, and hold out his arms. Now there was little point in bothering to purchase material; last season's gown would do for this as well. A widow of twenty-nine might be expected to marry again, and Doctor Armstrong, when he saw Fanny-Rosa after her return to Clonmere, some six months after her husband's death, said to himself that no one of her temperament and vitality would be likely to remain single for long. He was wrong. All that side of life was finished and done with. The future remained, with one day Johnnie master of Clonmere. Mrs John Brodrick was a person of importance. One day, surely before very long, her father-in-law would die, and Johnnie would come in for the estate and the money. Fanny-Rosa would be mistress of Clonmere. It would be she who would give all the orders, pay the wages, have the handling of Johnnie's purse; and his fortune would be enormous, no doubt, for the copper was bringing in vast sums, and Mrs John Brodrick, running the estate for the benefit of her son, would be a someone of considerable significance in the barony. She had never forgotten that she was the niece of the Earl of Mundy, and now and again she would remind Eliza and Barbara of the fact, just dropping a casual word or two, but those words sufficient to bring them to some sense of reality, if familiarity with her presence had caused them to neglect it.

Little by little she began to talk of what she would do to Clonmere when the house became hers, or rather Johnnie's, which Barbara and Eliza felt was rather premature. Their father was not yet seventy and enjoyed excellent health, and there seemed small prospect of his making way for his grandson for several years to come.

"It is a pity," said Eliza one day to Barbara, "that Fanny-Rosa talks so incessantly as though Clonmere belonged to her. For my part, I find she has become very altered since John died. She has lost much of her gaiety, and is overbearing "

"Poor Fanny-Rosa," sighed Barbara; "we neither of us know quite how much she misses John. We must be patient and not mind; and don't forget how devoted she is to darling Johnnie."

"I say nothing against her devotion to Johnnie," replied Eliza, "but I find it rather trying when Fanny-Rosa gives orders in the stables, and has my horse saddled for herself when she wishes to ride."

"You forget," said Barbara the peace-maker, "that Fanny-Rosa has been used to giving orders too. She did everything at Lletharrog, and a married woman who has had a house of her own is lost without servants to command. I am always finding her in the kitchen, countermanding my instructions, because she tells cook that certain dishes are bad for the children's digestion, and as she is probably right, I say nothing. Whatever she does, do let us avoid any unpleasantness."

"It amazes me that father does not become annoyed at times," said Eliza. "She flatly contradicts him at dinner very often, which was a thing he never would accept from any of us."

"Fanny-Rosa has travelled, which you and I have never done," said Barbara, "and she has also read many more books. And I have frequently noticed that men will argue quite amicably with women who have had husbands, when they will snub unmarried women like you and me. I suppose they have some sort of superior knowledge of life that we do not possess."

Eliza sniffed. She hated to be reminded of spinsterhood and her middle years. But her brother's widow had come to live with them for good, and Barbara was right, it was no use having any unpleasantness. So "Mrs John", as she was known to the servants, began to take a more prominent place in the running of the household than either "Miss Barbara" or "Miss Eliza", but in a different way. Meals that were late and rooms that were undusted meant little to her, but if pastry appeared on the table when she had ordered a milk pudding she would storm into the kitchen and shout at Mrs Casey, shaming her before the other servants, and if some article of dress or a trinket was missing from her dressing-table (and no doubt fallen behind it, for Fanny-Rosa had no sense of order in her room) the housemaid would be summoned and upbraided as a thief, and possibly be sent from the castle at once, without Barbara's permission or even knowledge that any such scene had occurred.

Her children were never quite sure of her. She would spoil them lavishly one moment, and scold the next; and, after their grandfather, the most dominant figure during those years of childhood at Clonmere would be the bewildering, changeful personality that was their mother, some-times an angel with smiling eyes and a cloud of hair about her face, at others a wrathful demon, a fury from a fairy-tale, with a voice that uttered angry sounds.

The only person to beat Johnnie was his godfather, Doctor Armstrong, or "uncle Willie" as he was known to the children, and Johnnie never forgave him, because the beating, for the first time in his life, was undeserved.

Aunt Barbara had not been well, she was always coughing these days, and uncle Willie had come to see her. She had been making a shawl for a sick woman up at Oakmount, and her wool had been left in the draw-ing-room. Uncle Willie, requested by aunt Barbara to fetch the shawl so that she could continue working upon it while laid up in her room, found the wool tangled and dirtied beyond repair, and the shawl torn in shreds. The servants, when questioned, admitted to having seen "Master Johnnie" playing with the wool after breakfast. Johnnie was summoned by his godfather and accused of doing wanton mischief. In vain he pro-tested that he had only touched the shawl for a moment and then put it aside, saying that no doubt the nursery puppy had broken loose and done the damage, for which he was very sorry. He would not have displeased aunt Barbara for the world when she was unwell. His godfather refused to believe him, and told the boy that he was lying.

Johnnie flushed scarlet. "I am not lying, God damn you," he said (he was just turned ten at the time) and made to leave the room.

Uncle Willie laid hold of him, and being a strong, powerful man, he was able to control his struggling godson.

"You deserve a beating for the mischief and for lying to me," he said firmly, "and that the matter may sink in I shall do the business in front of the servants, so that they may know you for a spoilt, ill-tempered, unmannerly boy."

And there in the stable yard, before Casey, and Tim, and Thomas, and the women gaping from the kitchen window, Johnnie's breeches were taken down, and his hind-quarters bared to the world, while his god-father gave him a dozen hard strokes with his cane.

Johnnie was too stupefied to cry, but when the performance was over and his godfather had walked back into the house Johnnie suddenly real-ised what had happened, that his breeches were hanging about his ankles, and that the kitchen girls were sniggering behind their hands. The shame of what he had undergone came over him in a flash, and plunged into misery that he had never known in his life before, he ran up to the woods and flung himself upon the ground, weeping tears of bitter humiliation. Never, never again could he go back to the house. Never could he face Tim or the servant girls. The indignity, the injustice, the stark horror of the whole proceeding! Passionately he prayed for uncle Willie's death, and that some kind fate would overtake him too, and bear him away from

Clonmere. It became dark and cold, and still the boy lay out in the woods, his handsome face swollen with anger and grief and pain, while the weals on his backside began to smart and prick, and the load in his heart became heavier. His mother would pity him, and no doubt be angry, furiously angry, with uncle Willie, but she would pity him none the less, and want to put lotion on his sore buttocks. But he did not want her pity, he wanted her admiration and her love. He wanted her to think that he, Johnnie Brodrick, was the most wonderful person in the world, not merely a small boy whose breeches had been taken down in front of servants. His mother would not understand the agony and shame that held him now, the sense of impotence. And desperately, his head in his hands, the tears pouring down his cheeks, Johnnie cried, "Oh, why did my father die? He would not have treated me thus. . . ." Dimly, for his boy's memory was short, he saw the tall, dark figure of the man who had been his father, he saw the smile, he felt the pat of his hand on his shoulder, he heard the low, quiet voice, and for the first time he was aware of bereavement, he who had realised little or nothing of it when his father died.

Presently he fell asleep, exhausted by emotion, and here it was that Baird found him, on his way home through the woods to his cottage, and being an old, kindly man with some perception, he carried the boy back to his cottage, saying nothing of what had taken place, although the servants had told him the whole story, with many embellishments. He gave the boy half of his own dinner, and allowed him to go round trapping afterwards, carrying the ferret in his hand. By nine o'clock Johnnie had recovered something of his former spirits, and was happy enough to borrow Baird's lantern and go home to bed. He went indoors by the side entrance, and crept upstairs to the bedroom he shared with Henry, fearing that his mother or his grandfather might hear him and demand an explanation of his absence at dinner.

"I've been trapping with Baird," said Johnnie loftily, taking off his clothes. "I have had a most interesting day. The ferret made no attempt to bite me, and I was not in the least afraid of him."

"Lucky beggar," yawned Henry; "you might have taken me with you. It's been very dull here. Fanny and Edward were playing at houses, and I don't care much for that; it's too babyish."

"Did my mother ask why I was not at dinner?" said Johnnie carelessly.

"She was not at dinner herself," said Henry sleepily. "She had gone over to Andriff to see aunt Tilly and the new baby. And uncle Willie told aunt Eliza that he thought you might not be in, and she was not to worry if you were late."

This showed a glimmer of understanding on the part of uncle Willie, thought his godson, but for all that he would never be forgiven.

"Was that all uncle Willie said?" asked Johnnie.

"I don't know," said Henry; "he went away after seeing aunt Bar-

bara. I ran beside his horse for a little way. Will you take me to see the
ferret to-morrow, Johnnie? It would be such sport to go together."
"I don't know," said Johnnie grandly. "I don't think you are quite
old enough for ferrets."
And with that he turned on his side and was soon asleep. But he was
careful the next morning to dress with his back turned well away from
his brother, and went down to prayers in some anxiety, for fear he should
read contempt on the faces of the servants. He realised, however, that
uncle Willie had said nothing of the business to the family. He was
greatly relieved, and his relief took expression in bullying the younger
children during the rest of the day. He boasted loudly about his prowess
with the ferret, so that Fanny's and the boys' admiration for his skill
would cover his own shame at yesterday's disgrace, and, although the
day passed happily enough and without incident, he seemed to hear a
mocking voice inside himself, whispering that he was in reality no very
heroic figure, but a silly child, unbreeched before servants, and one day
all the world might know. He listened with interest when his mother
that evening mentioned something about "how the library would be his,
when grandfather died."
"But my aunt Barbara would surely use the library before me?" he
said. "After all, she is the eldest person in the house after grandfather."
Fanny-Rosa laughed at the serious, childlike logic of her son.
"Age has nothing to do with it," she said. "When your grandfather
dies Clonmere will be yours. You can do what you like with the rooms."
"Do you mean I shall be the master, like grandfather is now, and the
servants all have to do what I tell them?"
"Of course, my darling."
"And could I forbid uncle Willie the house, and set the dogs on him if
he dared to enter it without my giving permission?"
Fanny-Rosa laughed again. "I think it would be an excellent plan if
you did," she said. "Uncle Willie can be very disapproving and tiresome
at times, and it would amuse me greatly to see him run for his life."
"Don't you like him, mother?" said Johnnie, greatly daring.
Fanny-Rosa did not answer for a moment.
"I don't dislike him, of course," she said, "but I have never cared
much for his dictatorial manner. He presumed so much, because of his
friendship with the family. And after all, he is nothing more than a
country doctor. Most people would not receive him at all."
"Is it inferior to be a doctor?" said Johnnie.
"Well, it's one of those professions that gentlemen usually avoid. The
Services and the Church are the only real professions. Actually, it is
much better to have none at all, and just own property, as you will do."
"Perhaps," said Johnnie, after a moment or two, "my grandfather will
die next month, and I can set the dogs on uncle Willie."
The idea, once fixed in his mind, took firm root, and often he

would ply his mother with questions as to how they should live, and what they would do, when the great event took place. It seemed to Johnnie that to become master of Clonmere would take away the stain of that beating that rankled in his memory. The servants would never dare laugh at him then. He began to watch his grandfather carefully for signs of failing health. Sometimes he would enquire anxiously at breakfast as to how his grandfather had slept, and Copper John, unused to such solicitude from his eldest grandson—for it was Henry, like his namesake, who possessed the manners in the new generation—began to think that perhaps after all young Johnnie had some natural feeling, and might become a companion by and by. He often felt lonely, these days, did Copper John, with his two sons dead, as well as his little Jane, and Barbara practically an invalid. One day he took the boy with him on a visit to the mine, and was amused at many of his questions, particularly when he enquired of Captain Nicholson whether his grandfather would die if he was pushed down the shaft.

"I'm afraid he would, Master Johnnie," said the mining captain, and Copper John was quite touched when his grandson looked thoughtful, and remarked that no doubt there were many dangerous characters about, and his grandfather would do well to keep his stick with him.

"When you are older," said Copper John, as they rode home together, the boy mounted on his pony, "you shall come with me to the mines and help me keep the fellows in order. There is plenty of work to be done."

"I will come with you now, grandfather," said the boy eagerly. "I should very much like to go with you every day."

Copper John laughed, and seemed amused at his flushed, black-haired grandson, who was suddenly beginning to show an interest in the life about him. "Time enough for that when your schooling is over," he said. "Your uncle Henry went through Eton and Oxford before he knew much about the mining business."

"But, grandfather . . ." began the boy, and then stopped, for he remembered that he could scarcely remind his grandfather that by that time he would have been in his grave for years, and he changed his sentence, and said intead, "I trust you are not over-tired from your ride?", and Copper John said "No, indeed not, I could ride double the journey and feel nothing of it," which seemed to impress the youngster, for he looked thoughtful again At any rate, mused Copper John, the lad was becoming civil at last.

That autumn Fanny-Rosa had her young family painted. The picture was hung upon the walls of the dining-room, on the opposite side to Jane's portrait. The group is an attractive one, of the five children in their red velvet pantaloons, playing in the garden of Clonmere. Little Herbert, sitting upon the ground in his petticoats, smiles gaily, and so does Edward, with his crop of curls. Henry is more thoughtful, and Fanny, with all the responsibility of being the one girl of the family, is a trifle pale, a trifle wan. Johnnie dominates the group, Johnnie with his bow and arrow, his careless tumbling hair, his proud obstinate handsome face. He looks out upon the world with arrogance and bravado, as though he is determined to show the people who might one day look upon his portrait that Johnnie Brodrick of Clonmere cares for nothing and for no one.

2

When Johnnie was fourteen he was sent to Eton. With each succeeding holiday Fanny-Rosa took up more space for herself and her boys. Barbara, by now a hopeless invalid, seldom left her room, and gave up all the housekeeping into her sister-in-law's hands. Eliza put as good a face upon the matter as she could, but was inclined to spend more time in Saunby these days than she did at Doonhaven. As for Copper John, he carried his seventy years as though he were still barely sixty, and although his thick hair was now white, his figure more bent than it had been, his mind was as keen as ever, and he transacted the business of the mines with the thoroughness and the efficiency of a man half his age. He became possibly a little more formidable to his grandsons as the years passed. There was something awe-inspiring about the grim, set face, the square shoulders, the massive jaw, that seemed symbolic of God Almighty, and when he took his place at the head of the breakfast table, with the open Bible in front of him, the boys would have the uneasy feeling that the Great Presence had indeed descended upon Doonhaven, and with one fierce glint of his eye might sweep them all into everlasting destruction. "I am Alpha and Omega, the first and the last", the solemn voice would announce, and young Herbert firmly believed that his grandfather spoke about himself, and waited for a dove to fly down and circle over his head, as it did in the frontispiece of his prayer-book. Fanny, who was naturally of a timid disposition, was frankly terrified of the old man, and vanished to her room whenever she caught sight of him. Henry was the only member of the family who appeared to be on normal terms with his grandfather. He was a frank, engaging child, with a charm peculiar to himself, and strikingly like the uncle Henry he had never known. Perhaps it was this likeness that made Copper John lean more kindly to the boy than he did to his other grandsons, and during the summer holidays he would sometimes walk with the lad about the grounds, the inevitable stick in his hand, his shovel hat upon his head, while Henry asked his opinion on the political affairs of the day, to the old man's silent amusement. Johnnie by now was frankly antagonistic. The commanding voice at dinner, which would allow none other to speak while he himself was speaking, was a source of irritation. Johnnie, bored, restless, longing to escape from the table and saddle his pony, would mutter to himself, "Get on with you, you damned old fool," knowing that his grandfather's hearing was not what it had been, and taking a silent delight in watching the look of terror on his sister's face when she heard the whisper. The days of practical jokes were over. A fellow who goes to Eton does not put white mice under the servants' petticoats, or balance jugs of water upon the door, but there were other amusements these days that the adult world disapproved of just as much as they had done of the practical jokes, such as smoking in secret behind the stables, and drinking ale with the village lads in Doonhaven.

It was exciting to climb out of the pantry window after dark, when he was believed to be in bed, and go off to the park and meet Pat Dolan, and Jack Donovan, and one or two others, all several years older than himself, but far more ignorant, or so they pretended to be. Lying on their backs in the long grass, with pipes in their mouths (which, truth to tell, made Johnnie feel a little sick), the "young gentleman" would hold forth upon life at Eton, and the number of his friends, and how his tutor could do nought with him, and how he proposed to leave before he was eighteen if he wanted to. "When the old man dies all this will belong to me," Johnnie would say airily, with a wave of his hand. "I shall invite you fellows up to the castle if I want to," and there would be much sniggering from the youths, much flattery and calling of him "a splendid sport, the pick of the pups", words which sent a glow of pride through Johnnie, whose friends at Eton were not as numerous as he would have the village lads believe. In fact, Henry appeared to do very much better in three weeks than Johnnie had done in three years. He adapted himself to the strange world of public school with an ease and grace that his elder brother envied, and Johnnie, resentful of discipline, loathing work, and fresh from a passionate quarrel with a boy who had been his best friend and now forsook him for another, would see his younger brother laughing and contented, befriended alike by his tutors and his companions, and he would wonder miserably what was wrong with himself that he must be at such constant war with everything and with everybody.

"I loathe Eton," he told Henry, on the way home to Clonmere for the long summer vacation, just after his seventeenth birthday. "I've a good mind to ask mother if I can leave. There's no one in the house now worth speaking to, and I find the life there incredibly tedious."

"It was a pity you never took up rowing," said Henry. "It's been half my fun, and all the most amusing fellows row. I'm going to join the beagles next half. Both Locksley and Middleton have asked me to spend a week with them before we go back, and I should rather like to go. Locksley's father has the best shooting in England."

Johnnie was silent. No one had asked him to spend a week when he was only fourteen. He had been to one or two fellows' homes, but he had never particularly enjoyed himself. Friendships seemed to be a burden to him instead of a pleasure. He glanced at his brother, smiling to himself over the paper he was reading, and suddenly saw his own reflection in the window, sombre, scowling, moody, and the contrast depressed him. If that was how he looked always, no wonder, fellows found him unattractive.

His mother, as usual, restored something of his self-confidence.

"My darling boy," she exclaimed, throwing her arms about him, "how you have grown in the last three months! Why, you are almost a man. It's surely absurd that you should still be at school, poring over lesson books."

Johnnie hugged her with affection. It was good to have your own thoughts spoken aloud by somebody else. His mother was a wonderful person, but why in God's name had she got a stocking wound round her head, instead of a cap, and surely, with her brilliant hair, that had grown even more brilliant since last holidays, it was a mistake to wear a crimson jacket? She was fatter, too, than she used to be.

"I'm glad you think it a waste to be poring over books," he said. "The fact is there is nothing to be gained by my staying on at Eton, and I want to leave."

"Of course you shall do so," she said. "I shall speak to your uncle Bob about getting you a commission in the Dragoons. You know your poor grandfather is dead?"

"What?" Johnnie shouted in excitement.

"No, no," said his mother quickly, glancing over her shoulder. "I mean grandfather Simon. Uncle Bob is over at Andriff now, trying to set the place to rights. Everything was in incredible confusion, of course."

"I wish," said Johnnie in low tones, "that it had been grandfather Brodrick."

"So do I," said his mother; "but what's the use of discussing that? Anyway, grandfather Simon died very happily. He went to bed the worse for drink as usual, poor darling, and set fire to his blankets. His pipe must have fallen out of his mouth, and when the servant went to his room he was nearly suffocated by the fumes of tobacco, and whisky, and smoke, all mingled together. The dear old man seems to have been asphyxiated by his own breath. The servant said he looked very peaceful."

"I suppose Castle Andriff goes to uncle Bob?" said Johnnie.

"Yes, and whatever money there is, which can't be more than two-pence. He has left all his port to you, by the way."

"Oh, come, that's something," said Johnnie. "Can't we get it over to Clonmere, and put it away, so that grandfather does not know anything about it?"

His mother laughed, and for one moment looked like the Fanny-Rosa of other days, as she closed one eyelid, and put her finger on her lips.

"It's there already," she said. "I've got it stacked away in one of the attics. Your grandfather will never find it. And anyway, I'm mistress of the house these days; no one would dare to ask any questions."

"How is aunt Barbara?" asked Henry.

"Much the same," said his mother. "She never leaves her room, and eats about as much as a sparrow. Uncle Willie says she can scarcely live through the winter. Of course she ought to be in a milder climate, but she has not strength enough to move."

"What age is she, mother?" enquired Johnnie.

"Your aunt? Oh, I suppose she is not more than forty-eight."

"My family seem to die uncommon young," said Johnnie. "You'd say there was a curse on the lot of us."

"There does not seem to be a curse on your grandfather," said Fanny-Rosa. "Do you know—of course it's only gossip—but I hear the mines are bringing in as much as twenty thousand a year? And still we have cold supper on Sunday nights, and no fires before October. I really can't stand it these days, and have Thomas bring turf up to my room, and a tray too, if I'm feeling hungry. Don't stare too hard at the new housemaid, by the way. She has squint, and is not quite right in the head."

"Why, whatever happened to Meg?"

"Oh, she and I had a flaming disagreement, and I sent her packing. They say now in Doonhaven that the girls won't come out to Clonmere, because I am so difficult. Did you ever hear of anything more absurd? Why, I am the easiest mistress in the barony. As for looking under the beds, I would not dream of it. I'd be too afraid of what I should find."

The two boys laughed. What an entertaining companion their mother could be when she chose, with her easy laugh, her slanting eyes, her expressive gestures, and what did it matter after all if she did let her complexion go to hang with all those freckles, and never brushed the flaming curls, and wore that ridiculous stocking round her hair to keep it in place?

"I've started a great scheme in Doonhaven," she went on, "and that's to be teaching the young girls of the village how to make lace. Some half-dozen of them come up to the castle every Thursday."

"What on earth for?" asked Johnnie.

"Why, it's a form of culture, isn't it? And what would they be doing with themselves otherwise? Lying under the hedges with the lads, no doubt. As for the reverend father, he called upon me in great anger, as you can imagine. 'It's devil's work, Mrs Brodrick,' he said to me, 'for you to be giving these girls ideas above their station. You'll have them all discontented with their lot before you've finished. And if you want to do good works,' he said to me, as I bowed him from the door, 'you'd do better to leave the young women of Doonhaven alone, and look to your sister's bastards.' I called him something he would not forget in a hurry. . . . Poor aunt Tilly! don't I send her a parcel of old clothes every Christmas? She has eleven children now, all running barefoot in the streets of Andriff. You'd think Sullivan would make shoes for them, being a cobbler by trade."

The drawing-room at Clonmere had all the old disorder of Lletharrog. There were bits and pieces of lace lying about the floor and on the chairs, and the vases were filled with dead flowers that Fanny-Rosa kept forgetting to throw away. Parcels of books lay on the writing-table, the paper and string beside them, Fanny-Rosa was constantly sending for books, and then neglecting to read them when they came. The latest puppy had messed on the carpet, and no one had cleared it up, and there was a lot of sticky toffee in a corner of the sofa that had doubtless fallen out of Herbert's pocket. Johnnie and Henry went along the passage to say good evening to their aunt. She was lying by the window, her face very pale and wan, but the same gentle, patient aunt Barbara she had always been, with kind enquiries after their health, and how much she wished she could have felt up to joining them for dinner, but alas, she had not been downstairs since they were home last. She did trust, she said, that their beds were aired. The room in the tower was inclined to be damp, but of course their mother would have given orders for the linen to be warmed, which Johnnie very much doubted, but did not say so. Then she began to cough again, a distressing, tearing sound, and Henry, with his usual tact and good manners, pretended to examine a picture on the wall with great interest, while Johnnie was seized with a horrible nervous fear of laughing. Outside in the passage he collapsed, stuffing his handkerchief in his mouth, and Henry, shocked and upset, begged him to be quiet.

"How can you?" he said. "She can't live much longer. It's horribly sad."

"I know that, you damned fool," said Johnnie. "I'm every bit as fond of aunt Barbara as you are. But the sound of the cough . . ."

And once again he proceeded to rock with silent laughter, the tears running down his cheeks, until Henry too became infected, and they ran down the stairs into the garden, half hysterical, and nothing less than a cold plunge into the creek restored Johnnie, who scattered his clothes in a heap by the bank and dived in without a thought.

It was a good thing, thought Henry, that their grandfather was not returning until the next day. What would be more awful than the sudden sight of him rounding the drive and seeing Johnnie there in all his nudity? They would none of them hear the end of it until the holidays were over.

"Come out, you madman," he called. "One of the maids from the house might see you."

And he glanced apprehensively over his shoulder.

Johnnie shook himself like a dog, and grinned up at his younger brother. He had no towel; he must dry himself on his shirt.

"What a treat for them if they did," he said. "I bet that pretty one in the kitchen would like to have a look at me."

"Conceited old idiot," replied Henry. "What have you got to be proud about?"

Johnnie laughed, and did not answer. He began drawing on his clothes and whistling to himself. The sullen gloom that he had experienced coming away from Eton had gone. His mother had said he could leave at

146

HUNGRY HILL

Christmas and uncle Bob would get him a commission in the Dragoons. He would go abroad and smash a lot of people up, and poor old Henry would still be a schoolboy in tail-coat, with Lights Out at ten o'clock. . . .

"Just in time," murmured Henry, as aunt Eliza came out of the house and down the bank to greet them.

"Dear boys," she said, giving them each in turn a rather flabby cheek, and an odour of moth-ball, "how delighted I am to see you. Darling Johnnie, such a young man, and Henry, quite a big boy too. You soon won't want to talk to your old aunt."

"Don't say old," replied Henry gallantly, "you look as young to me as ever you did. How's the sketching?"

"I've done one or two quite pretty little scenes, which I shall show you both some time. Johnnie, you would not care to go to Slane tomorrow and meet your grandfather? The steamer will not be coming for two or three days, and he has no business to keep him in Slane, apparently, so wishes to come down by road. Tim will drive you in the carriage."

"I don't mind," said Johnnie.

"I'm sure your grandfather would appreciate it. He has not seen you for six months, you know."

"Doesn't he get very lonely all alone in Saunby?" said Henry, as they went into the hall. "I can't think what he does with himself, without the mines to watch that side of the water."

"He goes into Bronsea twice a week still," replied Eliza, "and over to your old home at Lletharrog now and again. It's such a good thing Mrs Collins is so excellent a housekeeper, and knows how to look after him. With your aunt Barbara an invalid it would be impossible for me to be with him in either place. I seem quite tied here these days."

"You wait until I get my commission, aunt Eliza," said Johnnie. "I shall invite you to London, and will spend my leave with you. Would you like me in a red coat?"

"I should indeed, Johnnie darling. All the young women would be most envious of me. Is dinner ready, Thomas? I am famishing."

"Mrs John she says an hour later today, Miss Eliza; she wanted to finish some embroidery."

"Oh dear, what a nuisance! The hours of the meals are changed every day. Yesterday when I came in from my walk the dishes were cleared away, because she took it into her head to eat earlier. I never know where I am."

Johnnie peeped in at the library door. The room was bare and spartan, with the cold chill of a room that has not been used for many months. But his grandfather's presence clung about it still. Even the smell was the same: leather, and pens, and paper. There was something forbidding about it, like church. What a contrast, thought Johnnie, as he ran upstairs, to the babel of the drawing-room, where Fanny-Rosa, flushed and heated, was pinning a dress pattern on to her daughter Fanny, and scolding her at the top of her voice for fidgeting, while Edward and Herbert, climbing over the furniture and locked in combat, were watched with delight and appreciation by two barking spaniels.

The following day Johnnie set out for Slane, in high humour because Tim let him drive the horses—or rather, he had commanded Tim to hand him the reins. Old Casey had been dead for some years, and the one-time groom, now a married man of nearly fifty, sat beside his young master in some trepidation. Master Henry could be trusted with the horses. He had a natural way with animals, like his father before him, but Master Johnnie had no patience at all, and would tug at the creatures' mouths and flick his whip so that the gentlest animal became a prey to nerves.

"Let the horse do the work, Master Johnnie, leave him alone," said Tim, but Johnnie, who found the pace too slow, was for urging the beast onward.

"Why don't you drive a hearse, Tim? You'd be more suited to it," he said. "Come on, you lazy devils, you're both so fat you can scarcely crawl, like this damned fool who looks after you."

"And that's no fine way to talk, Master Johnnie, to one who knew you when you were a baby."

"Ah, you know my bark is worse than my bite, Tim. I wouldn't hurt your feelings for the world," said Johnnie, and he felt in his pocket for a piece of silver. "Here, you can drink perdition to me when you get to Slane."

"I don't like to take it, Master Johnnie."

"Don't be ridiculous. It isn't every day you drive me to Slane, is it? Make the best of it, while you can."

It was fun to be all on his own in the city, with the horses and the carriage put up at the hostelry, and his grandfather, on enquiry, closeted with the manager of the bank, and likely to remain with him for two hours at least. He wandered down by the river and watched the shipping, and the sounds and the smells of Slane were good to him, because he felt well, and carefree, and was seventeen, and had money to burn in his pockets. He rounded the corner of a street, and ran slap into two of the fellows from Doonhaven. One of them was Jack Donovan, son of Sam Donovan who kept the shop on the quayside, a tall, well-set-up young man, some half-dozen years older than Johnnie, with ginger hair and prominent blue eyes.

"Why, here's wonders," said Jack Donovan, "young Mr Brodrick in person. Me and Pat was only saying to one another, it was time you were home from your fine school across the water."

"How d'you do," said Johnnie languidly, handing him two fingers. "Where are you fellows going? I'm waiting for my grandfather, and have two hours to spare in which to kick my heels."

"Ah, we'll show you Slane," said Jack Donovan, with a wink. "Sure, it's a grand city when you know your way about. Let's wet our tongues while we think about it."

"You'd better not be seen with us in a public-house," said the other boy. "Maybe your grandfather will get to hear of it, and lam into you."

"I'll do as I damn well please," said Johnnie. "Lead on, you two, I'm as thirsty as a tinker."

He knew very well that if he was discovered in the company of the two fellows there would be the devil to pay, especially as one of them was a Donovan, because for some reason or other his grandfather disliked the Donavons, and so did both his aunts, and his mother too. Their dislike made him the keener to be friendly. Soon the three boys were seated round the bar in one of the numerous "publics" in Slane. The atmosphere was stifling, and the place was crowded. There was a fair somewhere in the town, and many of the country people filled the public-house, old men telling interminable stories, shrill, arguing women, and bright-faced country girls with shawls round their heads.

"What will you have? Whisky?" asked Jack Donovan.

"Yes, if you do," said Johnnie boldly.

At home he drank ale, when he could get it, and sometimes a meagre glass of port when his grandfather had the thought of passing the decanter.

"That's the way of it," said Jack Donovan in admiration, as Johnnie threw down his measure in one gulp, and tried to appear composed. "Why, you'd like another, I'll be bound. Here, Pat, another whisky for this handsome young gentleman."

Johnnie took his second dose more slowly. God, it was good, though. Damn good. Put life into a fellow. And guts too. He'd be damned if he would go back to Eton next half. Uncle Bob should get him a commission right away.

"I'm joining the Dragoons in a few months," he said, watching his two companions.

"That's the life," said Jack Donovan. "Ah, you'll look brave, Mr Johnnie, carrying the King's colours. Why, I declare I've a mind to go with you. Have another whisky?"

"I don't mind if I do," said Johnnie, "on condition that I pay."

"Here's your health, then," said his companion, "and the best of luck to the finest young cock it's ever been my chance to meet, and that's God's truth, I'll have you know. Are you twenty-one yet?"

"Seventeen," said Johnnie.

"Now you're lying to me. By all the blessed saints in heaven, you are lying to me. Is he not, Pat?"

"I assure you I am not. I was seventeen in May of this year."

"And drink whisky the way you do. That's something to be proud of. I'd swear you were twenty-one. See that maid looking at you through the window there? She would swear you were twenty-one too, wouldn't she, Pat?"

There was much laughter and swaying about on the stools beside the bar, and Johnnie, surprised that he could still sit straight, laughed across at the girl in the shawl, who smiled back and beckoned.

"Ah, now he's made a conquest, now he's lost to us," lamented Jack Donovan, raising his eyes to heaven. "But maybe if he's only seventeen he'd do best to leave Betty Finnigan alone. She won't take them quite so young."

"What do you mean?" said Johnnie.

The fellow's laugh was suddenly becoming offensive, and he disliked his ginger hair. Perhaps, after all, his grandfather was right not to care about the Donovans. The room was getting damned hot too, and all the people making a hell of a noise.

"I bet you don't put Betty Finnigan where she should be as quick as you knocked down those two whiskies," said Jack Donovan, thrusting a grinning face far too close to his own.

"Oh really? What makes you think that?" said Johnnie.

"Because they don't let you do those things at your fine school across the water," said Jack Donovan. "Anyone can slip a glass of whisky down his throat, but it takes a man to have a woman."

There was another great burst of laughter, and some of the other people in the public-house turned round and stared at Johnnie.

"Have your fun, boy," said an old fellow, waving his glass. "These young sparks are jealous of you, that's the plain truth of it, isn't it, Betty?"

The bright-eyed girl in the shawl nodded, and smiled again at Johnnie.

He rose slowly to his feet, and looked down at Jack Donovan.

"Thank you for your company, Jack," he said. "One of these days we'll drink together again. Meanwhile, I have another appointment." He slammed down some silver on the bar, and put his hat on the side of his head. "Am I going your way, or are you going mine?" he said to Betty Finnigan. . . .

It was five o'clock by the time Johnnie stood once more outside the bank. It was closed and barred, and the shutters drawn. His grandfather must have left fully an hour ago. Perhaps he would be waiting for him at the hostelry. Well, let the old bastard wait. It would not hurt him. Strange, thought Johnnie, how he did not feel nervous of him any more. His grandfather might look upon him with those grim, cold eyes of his, he might summon him to the bleak, cheerless study, and still he would not care. What had given him this feeling of cool confidence he could not say. Maybe it was the whisky he had taken, maybe it was the feel of the girl in his arms, maybe it was just the fact that he was seventeen, that he was Johnnie Brodrick of Clonmere, and if anyone dared to contradict him he would knock his back-teeth down his jaw, that made it impossible ever to be afraid again of an old man of seventy-five who should have been in his grave years ago.

When Johnnie came to the hostelry he found the carriage drawn up outside, and Tim standing by the horses' heads. His grandfather was by the open door of the carriage, his watch in his hand.

"Good afternoon, sir," said Johnnie "Have I kept you waiting?"

It was queer. He wondered if he had grown much during the last months, because he was now taller than his grandfather. Or was it possible that the old man had shrunk? Surely he leant more on that stick of his than he used to do? Copper John looked at his grandson, and replaced his watch in his waistcoat pocket.

"I was just about to leave Slane without you," he said shortly, climbing into the carriage and seating himself in the far corner. "Well," he said, after a moment, "what have you been doing with yourself?"

Johnnie took his handkerchief out of his pocket with a flourish, and blew his nose. It would be delicious, he reflected, to throw caution to the winds and tell the truth, and then watch the expression on his grandfather's face. He fought down inside himself a wild desire to laugh.

"I spent the afternoon, sir," he said, "appreciating the beauties of Slane."

His grandfather grunted.

"You were in the city shortly after two o'clock," he said. "You must have walked three times round the place, and seen all there was to see by four. Open the window your side, my boy; the air is very close in here."

He smells the whisky in my breath, thought Johnnie; now there'll be the devil to pay. I shall have to tell him I felt faint, and was obliged to go into a public-house and lie down. Once more the outrageous laughter rose in his throat. His grandfather said no more, however. He seemed thoughtful, preoccupied, and rather unlike his usual self. Perhaps his interview with the manager of the bank had not been a happy one. It was hardly possible, though, with the copper mines bringing in twenty thousand a year. But his mother was always prone to exaggeration. Possibly the tale was completely untrue, and things were going badly. Anyway, it was not his affair, thought Johnnie, and yawning, he closed his eyes and leant back against the cushions of the carriage, one hand on the window-strap for balance. He felt delightfully sleepy, incredibly content, and if that was the result of whisky and Betty Finnigan, what the devil would he be feeling like in a few years' time, after he had seen service in the Dragoons? The world was not such a bad place, after all. In a very few minutes he was fast asleep, his face flushed, his black hair tumbled, and looking, if the truth be told, considerably less than his seventeen years.

He did not wake until the carriage rattled down into Doonhaven itself, when he came to with a start, recollecting the presence of his grandfather beside him, and was much relieved, and not a little surprised, to find that his grandfather had also slept, and therefore could not upbraid him for being an idle dog and a dull companion.

It was a great temptation to tell Henry how he had spent his afternoon in Slane, but something prevented him: a faint suspicion that his younger brother, instead of shouting approval and patting him on the back, might draw away from him, puzzled, rather put off, and perhaps think less of him than he had done before. The family had dined, of course, and his grandfather had done so in Slane, so Johnnie, feeling that he could eat the house, fell upon the cold supper laid aside for him in the dining-room, and made non-committal replies to Henry's eager questions about the afternoon.

The younger boys and his sister had already retired to bed, and when Johnnie and his brother went upstairs to the drawing-room to say goodnight, he found his grandfather standing before the mantelpiece, with a curious, rather embarrassed, expression on his face. His mother was seated in the chair by the window, and his aunt Eliza opposite her, and they had both put aside their work and were listening to the head of the house. Good Lord, thought Johnnie, he has found out about me this afternoon and is telling them. . . .

"Wait a moment," said his grandfather. "Both you boys had better hear what I am about to inform your mother and your aunt. Sit down, will you?"

His grandsons obeyed. Copper John coughed, and clasped his hands behind his back.

"I don't want to make a long story," he said, "but will acquaint you in a few words with what has happened. I only propose to make a short visit this time, in order to see the mines and discuss the business there, and shall then return to the other side of the water. I shall, in the future, continue to reside there rather more frequently than I have done in the past, making, with your permission, Fanny-Rosa, my headquarters at Lletharrog. Eliza can use the house at Saunby, when she feels at liberty to do so. This house, of course, will be kept open for the entire family, and my grandchildren will continue to make it their home."

He paused, and coughed again. Eliza seemed puzzled, and glanced across at her sister-in-law.

"What will you do, father," she said, "all alone at Lletharrog? It is rather far for you to keep going backwards and forwards to Bronsea. That is why you moved to Saunby in the first place."

"I shall not be alone, my dear," said her father, "that is what I wish to tell you. Mrs. Collins consented to become my wife three weeks ago. We were married in Bronsea, and moved out to Lletharrog afterwards. She is a dear, good, faithful woman, and devoted to me. I am very glad indeed to call her Mrs Brodrick, and I hope you will do the same."

For a moment there was a great and dreadful silence. Then Fanny-Rosa said "Good God!", and Eliza burst into a torrent of weeping.

"Oh, father," she said, "how could you! Mrs Collins, your cook, how shaming, how disgraceful, after all these years! What will people say, all our friends in Saunby? They will never speak to any of us again."

"One thing is certain," said Fanny-Rosa: "the news of this will kill Barbara. We shall have to keep it from her somehow."

"Barbara knows already," said Copper John quietly. "I told her this evening when I went to her room. She appeared fully to understand."

"If she had not become an invalid this would never have happened," wept Eliza. "It is because she lay here, with me looking after her, that you became so dependent on . . . on that woman—I never will call her Mrs Brodrick, father, it is too much to expect."

And once again she was choked by tears.

"Of course," said Fanny-Rosa, "your father is entitled to do as he pleases. It is not as though Mrs Collins is a young woman, who might . . . What I mean to say is, this new arrangement cannot affect Johnnie in any way, I suppose?"

"I assure you," said her father-in-law, "that Johnnie's interest will be affected in no way whatsoever, nor yours, Fanny-Rosa, nor yours, Eliza, nor those of any member of my family. I am seventy-five years of age. My wife is fifty. I shall, very naturally, make provision for her in my will, but nothing that I leave to her will be taken from any of you. As to our friends in Saunby and elsewhere, Eliza, you need not worry on that account. We shall live very quietly in Lletharrog, and Mrs Brodrick will never move anywhere else. It is not even necessary for people to know that I have married again, if you do not wish to tell them. I do hope and trust that none of my family will feel ill-will towards the woman who has so kindly consented to become the one companion of these last years of mine."

No one answered. He looked from one to the other, and then across at his two grandsons. Thomas came in to draw the curtains. As he drew them with a click across the window there was something of finality about the sound, thought Henry, like the end of an epoch. Nothing would ever be quite the same again. Clonmere would continue, he and Johnnie and the boys would come there to spend their holidays, but their grandfather would not be with them. The library would be empty, the hall table bare of the nobbled stick and the shovel hat, and in the little farmhouse at Lletharrog across the water his grandfather would be sitting opposite his cook, that large-faced, cheerful woman with the red hands, who made such excellent scones, and had that awful sing-song Bronsea accent. . .

It was horrible, thought Henry, it was vile. His grandfather, whom he had feared and respected so much, to come crashing down like this from his pedestal. It was as though God himself had suddenly become degraded. Poor aunt Barbara, poor aunt Eliza; how wretched and miserable they must be feeling! He would have to be especially nice to them from now on, and keep those youngsters from making too much noise.

Thank the Lord, thought Fanny-Rosa, that he has decided to live at

Lletharrog and not bring her here. It won't affect any of us, and I can do as I please with this place. A mercy she was not a young woman, who would produce a family. Old men were such idots, and one never knew. . . .

It's all very well, thought Eliza, to say I am to have the house at Saunby. There is nothing I should like better, provided he allows me enough money to run it, but he is always so close, and anyway I cannot very well leave Barbara, although I am certain it is only a matter of a month or two now. But I must try to be firm, and get him to allow me sufficient to live in some sort of style in Saunby. After all, I shall be the only one to survive of all his children.

"If," said Copper John slowly, "no one has anything more to say, I will wish you all a very good night. We will meet at breakfast at eight o'clock. I shall be going up to the mines as usual."

He kissed his daughter and his daughter-in-law, and shook hands with his grandsons, and went from the room.

Johnnie could hear him walk downstars and shut the library door behind him. Poor lonely old bastard, thought Johnnie; poor old devil, with no one to give him comfort all these years, his wife some thirty years in her grave, and his sons and his daughters dying off one by one. This is the fellow I've hated and been afraid of for as long as I can remember, and he's human after all. He's like me, he wants the same things, the same comfort. He is not God Almighty, and never has been; he is only a poor, tragic, lonely old man. And good luck to him, thought Johnnie, good luck to him and his cook; mother and the aunts could look as shocked as they liked and say what shame it brought upon the family. They did not know what the old man must have suffered, they did not understand. . . .

"I say, it's pretty awful, isn't it?" said Henry, as the two brothers undressed and got into bed.

"Rot!" answered Johnnie; "why shouldn't he do what he wants?"

"It will seem so queer," said Henry, "to come here for the holidays and not to see grandfather. I hate changes. I like things to go on being the same."

Johnnie did not answer. He lay on his back with his hands behind his head, and through his mind, in a turmoil, raced the events of the afternoon. Driving the horses, walking the streets of Slane, seeing Jack Donovan and his friend, going into the public-house, having those drinks, and that girl. And then his grandfather's news on top of it all, seeing his tragic, lonely figure, and the thought of leaving Eton, of going into the Dragoons in a few months' time perhaps, of fighting abroad.

Henry was soon asleep, but perhaps because he had slept in the carriage coming home, Johnnie tossed and turned on his bed, his mind more wakeful, more disturbed as the hours passed, and always he seemed to see the grinning, ginger-headed Jack Donovan thrusting his offensive face close to his own and asking him to have another drink. When the stable clock struck three Johnnie sat up and threw aside his bed-clothes. Henry did not stir, and the house was still and quiet.

"I wonder," thought Johnnie, "if there is any whisky in the cellar."

He went out into the corridor, and crept to the top of the back-stairs. They felt cold to his bare feet. He listened a moment, and heard no sound. Stealthily, furtively, he felt his way in the darkness to the kitchen regions. Somewhere a clock was ticking. He put his hand out and touched the cellar door. And for once in his lifetime Thomas had neglected his duties. The key was in the cellar door. . . .

3

On the second of December, 1856, a cab turned into St James's Street from Piccadilly, and from thence into Pall Mall, stopping at length before number 17a, which was at that time bachelors' chambers. It was a dark, wet evening, and the driver rang the bell and waited for the janitor to answer it before he opened the door for his passenger to alight. "Dirty night, mum," he said conventionally, holding out his hand for his fare. And as she dropped the silver into it and said "Thank you, my good fellow," with an air like a queen, he grinned, and watched her climb the steps of the building, for she could not have a notion how she looked, with that bright purple velvet cloak round her shoulders and the bonnet that was meant to be the same colour perched sideways on her brilliant hair. Mark you, he said to himself as he whipped up his horse and clattered away down the wet street, I dare say she was a rare good-looker in her day, and there were not many women about who tipped half-a-crown, or men either, for that matter.

"Captain Brodrick is not yet returned, Madam," said the janitor. "He said if you came you was to wait, he would not be very long. He's having a hair-cut, I believe, Madam, down in Jermyn Street."

"I hope then," said Fanny-Rosa, "that he doesn't let himself be cropped like a convict. What's the use, I say to him, of having a head of hair like his, and then shaving it off, as though he were doing time? Pray light the gas. The room is like a morgue. What does Captain Brodrick do with himself in such a poky place, I wonder? But I suppose you won't tell me if I ask?"

She laughed, and peeled off her gloves.

The janitor looked uncomfortable. The lady was Captain Brodrick's mother, and though she seemed somewhat unconventional, it would hardly do to discuss the Captain's behaviour. He watched her as she adjusted her bonnet in front of the looking-glass, and, opening a small handbag, flecked some white powder on her face. The result was not very happy. Fanny-Rosa caught his eye in the looking-glass.

"What's the matter?" she said sharply.

"Nothing at all, Madam," replied the janitor, and, bowing, he closed the door behind him.

"Damn fool," muttered Fanny-Rosa, and smoothed away the excess of powder. She gave a twitch to her cape, and fastened the brooch on the face of it. It was a handsome diamond brooch, Johnnie's regimental badge. The pin was always coming undone. She knew she would lose it one day. She began to walk round the room, picking up the objects on the mantelpiece, opening boxes and examining pictures. Johnnie's desk was shut, but the key was in the tobacco jar on top of it. Fanny-Rosa opened it, humming a tune to herself as she did so. Papers, and envelopes, and pieces of blotting-paper scattered in all directions. "Hopelessly untidy," murmured his mother, "exactly like me." There were several bills, none of them paid apparently, and all to account rendered. Fanny-Rosa read them all. There were one or two invitation cards, which she scrutinised, and a letter, obviously written in a feminine hand, accusing him of neglect and signed "your loving little Doodie". Fanny-Rosa smiled. "Loving little fiddlesticks," she thought. In one drawer she found a doctor's prescription which intrigued her but unfortunately could not be deciphered, and a box of pills that she smelt and tasted but found disagreeable. A step outside startled her for a moment, and she slammed down the desk and began to hum loudly and turn again to the looking-glass. But it must have been the janitor going about his business. The rest of the desk was disappointing. The drawers were filled with maps and military text-books and orders. Fanny-Rosa turned her attention to the cupboard. It held clothes. Johnnie's great-coat, and his service jacket, and his top boots. Nothing of interest there, although she liked to touch his clothes, and she let her hand rest lovingly a moment on the service jacket, with the ribbon on the breast. Poor darling! he had worn it out in that terrible Crimea; it was a wonder he had not been frozen to death. Idiotic fiasco. Why anyone had ever gone in for the thing was a wonder to her. . . . Hullo, what was this? Something in straw stuffed behind the boots. Just what she expected. A bottle of port. And here was another, and another. All empty. She wondered where he kept the full ones. She shut the cupboard, and opened the door into the little bedroom beyond. Nothing here, except his bed, and his wash-basin, and a chest-of-drawers. She hesitated a fraction of a second before opening the bedside cupboard. In it she found a bottle of whisky, half full. She shut it again, and went back into the sitting-room.

"If he must drink," she said to herself, "why doesn't he put it all out on the sideboard? There's nobody to see. Besides, I would not mind a glass of port myself."

She drew her chair close to the meagre fire, and poked at the coals. Men had no idea of comfort, especially army men. They got so used to early hours and iron beds and general dreariness that they never seemed to expect anything else. Edward was just the same now he had entered the regiment too. Henry was different. He was the only one of the boys who really knew how to live. And Herbert, leaving Oxford to go and be a curate in that Liverpool slum, was quite beyond her. He had been such a bright, amusing little boy too. As for Fanny, well, it was exactly like her to marry a clergyman. Not that she had anything against Bill Eyre; he was a most worthy creature, and had some money too, and after all the Eyres were one of the oldest families in the country. But there was something about a clergyman. . . . In fact, Fanny-Rosa never quite knew how they brought themselves to marry, far less to breed. When she thought of upright, worthy Bill, and her own timid, rather dull little Fanny, she could not begin to imagine . . . Still, there it was, and a baby expected in three months. She wondered how she would feel as a grandmother. What a time Johnnie was being! He had no doubt gone in somewhere for a nip, poor lamb. What a lot of trouble it would save if he would only be open about it, and would come back here, and both of them sit to a bottle together. Those were his swords in the corner. She never knew if they were for show, or if soldiers really used them in battle. Johnnie told such ridiculous tales of blood and slaughter that she could not believe him. Here he was though. The door burst open, and the darling boy came into the room.

"Forgive me, I've kept you waiting," he said, going to her at once and taking her in his arms.

"Have they cropped you now?" she said, turning him about, and he laughed, showing his dark head, and bent it for her to kiss.

"If you had your way, mother, you'd have my hair on my shoulders still," he said.

Johnnie at twenty-six was much the same as he had been at seventeen, but taller, broad-shouldered, though not as tall or as broad as his brother Henry, who outstripped him by two inches. His face had coarsened somewhat, his mouth had become more obstinate, and the expression in his eyes a little arrogant, a little watchful, as though he expected criticism and would squash it before it came.

"Well, what's all the excitement?" he said. "Why am I to take everybody out to dinner?"

"A celebration," said Fanny-Rosa. "It's really rather an honour. Henry has been made high sheriff for Slane, and he's only twenty-four."

"Good Heavens!" said Johnnie. He was silent a moment, and then he laughed. "I always did know Henry had the talent of the family," he said. "He won all the honours he could at Eton, and I did not achieve any. By all means let's celebrate. I don't grudge him his success. High sheriff of Slane, is it? We must pull his leg about it."

Fanny-Rosa was relieved. Sometimes she was just the smallest bit anxious that darling Johnnie might be jealous of his younger brother's triumphs. Everyone seemed to be so fond of Henry, in this country as well as across the water. He had hosts of friends. And wherever she went, whether it was over there, or to stay with Eliza in Saunby, or here in London, people would seem interested when they heard her name, and say, "Are you the mother of Henry Brodrick? But how delightful to meet you! We are so devoted to your son." She was glad and proud, of course, and Henry was a dear no doubt, and very charming and good-looking, but she wished sometimes that it would be the other way about and someone would say, "I met your eldest son, Captain Brodrick, last week. What a splendid fellow he is!" But no one ever did say that. Only once, in London, had she come across a man who knew Johnnie, and he had been very non-committal. "Oh, yes," he said, "I did serve with him at one time, before the war. . . . Haven't seen him since," and then changed the subject. Once she had asked Edward, soon after her younger son had joined the regiment, whether there was any unfair feeling against his eldest brother. Edward had looked most uncomfortable.

"I don't think so exactly," he said, "but you see, poor old Johnnie has such a deuce of a temper, and he rubs fellows up the wrong way sometimes. They don't mind him being as wild as a hawk, but they do object when he has too much port after dinner and calls every one he sees a swine and a bastard."

"Yes," said Fanny-Rosa, "yes, I see. . . ."

And yet, she thought, looking as this eldest son of hers as he brushed his hair before the mirror in his bedroom, how charming he could be when he wanted to, how affectionate, how lovable, and she was certain that his brains were the equal of Henry's, but he did not bother to use them, any more than his father had done. As for his temper, well, that was her legacy, and anyway it showed spirit, a determination not to be beaten.

"We had better be going, Johnnie," she said. "I told the others seven-thirty."

"Very well," he answered. "There is a cab waiting, Dobson will see you into it. I shan't be a moment."

She went out into the hall, and, glancing back over her shoulder, she saw through the chink of the door that her son had opened the cupboard against the wall.

"He's going to have a glass of port," she thought. "I wonder how much he gets through in the day."

The janitor held the carriage umbrella over her head, and she stepped into the cab, Johnnie joined her in a few minutes. He was flourishing a handkerchief, and a wave of eau-de-Cologne filled the cab.

"What does this party consist of?" he asked, stretching his legs on the seat opposite.

"Only ourselves," she said, "and Henry, and Edward, and Fanny, and Bill, and Bill's sister Katherine, whom I think you have not met."

"Is she as dull as Bill?"

"Don't be unkind about your brother-in-law; I'm devoted to him. Katherine is most charming. I rather fancy Henry has an eye on her. Be civil and charming to everyone, for my sake. And don't make any remark about Fanny's appearance. She is very sensitive."

"Why the devil does she go out in public then?"

"She only does so tonight because of Henry. Then she and Bill are going off to Clifton, to await the arrival."

"What a confounded wet night it is!" said Johnnie, peering through the glass, and rubbing it with his handkerchief," and where in hell's name does this fellow think he's going? I swear he's taken the wrong street. Here, you blithering idiot. . . ."

He lowered the window, and began shouting at the driver.

Fanny-Rosa leant back and said nothing. This always happened, driving with Johnnie. Never yet had any cabman taken the right route. By the time they reached their destination he had cast doubt on the cabman's parentage, his personal morals, his cleanliness, the fidelity of his wife, and all to the unfortunate fellow's face. She began to wonder whether there would be a fight when they reached Portman Square. But Johnnie suddenly changed his tone, gave the man an enormous tip and said he would not have his job for anything in the world, and giving his arm to his mother, he conducted her into the hotel, leaving the cabman red in the face, stupefied, and dumb. Henry and Edward were waiting for them.

"The others will be down directly," said Henry; "the girls are tidivating, as usual. How are you, old fellow! I can't tell you how pleased I am to see you."

He shook hands with Johnnie, and kissed his mother The two brothers had not met for nearly a year.

"Greetings to the Sheriff of Slane," said Johnnie. "And how's the law going, and the politics, and all your other interests?"

"Pretty well," smiled Henry. "I believe in dabbling in as many things as possible. They want me to contest the seat at the next election, but I think I'll wait a few years before I do that."

Enterprising chap, thought Johnnie. Always a finger in somebody's pie, but never being irritating about it. Here came Fanny, poor girl, looking grotesque, and the worthy Bill, and . . .

"This is Katherine Eyre," said Henry. "My brother Johnnie."

Charming, his mother had said, Johnnie remembered, but she had not told him she was beautiful. The smooth, dark hair, gathered in a low knot on the nape of her neck, the serene brown eyes, the cream-white texture of her skin, the whole impression of her, he thought, suggesting repose and quiet, someone withdrawn into herself who brought peace to the beholder. He found himself at a loss for words, and because he was not used to feeling shy before women he began to bluster, to give orders to the waiter in a loud voice, and when they came into the dining-room he complained about the position of the table; it was cramped against the wall, they must have the one in the opposite corner instead. Henry took charge and

mollified the waiter. He gently teased his brother and changed the
conversation, and soon they were all seated, Johnnie on the left of
Katherine Eyre, and, rather than that she should think him a dullard
and a boor, he at once plunged into a fantastic tale about the Crimea
—she had asked some question on the war—hoping to impress her with
its extravagance

"I should like," she said, "to have been out there and helped Miss
Nightingale. Not so much because of the nursing—I hardly think I could
have stood it—but because so many of the men must have felt lonely and
unhappy and would want comfort."

She looked at him and smiled, and he turned away, crumbling a piece
of bread, because he was reminded suddenly of himself in that appalling
shambles at Sevastopool, taking a very different sort of comfort in the
arms of a slant-eyed, rather dirty little refugee, and how he had gone
without whisky for five days and nearly died in consequence.

"I don't think," he said, "you could have done much good . . ."

And then he saw Henry staring at Katherine Eyre across the table.
with such tenderness and adoration that Johnnie felt a strange despair
come upon him, a feeling that he was an outcast, a pariah dog, who had
no business to be sitting here with his brother and Katherine Eyre. They
belonged to another world, a world where people were normal and
happy, and had faith and confidence in the future. And above all faith
and confidence in themselves.

"Here," he said loudly, "no one's drinking anything. Aren't we going
to toast the Sheriff of Slane?"

And he thumped on the table for the waiter to attend them. The
other people dining in the room turned round at the sound of his
voice.

"Henry," he said to Katherine Eyre, "gets his way by being polite to
people. I get mine by doing the opposite."

She did not answer, and once again he felt depressed and lost, not
because there was any sign of disapproval in her eyes, or condemnation,
but because the sight of her sitting there beside him made him wish to be
different, someone who was quiet and peaceful like herself. He felt that
very possibly she considered it unimportant whether people got their own
way or not, and that in any case to shout and to bluster was something
she would never do.

There was his mother laughing and talking to Bill. She enjoyed life,
anyway, and would continue to do so whatever happened, and Bill, that
honest parson, chatted back politely to his mother-in-law, though no
doubt he did not care about the dyed hair and the powdered face.
Fanny, giving birth any minute, was like a mouse, and always had been;
no chance of her ever breaking the peace; and Edward and Henry
discussed the affairs of the day as though the words Conservative and
Liberal meant anything at all. No, he was an outcast, and always would

be, and no doubt everybody here, except perhaps his mother, wished that they could have dined without him.

"Well," he said, leaning back in his chair, "we have toasted Henry's future as a sheriff, what about toasting mine as a civilian?"

There was a pause in the conversation. Everybody looked at him.

"What do you mean, darling?" said Fanny-Rosa.

"Only that I am leaving the regiment," said Johnnie. "I sent in my papers today."

At once a torrent of questions were flung at him. What did he mean by it? and surely it was a pity, he had always said the life suited him, and one conventional phrase after the other. Only Edward, the other soldier present, made no comment. And Fanny-Rosa, with sudden intuition, wondered whether Johnnie had been requested to leave. . . .

"Oh, I'm fed up with the service," said Johnnie. "All very fat and fine when there's some fighting to do, but to stand about all day on a barrack square is not my idea of amusement. I've had it in my mind to leave for some time. What will I do? I haven't the slightest idea. I shall probably go abroad. Anyway, what the devil does it matter? The fact is, Miss Eyre, I find it rather degrading, and not particularly profitable, to be six-and-twenty years of age with deuced little to live on, waiting for an old man of eighty-four to die and leave me all his money."

The speech made an uncomfortable impression. His sister blushed, and glanced at her husband. His mother smiled a shade too brightly and began talking rather loudly to Henry about his plans for Christmas. Only Katherine Eyre appeared unmoved. She looked up at Johnnie, her eyes grave and kindly.

"It is a very difficult position for you," she said, "and must make you feel so unsettled. Don't go abroad, though."

"Why not?" said Johnnie.

"I don't think you would be happy."

"I'm not happy anywhere."

"Whose fault is that?"

"Nobody's. It's my misfortune to be cursed with the nature I have "

"Don't say that. You are really the most kind and generous person. I have often talked about you to Henry. He is very fond of you."

"Is he? I doubt it."

"You like to make yourself out worse than you are. That's foolishness. You ought to come across the water, and take an interest in your country."

"What has my country ever done for me?"

"It's given you your life, for one thing."

She laughed, and his heart smote him because she had so little knowledge of his true character, his selfishness, his vices, his utter want of principle.

"I've always understood," he said, "that I was a seven months' child. Perhaps that is why I lack all the virtues. And the nicest member of my family died the day I was born, my aunt Jane, who might have made something out of me. She was to have been my godmother. I think you are a little like the portrait of her that hangs in the dining-room at Clonmere."

"I suppose," she said, "that you would not like me for a godmother instead?"

He stared at her suspiciously. What the devil was she driving at? The words would have sounded flirtatious, inviting, from anyone else, or deliberately provoking from an older, clever woman. But from Katherine Eyre they were unique, because they were sincere. She looked at him with her calm brown eyes, and once again she smiled.

"Are you afraid I should play the governess?" she said. "I promise you I would never do that. But if my godson had twists I should want to help him unravel the knots."

Johnnie had forgotten the rest of his family, forgotten the people in the dining-room and the passing waiters, the bustle and confusion. It seemed to him that there was no one but his tortured, angry, resentful self, and the blessed, healing presence of Katherine Eyre.

"You are a very unusual person," he said slowly. "I wish to God I had met you before."

"We are going to see a lot of one another from now on," she said, "so the future will make up for the past. You must come and stay with us in Slane."

Why, wondered Johnnie, was she so gracious to him, so kind, as though it mattered to her what became of him, as though she cared for him in some strange personal way, who had only met him an hour before? If he could think for one moment that there was to be someone in life who would bother about him, help him, smile at him, talk to him, why then there was hope indeed. She had asked him to stay in Slane? Did the Eyres live in Slane? He could not remember. How unusual she was, lacking all ordinary convention, and yet bearing no resemblance to the fluffy little coquettes with whom he amused himself in London. Yes, he would go back to his own country, he would stay with Katherine Eyre and her family in Slane, and perhaps, after he had seen a bit more of her, there would be some purpose in living after all. She would be merciful and kind, and if he shouted, and swore, and drank, and lost his temper, she would forgive him. That was what he needed more than anything in the world. Forgiveness. Mercy.

And now Henry was getting up with a glass in his hand, looking proud and happy. His brother supposed there was to be another toast. And Henry said:

"Mother, Fanny, Bill, Johnnie and Edward, I have another announcement to make. Today I am the happiest of men because Katherine has promised to marry me. And the wedding is to be in Slane, in two months' time."

Everyone was smiling, everyone was talking at once, and there was
Edward patting Henry on the back, and Fanny leaning across to
Katherine Eyre and kissing her, and his mother saying "But Katherine,
my dear, how very delightful," and Bill apologising for two Eyres in
their family all within twelve months. Johnnie heard his own voice
loud and hearty, saying, "Congratulations, old boy; you deserve to be
happy, God bless you," and suddenly the atmosphere became unbearable—the pleasure on all their faces, the quick discussion of plans, the
women, all excited and eager, talking about wedding-dresses and brides-
maids and God knows what, and Henry looking across with confidence
and pride at this Katherine who was to be his bride, his comfort, his loved
one. . . .

"You'll be my best man, old fellow, won't you?" said Henry, and
Johnnie pushed back his chair and got to his feet.

"Not on your life," he said rudely. "I don't know how to behave in
church; you'd better get Edward, or summon Herbie down from Liverpool, then there'd be two chaps there in dog-collars. No, I'll stand in the
street outside, and thrown an old slipper at your carriage as you drive
away"

He saw the sudden hurt expression in his brother's eyes, and the
inevitable flicker of a question, "What's wrong with Johnnie now?" that
he had seen so often before, as a child, as a boy, as a man. It's no good,
thought Johnnie; I always hurt people, I always make them unhappy; I
spoil every party; it would be much better if I went. I don't belong to
this sort of happy family atmosphere anyway. Let Henry marry his
Katherine. He is the right sort of fellow for her. They will make one
another happy. And she will give him peace and understanding. As
for me, I can make my own peace, in my own way, and if it's black
oblivion from a bottle or a tart, what the hell does it matter to anyone?

"Sorry to break the evening," he said, "but the fact is I've just remembered I promised to see someone at nine. And anyway, you'll all enjoy
yourselves far better without me." He drew a couple of sovereigns from
his pocket and dropped them on his brother's plate. "My dinner," he
said. "Goodnight, mother."

And he walked slowly out of the dining-room, conscious that people
were turning to stare at him and one or two were smiling, were raising
their eyebrows, and one of them lifted a glass significantly. God damn
them, he thought, God damn and blast the whole bloody lot of them.

Mechanically he took his hat and his coat and his cane from the
attendant in the vestibule. The rain had ceased and there was a wind now,
cutting and cold. He walked down the street; here came three fellows
arm-in-arm, walking up the pavement towards him. He expected them
to break apart and give him passage, but either they did not see him
or they did not choose to do so, and without hesitation he walked into
the midst of them, throwing one into the gutter, and the other against the

wall, and the third he elbowed into a lamp-post. "Now go and learn manners, will you?" he cried, and the three, too astonished to retaliate, shouted after him, and one man bellowed out for a policeman, but by the time his call was answered, and a crowd had collected, Johnnie was away down the middle of the road. "Where am I supposed to be going?" he said to himself, and then he remembered his excuse to the family, the engagement at nine o'clock. Well, it was true, now he came to think of it; his colonel was giving a reception at his house in Grosvenor Street. The same pompous old fool who had hummed and hawed that morning, and said that under the circumstances, and it was very painful for him to have to say so, but he hoped Johnnie would realise . . . In other words, Johnnie had better leave the regiment before he found himself chucked out. All right. Johnnie would do so. And damned glad of it into the bargain. He reached in his pocket and brought out the invitation card that had lain on his mantelpiece before the interview took place. "Colonel the Hon. George Greville and Mrs Greville at home." He read it once more under the light of a nearby lamp.

"They shall have the pleasure of my company, if they so desire it," he said. He rocked unsteadily on the pavement, smiling to himself, and on the opposite side of the street a cab rumbled by. He summoned it with a flourish of his cane. "No. 11 Grosvenor Street," said Johnnie.

It was rather pleasant leaning back in the cab, with his head against the cushion, and it seemed to him that the cab arrived in Grosvenor Street far too soon. He climbed carefully from his seat, and paid his fare. The lights shone brightly from the house, and there was a red carpet down from the front door to the pavement. A crowd of people had collected outside in the street to watch the arrival of the guests. The door opened for a moment to admit one of Johnnie's brother officers and his wife, and then closed again.

" 'Ere, ain't you got a wife, mister?" said a girl at Johnnie's elbow. He took off his hat and bowed.

"Unfortunately not," he said, "but would you be good enough to accompany me instead?"

The girl screamed with laughter. She was a little painted prostitute who had walked up from Piccadilly to see the fun.

"What would they say to me if I went inside?" she chaffed.

"That's exactly what I would like to know," said Johnnie. "Will you come with me? Or are you afraid? I'll give you five pounds if you do."

The girl laughed nervously, and another woman, her companion, pulled at her arm.

"Come away," she said. "Don't you see the gentleman's tipsy?"

"Tipsy be damned," said Johnnie "I'm roaring drunk if you want to know. Here, what about this?" And he shook five sovereigns in his hand.

"All right, I'll do it," said the girl boldly. "Let go, Annie, will you?"

Johnnie offered her his arm, and rang the bell. Once more the door opened, and a powdered footman stood within the entrance. A hum of voices greeted Johnnie and his companion. Men in uniform and women in evening dress thronged the stairs. At the head of the stairs on the landing, Johnnie caught a glimpse of his white-haired colonel and his stately wife.

"What's your name, sweetheart?" said Johnnie to the girl beside him.

"Vera," said the girl, hanging back, "Vera Potts. . . . You're not going to take me up there, are you, mister?"

"I most certainly am," said Johnnie. He handed his hat and coat with a bow to the second footman, who was whispering to his colleague in great agitation. "Have the goodness to announce us," said Johnnie, moving forward to the stairs. "Captain Brodrick and Miss Vera Potts. Hullo, my dear Robin, how are you? And your wife? Delighted to meet you. I don't think you have met Miss Potts. Miss Potts. Captain Sir Robert and Lady Frazer. This way, Vera my dear. . . ."

People were falling back against the stairway as Johnnie elbowed his way forward, the girl still clinging to his arm. Johnnie himself could see with difficulty, but he was aware of many heads turned towards him, of several blank expressions, of someone calling to him from the hall below in a voice of extreme urgency, but he felt himself possessed of great power and self-confidence. Now his colonel's head was turned towards him, and the conventional smile of greeting froze on the lips of the colonel's wife, as her outstretched hand, in its long white glove, fell before the grubby paw extended to her by her uninvited guest.

"Good evening, Mrs Greville," said Johnnie, "good evening, sir. May I present Miss Vera Potts, of the old firm of Potts, Piccadilly?"

"Please to meet you, I'm sure," said his companion.

Mrs Greville had the distant, far-away expression of one who has received a blow between the eyes, and for one moment Johnnie thought she might faint. But she recovered magnificently, she bowed, she murmured.

The colonel was unmoved. He greeted Johnnie with courtesy, and shook hands with Johnnie's companion. Only the little pulse beating in his forehead betrayed his inner feelings.

"Morton," he said, to a crimson-faced young subaltern at his elbow, "I think Miss Potts would be happier outside. Would you have the goodness to see her to the door? There is another staircase, through the landing there, on the left. Thank you. And will you, Frazer, and somebody else, hail a cab and take Brodrick home? I am afraid he is not very well. . . ."

"On the contrary," said Johnnie, "I am exceedingly well. And I myself will conduct Miss Potts to her friends. Good evening, sir."

He bowed, he offered his arm once more to his companion, and together they sailed down the staircase and into the hall, stared at by a hundred faces; and so his hat and his coat and his stick again, and out on to the red carpet with the door slamming behind them. . .

Later, much later, Johnnie pulled aside the curtains in his room in Pall Mall. The morning was foggy and grey. For a while he could not remember what had happened the night before, and he reached for the flask in the drawer of the dressing-table. He felt better after a moment or two, and his eye fell on the sleepy form of Vera Potts, who was lying on his bed. Strange, he had no recollection of anything after leaving Grosvenor Street. He went into the sitting-room and stared vacantly about him. There was his coat, and the much-trimmed hat of Vera Potts, and the fur she had worn about her neck. He took another sip from his flask. Then he noticed a telegram lying on the desk. He put out a shaky hand and opened it. When Vera Potts came into the room, looking for her things, she found Johnnie sitting before his desk, the telegram open in his hand. He was staring straight in front of him.

"What's up?" she said. "Not bad news, is it?"

He did not seem to hear her. He was watching the grey December fog break upon the world outside.

"My grandfather's dead," he said slowly. "That means Clonmere is mine."

4

The funny thing was that he still felt that the library belonged to the old man, and when he opened the drawers of the great roll-top desk, or turned a key in the book-case, he did so with a certain uneasiness, as if Copper John might walk into the room at any moment, and stand there with his hands behind his back, his eyes narrowing under his thick eye-brows, and demand in cold, measured tones what his grandson was about. The place smelt of him. It was grey, austere. And Johnnie knew that he could never sit there, never write letters with any sense of ease because of the shadow of his grandfather, looking over his shoulder.

The thing was ridiculous, of course. His grandfather had not been to Clonmere for more than six years. And Johnnie tried to picture him, that old deaf man of eighty-four, living with his housekeeper-wife at Lletharrog, waiting for death to claim him, seeing no one, writing to no one, except once a month with great regularity to the manager of the mines on Hungry Hill. Surely there was nothing fearful about that distant figure, sitting day after day in the living-room of the farm-house? And yet Johnnie shuddered, for no reason, and he would shut up the roll-top desk, and push away the chair, and leave the library to the cobwebs and the dust, and go out into the sunlight. There was a queer anti-climax in returning home. All his life he had waited for this moment, dreamt about it, planned for it, and now that it had come the savour was lost to him, the excitement was no longer there. "It's come too late," he thought, wandering about the grounds, listening abstractedly to what the agent had to say. "It's come too late. I no longer care. This should have happened ten years ago, then it might have been worth while." The agent had an irritating manner; he was a fellow called Adams. Johnnie did not know him, and he kept referring to Henry all the time, as though the place had come to him, and not to Johnnie at all. "Yes, Captain Brodrick, your brother, Mr Henry, ordered those trees to be planted; he was staying here last summer, with the other young gentlemen, when you were abroad." And then, "Mr Henry suggested that the farm-buildings should be repaired, and he settled the dispute between old Baird and the new man; he decided Baird was really too old for the job, and he engaged the present man, Phillips." And, "Mr Henry used to go up to the mines fairly frequently. I rather think the letters referring to the business have been going to him."

No doubt, when he was in the regiment, and with his grandfather living in retirement at Lletharrog, Henry had given an eye to the place; but now his grandfather was dead, and Johnnie was the head of the family, Henry could mind his own business.

"In future," he said curtly, "all communications in regard to the estate or to the mines are to be brought direct to me."

The tenants kept asking after Mr Henry too, looking a little doubtfully at Johnnie, as if he had no business to be there, and was a stranger. Up at the mines it was the same. The former mining captain, old Nicholson, had retired long since, and his place had been taken by a manager, Griffiths, who showed him the accounts willingly enough, and appeared efficient and civil, but who when Johnnie asked some question about machinery, said "that Mr Henry considered the plant wanted renewing, and perhaps Captain Brodrick would be seeing his brother, and find out what steps he had taken in the matter."

"My brother," said Johnnie, "is particularly busy at the moment getting himself married, and anyway the management of the mines has nothing whatsoever to do with him."

"Of course, now you are home, Captain Brodrick, it is a different matter," said Griffiths hastily. "No doubt you will see to things personally."

And he began talking technicalities, and showing Johnnie figures, none of which meant anything much to Johnnie. But rather than betray his ignorance he nodded his head now and again, and asked questions, and put some sort of bold face on the matter so that the manager would learn his lesson.

"I'm damned if I'm doing to be dictated to by Henry or anyone else," thought Johnnie, and on returning to the castle he had all the servants in and cursed them, just to show them that he was not going to stand any nonsense. He was irritated when old Thomas informed him that if the Captain did not require his services he would go and look after Mr Henry and Mrs Henry, in the house they had taken in Slane.

"Go by all means, if you want to," he said. "I don't want to be served by people who dislike me."

"It's not that, sir," said the old servant, looking uncomfortable; " 'tis only that I know Mr Henry's ways, and that with your being out of the country so long, I might not please you."

So Thomas departed to Slane, and so did one or two of the other servants, and Johnnie, in exasperation, sent for the batman who had looked after him in the regiment. He took charge of the house immediately, and shortly afterwards Fanny-Rosa arrived, with three more servants and all her luggage, and two or three dogs, announcing that darling Johnnie could not possibly live at Clonmere all by himself, of course she was going to look after him.

"You know, my darling," said Fanny-Rosa, tucking her arm in her son's, and walking up and down before the house, "what you ought to do is to marry. Some nice quiet, placid creature, who would give you dozens of children, and be about the place if you wanted her, but with no mind of her own to make an irritation. She would not get in my way or in yours. There must be someone in the country who would answer the purpose. Good family, of course. None of your upstarts."

"I dislike quiet, placid women," Johnnie said, "and so do you; and anyway I'm too much of a ruffian for any woman to marry, so we won't discuss it."

"Henry and his Katherine are ideally happy," said his mother. "It's a pity you can't be the same. A wife would steady you, give you more of a background. I'm not a fool. I know what I am talking about."

"I've no desire to be steady," said Johnnie, "and if you are going to start lecturing me I shall remind you that this house is mine, and not yours."

Fanny-Rosa glanced at him sideways. Queer how mention of Henry and Katherine always made him stick out his jaw and smoulder.

"Don't be absurd, darling," she said, "you know I never lecture."

But she made a silent resolve to question this servant of his discreetly some time as to how much whisky his master was consuming, and where he kept the key of the cellar, and what he did with himself every evening, and whether he received many letters. The great thing at the moment was to keep Johnnie occupied. Fanny-Rosa wrote invitations to every neighbour within thirty miles inviting them to Clonmere to shoot before the season finished. Her brother, Bob Flower, who had married and settled down in Castle Andriff, her cousin, the Earl of Mundy, her other cousins, the Lumleys—everybody who might be induced to make some sort of companionship for Johnnie, was pestered with letters and invitations, all claiming that "darling Johnnie was longing to see them," and on accepting the invitations and going to Clonmere the guests would be greeted by their talkative, flamboyant hostess, dressed in every describable colour to clash with her vivid hair. Later, considerably later, in the day, they would be joined by their somewhat flushed and slightly incoherent host, who would be hearty and aggressive in turn, one moment laughing boisterously, the next plunged for no apparent reason in sullen gloom. And the guests would be diffident, embarrassed, uncertain whether they were expected to shoot or to order their carriages and go home. At any rate, when next invited to Clonmere they would find themselves otherwise engaged.

"Extraordinary people are," Fanny-Rosa would say. "Last winter, when Henry and Herbert were here, they had friends over to shoot two or three times a week, inviting themselves. And now the same lot are full of excuses about the roads and the distance."

"It's not extraordinary at all," said Johnnie; "it only means that they liked coming to see Henry and Herbert, and they don't care about coming to see me. For God Almighty's sake stop asking them. I can invite my own friends."

And he would wander around with the keeper, and one or two of the tenants with whom he had struck up a queer familiarity, because there was no one else.

It was on one of these occasions that he came across Jack Donovan, whom he had barely set eyes on since he was a boy, and who brought back vividly the long-forgotten episode in the public-house in Slane. The fellow was little changed, still carroty-haired and impudent, and he stuck out his hand at once to Johnnie and asked after his health, although the gun under his other arm showed only too plainly that he had been poaching.

"Ah, now you've come back to us again, Captain, we shall see some sport," said Donovan. "That's what I was saying down in Doonhaven to the boys; there'll be lively times ahead. Here's the gentleman that will give some entertainment to the countryside."

Johnnie laughed, although at first he had felt like hitting the fellow.

"You'd better join us, Jack," he said, "and find the hares for us."

"I'll find you hares," said the other, with a wink. "I know the ground like the back of my hand, but I've been obliged to come here quietly, Captain, while you've been from home. It was Doctor Armstrong had the shooting here, and he's no friend to me or my family."

"Never mind Doctor Armstrong," said Johnnie; "you can come and shoot as my guest for a change."

The thought that his godfather disapproved of Jack Donovan was enough to make Johnnie claim the man as a friend at once. Uncle Willie had already made one or two brief appearances at Clonmere, each time adding another pin-prick to Johnnie's mounting irritation. Did Johnnie propose to do this, did he intend to follow his grandfather's example in that, and had he asked his brother Henry's advice about the other? The truth of the matter was his godfather presumed too much on old times' sake. He was over sixty, and past his job, thought his godson, and if he was not very careful Johnnie would have him thrown out of the place and the practice given to a younger man.

"What are you doing for yourself these days, Jack?" he asked, and the man shrugged his shoulders.

"You might well ask me that, Captain, with my elbows coming out of my coat, as you can see for yourself. There's no trade left in the place at all, and my father's old shop that I have there on the quayside falling about my head. We're thinking of going to America, me and my sister Kate. There's nothing doing here at all."

"You don't have to do that," said Johnnie. "I'll find something for you at Clonmere. Now I come to think of it I want someone to live in the gate-house at the top of the drive. I sacked the people only last week for being uncivil. You and your sister had better move in."

Jack Donovan looked up at him, his light blue eyes suspicious.

"Ah, you're making a game of me, Captain."

"I am not. Why shouldn't you live in the gate-house?"

"Sure, it's for you to say. The place belongs to you, Captain, and you can have what tenants you like, now old Mr Brodrick is dead. He would never have had one of us Donovans in his gate-house, I can tell you that."

"All the more reason to have one now," said Johnnie, "and if anyone dares say anything against it, you can refer them to me."

He thought very little more about the matter, until in a few days' time the agent came to him in a state of great indignation, and said that Jack Donovan from Doonhaven, and his sister, had had the impudence to move their things into the gate-house, which he, the agent, had promised to one of the Captain's tenants from Kileen, and would the Captain please give orders for them to leave immediately?

"Certainly not," said Johnnie, delighted to make the agent lose face. "I have given permission to the Donovans to take over the gate-house."

"It is not at all customary . . ." began Mr Adams, but Johnnie told him to go to the devil and went out of the room. That evening at dinner his mother brought up the subject again.

"What is all this nonsense about those dreadful Donovans trying to seize the gate-house?" she said. "The servants are full of it. You're going to turn them out, of course."

"I shall do nothing of the sort," said Johnnie. "Jack Donovan is a very good fellow, and happens to be one of the few people on the estate who appear to like me. They shall live in the gate-house as long as they want to."

"But, Johnnie," protested his mother, "the Brodricks have never had any sort of truck with the Donovans, you must know that. They are a horrible family. Your father caught his death from visiting one of them. For that alone I can never forgive them."

"Because my father had the misfortune to catch diphtheria from one of the Donovans is no reason for me to dislike this generation," said Johnnie. "I should have thought you would have had more sense. The most reasonable thing to do would be for you to go and see Kate Donovan, and ask if she is comfortable."

"My darling boy, I've never spoken to any of the family yet, and I'm certainly not going to begin now. If she's the sly-looking creature with flaxen hair I saw walking down the drive this morning, I don't think much of her. You ought to have had the Mahoneys at the gate-house. I like Mrs Mahoney. Why didn't you ask my advice in the first place?"

"Because I prefer to use my own judgement," said Johnnie shortly, reaching out for the decanter.

"It's a great mistake," said Fanny-Rosa, watching the amount that went into the glass, "to bring people up from the village who are nothing to do with the estate. I tried it with servants, and it never worked. After all, I ran this place at first, more or less on my own and later with Henry's help, all the time you were with the regiment, and I do know something about it by now. Why don't you finish the decanter while you're about it?"

Johnnie put down his glass and faced his mother across the table.

"I think it is time," he said, "that you and I came to some sort of understanding. For years we used to talk about living here together when my grandfather died, didn't we? And now it has happened, and here we are. And you know, and I know, that it's a failure. It does not work. What do you propose to do about it?"

"What do you mean?" said Fanny-Rosa.

"Only that would it not be rather better for both of us if you went and lived somewhere else?" said Johnnie.

For a moment Fanny-Rosa did not answer. She played with the table-cloth in front of her, and there were two vivid spots of colour high on both cheeks. Johnnie watched her moodily, hating himself for what he had done, but knowing that he would never now take back his words.

"I see," said Fanny-Rosa. "I've been getting on your nerves. It was a good thing you told me. Mothers are so blind."

She got up, and walked over to the fireplace, and stood for a while with her hands to the blaze. Johnnie suddenly remembered her as she had been twenty years ago, with that same cloud of hair, now dyed and patchy, falling about her face, and how, when he was a little boy, she had swept him up in her arms and held him close. He could remember the scent she used then, and the lovely cool smell of her skin. Now her chin sagged a little, and the powder, so carelessly applied, had sprinkled upon her dress, so that there were spots of it on the satin. His heart ached, and savagely, in his mind, he cursed the years that had come between them, that could never now be bridged; years that had changed her from a laughing, careless girl to this rather ridiculous figure of middle-age, that touched him only because of the past, not through the present.

"Well, don't let's make a tragedy of it," she said lightly. "If you would rather be alone, thank heaven you said so in time."

Johnnie wheeled round his chair, and stared with her into the fire.

"You don't understand," he said. "It is a tragedy. For years I used to think about this, and you being here with me, and what we would do together. And now that we are here, it's a God-damn awful failure. Isn't that the greatest tragedy that can happen to anyone?"

They gazed into the fire, he with his glass in his hands, she with one hand upon his shoulder.

"I wonder," she said suddenly, "what would have happened if your father had not died."

And there was something in her voice that caught at his heart and made him look up at her swiftly and take her hand. But when he swung her round her face was smiling, there were no tears, and she began talking very rapidly about finding a little villa, perhaps in the south of France, for the autumn and winter. She had often thought she would like to do so. As a girl, she said, she had always spent winters abroad, in France and Italy. It had been most amusing; the only thing was that of course it might be rather expensive. . . .

"Blow expense," said Johnnie. "You know perfectly well that I should allow you anything you want. All that we can arrange."

"Darling," she said, "how sweet and generous of you," and she patted him on the head, which was worse, he thought, than if she had stormed and raved at him. "I wonder if Eliza would care to come out with me," she said, "as a change from Saunby? We could stay at a hotel and look for a tiny villa together. I think I shall write to her tonight. I should prefer Monte Carlo to anywhere else. More going on . . ."

And she opened the door and left him in the dining-room alone, and he thought suddenly how after all these years he knew nothing of his mother, nothing of her mind or her heart. And whether he had broken that heart by his words this evening, or whether she had none to break, was something that he would never know, or anyone else. No one but Almighty God would ever look into the soul of Fanny-Rosa and read the truth.

The next morning he woke full of remorse for his hard words of the evening, and went along to his mother's room to apologise and ask her to stay. He had been drinking too much, he said, she must not take any notice of what he had said; but he found her surrounded by boxes and books and every describable article, clothes long put away, hats, sashes, gloves, relics of the years that had gone.

"So amusing," she said. "I keep coming upon things I had forgotten. Here is a little old hat that I wore when I became engaged to your father," and she picked up a crumpled straw object, the size of a saucer. "It might do for the kitchen-maid on Saints' days," she added, tossing it aside. "Here is your first shoe," she laughed, showing him a scarlet baby slipper. "I must not throw that away. You only wore it a few weeks, your foot grew so quickly. Look at this satin gown. I had it new to wear in Bath, where your father and I once spent a week of tremendous gaiety, and then I started Edward shortly afterwards and was soon too large to put it on. Most annoying, I remember. With a little alteration it would do very well for me now." She held it up against her.

Johnnie watched, despair in his heart. There was so much sadness, it seemed to him, in all these things that had once been part of her.

"I think we were very foolish yesterday," he said. "You had better change your mind and stay."

"Oh, nonsense," she answered; "it's a great mistake to go back on a decision. I learnt that many years ago. Besides, I am beginning to look forward to my little villa. I shall enjoy seeing a lot of people again, and going about. You are treading on that muff, darling. Would you mind moving?"

And he thought that perhaps after all she was not acting, she really had a wish to go, and, because that seemed to him almost more tragic than if she had longed to stay with him, he went downstairs to the dining-room and drank half a bottle of whisky. In a week's time she had gone. . . .

Johnnie shut himself in the house and saw no one. The weather was bad, it rained day after day. The mist would hang about the creek and hide Doon Island, and Johnnie, staring from the windows, would watch the mournful, driving rain, hear the sucking sound of it in the gutters, and see the low, grey clouds sweeping over Hungry Hill. Then, because there would be nothing else to do, he would go out into the rain and walk up the drive through the park, and go into the gate-house and talk to Jack Donovan. The man amused him; he had a coarse, easy sort of humour, and a fund of stories about the people of Doonhaven that appealed to Johnnie's warped sense of the ridiculous. Probably most of them were untrue, but that did not matter. And Johnnie in his turn would relate his experiences abroad, generally the more discreditable ones, because they made Jack Donovan laugh the loudest. The time he had broken into a harem in Turkey and made love to a veiled lady when her husband was away from home was a favourite one with the Donovans—because Kate Donovan too would be of the company, watching him round the corner of her eyes while she pretended to cook her brother's dinner. She had smooth fair hair, almost white in colour, parted in the middle, and Jack told Johnnie that it reached below her waist and she could sit on it.

"Let's have a look at it," said Johnnie, and she pretended to be shocked at once, refusing and making a pother about it, but her brother urged her.

"Go on, Kate; you should not be so proud before the Captain."

And after much persuasion she let it down, peering through her hands at Johnnie. It transformed her at once from a rather ordinary young woman to something original and intriguing, and Johnnie thought what a delight it would be to wind his fingers in the hair, twist it into knots, and make play with it.

This sight of Kate Donovan with her hair down gave him an excitement, and soon almost every day he would wander up to the gate-house and look in and have a chat with the brother and sister. The little stuffy kitchen, with its smell of cooking, its dingy lace curtains, its tawdry crockery, its china figures of the Virgin and St Joseph on the mantelpiece, and the large wooden crucifix on the wall, became more homely to him and more comfortable than the cold, empty rooms down at Clonmere.

Gradually Jack Donovan took to being out when Johnnie came. His sister would bring a bottle of whisky from the cupboard, and a glass, and pour it out for him, saying the afternoon had a chill to it. Johnnie would watch her over the rim of his glass, amused by her pretence of shyness, which he knew very well was assumed, and then he would ask her to take down her hair, and after much shaking of her head and turning away from him she would do so. It would be quiet in the kitchen, with no sound but the ticking of the clock, and Johnnie, with the whisky inside him and Kate Donovan on his knee, would feel a pleasant lethargy steal over him, as he played with her long flaxen hair. How much more comfortable it was to be doing this than sitting all alone in the dining-room at home. Through half-closed eyes he would see the picture of the Pope on the wall opposite, with the rosary beneath, and the incongruity of what he saw compared to what was going on in the kitchen made the laughter rise within him, so that he would hasten to bury his face in Kate Donovan's hair and hide his amusement from her.

Sometimes, back at Clonmere, he would suffer from reaction. It was really rather lamentable, he would think, to go up every few days to his own lodge and make love to his lodge-keeper's sister. Conversation with Kate was impossible, she had none; he went to see her for one purpose only. It was a way of passing the early autumn days of 1857.

He would suffer from reaction most when he paid his occasional visits to his brother's house, East Grove, in Slane. A longing would come over him, that had neither rhyme nor reason, to see his brother's wife Katherine. As soon as he entered her house he would be aware of a sense of peace that he experienced nowhere else. She would come to him, across the drawing-room, and give him her hands, and say, "I am glad to see you, Johnnie. You are going to stay the night, of course," and would take no denial. Thomas would carry his bag to the spare room upstairs, and then tea would be brought, and he would sit beside Katherine while she poured it out, watching her hand on the tea-pot, the curve of her shoulder, the long, slim neck, the exquisite, calm profile.

"What have you been doing with yourself, Johnnie?" she would ask, laying a hand on his knee and looking in his eyes, and he would be filled with sudden loathing for his life and everything he did. Loathing for his useless, hopeless days, the lying in bed in the mornings, the futile pretence of seeing Adams the agent, the sitting alone in front of the whisky bottle in the dining-room, the walking up to the gate-house and the sordid fumbling interlude with Kate. The return to Clonmere and the whisky bottle once again. He gazed round the drawing-room of East Grove.

It was comfortable, kindly, with the fire in the grate and the polished brass fender. The carpet was a soft green, and the shining chintzes had apples in them. There were flowers on the table, flowers on the mantel-piece. Katherine had some work on her lap, for she was expecting a baby shortly, but this work she put away, because, she said, such domestic sights were not particularly interesting to the beholder.

"I wish, Johnnie," she said, "you would leave Clonmere for a time and come and stay with us. I should love to have you here, and when Henry is out—which he is very often—you would be a companion. I don't seem to see very much of my godson."

"I should like it," said Johnnie, "more than anything."

"Well, then?"

He shook his head.

"No," he said stubbornly, "two people who are happy, like you and Henry, don't want a third coming in to spoil the harmony."

"Don't be foolish, Johnnie," she said. "It would only make us happier if we thought you were being happy too. It's lonely for you in that big house all alone, and although I am not going out and about much just at the moment, we could read together, and I would play to you, and Henry would love to have your company when he returned in the evening."

Johnnie thought what it would mean to sit here, day after day with Katherine, in the peace and quiet of Katherine's house. Just to sit and watch her hands, folded as they were now, would be enough. Just to listen to her calm voice, and now and again to have her eyes smile at him, as she glanced up from the book she would be reading.

Presently, when Thomas had removed the tea, Katherine went to the piano and played very softly. She seemed so remote, so detached from the world, as she sat there on her music-stool, looking away towards the window. What does she think of, Johnnie wondered. What goes through her mind? Does she give to Henry the peace she gives to me? He closed his eyes, and as he listened to her playing, Johnnie created the illusion for himself that this was his room, his house, and his wife who was sitting there at the piano, and that when she had finished she would come and bend over him, and touch his hair, and ask him if he was content. Then the door opened, and Henry came into the room, radiant, smiling.

"Hullo, old fellow; this is a surprise," he said, and Johnnie rose from his chair, a guest in his brother's house, the dream shattered into foolishness.

Katherine closed the piano and went at once to her husband. He kissed her, and stood talking to Johnnie with his arm about her.

"How do you think she's looking?" asked Henry proudly, and without waiting for an answer he plunged into an account of his day, telling some amusing story about the civic luncheon he had been obliged to attend, where the honourable member for the city had made a tactless speech.

"I suppose," said Katherine, "you smoothed the whole thing over, and invited all those who were offended back to dinner?"

"I did nothing of the sort," said Henry. "I wished the affair well done with, so that I could get home to my wife."

And once again he bent his head and kissed her, and Johnnie saw her look at his brother with an expression that brought a pain to his heart.

"She loves him," he thought, "he makes her happy," and as he dressed for dinner, and heard them talking to one another in the room next to his, he thought suddenly of all the women he had never loved, who had made a momentary excitement and no more. What a dreary, worthless little procession they made through the years, ending now with Kate Donovan in the gate-house kitchen. Oh God, he thought wearily, if everything had been different, if I'd never gone into the regiment, never been through that blasted senseless war, but stayed here in the country, met Katherine and asked her to help me. Perhaps she would have married me instead of Henry. We would have lived together at Clonmere and she would have had my children, not his; and she would have looked at me in the way she did at Henry ten years ago.

There was a little pot of flowers on his dressing-table—she must have arranged them there before he came up to dress for dinner—and a book beside his bed, and a fire in the grate—signs of her care, her thoughtfulness—and there was a neatness and a comfort about the room so different from his own bleak bedroom at Clonmere. In the room next door he pictured Katherine sitting before her mirror, brushing her hair, while Henry wandered in, fastening his collar and tie, the intimacy between them a natural happy thing, making them closer to one another than before. It was something that he would never know, this sharing of life between a husband and wife. The only memories he had were sordid, grey. . . .

Dinner at East Grove was at seven o'clock. The candles were lit on the polished table. A parlour-maid helped Thomas hand the plates. And Johnnie, seated beside Katherine, compared her ways and his brother's once more to his own, when, sprawling alone in his dining-room, he would be faced sometimes by a stained cloth and tepid food, and after cursing the servant until the man was white with fear, he would decide not to eat at all, and stretch out his hand to the decanter instead.

When Katherine had risen and left the brothers together, Henry glanced across at him, with a curious half-shy expression, and said: "I suppose you would not care to make me your agent, would you, Johnnie?"

"Why, what's the matter with Adams?" said Johnnie.

"I don't mean you should dismiss Adams," replied Henry, "but allow me to act as—well, as overseer, for want of a better expression. You're letting the place go rather to pieces, you know, old boy, and it seems such a pity, when I think of all the care and trouble and expense put upon it by grandfather. Don't be annoyed with me for saying this. I've wanted to speak to you about it for some time."

Johnnie flushed, and stuck out his jaw.

"I don't know what you're talking about," he said. "The place is run in the way I like it to be run, and that's all there is to it. As a matter of fact I think very little of Adams, and I shall no doubt be my own agent in future. You would probably find it more trouble than profit."

"All right," said Henry swiftly. "We'll say no more about it. I only suggested it, as I thought it might help, and take some of the business off your shoulders. Been up to the mines lately?"

"I have not," said Johnnie, lighting his cigar. "There is nothing to go to the mines for. The only interest to me is to see what gets paid into my account at the bank. Why do you ask?"

"No reason. Only that I believe it encourages the fellows employed there if they feel the owner takes a bit of interest, and enquires after their welfare, and the work too, now and again."

"Any other advice?" asked Johnnie.

Henry pushed the decanter towards him.

"Only to go a bit slow on this, old fellow," he said, "and see rather less of the Donovan family."

Johnnie laid down his cigar.

"Who the hell's been talking to you about the Donovans?" he said.

"You know what this country is like for gossip," said Henry. "What goes on in Doonhaven is all over Slane in a couple of days. Jack Donovan isn't much of a chap, you know. He has a bad record for poaching and pilfering generally. And he's been heard boasting in the public-houses here that his sister has you by the ears, though he didn't use quite such a polite expression."

"God damn everyone," shouted Johnnie. "Why the hell can't people leave me alone?"

"They would leave you alone," said Henry, "if you would leave the whisky alone."

Johnnie leant back in his chair and stared at his brother.

"It's damned easy for you to talk, isn't it?" he said. "You are happy and married to the woman you love. There's precious little for you to worry about. You have your Katherine. Let me enjoy my Kate."

He laughed, and poured himself another glass of port.

"I'm sick and tired of people telling me what to do," he said. "I suffered from it in the army, and I'm not going to stand it in civil life."

"I'm not trying to preach at you," said Henry quietly. "I'm only telling you to beware of Jack Donovan. If you choose to have an affair with his sister I can't stop you. But do keep your head."

"The Donovans are my friends," said Johnnie. "They're the only people in this country who have showed any friendliness to me since I came back to it."

"Very well," said Henry. "I won't say any more. Let us go into the drawing-room and ask Katherine to give us some music."

Yes, it was easy enough for him, thought Johnnie, watching his brother turn the pages for Katherine at the piano, while she looked up at him and smiled. To-night they will be together, she with her head on his shoulder, and to-morrow he will wake, and Katherine will be beside him. And the next day and the next. When he is irritable she will soothe him. When he is tired she will rest him. When he is gay she will join in his gaiety, and when he is solemn she will be solemn too. They belong to each other, she is going to have his baby. And I belong to nothing and to no one; I'm nothing but a useless, ill-tempered drunkard, whose only amusement in life is to make love to my lodge-keeper's sister.

"Johnnie," said Katherine suddenly, looking up from her music, and smiling across at him, "you are going to stay a little while with us, are you not?"

And Henry, with his hand on her shoulder, glanced at him too.

"Yes, Johnnie, I wish you would. I'm out a great deal, and I should like to think of you here with Katherine. I know you would be happy. I know she would look after you."

Johnnie watched them, Katherine at the piano with the lamp-light shining on her smooth dark hair, and Henry his brother, playing half-consciously with the lace on Katherine's collar. The little gesture familiar, intimate, broke into Johnnie's dream.

"No," he said, "no, I shall leave you both in peace and go back to Clonmere."

5

When Johnnie returned home one of the first things he did was to dismiss his agent Adams, telling him that in future he would look after the estate himself. This would show Henry, and anyone else who chose to criticise him, that he was not so incompetent as they liked to believe. For a month or so he rose earlier in the morning, answered his letters, walked or rode round Clonmere, and even went up to the mines once or twice a week. Then he had the misfortune to catch a chill and be laid up for several days, and as he lay alone in his dreary bedroom, with only his man-servant to minister to him, depression once more came upon him, and his energy of the past few weeks seemed futile and absurd. What good did he achieve, after all, by riding up to Hungry Hill and sitting in the counting-house? He merely wasted Griffiths' time. During the hour he would spend in the place, the manager would be fretting to be gone. And it would be the same about the estate. He was certain his tenants disliked him. No one gave him a welcome, except the Donovans. And by God, he thought to himself, tossing on his bed, they are my only friends; no one else cares one ha'porth about me. I could lie here and die before anyone came to see me. His godfather, Doctor Armstrong, looked

in upon him one morning, and read him a lecture on self-indulgence.
"You've only yourself to blame for the condition you are in," he said,
without an ounce of sympathy, and sat for fully twenty minutes declaim-
ing the evils of alcohol. Then he departed, and Johnnie, feeling rather
worse towards evening, bade his man bring up a bottle of port from the
cellar, after which he was sufficiently recovered to put on a dressing-
gown and eat cold bacon and potatoes by the fire in the dining-room,
where Jack Donovan, full of sympathy, sat with him to bear him company.

"Here's Kate been fretting herself sick for the sight of you these past
few days," he said, "and nothing would content her but that I should
come up myself to the castle to see the Captain. How do you feel, then?"

"Like hell," said Johnnie.

"It's lying here by yourself that does it, Captain. As for physic, the
man has yet to be born that drew any strength from the stuff. It's what
you have there in the bottle that will do you most good."

"That's the way I like to be spoken to, Jack. By heaven, you're the
only friend I have."

"True for you, sir. It's what Kate was saying to me only this morning:
the Captain's fine friends and relatives would let him die before they gave
him a thought. I tell you what it is, sir, you have too much spirit for
them, that's the trouble. You like to go your own way, and why shouldn't
you? Here's that dirty fellow Adams going round saying you don't know
one end of your property from the other. I'd scalp the brute."

"Oh, he says that, does he?"

"Sure, 'tis out of spite because you took the agency out of his hands. I
can tell you one thing, Captain, and that is I'll give you a hand any day
with the property, when you haven't the mind to be bothering with the
place."

"That's very good of you, Jack."

"Ah, don't mention it. No trouble at all. I dare say I can squeeze
more out of the place for you than Adams. What do you say to Kate
coming round and straightening things up for you here in the house?"

"I'd be very obliged if she would," yawned Johnnie. "None of my servants here flicks a duster in the rooms from one day to the next."

The port was taking effect, it was making him sleepy, and satisfied,
which the medicine of his old fool of a godfather would never have done,
and it was pleasant, thought Johnnie later, lying in his bed once more,
with a fire lit in the grate, to see Kate moving noiselessly about the room,
drawing the curtains and shutting out the grey November afternoon,
folding his clothes and putting them away, and afterwards, when he was
practically asleep, creeping to his side and lying down on the bed beside
him. He thought of East Grove, and his brother and Katherine sitting
down now to their tea in the drawing-room, and later Katherine playing
the piano, and Henry sitting back in his chair, turning it so that he could
watch the lamp-light on his wife's hair.

"He has his Katherine," thought Johnnie, "I have my Kate. What the hell do I care?"

And pulling Jack Donovan's sister close to him he sought oblivion, while the rain began to patter again on the closed window and the darkness fell.

It was easy, as the winter passed, to rely more and more upon the company of the Donovans. Jack had a shrewd, rather cunning business head upon him, and in less than no time, Johnnie noticed, he had the affairs of Clonmere at his finger-tips. He dealt with the tenants, he paid the wages, he took upon his shoulders all that his master could not be bothered to do.

"I don't know how I'd manage without you now, Jack," Johnnie would say to him. "You save me all the work that bores me stiff, and I don't have to worry any more whether the fellows dislike me or not."

"Dislike you?" said Jack Donovan. "Why, Captain, you're the best-liked gentleman that's ever borne the name of Brodrick. Aren't there men and women down in Doonhaven that speak to you who never spoke to your brother, or your grandfather? Even Father Healey himself said to Kate the other day the Captain is a credit to the country."

It was indeed rather remarkable, thought Johnnie, that the priest of the district, who to the best of his belief had never in his grandfather's time had as much as a nod from any member of the family, far less entered inside the park, should now smile and bow to the present owner of Clonmere, and even take tea with him in the stuffy kitchen of the gate-house. He was really, Johnnie decided, quite a good sort of fellow, and he found himself fumbling for five pounds to give to the priest for distribution among the poorest families in the district.

"Never before," said Father Healey, counting the coins carefully, and putting them away in a shabby leather purse, "never before has a Brodrick given a thought to any of the poor stricken members of my flock. And there's my church, with the roof soon to fall in, and how am I to find the money to repair it?"

Johnnie remembered his balance in the bank, swollen by the copper from Hungry Hill, and promised a cheque to Father Healey.

"Didn't I tell you the Captain was a gentleman, father?" said Jack Donovan, peering over the priest's shoulder to see the amount of the cheque, "He's as simple-hearted as a child with his money, and twice as generous. Kate, pour the reverend Father another glass of whisky, and the Captain too."

"Not for me, child, not for me," said the priest, holding up his hand. "I must be on my way. It is a joy to see a man of your position," he added, looking at Johnnie, "happy in such humble surroundings, and with so little thought of the honour he does those he visits."

"I should be lost without Jack and Kate to look after me," smiled Johnnie.

"And they would be lost without you," said Father Healey. "Here is Kate, a dear child I have known from her birth, with a mind and heart as innocent now as the day I baptised her, and showing you, I am well aware, a devotion that could not be equalled by the highest in the land. It would be a terrible thing if such devotion were ever to be cast aside as worthless, and an innocent heart betrayed."

"What the devil does he mean?" thought Johnnie, but he shook hands with the priest, and assured him that neither Jack nor his sister should ever want for anything while he was living at Clonmere.

"I believe you," said Father Healey, opening a vast umbrella to shield his stout person from the rain. "You have given proof of your honour and generosity to me in person, and this blessed child, with no parents living and only her brother to care for her, trusts herself in your hands."

And leaving the gate-house he turned down the hill towards the village.

"Ah, he's a great saint, the reverend father," said Jack Donovan, glancing at his sister, "and has a tenderness for Kate. He'd die rather than see her wronged, just as I would myself. I tell you, Captain, if I ever saw my sister shamed I'd strangle her with my two hands. And you know that, don't you, Kate?"

"Yes, Jack," said his sister softly, looking meekly at the work on her lap.

"There's some gentlemen, Captain, believe it or not," said Jack Donovan fiercely, "who would seize advantage of a young woman's innocence and make game of her when her brother's back was turned, and the poor creature herself as ignorant as the babe unborn. Why, it's disgusting."

Johnnie shrugged his shoulders, and finished his glass of whisky. Surely Jack was not going to feign ignorance at this late hour of all that had taken place under his roof during the past months? As for his sister's innocence, anyone less innocent than Kate the second day she had put her hair down in the kitchen would be hard to find.

"You had better come down to the castle in the morning, Jack," he said briefly, rising to his feet. "Phillips has brought me in a bill for meal and cattle feed I can't make head or tail of."

"Won't you stay for a bite of supper, Captain?"

"No, I don't think so. Goodnight, Kate."

He arrived home to find a letter from Katherine, reproaching him for his neglect of East Grove for so many weeks. She had hoped so much, she said, that he would have paid them a visit at the New Year, and he had never done so. His goddaughter Molly was flourishing, and Henry very proud of her, and as Johnnie would not come to see them she proposed that they should visit Johnnie. If Henry brought his gun next Saturday would there be any woodcock left, and any hares on Doon Island? Her brother, Bill Eyre, was with them, and would come too.

The letter put Johnnie in a fever of unrest. The house was disreputable. No comfort for Katherine; she would be cold and miserable, she could never stand the place for a day. Yet how dear to see her again, to have her sitting in his drawing-room, if only for a couple of hours.

During the few days before Saturday came he threw himself with a fury of energy into the business of getting the house into shape. Servants were cursed, dismissed, and taken into service again, all within the hour. He walked round the grounds with his keeper, arranging the shoot. He even sent out invitations to his godfather, Doctor Armstrong, and one or two other people in the district, to make more sport for Henry.

"I'll let them know," he said to himself, "that I can put on as good a show as my grandfather ever did."

The morning of the great day was crisp and fine, and Johnnie, up earlier than he had been for several weeks, walked down to the creek and looked across at the snow-tipped crest of Hungry Hill. The sun shone into the windows of Clonmere, the doors were opened wide, and the dining-room table, laid for cold luncheon, looked clean and inviting for the first time for months.

The old pride in his home, that he had known as a small boy when he had coveted Clonmere from his grandfather, returned once more. He would show Katherine that he was not utterly despicable, that he was master of his house and of himself, and she would understand why he wished his home to shine for her this day. He went inside to give a last-minute direction to his servant, and was told that Mr Donovan was waiting to see him in the library. He frowned; he had hinted to Jack a few days previously that he would be obliged if his agent and his sister made themselves scarce while his brother and sister-in-law were staying. Henry did not care for Jack Donovan, and Henry, being his guest, must be deferred to for the period of the visit.

"What is it, Jack?" he said "Is anything wrong?"

The agent's face was very solemn His ginger hair was plastered down with grease, and he was wearing his Sunday clothes.

"Kate's very low, Captain," he said gravely. "She's wondering whether you can slip up to the gate-house and see her?"

"Of course I can't," said Johnnie irritably. "You know I have Mr Henry and his wife coming, and several other people. I shan't be coming to the gate-house until they have all gone. My brother may be here for several days."

Jack Donovan's face became gloomier still.

"She'll take it very bad, sir," he said. "In fact, I don't know what to do with her, and that's the plain truth of the matter Not a wink of sleep last night for the pair of us. And she crying and taking on so, I thought I should have to send for Doctor Armstrong. I am glad I did not, with him coming here to shoot today."

"What the devil's the matter, then?" said Johnnie, glancing impatiently at the clock "The party will be here any minute."

Jack Donovan coughed, and ran his cap along the edge of the table.

"Women take such fancies into their heads at these times, Captain," he said. "Say what I would, she wouldn't listen to me. 'I'll destroy myself,' says she. 'I'll throw myself into the creek, if he turns his back on me now.' 'You be quiet, Kate,' says I. 'The Captain is too good a friend to treat you, a respectable young woman, like he might a poor creature of the streets. He'll see you righted, depend upon it, before the mischief is spread abroad to cause a scandal through the country by which he could not hold his head up before the gentry.' "

Johnnie banged his fist down on the desk.

"Look here, Jack," he said. "What in the name of God are you driving at, and what's suddenly come over Kate to behave in such an astounding fashion?"

"Why, sir," said his agent, opening his eyes wide in astonishment, "you surely know Kate is in a certain condition, and has been like it, she tells me, these past two months?"

Johnnie stared at his agent heavily, his mind in a turmoil.

"This is the first I've heard of it," he said.

Jack Donovan went on rubbing his cap along the desk.

"The poor creature is that distraught she scarcely knows what she's about," he said. "The reverend father is with her now, praying beside her. It's my belief she'll have no comfort, though, until she's seen you."

"I can't see her, it's impossible," said Johnnie excitedly, pacing up and down the room. "Surely you can explain the position; she knows perfectly well that my brother and his wife are expected. Is she sure of her facts? How does she know about this—this damned business?"

"Sure, her old auntie down in Doonhaven told her it was certain. I tell you, Captain, it's enough to break a man's heart. Here's this young woman, my sister, given herself to you without thought of the consequences, and likely to kill herself unless we can find an honourable end to it all."

There was a sound of wheels upon the drive, and Johnnie, glancing out of the window, saw his brother's carriage drive up to the door.

"Look here, Jack," he said desperately, "I can't deal with this matter now. . . . Go out, by the back door, and don't show yourself here until I send for you. Take yourself off, man, for God's sake."

He fumbled in his coat pocket for his flask, and drank the contents, and then went out on to the drive to greet his brother, his heart beating, his whole mind in an agony of anger and distress.

"Dear Johnnie," said Katherine, stepping down from the carriage, giving him her hands; and the sight of her, cool, beautiful, serene, with her calm madonna face, made a damning contrast to the hasty image he had conjured of a flushed, dishevelled Kate in the back bedroom of the gate-house.

"Are you all right, old boy?" said Henry. "You look a bit upset?"

"Of course I'm all right," said Johnnie swiftly, "How are you, Henry?

And Bill, too? Brought your gun, I hope? Good. Where's the doctor? There are one or two others coming. Let's start walking through the woods, shall we? Wait though. I haven't shown Katherine her room."

His manner was so agitated, his speech so inconsequent, that Henry and Bill Eyre exchanged a glance of understanding.

"Don't bother about me, Johnnie," said Katherine. "I shall be perfectly happy if you want to get off to your shoot."

"Damn the shoot," said Johnnie; "your comfort is the only thing that matters," and he started pulling the bell-rope in the hall so violently that it broke.

"I think it would be best if we left Katherine to do as she pleases," said Henry smoothly. "Here come uncle William and the others, and there's Phillips and the beaters. What about getting into the air, Johnnie old man, and cooling down a bit?"

Everything was going wrong, thought Johnnie. It was not thus that he had planned the day. Katherine was now to be left alone, apparently, instead of coming with them, and surely he had told that blasted idiot Phillips to meet them up by the farm where they were to shoot first, and not come down here on to the lawn in front of the house with that ragged collection of youths and urchins who looked as if they had been grubbing in the barn after rats? The strong drink he had taken, on top of his interview with Jack Donovan, and the pent-up excitement of Katherine's visit combined, put his temper quite out of control.

He started to shout and rave at the keeper, who had chosen, for some unknown reason, to get himself up like a scarecrow, and was wearing a pair of very old darned breeches, with a patch in the seat, instead of the new corduroys that Johnnie had ordered especially for the occasion.

"By heaven!" said Johnnie. "This is too much, when a fellow disobeys my orders to such an extent," and hardly knowing what he was about he lifted his gun and fired straight at the unfortunate fellow's backside.

The keeper fell forward on to his face, with a cry of pain, and Johnnie, dazed and bewildered, watched his godfather and Bill Eyre rush forward to the man's assistance. Henry took hold of his brother's arm and led him back into the house.

"I don't think any damage has been done," he said, "but under the circumstances I think it would be best if you stayed at home, and allowed me to conduct the shoot. That is, if we decide to shoot at all after what has occurred."

The affair had happened so suddenly, and was so ludicrous, that Henry hardly knew whether to laugh or to be angry, but there was something tragic, almost frightening, in the expression on his brother's face, and he did not like to leave him alone.

"I'll call Katherine," he said; "she'll stay with you."

And he went into the hall and looked up towards the landing.

"No," said Johnnie. "No. . . ."

He felt sick and tired and bitterly ashamed of having made such an exhibition of himself, and to have Katherine know of his behaviour was the last thing he wanted in the world.

"Here," he said, calling to his brother and feeling in his pocket for a couple of sovereigns, "give the fellow this—tell him I'm sorry—and go out and enjoy yourselves, if you can. It's as well I don't come with you. Even if nothing had happened, I should have spoilt your day. . . ."

Now his futile ridiculous anger was spent he was exhausted, he wanted to forget everything and everybody. He went into the library and shut the door, and sitting down in his grandfather's hard upright chair he buried his face in his hands. He could hear Katherine's soft footstep in the bedroom overhead, as she unpacked her clothes, and presently the distant sound of shots came from the woods above the castle. The house was peaceful, still.

And then he remembered the stuffy kitchen at the gate-house, the crucifix and the rosary on the wall, and Jack Donovan, and Kate, and Father Healey. The miserable tangle he had got himself into, shaming and sordid, filled him with despair, and bitter, useless anger. He could picture the family at the gate-house, the old aunt from the village, probing, questioning her niece, and Father Healey, with his rosary dangling over his fat stomach, muttering prayers beside the hysterical Kate. The thought of seeing her, or touching her, revolted him. It was humiliating and degrading that those hours of drunken oblivion should result in this claim upon him, and that a woman for whom he cared nothing should feel herself bound to him because of what had passed between them. Again he heard Katherine's footstep overhead, and her low voice as she said something to the housemaid, and he remembered his visit to East Grove last summer, when Henry, proud and happy, had confided to him that Katherine was expecting a baby before Christmas. How tender his brother had been, how anxious, how full of solicitude, insisting that his wife should rest upon the sofa, should not tire herself in any way; and it had made a pang at the time in Johnnie's heart because of the closeness they must have for one another. He envied his brother, envied the calm serenity of his life, the still, untroubled progress of the months while Katherine waited for her baby to be born, and Henry's pride, his unaffected joy when his daughter came into the world. And now, at the end of Johnnie's drive, at the gate-house, was a woman in precisely the same state as Katherine had been nearly twelve months ago, because of Johnnie. The knowledge of it revolted him, made him shudder; he never wanted to look at her again.

How many times before this must have happened, in his own family, amongst his own forbears; and he remembered the tale of his great-grandfather and the sons he had scattered about the countryside. Perhaps he had thought little of it, and ridden through Doonhaven and thrown a coin to a dark-haired brat grubbing in the street, knowing it was

his, and thought no more about it. Not Johnnie. He could not live thus.
He could not live at Clonmere and know that there was a slatternly, unattractive Kate hiding herself in her brother's shop in the village, and
later know of a child, with his own blood in its veins, calling Jack
Donovan "uncle".

Oh, God, how sordid, how lacking in beauty was this life he led! Was
there no way out of it, no finish to the business? He looked at the gun he
had laid aside, propped against the wall. Yes, there was always that way.
But suppose it did not work? Suppose he made a mess of it, as he had
made a mess of everything else, and all he did was to blow half the side of
his face away and continue to live? Johnnie touched the gun, ran his
hand along the barrel. Perhaps he would not miss, after all. But he
lacked the courage, that was the fact of the matter. He would have to
obliterate fear with whisky before he set about it. He opened the long
drawer in his grandfather's desk, and pulled out a bottle that was about
a quarter full. Not enough there, he thought, to make a proper job of it.
And then, as he was uncorking the bottle, the door opened and Katherine
came into the room. She stood on the threshold, looking at him, and he
stared at her foolishly, the bottle of whisky in his hand.

"I'm sorry, Johnnie," she said. "I came to find a book. I thought you
had gone out shooting with Henry and the others."

She turned away, quietly, with delicacy; it was as though she had suddenly come upon him in his bath. He put the bottle away in his desk, and
shut the lid.

"Please don't go," he said. "I—I want to talk to you."

She turned round once more, watching him with her grave, kind eyes.
What must she think of me? he wondered.

"The day has gone wrong," he said—"my fault, as always. The others
have gone shooting without me."

She came over to him, and put her hand on his shoulder.

"What went wrong, Johnnie?" she said. "Can I do anything to
help?"

Anything to help. . . . There she stood beside him. He had only to
make one move and she would be in his arms. Katherine, the remote and
distant one, with her madonna face, her soothing, gentle hands.

He turned away abruptly.

"No," he said harshly, "you can't help. Why should you? Nobody
can. Why don't you go and join Henry and your brother?"

She did not move. She went on standing there, looking at him.

"You're unhappy," she said, "and when people are unhappy they do
foolish things."

He saw her glance at the open drawer from which he had taken the bottle
of whisky, and from there towards the gun, propped against his desk.

"Well?" he said aggressively," what about it? Wouldn't it be simpler
if I put an end to myself? No one would care."

"There you are mistaken," she said. "Many people would care. Your mother, Henry, your other brothers, and Fanny. All your friends."

"I have no friends," he said.

"I thought I was your friend," she answered.

He did not say anything for a moment. Katherine his friend. . . .

"You have Henry, and your baby, and your home," he said. "Why should you bother about me? I'm not worth it, anyway."

"One does not love people for what they are worth," she said gently. "One loves them for themselves."

What did she mean? When she said the word love, did she mean pity? Did she discuss him with Henry when they were alone together, saying, "Something must be done about him"?

"If you think you can reform me at this late hour you're wasting your time," he said.

She went over to the window and stared out across the garden.

"This could be such a happy, peaceful house," she said, "and you don't allow it to be so. You put your sad, angry thoughts about it."

"It would be happy and peaceful if you lived here always," he said, "instead of coming for one night."

"You mean," she said, smiling, "that my cheerful thoughts would dispel your gloomy ones? I wonder if they would be strong enough."

Her profile was turned from him again towards the window. That is how I would have her painted, he said to himself, if she were mine—standing so, with that wrap about her shoulders, and her hair gathered low on the nape of her neck.

"Anyway, you will live here one day," he said, "you and Henry, after I am dead. And your portrait will hang on the wall in the dining-room, beside aunt Jane and the picture of us all as children Perhaps it will bring back the peace that I have destroyed."

She looked at him gravely, and he wanted to kneel beside her and hide his face in the folds of her gown like a shame-faced lad.

"You may marry, Johnnie," she said; "you may have children."

Her words stung him to the reality of the present. Once again he saw the gate-house kitchen, the priest, the weeping Kate.

"Never," he said violently, "never, I swear it."

The horror of his position came upon him with renewed force; he began walking up and down the room, running his hands through his hair.

"I shall have to leave Clonmere," he said, "I shall have to get away. I can't possibly stay now this has happened."

"What has happened, Johnnie?" she said.

He had spoken without thinking, and now he stopped short, flushed, and guilty, and confused. What in heaven's name would she think of him if she knew what he had been doing these past months, culminating in the present degradation at the gate-house? She would be aghast, revolted. . . .

"If you have done something you are ashamed of," she said quietly, "why don't you ask God to help you?"

He stared at her hopelessly.

"The Almighty has no time for people like me, Katherine," he said. "If he did I should not be in the mess I am now."

And suddenly he was aware, fully and unmistakably, of the great gulf between them, which because of his years of guilt, and vice, and self-indulgence, could never be bridged. He saw the gentle pattern of her life, calm, and quiet, and untroubled, believing in God because she was naturally good, naturally free from temptation and trial. She told him, with simplicity, that one day he might marry, not knowing that the only woman he would ever want as a wife would be herself, the only children he could ever bear to hold the children she might have given him. Would he ask God to help him? Yes, if Katherine had taught him how to pray, if Katherine had knelt beside him every night, if Katherine had been the mistress of Clonmere, his wife, his loved one, then indeed there would be peace in his house, and peace in his heart too, and godliness, and joy. Should he tell her, he wondered? Should he risk everything and confess his love, his misery, his shame?

"Katherine," he said slowly, and came towards her, his hands out-stretched, his eyes beseeching, and he saw the sudden understanding in her eyes, the blinding flash of intuition, as she turned white and leant against the wall.

"Why, Johnnie," she said in wonder, "why, Johnnie. . . ."

And then there was a sudden footstep beneath the window, the crunch of gravel, and the sound of Henry's voice, gay and confident, calling to his wife. She turned, and went out of the library, leaving him alone. He stood there staring at the place where she had been.

6

Johnnie sat in the cabin of the "Princess Victoria", in Slane harbour, waiting for the steamer to weigh anchor. His manservant had stowed away his trunks and baggage beneath the berth, and had taken himself off to his own quarters. The vessel rocked slightly, and now and again, through the open port-hole, came the mournful hooting from another ship progressing down the harbour. From the deck above came the tramp of feet, and an occasional whistle. Through the darkness glimmered the lights of Slane. There was a draught coming from the port-hole, and Johnnie's ulster, hanging on the door, swayed backwards and forwards. His light portmanteau, placed on a chair by his servant, slid gently to the cabin floor. The label upon it stared up at the owner. "Captain Brod-rick. Destination London." And then what? Johnnie shrugged his shoulders. London and beyond. . . .

He had only a hazy recollection of the past few weeks, and an imperfect memory as to how he had got himself upon the "Princess Victoria" at all.

He had written dozens of letters. That was the chief thing that stood out in his mind. He had sat down to his grandfather's desk in the library at Clonmere and written letters to everyone who knew him, letters asking forgiveness of his relatives and friends. Why had he done so? He did not know. He could not remember. But that the letters had been written and dispatched was as clear as the fact that he was now on board the "Princess Victoria", because some of the answers to them lay upon the berth beside him. The vessel, proceeding down-stream, hooted again, mournful, insistent. Johnnie got up and closed the port-hole, and reached for the flask in his ulster pocket. Five hours until midnight. . . . And then farewell to Slane, farewell to this country of mist and tears, and away to what future, what ultimate destination, only the Almighty in his heaven knew.

Johnnie picked up one of his letters at random. It was from his brother-in-law, Bill Eyre, and was written from the parsonage at East Ferry.

"MY DEAR JOHN," it ran,

"I thank you from my heart for your most kind and considerate letter. I feel too deeply my own weakness and sins of omission not to pity and pray for you, who are now so greatly tempted. I have not allowed a single day since leaving your house to pass without imploring the Holy Spirit's inspiration and direction for you. God forbid that I should cease to pray for you. And now, my dear Johnnie, don't think I am taking an unwarrantable liberty in beseeching you by all the mercies of God, by the value of your immortal soul, by all you hope of a future state, by every consideration which is dead to you, to abstain from your soul and body destroyer (drink). Oh, my dear Johnnie, how I tremble, fearing some awful calamity may occur which might bring you to an early and dishonourable grave. No words can express the agony I felt, for your family's sake, during that last visit to Clonmere, when I saw you hastening to an end too dreadful to think of, and observed the fearful excitement under which you laboured at that time. I am sure you will not take offence at anything I have written. My dear Johnnie, commending you to the care of your heavenly Father, and again imploring his grace for you, believe me your most affectionate brother-in-law,

"BILL EYRE."

Johnnie threw the letter aside, and took another drink from his flask. He picked up a second letter from the pile. This was from Henry.

"MY VERY DEAR JOHHNIE,

"I have had a long talk with uncle Willie Armstrong about you and matters in Doonhaven. The lady may leave this country for America, if Jack Donovan and Father Healey will let her. But I much fear that these two people are playing a very deep game. They want you to marry her, make you a R.C., and get the property into their hands.

You may be angry with me for writing this, and you may also be angry when I beg of you, as your brother and friend, to make Jack Donovan and his sister leave the gate-house. I wish he would leave the country, and if not, be out of your sight and out of your way as much as he can. I beg and pray of you not to drink; all will be well if you do not. The many talents God has given you ought not to be thrown away. Give it up, old fellow, and make yourself, and every friend (and they are not a few), happy. . . ."

There was more of it, but Johnnie put it down, and took up a third. This was from his godfather.

"I have seen Kate Donovan, and she is willing to leave the country in a few months' time. There is no evidence at all as to her condition. Donovan professes his willingness to agree to any arrangement it may please you to make with regard to his sister, and I suggest that the next step is for them to quit Doonhaven, and for you to authorize me or your brother to pay their travelling expenses to wherever they think fit to go, and when I hear from them that they have arrived at their destination, Henry or I will state, through you, what you are prepared to do for their benefit. My reason for this, of course, it will be perfectly superfluous for me to tell you, as you will see at once the advisability of not perpetrating a scandal by the presence of the parties in the place where such scandal occurred. Your absence, however, will conduce most of all to the proposed arrangement. I am every hour more confirmed that you ought to remain away for some time. Believe me, dear Johnnie,

"Yours ever,
"WILLIAM ARMSTRONG."

How glad they must all be, thought Johnnie, in the secrecy of their hearts, to be rid of him, and what a fine, noble exit he was making, running away from responsibility like a rat, leaving other people to clear up the mess he had made. He was certainly heroic, was Captain John Brodrick, late of Clonmere Castle, Doonhaven. And here was the gem of them all, here was the scrap from his aunt Eliza.

"MY DEAR JOHNNIE,
"Do not make me unhappy in talking as if there was anything to forgive between us, as I assure you most solemnly there is nothing on earth that would give me greater delight than to promote your happiness in every way. I suspect that your affections are concerned in some way at the moment, causing you to write as you have done, and I only wish that the lady whom you honour, whoever she is, could reciprocate your feelings, for all our sakes. I know not how to thank you sufficiently for making me a present of £100, and also for the loan of the £300 I

had from you previously. I have always considered you the kindest and most honourable of my nephews, and the longer I live the more reason I have to do so. My dear love to you, and my sincere thanks for all your kindness.

"Your affectionate aunt,
"ELIZA."

Johnnie laughed. The kindest and most honourable of all her nephews. . . . He picked up the bunch of letters, and threw them in a corner of the cabin. Someone tapped on his door.

"If you want to stretch your legs ashore, sir, the last boat is just due to leave," called the steward. "She will be bringing the pilot aboard shortly after eleven, and you could return with him."

Johnnie glanced round the lonely, dingy cabin that was to be his home for the next forty-eight hours.

"Thank you," he said. "I shall take advantage of it."

The lights of Slane beckoned across the water, and Johnnie, his hands deep in his ulster pockets, thought of the one letter he had not written, therefore receiving no answer in return.

What could he have said to her that was not better expressed by his silence? Since that morning when he had looked at her in the library, and she had understood, and had gone from the room, they had not been alone together. The day had passed, and the night, and nothing more was said; and in the morning she had gone. They had all departed—Henry, and Katherine, and Bill Eyre, and his godfather—and the words he had wished to speak were never uttered, the help he yearned to ask for would never be given. Captain John Brodrick. Destination London. . . .

He wondered, standing there on the quayside, whether she was sitting now in the drawing-room at East Grove. Perhaps she was playing the piano, and Henry was lying on his chair before the fire, listening to her. He began to walk, heedless of his direction. And staring straight in front of him, brushing the people from the pavements as he was wont to do, he found himself presently standing before her house, with no knowledge of how he had reached it. The curtains were drawn across the windows, and a chink of light came from the shutters. He stood there, his hands in his pockets, looking at the door. A cab passed along the street, and in the distance he could still hear the muffled river noises—a whistle, the clanging of a bell. He went forward and lifted the knocker on the door. In a few minutes it was opened by Thomas, who peered at him through the darkness without recognition.

"Is Mrs Brodrick at home?" said Johnnie.

Then Thomas gave a start, and opened the door wider.

"I didn't see it was you, sir," he said apologetically. "No, I'm afraid Mr and Mrs Henry have gone out to dinner."

"Never mind," said Johnnie, "it doesn't matter."

"Would you care to come in and wait, sir? They may not be home until after ten. There's a nice fire in the drawing-room."

Johnnie hesitated. Even here, standing on the threshold, the peace of the house enfolded him, the kindliness, the warmth.

"Perhaps I will, Thomas," he said slowly.

The man showed him into the drawing-room and withdrew, shutting the door behind him, first turning up the lamps and poking the fire.

Johnnie went and sat in Henry's chair. Opposite him was Katherine's chair where she had sat before she went out to dinner, because on the chintz cover was the imprint of where she had been. There was her needlework on the low stool before the fire, and a book she had been reading. In the corner of the chair was a little white woolly lamb. She must have been sitting with her baby daughter on her lap, showing her the lamb, while Henry, in the chair where Johnnie sat now, leant back and watched them both. Then the nurse would have come down and taken the child up to bed, and Katherine, moving on to the stool to have the warmth of the fire, would take her needlework and talk to Henry, ask him questions about his day. Then they would go upstairs to their room and dress for dinner, Henry grumbling a little, perhaps, because of the inconvenience of turning out, but content enough at heart because he always enjoyed himself wherever he went, on all occasions.

Katherine would wear the white gown she had worn that night at Clonmere, and before leaving the house she would look into the drawing-room a moment to see that the lamps had been turned down and that the guard was before the fire. He could see her standing there by the door, the light in the hall shining in her hair, her cloak about her shoulders, and she would leave behind her something of herself, fragrant, indefinable, the blessed peace of her presence that he felt now, as he sat there, in the chair that was not his. . . . But it was not any use sitting there, because he had to go away, he had to go to the ship and across the water and not return again, perhaps, for months, for years. It was no use sitting there in this house that did not belong to him.

He got up, and looked for the last time about the room. He touched the piano that was hers, the keys where her fingers had rested. He went over to her desk and saw the neatness of it, the stack of smooth white paper, the little scarlet pen. He wanted something of hers to take with him, and on a sudden impulse he picked up the small black leather volume that was lying on the top of the desk. It was a copy of the New Testament. He put it in his pocket, and going out into the hall, he lifted his coat and his hat from the chair where Thomas had placed them. The hall was deserted. Thomas had gone back to the kitchen. The grandfather clock ticked slowly in its corner. It was five minutes to nine. Two hours before the pilot boat would return to the ship. Johnnie opened the front door and again stood looking up and down the empty street. There were other places in Slane where there would be warmth and comfort, places where he might forget the dark, dreary cabin of the "Princess Victoria" and the grim finality of the labels on his luggage, "Captain John Brodrick. Destination London". A little wind blew round the corner of the street, and the door of Henry's house shut behind him with a slam. Farewell to Slane. Farewell to his country. Johnnie laughed, thinking once more of aunt Eliza's letter, and turning his coat collar up against the wind, and pulling his hat over his eyes, he began to walk up the street towards the city.

.   .   .   .   .

It was to East Grove that the police came, two days afterwards. They arrived while Henry and Katherine were having breakfast, and the inspector asked to speak privately to Mr Brodrick. Henry came out into the hall immediately, leaving Katherine in the dining-room.

"You are a relative, I believe, sir, of Captain Brodrick?" said the man.

"I am his brother," said Henry. "Is anything the matter?"

The inspector explained to him, in brief words, what had happened. Henry went with him at once. They were narrow and dark and not of great attraction, the back streets of Slane, and the house to which the inspector brought him was grey, with a cheap, garish look about the beaded curtains at the window. A frightened-faced woman was waiting for them in the hall.

"It's not my fault," she began, on sight of Henry. "I've never had anything happen in my house like this before, and you know it, Mr Sweeny. You can't get me into trouble about it."

Her voice was shrill and nervous. The inspector bade her hold her tongue. He led Henry upstairs to a bedroom on the second floor, and taking a key from his pocket he unlocked the door. The room was in disorder. Johnnie's boots were in one corner, his clothes in another. There were some half-dozen empty whisky bottles, balanced with great nicety, one on top of the other, in the middle of the floor, and round the neck of the highest was a woman's garter, crimson in colour, made of shabby silk. Johnnie himself lay on the bed, half-dressed. He looked in death more peaceful than he had ever done in life. The sullen, angry expression had gone for ever. His eyes were closed, as though he slept, and his black hair was thick and tumbled like a little boy's.

In one hand he clutched an empty bottle, and in the other the New Testament.

BOOK FOUR

HENRY, 1858-1874

I

I T W A S winter again at Clonmere, and the cap of Hungry Hill was white with snow. The sun shone brightly, and there was a crisp, fine tang about the air, a sense of lightness, as though the old, wet melancholy of autumn was laid aside forever and forgotten, while this new cold clarity heralded the spring. The fallen leaves in the park were dry, and crinkled with the frost. The naked trees lifted black branches to the blue sky, and the short grass before the castle was dusted with silver. The tide ebbed swiftly from the creek, the surface of the water whipped with a lively ripple, and the thin smoke from the castle chimneys rose straight in the air like a column.

Tim the coachman drove the carriage round to the front door, and climbing from his seat, stamped up and down before the horses, blowing upon his fingers. It was Sunday, and he was to drive Mr and Mrs Henry to the little church at Ardmore, as was their custom. It was a pleasant thing, thought Tim, as he waited for his master and mistress, to have the life about the place natural and normal once more, almost as though the old gentleman himself was alive again, and the first Mr Henry and Mr John and poor Miss Barbara and Miss Jane all back again and living, instead of being, some of them, these thirty years in their graves. The intervening years seemed to have slipped away, and Tim, who would be sixty next birthday, would often find himself casting his mind back to his early days as stable-boy under old Baird. He would find himself confusing the present generation with the one that had gone before, and he would shake his head and sigh, and bid "Mr Henry" guard against the cold air for fear it should bring back his cough, confusing him with the uncle who had been dead for thirty years.

Here he came now, Mr Henry, his master, dressed for church, with his tall hat in his hand, and his gloves and his stick, looking for all the world as his uncle Henry had looked, all those years ago. And hadn't he the same way with him too, the same winning smile, the laugh, the friendly touch on the shoulder? And he would walk around the place on a Sunday afternoon, with his hands behind his back, in consultation with the agent, just as the old gentleman had done, when he was alive. He rode every morning to the mines too, and drove into Slane once a week, and indeed there was a fixed routine of living that pleased the coachman after so long a spate of muddle and disorder.

How different Mrs Henry was in every way from the other Mrs Brodrick, Mr Henry's mother. No pride here, no wild temper, no driving of her servants to distraction with the changing orders and the demands she put upon them, but a quiet, sweet reasonableness with every request she made, and a firmness of purpose that made the silly chatterers in the kitchen know their place.

There was peace "at the back" at Clonmere, where there had been nothing but strife and grumbles and discontent for years. She put her touch upon every room in the castle, did Mrs Henry, and the room was lighter for it.

"You'd say," said the cook, "that she had a healing hand."

Gone was the acccumulation of dust and disorder, of litter and rubbish, that Fanny-Rosa had allowed; vanished was the chill discomfort, the grey misery, that Wild Johnnie had accepted. The rooms were swept, the fires were lit, the windows flung open to the air. Once more flowers and fruit were brought in to the house, once more the grass was cut, the paths were weeded, the shrubs were pruned, as they had been when Barbara, as eldest daughter of the house, kept Clonmere for her father. The house "belonged" once more.

The mistress stood now on the doorstep beside the master, bidding Tim good-morning, and they looked, thought the coachman, the handsomest couple in the country. She was nearly as tall as himself, and with the warm cape wrapped round her, and her smooth, dark hair showing from her bonnet, she might have been a queen.

"How are we for time, Tim?" asked Mr Henry.

"It's just turned the quarter, sir," replied the coachman, holding open the door of the carriage.

The master was a great stickler for time, like the old gentleman. It would never do to be late for church. But he had a graciousness about him and a courtesy, quite different from his grandfather.

And now the mistress was seated in her corner of the carriage and the master was tucking the rug round her, putting her feet in the footwarmer, the whole done with such a loving care and so much gentleness that Tim remembered the talk at "the back" of how there was another baby expected before many months. The nurse was standing in the open doorway, holding little Miss Molly in her arms, the child waving a plump hand to her father and mother. And then Tim climbed up to his seat and gathered the reins in his hands, and the carriage bowled away down the drive, under the archway past the rhododendrons, and swept round beside the creek and through the woods to the park.

Henry held Katherine's hand under the rug and wondered, for the five hundredth time, perhaps, what she was thinking about; so detached, so remote, her calm, quiet manner different in every way from his own eager impetuosity.

"Are you warm enough?" he said anxiously, peering into her face. "Are you sure you feel equal to the drive?"

"Yes, of course," she answered, warming his heart with her smile. "I feel very well indeed. And I could not bear to miss the weekly drive to Ardmore, you know that."

He leant back again in the carriage, reassured.

Uncle Willie Armstrong had impressed upon him to be careful with her.

"Your mother," uncle Willie had told him, "gave birth to all you boys without turning a hair in the process. She had all the toughness of old Simon Flower. But if you're going to follow your father's example and rear a large family, I advise you to do it rather more slowly than he did. Your Katherine is a much more delicate plant than Fanny-Rosa Flower."

And here they were, with young Molly barely a year old and another one already on the way. But perhaps uncle Willie Armstrong was inclined to fuss. . . . Henry gazed out of the carriage window. The trees at the far end of the park, close to the road, were looking a bit shorn after their lopping in the autumn. Still, they would be all the better for it, and would be well enough in two or three years' time. Katherine was bowing and smiling at Mrs Mahony at the gate-house. Henry purposely turned his head away. The gate-house brought unpleasant thoughts, reminders of something that was best forgotten. Jack Donovan and his sister had left the country and gone to America, no trace of them remained in the little lodge at the entrance to the drive, and yet whenever Henry passed through the gates he would remember, for all his wishes to forget, the insolent, familiar manner of the fellow when his fare was paid to him, the furtive, crafty expression of his sister, and through them both the helpless, tragic eyes of poor Johnnie the last time he had seen him at Clonmere. No, those things were not the best food for thought on a Sunday morning, and Henry, once more caressing Katherine's hand under the carriage rug, began to chatter lightly and gaily about nothing at all, of the shooting party the week before, of Petty Sessions the following Tuesday in Mundy, of a letter received from his mother Fanny-Rosa from Nice the day before.

"You noticed," he said to Katherine, laughingly, "that it was full of the usual extravagances. I believe she is having the time of her life."

"I wonder," said Katherine.

"Oh, dearest, you don't know my mother sufficiently well to judge. I quite thought poor Johnnie's death would break her completely, but I am inclined to think, after the first shock of it wore off, she dismissed the matter from her mind and poor Johnnie too."

"Your mother is not so superficial as she would have everyone believe," said Katherine. "She pretends to other people, and to herself as well."

"My mother pretends to no one," said Henry, "you can rest assured about that. No, she has her little villa, and her foreign counts, and her casino, and is very well content. Look, there is that disagreeable Mrs Kelly actually curtseying to you. What have you done to the people of Doonhaven? I have never known anyone of that family smile at a Brodrick before, unless it was to do something very dirty afterwards."

"Perhaps," said Katherine, looking sideways under her bonnet, "the Brodricks never smiled at the people of Doonhaven."

"I am quite certain they did not," said Henry, "and that is why the first of them was shot in the back. What do you think of the new road out to the mine? The new surface is a capital affair, quite different from the old gravel that became almost impassable in winter. Grandfather would have been pleased with it."

"I think, with you, that it is a great improvement, but I should like it better if the miners' houses had been taken in hand at the same time. Some of those huts are a disgrace. I cannot bear to think of little children being obliged to live in them."

"Are they really so bad?" asked Henry. "I'm afraid I have never been through them, and have only concerned myself with the efficiency of the mine. I can easily give order to have the wood strengthened, and the worst places painted. That should keep out the cold and damp."

"Why not give orders to have them pulled down altogether, and brick houses built instead?" said Katherine.

"Dear heart, that would cost a lot of money."

"I thought the mines made such an enormous profit last year?"

"So they did, but if we once start pulling down the miners' huts and building them small palaces, there will be no profit at all."

"Now who is exaggerating?" smiled Katherine. "The miners don't ask for palaces, Henry love. They only ask for a bit of warmth and comfort, which, considering how hard they work for you, I think they deserve."

Henry pulled a face.

"Now you make me feel a worm," he said. "Very well then, I shall go into the matter, and see what can be done. But I warn you they won't be grateful. They will say, in all probability, that they prefer the old wooden cabins."

"Never mind about gratitude," said Katherine, "at least those little children will be warm. . . . Hungry Hill has a smiling face today. Do you see the sun on the ridge? It looks like a crown of gold."

"Hungry Hill has too many moods for my liking," said Henry. "The bad weather before Christmas interfered with the work, and a whole shipment of copper was held up."

"Nature works slowly, in her own time," said Katherine, "and if you become impatient she gets angry. Why, there is Tom Callaghan walking to church. His horse must be lame. I wonder he did not wait for us to pick him up in Doonhaven. Tell Tim to stop the horses, dear."

Laughing, Henry climbed out of the carriage, and called out to the curate, who was walking ahead of them, covering the ground with immense long strides.

"Tom, you madman," he shouted, "what do you mean by not waiting for us? Come and take a seat beside Katherine. We are seriously affronted."

The young curate turned, and smiled. He was a great big fellow, with a fine handsome face and a brown beard.

"The morning was so lovely," he protested, "and Prince wanting a shoe, so I promised myself the treat of a walk. The first few miles were delightful, but I was just beginning to think myself a martyr."

"You can make the sermon shorter in consequence," said Henry. "Come, jump in and bury your pride. Katherine is quite disgusted with you."

"I have never known Katherine disgusted with anyone," said the curate.

Tom Callaghan was an Oxford friend of Henry's who, with a very small amount of persuasion, had accepted the appointment of curate to the living at Doonhaven, and whose weekly duty was to take the service at the furthermost church in the parish, the little church by the sea at Ardmore. He could have done much better for himself across the water, but his affection for Henry was such that he preferred to bury himself in isolation, to be near his friend, rather than win esteem and prosperity in a large town.

"What do you think is her latest whim?" said Henry. "Nothing more than that I should pull down the miners' huts and build them brick cottages instead. I shall be ruined."

"An excellent plan," said Tom decisively. "First, because those huts are a disgrace. And secondly, because you have more money than you known what to do with."

"That," agreed Katherine, "is what I am always telling him."

"The trouble is," said Henry, "that you both have Nonconformist consciences. And you try to give me one too. My grandfather would not have listened to you."

"From what I hear of your grandfather," said Tom, "he was a godless man. At least you do not work the mines on Sundays, as he used to do."

"And that also was Katherine's doing," smiled Henry. "I tell you, Tom, I have married into a family which has so many principles that they quite bewilder a fellow. Take my advice, and avoid 'em like the plague."

"I would rather be good like the Eyres than clever like you Brodricks," said Tom Callaghan. "The only reason you are not as hard a man as your grandfather is because you had the sense to marry Katherine. Here we are at church, and there will be three other people in the congregation besides yourselves, I have no doubt."

The little church stood quite alone, windswept and solitary, looking out over the wide waters of Mundy Bay. But for all its stark position, exposed

to the four winds and the rains of winter, there was something comforting
and strong in its grey solidity, something ageless in the lichen that clung
about its walls. Inside all was peaceful, all was quiet, as though no evil
thought, no hard memory, could penetrate the still serenity. The gales
might blow, the floods might come, but the church of Ardmore would
withstand them all, a small bastion in eternity.

Henry, kneeling beside Katherine, watched her calm profile, her dark
eyes turned to the altar, and he thought how no man but himself would
ever know how beautiful she was, how true, how tender. Was Tom
Callaghan right? Would he be as hard a man as his grandfather but for
Katherine? The thought was an uncomfortable one, and, like all uncomfortable thoughts, he dismissed it as absurd. He was not hard. Tom
must have been joking. He had always, as far back as he could remember,
thought about other people before himself. Put duty before pleasure,
right before wrong. He could say, in all good conscience, that he had
never done a low, foul, or evil thing. True, he had been lucky, successful
and happy in his work and his friends; but luck, after all, was a gift from
the Almighty, and anyway he was grateful for it. No, Johnnie had been
the hard member of the family. Johnnie had been the selfish, ruthless
one, spreading misery, poor devil, wherever he went. Tom Callaghan
ought to have known him.

And Henry, making the General Confession in a loud, clear voice as
was his custom, "we have erred and strayed from Thy ways like lost
sheep", thought, as he always did, that really the words did not apply to
him, or any other normal law-abiding fellow who lived an honest life
and did his duty to God and the Queen. They applied to the thieves,
and the adulterers, and the drunkards, who never even bothered to come
inside a church.

When the service was over, and Tom Callaghan was changing in the
vestry, Henry and Katherine went and stood in the churchyard and
looked down upon the sea. The long rollers from the Atlantic swept past
them up the bay. A robin was singing from a gorse bush beneath them,
his song plaintive yet sweet, strangely nostalgic in the cold, clean winter
air.

"I am glad we had Molly christened here," said Katherine. "We will
do the same with the next baby, and with all our children. And when
the time comes for us to go, I should like you and me to lie here, dearest,
together."

"Don't be morbid," said Henry, drawing her to him. "I hate discussions about death. Kiss me instead. There goes the 'Emma Mary',
bound for Bronsea. They must be taking advantage of this weather,
otherwise they would not have sailed on a Sunday. She's well laden, isn't
she? Nearly one hundred tons of copper there, my girl."

"Never mind the copper," said Katherine. "Will you remember my
wish about this little churchyard?"

"I refuse to commit myself about anything so damnable," said Henry, "and don't let's stand about any longer, you will catch cold. Look, there is old Tom waiting for us by the carriage. What a dear fellow he is, and how glad I am he has come to live down here. In fact," he continued happily, drawing Katherine's arm through his, "I can think of nothing more delightful than to have all one's best friends in the neighbourhood. Tom, old boy, you preached a capital sermon, just what I might have said myself if I were in Orders, and to show my appreciation I propose to build you a house You can't possibly go on living in that miserable cottage in the village."

"Indeed I can."

"Indeed you can do nothing of the sort. Don't argue, I dislike argument before lunch. And to convince you that I mean business I will show you the site I have in mind. It came to me when we were singing 'Rock of Ages'. Just after you turn out of Doonhaven, before you come to the rise in the road and the Oakmount cottages, there is a fine piece of ground nearly level that will make an excellent foundation. We will call it Heathmount, and as soon as the old Rector dies you shall have the living, and make Heathmount the Rectory."

"And Tom shall marry, and settle down, and his children will be able to play with ours," said Katherine.

"It certainly saves a lot of trouble when one's friends arrange the future," said Tom Callaghan. "Why not go to even greater lengths and write my sermons for me too?"

"I will do so," said Henry, "on condition that I preach them as well. It would give me great pleasure to use the text 'Render unto Caesar the things that are Caesar's', with reference, of course, to the usual arrears of rent."

The site of Tom's future home was duly pointed out and appreciated, and then the carriage turned in at the gates and down the drive to Clonmere, with hot luncheon awaiting them in the dining-room, the setters barking a chorus from the steps, the smoky tang of the piled turf fire filling the hall, the warm, familiar atmosphere of home, dearly loved, rising to greet them.

Little Molly, beribboned and in white, was brought down to dessert to sit upon her mother's knee, and Henry, pushing back his chair and stretching his legs, cracked walnuts to make her laugh. And, himself well filled with roast mutton and apple tart, he felt all the pleasing, drowsy contentment of a man whose idle afternoon stretches before him, to make it what he will

"I think," said Tom, watching his friend with a smile, "that you ought to consider yourself the luckiest of men. You have a fine property, a vast fortune, a flourishing business, a distinguished career up to date, an angel of a wife, a delightful baby daughter, and, in fact—nothing in the world you lack. If I were not a parson I should envy you."

"But because you are a parson you take care to preach at me instead," laughed Henry, "and no doubt wish to warn me not to lay up treasures upon earth, where moth and rust corrupt. It's no use, Tom, old fellow. I live in the world, and though I don't count myself a materialist I believe in using to advantage, and in enjoying too, what the world provides. There is no sin in that, as far as I can see."

"I think I know what Tom had in his mind," said Katherine. "When a man is happy and contented, with nothing going wrong, he is in danger of the deadliest of sins, which is complacency. No, Molly dear, no more sugar, you have had plenty. And more will give you a pain. You may play with Mamma's locket instead."

The child, who had puckered up her face, was soon distracted by the dangling chain and the little case that opened and then closed with a snap.

"Training starts, you see, Tom?" winked Henry. "Molly wants sugar, but is fobbed off with something else! No complacency there. I would let her eat all the sugar her small stomach could hold, and then wait for the inevitable pain. That would teach her a lesson, and she would not eat sugar again."

"That's where you are wrong," said Katherine, "Molly is too small to connect cause and effect. The pain, to her, would have nothing to do with the sugar. A baby must be distracted, then when reason dawns she must learn obedience, and the necessity of obedience."

"She has it all arranged," said Henry, "from the first lessons in A.B.C. down to the final examinations. I never knew anyone take the upbringing of children so seriously. I cannot remember my mother ever teaching us a thing. She certainly never corrected us."

"It's a wonder to me that you are fit for society at all," said Tom. "You take my advice, and leave the education of your offspring to Katherine."

"Very well," said Henry, "and if they don't come to heel quickly I'll flay the hides off 'em. One thing at least, they'll never want for anything."

"The next deadly sin," murmured Tom—"too much money. Poor Katherine, you are going to be fully employed, I can see."

Henry threw a nutshell at his friend.

"Supposing you leave my sins alone," he said, "and give me a word of practical advice instead. There's to be a by-election at Bronsea, as you know. Old Sir Nicholas Venning has died. I'm thinking of contesting the seat in the Conservative interest."

"Are you indeed?"

"It would give me a lot of fun, if nothing else, and the Brodricks have had connections in that county ever since 1820."

"And what does Katherine think?" said Tom.

"Katherine thinks that her husband's energy is such," smiled Henry's wife, "that if he does not plunge into politics it might be something worse. And it will keep him out of mischief."

"A truly wifely remark," said Henry. "No high ambitions for me, you observe, Tom. No hope or even suggestion that I might become Prime Minister. Just a kindly smile that it may 'keep me out of mischief'."

"I agree with Katherine," said his friend. "Go ahead by all means, make your speeches, give your dinners, kiss the Bronsea babies, and accept the rotten eggshells with a bow. I wish you all the luck in the world. And if you do succeed in finding your way to Westminster, I will cross the water too and listen to your maiden speech, and tell the people sitting next me that Henry Brodrick is my oldest friend. You might get me a bishopric in twenty years."

"Seriously, though," said Henry, "I might easily win the seat by a handsome majority, although it has been held by a Liberal for so long. The family will rally round me. Herbert at Lletharrog—I told you he had the living there, didn't I, and is living at the old house?—and aunt Eliza at Saunby. I can spin a good yarn about my Bronsea connections, although perhaps I won't say much about my step-grandmother who lives in the village and curtseys whenever she sees Herbert."

"I believe you are a snob after all," laughed Tom.

"Indeed I am not, but it doesn't do to produce the skeleton in the cupboard on a political platform. I tell you what, we'll take a house in London for the season, whether I win or not, and you shall come and stay with us. It will look well to be seen about with you, and will show that I have a respect for the Church."

"Can't you damp his ardour, Tom?" said Katherine. "We were talking of complacency, and there he stands before you, more pleased with himself than anyone living. Come, Molly, we will leave your papa and your uncle to discuss the world, and go and play with your beads by the fire in the drawing-room."

Later in the day, when Tom Callaghan had gone back to take Evensong in Doonhaven, and Molly had been put to bed, and the long curtains were drawn across the windows, Katherine lay on the sofa that had been Barbara's and was now moved close to the fire, and Henry sat on the floor beside her, her hand against his lips.

"Am I really complacent?" he said anxiously. "Are you getting tired of me?"

She smiled, and ran her fingers through his hair.

"To the first question 'yes'," she answered, "to the second 'no'. Oh, I don't mean complacent, dear one. But when a person is very happy he is apt to become less sensitive, less aware. And I would not like you to become too worldly, too preoccupied with business, and money, and the success of Henry Brodrick."

"I can't help being happy," he said, "married to you. Every day I love you a little more. And whatever I do, whatever I accomplish, is because of you; don't you know that?"

"Yes, dearest, I do, and it makes me very proud, but a bit worried too. You put me first in life, before God, and that is not right."

"God is not real to me as He is to you," said Henry. "You I can touch, I can hold, I can kiss, I can love. God is something mysterious, intangible. And so, in a humble way, you take the place of God."

"Yes, sweetheart, but people pass away, and God is eternal."

"Damn eternity. I don't want eternity. I want you, and the present, forever and forever." He leant across the sofa, and buried his head against her. "I can't help it," he repeated, "I can't help loving you. It's in my blood. My father was just the same about my mother, and although I barely remember him—I was only four years old when he died—I can recollect him standing by the creek, watching her as she played with Johnnie, and Fanny, and myself, and I shall never forget the expression in his eyes. My aunt Jane was another. If she had not been killed in an accident she would have died of a broken heart, grieving over some fellow on Doon Island. It's no use, Katherine, we Brodricks are made like this; you must accept it."

She held him close to her, and kissed the top of his head.

"I do accept it," she said, "but it makes me afraid, all the same."

He leant back, his head against her knee, and stared into the fire.

"I often wonder," he said thoughtfully, "whether poor Johnnie's despair was not due to a love affair gone wrong. Oh, not that Donovan woman, that was merely a sordid interlude, but something deeper. But who the devil could he have been fond of? I never heard him mention anyone."

Katherine did not answer. She went on stroking his hair.

"If only he could have married and settled down, it would have been the saving of him," continued Henry. "That ghastly end could have been avoided. Perhaps if you had met him first you might have married him instead of me."

He turned, half smiling, half sadly, to look at his wife. Her eyes were filled with tears, and she was staring into the fire.

"Sweetheart, what is it?" he said. "I've hurt you. I've made you unhappy? Selfish, careless brute that I am. I ought to remember you are not well. And here I've been, tiring you with family history. My poor darling, your face is white and miserable, what have I done?"

"Nothing," she said, "it's nothing, I promise you. Just a sudden foolishness."

"It's been a long day," he said. "You should have rested this afternoon, instead of walking with us through the woods. I thought it was too far for you at the time. And then lifting Molly about here, after tea. She is too heavy for you now. Does the other little one make a heaviness?"

"The other little one is quiet."

"I shall carry you to bed, then," he said. "Come, put your arms round my neck, and hold me close. Where is your book? That one, by the window there? Reach down for it, then. Mr Dickens again. What would you do without him? I shall read a chapter aloud to you, and then you must close your eyes and go to sleep, and have all the rest you can. Don't worry about the lamps. I will come down and put them out when I have seen you safely in bed."

He carried her along the passage to the room that had been Barbara's. He left her alone, and went back again to the drawing-room to blow out the lamps. How unlike Katherine to have tears; she who never gave way, who was so calm, so quiet. She must be very tired. There could be no other explanation. It was not possible that she should have anything on her mind. But when he had read her the chapter of the novel, and had laid it aside, he leant over her and taking her in his arms, he said, searching her eyes, and feeling for his words, "Tell me, darling, tell me the truth—are you happy with me?"

2

The Town Hall at Bronsea was packed to suffocation. There were fellows straight from the docks, still in their working clothes, with caps on the backs of their heads and pipes in their mouths, men from the smelting works and factories, and their women-folk too, with shawls about their heads, all them talking in the high, sing-song voice peculiar to Bronsea. Most of the working people intended to vote for the opposing candidate, Mr Sartor, the Liberal, and had only come to the meeting to indulge in the free fun of baiting the speaker, but there were a certain number amongst them who sported the blue ribbon for all that. Clerks from the shipping office who had met Henry Brodrick personally, seamen who had handled his cargoes back and forth across the water from Doonhaven to Bronsea, men from the smelting-works who had seen him and spoken with him, and the sprinkling of shop-keepers, small tradesmen, doctors, bank-managers and others, who considered it "genteel" to vote Conservative, because it put them in a superior class to the working men and women of Bronsea.

The noise was tremendous, with the clatter of tongues, whistles, and laughter, and then someone from the rear of the hall started up a hymn, and was at once joined by the large mass of people present; the chattering mob changed instantly into a massed choir, solemn and majestic.

Henry, eager and excited, his blue rosette in his buttonhole, his frock-coat immaculate and closely fitting his tall, broad figure, watched them impatiently, anxious to begin. Not that he could do much in such a gathering. They had come to mock him, rather than applaud or listen with any serious intent. There were the members of his family who had come so loyally to support him. Herbert, now vicar at Lletharrog, and his cheerful, dumpy little wife. Who, when they were children, would ever have supposed that Herbert, the baby of the family, with his lively ways and twinkling brown eyes, would become a parson? There was Edward, on special leave for the occasion, his curly hair standing straight on end as it always did, bending across to talk to Fanny and Bill Eyre, who had travelled the water for the event. Fanny with the inevitable little crushed expression on her face that she had worn as long as he could remember, which must have come from being the one girl amongst four brothers, for honest Bill Eyre was easy enough in all conscience. Heavens, what a muster of parsons—because of course besides Herbert and Bill there was the faithful Tom Callaghan, being very attentive surely to the pretty young woman at his side, some friend of Fanny's. Perhaps Tom was smitten at last, and would take upon himself the bonds of matrimony. Aunt Eliza, over from Saunby, bolt upright and very full of herself, with a lorgnette dangling from her bosom which she kept putting up to her eyes, observing the populace with an expression of extreme disgust, as if she found the proximity of the working people of Bronsea really rather trying, and something which Miss Brodrick, of Brodrick House, Saunby, was not accustomed to in the general way. And lastly Fanny-Rosa, his mother, who had come all the way from Nice; not, she said, in order to see her son get up on a platform and talk with his tongue in his cheek, but because she had not a stitch to wear and must buy clothes. Paris was too expensive, and in France the people were so grasping, they expected ready money for every order given, whereas in England people never bothered about such things; she could buy and owe for years, and if bills did come in it was easy enough to pretend the letter had been lost in transit.

Henry had let her prattle on in this fashion, when he met her in London and brought her down to Lletharrog to stay with Herbert, but he was perplexed by this careless talk of owing money from his mother, who, as he knew well, had a very liberal income and had been provided for in his grandfather's will in extremely generous fashion.

As for clothes, he never thought his mother cared what she wore. She was always a mixture of finery and slovenliness—witness her appearance this evening. A wrap of really exquisite velvet with a high sable collar put over a shabby black gown, the skirt of which trailed on the ground and had the hem undone and besmeared with dirt. Her top half was magnificent. The vivid hair was white now—this had come since Johnnie's death—and the slanting green eyes matched the emerald earrings; she might have been a queen. But the lower half, with that trailing hem, belonged to any slatternly woman from the market-place in Doonhaven. There they were, his family; and the best beloved of all was absent, because of course she could not possibly undertake the journey in her present state, the baby expected any day now. He knew her thoughts were with him, he could imagine her hand in his and her dear eyes upon him, and her voice saying, "My Henry must say to the people what he believes to be true, and not try to be amusing all the time."

The trouble was that he found it so much easier to be amusing than to be truthful, and anyway if he once began to take politics seriously it would be the end of everything. Here was the Chairman, ringing a bell for silence, and here was he himself, standing beside the Chairman, with heaven knew how many hostile eyes gazing up at him. But what did it matter, when all was said and done? This was just another way to pass an evening.

He was greeted with cat-calls, boos, and whistles, to which he listened with a smiling face and with his hands in his pockets, and then, drawing out a large stop-watch, he clicked it and proceeded to examine the dial with close interest, at which there was a great burst of laughter from the crowd, which became quiet.

"I must congratulate you," said Henry, "on being shorter-winded than other mobs I have had to deal with."

There was another wave of laughter, and Henry, putting up his hand to catch a scarlet rosette that one of the Liberal enthusiasts had thrown at his head, placed it on the other lapel of his frock-coat.

"No doubt the gallant fellow who threw this knows exactly what are the political opinions of Mr Sartor, the Liberal candidate," said Henry. "If he does, he is vastly my superior. I understand Mr Sartor has voted once one way, twice the other way, and three times the first way. He told you all the other day that when he was young he was a Tory. He said he imbibed Toryism with his mother's milk—which is interesting insomuch as it shows that he was nursed at home. . . . He also told you that the Tories were descendants of the Scribes and Pharisees, by which I gather he meant that the Tory party existed while the Ancient Britons were running around in their war-paint, throwing stones at Julius Caesar from the cliffs of Dover. If our historical friend would look back a little farther, I fancy he would find no difficulty in connecting the Tories with the idolatrous priests of Baal; I am not sure but that the Architect of the Tower of Babel might have been a Tory; nay, it is possible that the Tempter, who in an unlucky hour got possession of the ear of the much-deceived, much-failing, hapless Eve, may have been a Tory. Well, that being so, we have done with the Tories, who, it appears, are pretty well bowled out."

Herbert, his arms folded, smiled as he watched his brother. How this took him back to their boyhood and the Debating Society at Eton, Henry standing with his hands in his pockets and his head a little on one side, just as he was doing now, enjoying himself hugely and tickling his school-boy audience under the ribs. But soon he was wading into thornier subjects, interrupted, now and again, by voices at the back of the hall.

"You ask me to define a Liberal?" Henry called. "All right, I will; someone who is liberal with other people's money. As a matter of fact, there are no such things as Liberals now. There are only Constitution-alists and Revolutionists."

This caused a storm, of course, and Fanny, glancing uneasily over her shoulder, wondered how difficult it would be to reach the door if trouble broke out.

"Hoot twice as loud as that: I shall be delighted to hear you," Henry was saying. "There is nothing like excitement and difference of opinion to add zest to life. Why, if we had no differences of opinion we should all be in love with the same woman."

Another shout of laughter greeted this sally, and Tom Callaghan, pulling his beard, shook his head sagely and caught Bill Eyre's eye. This was all very good fun, no doubt, but not the way to win an election. Henry must have seen the glance, however, because before three minutes had passed he was deeply involved in the great question of the day.

"I am convinced," he said, "that institutions which have become venerable with time, and which are fixed firmly in the hearts and minds of the people, should not be ignored. The fact is that ignorance of what is really involved lies at the root of all these evils. The British Constitution is based on two pillars, the Church and the State. Those who would separate the Church from the State, and cause it to seek an asylum amongst the sects, would destroy the very essence of the constitution. Change merely for the sake of change is never desirable. Change and decay are invariably linked together."

How true, thought aunt Eliza, change and decay; it put her in mind of her father and those last long, dreary years of his during his retirement at Lletharrog, alone with that dreadful housekeeper who had got hold of him. Eliza was sure he had left her more money in his will than was fair, and it was monstrous the way in which the silver tea-service had dis-appeared. It should have been hers by right as the only surviving daughter; change and decay, how clever Henry was! . . .

"The improvement of the working classes must be founded upon religion," said Henry.

Tom Callaghan sat up in his seat. Ah, this was some of Katherine's doctrine. Henry would never have thought of it for himself.

"Education based upon any other foundation will be of no avail; but education based upon religion will raise the lower classes to their proper position in society. I hope and expect," Henry continued, "to see a great revival in the Church before long, if the clergy don't mistake the forms and ceremonies of an objective religion for the inner forms of Christianity."

Herbert blinked. Was this a sly hit at him? He had gone through an Anglican phase at Oxford, but that was over long ago. How very odd to hear old Henry talking in such a solemn way. Did he really mean what he was saying, or was it just to try the temper of his audience?

"We—the Conservative Party—have enfranchised the masses," Henry was saying, "and it is now our duty, it is the duty of every man, to spread

the blessings of education amongst the enfranchised masses. I am a firm
advocate of compulsory education. No man, in my opinion, has a right
to bring up his children as he would his pig or his beast."

How amusing, thought his mother Fanny-Rosa, to see Henry so serious
and talking such nonsense. It seemed only yesterday that he was running
up the staircase at Clonmere stark naked, his hands clapped on his small
behind, while she ran after him with a slipper, which she had no intention of using. Such a lovely afternoon, the children had taken all their
clothes off and played on the grass in front of the Castle. Barbara had
looked down from her room and had been so shocked, and begged her to
get them indoors before their grandfather returned. No doubt Henry
and the others had all been brought up like pigs; it had been so much
easier to let them run wild. . . . And suddenly she saw Johnnie, with
the Indian feathers in his black hair, peering at her from the rhododendron bushes, his bow and arrow lifted, and John saying to her, in his low,
quiet voice, "I can't beat him, whatever he does. We made him, you and
I: he belongs too much to both of us." But all that was finished, none of
that must ever be thought about, it was dead and gone, and so were they;
this was reality, sitting now in this crowded, uncomfortable hall, listening
to Henry.

"You know that I come from across the water," Henry said. "Well, it
is no disgrace to belong to the land of Burke, of Palmerston, of Welling-
ton, but I may say I am the third generation of my family to be adopted
by your countrymen. My grandfather and my father lived here, and I
lived here as a child, where my brother lives today. The bones of my
grandfather lie in this country. Perhaps one day I may do the same."

And then it was all over, and there was clapping and hissing and singing and shouting, and the Chairman holding his hand for silence and
proposing a vote of thanks, and the whole party breaking up and making
for the door, with no eggshells thrown and no wild applause either.

The family all drove to the Queen's Arms for dinner, and Henry was
congratulated and smitten on the back by dozens of people he did not
know and dozens more he did, and everyone told him he had the seat for
certain.

"So very reminiscent of my brother Harry, your uncle," said Eliza. "I
can recollect him making points in just the same way. And your father
lounging in a chair, with a puppy on his knee, taking not the slightest
notice. I was so glad you insisted that there must always be a ruling
class. Really, the people I come across sometimes in Saunby are quite
dreadful. No one would have called upon them in the old days."

"You ought to live in Nice," said Fanny-Rosa. "Nothing under a
Count there, they're as common as ditch-water. I liked your speech,
Henry, though I don't know why you want to close public-houses on
Sunday; it will only make men drink harder on Saturday night. As for
your remarks about the R.C.s across the water, you might have added

the old saying that 'St. Patrick was a gentleman, and born of dacent people'. Are we going to get anything to eat in this hotel?"

"You must excuse my mother," laughed Henry to Tom Callaghan. "Living in France has made her a gourmet, and she expects omelettes and salads every quarter of an hour. Waiter, will you please serve dinner as soon as possible?"

"I've never in my life been surrounded by so many parsons," said Fanny-Rosa, "except the time that the Bishop of Slane came to Castle Andriff to spend the night, and brought with him a chaplain and a couple of curates. My sister Tilly and I were brats of children at the time, and we stole into their rooms when they were all at dinner and threw their night-shirts out of the window, and their reverences slept as nature made them. . . . Don't look so shocked, Bill. You are a married man and must have slept without your night-shirt before now."

"You know, Mrs Brodrick," said Tom Callaghan, "Henry is much more like you than anybody realises. I've been told so often that he is the spit of his uncle Henry, and a chip off his grandfather's block, but I know now who gave him his quick tongue."

"Oh, we Flowers always had the gift of the gab," said Fanny-Rosa; "it enables us to slide through many difficulties. No, Herbert there is most like me of all my children, and he was so afraid at what he might become that he sought sanctuary behind a dog collar. As for Henry, people are right to compare him with his grandfather and his uncle. He has the shrewdness of the one, coupled with the charm of the other. Which will gain the upper hand remains to be seen. . . . Is it roast pork they're bringing us? I had a passion for it before Edward was born, I always say that's why his hair is so curly, but I haven't been able to touch it since. Tell the waiter to bring me fish instead."

The brothers winked at one another. Their mother was in rollicking form. Katherine was wrong for once in her judgement, thought Henry, as Fanny-Rosa raised her glass and pledged his future as a Cabinet Minister. She was probably happier than she had ever been in her life, and Johnnie was entirely forgotten. What a stunning picture she made too, with that crown of white hair, and the green eyes, and the emeralds, as long as you did not look under the table and see the dragging hem. What age was she now? Fifty-three or four; he was not certain. The party was a great success anyway, and even aunt Eliza became quite flushed and excited, and forgot to be disapproving. Fanny lost her inevitable anxious look, the parsons behaved like schoolboys on a spree, and Tom Callaghan's great booming laugh echoed through the room. If only Katherine had been there, thought Henry, the cup of happiness would have been complete. . . .

Polling took place the next day, and the result was to be known by six o'clock, and given out from the steps of the Town Hall. Henry passed the day in a fever of impatience. Now that the speech-making was over,

and the canvassing, and the driving about through the streets of Bronsea
in a carriage bedecked with blue ribbon, there was a great sense of anti-
climax. It was hard to wait about all day for the result. Somehow he felt
unable to take luncheon with the rest of the family, and he went out and
fed alone in a pub at the end of the town, where he hoped no one would
recognise him. He then walked the streets of Bronsea, observing that
nearly everyone he met appeared to be sporting in his buttonhole a red
ribbon, the Liberal favour, and he counted only a dozen blue rosettes
during the afternoon. Possibly his supporters had voted early, he told
himself, or anyway they were not the type to walk the streets. How ridiculous was the whole affair, and what a fool he felt to be so nervous! He
found himself outside the shipping office of Owen Williams, the firm
which handled all the copper business for him in Bronsea, and had done
so since his grandfather's time. He stepped in to have a word with the
younger Williams, a man somewhat older than himself, about the prospects for the coming summer. Here at last was someone with a blue
rosette. It was quite a relief to his mind, and Williams assured him that
when he had gone to vote soon after ten o'clock the street had been
blocked with carriages, the owners of whom had all worn the right
colour.

"It will be splendid to have someone like you to represent the borough,"
he said. "I promise myself a treat, and that's to come up to Parliament
and hear you make your maiden speech."

"But I'm not there yet," warned Henry.

"All over bar the shouting," said the other.

For a little while they discussed the mines at Doonhaven, shipping, and
the copper trade in general, and just as Henry was about to take his leave
Mr Williams said casually, by way of conversation, that Henry was the
second member of his family to pay him a visit that day.

"Why," said Henry in surprise, "how is that?"

"Oh, your mother dropped in during the course of the morning," said
Mr Williams, "looking wonderfully well, I thought. She wanted an ex-
tension of the loan, you know, and I said it would be quite all right, of
course."

"Loan?" repeated Henry.

"Yes, we advanced her five hundred pounds last quarter, at your request, if you remember, sending the cheque out to her in France, and she
wished for a further sum of the same amount. We deduct it, naturally,
from your account with us at the end of the year. That was the arrangement made with her, according to your instructions, she said."

Henry was bewildered. He had given no such instructions, and knew
nothing whatever of a loan to his mother. She must have done this behind his back, without any authority. . . . The younger Williams was
looking at him curiously. Henry pulled himself together with an
effort.

"Oh, yes," he said, "I do remember now. My mother and I came to some such arrangement. Well, I must be getting along. Glad to have seen you."

"Good-bye, Mr Brodrick, and good luck."

Henry walked back to the hotel, his mind in a turmoil. Good God, his mother to go like that and lie to the fellow Williams, instead of coming straight to him and asking for a gift. He could not understand it. Why, in heaven's name, did she need the money, and what the devil did she spend it on? He would have to find her and question her: it was impossible to keep this sort of thing to himself. If only Katherine were here, she would know how to deal with it.

Fanny and Bill were sitting in the lounge of the hotel, with Miss Goodwin, Fanny's friend, and Tom Callaghan in attendance as usual. Herbert was out somewhere. If Miss Goodwin had not been there Henry might have asked advice from Bill and Tom, but he could not discuss anything so painful and intimate before a stranger.

"Where's mother?" he said diffidently.

"In her room, I think," said Fanny. "Where have you been? We were all quite worried. You look so tired."

"Nerves," said Tom. "Poor old Henry has had everything in life go smoothly up to now, and he's not certain what today will bring forth."

Henry did not answer. He was in no mood now for mockery. He went upstairs to the first floor of the hotel and along the corridor to his mother's room, and knocked at the door. Although she had only occupied it for three nights, the bedroom was already a shambles. There were shoes strewn about the floor, clothes on all the chairs, and the inevitable litter of hairpins, gloves, velvet ribbons, and handkerchiefs on the dressing-table. Fanny-Rosa was sitting on the bed, on which she had placed her trunk, and was putting something away under a folded gown.

"The conquering hero," she smiled, as her son entered. "Have you got a pain in your tummy, my poor boy? Your father was the same before one of the greyhound meetings. All strung up and pretending he did not care a damn whether he won or lost."

"I haven't come to talk about the election," said Henry, sitting beside her on the bed. "I don't mind what happens, one way or the other. I've come to talk about you."

Fanny-Rosa raised her eyebrows, and leaving the bed she strolled over to the dressing-table and began to do her hair.

"I went into Owen Williams' just now, before coming here," said Henry, "and he told me you had seen him this morning, and borrowed five hundred pounds from the firm, giving him my authority for doing so. Also that you wrote for the same sum only last quarter. Mother dear, what is it all about?"

"My dear boy, you look just like a schoolmaster," laughed his mother. "You ought to be a supporter of Mr Gladstone, instead of his opponent.

Yes, that younger Mr Williams was most obliging. I am very grateful to him."

"But I don't understand," said Henry. "Why on earth did you not come to me for the money, instead of going behind my back and giving my authority for something I had not promised?"

"I thought it easier that way," said Fanny-Rosa, yawning. "Such a nuisance for you to be bothered."

"It's far more bother to learn that you are borrowing money from a shipping firm in such an odd way," said her son. "Don't you see, dear, it is not regular at all. In fact, not to mince matters, it's completely dishonest."

"I never understand these things," said Fanny-Rosa carelessly. "Any sort of money transaction always appears to me to be dishonest. I have no head for figures."

Henry watched her as she ran a comb through her cloud of white hair. She seemed to have no shame, she was as irresponsible as a child.

"Do you find it difficult to live on the income grandfather left you?" he said incredulously. "I understood that life in the south of France was so much cheaper."

"Oh, my dear, life is never cheap anywhere," said Fanny-Rosa. "What with little dinners, and going about, and one thing and another, I am always short."

She was being persistently vague on purpose, thought Henry; she was not going to commit herself.

"You have about twelve hundred a year from my grandfather," said Henry firmly, "and the rent of your villa, in English money, is about fifty pounds a year. Say your servants—there's a cook and a little girl, isn't there?—and your food cost you a hundred; clothes, the small amount of entertaining you can do, a further fifty; that's only two hundred pounds gone, mother, and a clear thousand in hand. What have you done with it all, that you have been obliged to borrow a thousand pounds from Owen Williams?"

"It goes, I tell you," said Fanny-Rosa. "Don't ask me how or why. I have not the slightest idea. Henry, dear boy, do put off that schoolmaster expression, it is so unbecoming, and when you greet your constituents directly you must be your usual smiling, charming self. You are sitting on my ear-rings, darling; throw them across to me, will you?"

She pleaded softly, looking at him out of the corner of her eyes, and shrugging his shoulders he rose from the bed, the ear-rings in his hand, and fastened them gently in her ear.

"You have hands like your father," she said: "now I know why your Katherine loves you. . . . May you always be happy together."

He stared at her face in the looking-glass. Was that a very small tear in the corner of her eye, and she smiling all the while?

"Mother," he said impulsively, "why don't you give up this life in the south of France, and come and live with us at Clonmere? Katherine would love to have you, and you know you belong there, to your own country."

Fanny-Rosa shook her head.

"Don't be absurd," she said lightly. "My present existence suits me to the ground. Everyone and everything so amusing. Anyway, it's a great mistake for a mother to live with her son. I tried it once, and I failed. Which of these bonnets shall I wear this evening?"

"Never mind about the bonnets. Mother, will you change your mind and come and live with us? You could have your own rooms, do exactly as you please, and no one would interfere with you."

"No, darling."

"Will you tell me then what you are doing with your money?"

"Oh, Henry, don't harp so. . . . Look, it's half-past five; we ought to be at the Town Hall. Run down and tell the others to get ready. I love your Tom Callaghan; so much more understanding than the usual run of parsons. You have always been lucky in your friends. Johnnie never made any. . . . Kiss me, my funny dear serious son, and don't worry about me any more. I won't bother Mr Owen Williams again, I promise you. This coming season will make up for last, I know it will."

"Why, what do you mean?" smiled Henry. "You talk like a shop-keeper, as though you expected to make some money."

She flashed him a vivid smile, and patted the side of her hair.

"Let's go and find the others," she said, "and don't forget to put a flower in your buttonhole. Praise God I have such good-looking chil-dren."

It was useless, thought Henry, as he followed her downstairs, to try to get anything out of her. She just put up barriers all the time. She smiled, and looked softly at you, and made some irrelevant remark, but what went on within that head of hers you would never know. And he won-dered whether his father, who had loved her so well, had found her the same, and whether, even when they were closest, she had eluded him. . . .

The family were waiting for them downstairs in the lounge, and cabs were ordered immediately to take them to the Town Hall.

The streets were congested, though, with everyone bent on the same errand as themselves, and the horses were obliged to proceed at walking pace, or they would have run down the people.

Henry directed the driver to take them round to the entrance at the back of the building, for to climb up the steps in front of the crowds assembled in the square was to court immediate recognition.

Even now they could hear the hum of excitement and the babble of voices, for all the world, said Fanny-Rosa, like a mob before an execution, and as the cabs turned into the little street behind the Town Hall they could see line upon line of excited faces, looking upwards to the balcony, laughing, shouting, with caps waving, and handkerchiefs flying.

"We must be even later than I thought," said Henry swiftly, "it looks to me as though the result is being given out."

He handed his mother and his sister from the cab, and leaving them to follow in the care of his brothers, Tom Callaghan, and his brother-in-law, he ran up the narrow staircase at the back of the Hall that led to the large board room on the upper floor. His heart was beating, and for the first time in his life his hands were trembling. He entered the room, which was filled with people and the excited buzz of voices. Outside the crowds were cheering their heads off. And there, in front of him, standing on the balcony, hat in hand, bowing to right and left, was Mr Sartor, the Liberal candidate. Something snapped for an instant in Henry's mind, and a momentary wave of bitter disappointment filled his heart.

"Oh, damn . . ." he thought to himself, "damn and blast. . . ."

And then he smiled, he walked forward with his hand extended, and Mr Sartor, the new member for Bronsea, turned and saw him, and beckoned him on to the balcony beside him. The Liberal had won by a majority of eight thousand votes.

"And so that's that," said Henry, when the applause had died away and the crowds had dispersed to make merry in the public-houses. "And I may as well confess now to my family that I never for one moment thought I would succeed. It's been an experience, and very great fun; now let us go back and have an excellent dinner, and forget all about it."

"Spoken like a sportsman," said Tom Callaghan, taking his arm. "I don't mind saying I'm disappointed. I should have dearly loved to have gone to Westminster and seen you talking the heads off all the fellows there. But never mind, it was not to be, and we shall have you home in Doonhaven."

"Better luck next time, old fellow," said Edward.

"Ah, there'll be no next time," said Henry; "this was my first and last venture into politics. I don't mind making a fool of myself once, but twice is too often."

He chatted lightly and gaily to cover his sense of defeat. His family must not think he minded, nor did he mind, he kept insisting to himself. The worst thing in the world was to be a bad loser. No, it was just a silly pin-prick to his pride, that was all. Henry Brodrick hitherto had got away with everything.

"I simply can't understand how anyone voted for that Mr Sartor," said Fanny-Rosa; "such a terribly unattractive man. Bad teeth, which I can't forgive. And absolutely no breeding whatsoever."

"The people of Bronsea don't mind that, Mrs Brodrick," said Tom Callaghan. "They felt he knew more about them than Henry did, and that's how he won the seat."

"Oh, it's easy to persuade a man who lives on bread and porridge that he is a suffering man," replied Fanny-Rosa, "but whether you can do him any good by telling him so is another matter."

"Politics is a gamble, nothing more nor less," said Henry, "and if you lose you cut your losses and forget the business, which is what I propose to do."

"Which shows your very good sense of balance," said Tom. "Your inveterate gambler never knows when he is beaten, and goes on until the thing becomes a disease and he can't stop. It's a form of mental escape, like drink, and runs in the blood-stream. But I don't know why we are so serious all of a sudden. Henry, old friend, even if you have lost the election, you conducted the affair like a gentleman, and I, for one, am proud of you."

"We are all proud of him," said his mother, patting his cheek, "and he looked so handsome too, standing on the balcony beside that dreadful little man. I am quite certain everyone must have wished they had voted the other way round."

And so the Brodricks returned to the hotel, all of them suffering from anti-climax but determined not to show it, and as they entered the lounge a page-boy came forward and handed Henry a telegram on a salver.

"Some facetious fellow sending you a condolence," said Fanny-Rosa. "Don't open it, it will only annoy you."

But Henry had already torn open the envelope, and was reading the message. He glanced up, his eyes shining, and waved the paper in front of his family.

"To hell with politics," he said. "Who cares a damn for 'em? I've got a son, and that's the only thing that matters."

They crowded round him, looking over his shoulder.

The message was brief, but very much to the point.

"Don't be disappointed if the election goes against you. Your son was born today, and we both want you home. He is exactly like you, and I have called him Hal. My love and thoughts are with you. Katherine."

"Haven't I always said," smiled Henry, "that she is the only woman in the world? Call that waiter, Tom. I may have been defeated today at Bronsea, but by God, we're going to drink champagne tonight."

3

There was a measured serenity about those days; they had a natural rhythm to them, a slow movement, and events succeeded one another as the seasons did, with no sudden disturbance breaking the calm sequence. Life was something certain and secure, and Henry, breakfasting on a winter's morning, would know that the following winter would be the same, that the accustomed routine would be taken up and followed, and so on through the spring, the summer, and the autumn, the months would give him what he desired, his plans would come to maturity and be fulfilled. The winter and spring would be spent at Clonmere, and then, at the end of April, Henry and Katherine and the children would cross the water, and spend the season in London. It was delightful, he used to think, after the long, slow, peaceful winter at Clonmere, suddenly to hear traffic again, the hum of London, to be made aware of the existence of millions of people, to stroll across the Park on a May morning, chatting on the way with those of his friends whom he might meet, and then down to his Club in St. James's, to read the papers, talk again, and while away the time until he was due to meet Katherine for luncheon with friends in Berkeley Square, or Grosvenor Street, or wherever it was. And the luncheon would be amusing, fifteen or twenty people very often, most of whom he would know, and if he did not it was always enjoyable to meet new faces. Then, in the afternoon, the usual outing of the season, whatever it should be. Pictures, or a concert, or a race-meeting, or to Ranelagh, but back always, if it could be managed, to the house by five o'clock, because Katherine wished to spend this time with the children, and fretted if she did not. Besides, it was good for her to rest before dining out again in the evening. He liked the hour between six and seven, when, sitting in his chair before the open window in the drawing-room, the brightly painted window-box gay with flowers, he would browse over the events of the day. The joy, talking for the sheer delight of talking, thrashing a subject until it was in shreds. A sense of well-being would envelop him, and smiling, Henry would go upstairs to dress for dinner, and presently Katherine would call to him from her room, through the open door between them. The friends to whom they were bound would give them an excellent dinner, and afterwards there would be music, some lion or other invited for the purpose, and so home to bed round about midnight, well fed, contented, and tomorrow the whole thing beginning over again. Katherine would look very beautiful on these occasions, and he would feel so proud when they were announced, to see the heads turn in their direction, as Katherine led the way across the floor towards their host and hostess, her gown rustling slightly as she walked. The way she looked, he thought, the way she moved, the way she held her fan in her gloved hands, the smile, the angle of the head, put her in another class from every other woman; there would be no one in the room to touch her. And perhaps someone would come up to him with outstretched hand. "Good heavens, Henry, I haven't set eyes on you since Oxford days," and there would be the recognition, the momentary greeting, and then, "You have never met my wife. Katherine, this is a very old friend of mine."

"You know," his hostess would say at dinner, in her gay, mocking, fashionable way, "everybody says that you and your wife are the handsomest couple in London. People queue up to watch the Henry Brodricks drive to church on Sunday morning." And lots more of this nonsense, every day, which Henry told himself he took with a pinch of salt, and yet it was pleasing to be admired, to know that he and Katherine were bracketed together in this manner.

Henry kept his vow and did not play with politics again, but he continued to be a keen Conservative, and when in the neighbourhood of
Bronsea he was generally induced to make an appearance at some banquet or other, and entertain the company with his quick wit and lively
stories. In '67 he was made High Sheriff for the county, and this necessi-
tated a rather long sojourn in Saunby, the family taking up their quarters
at Brodrick House for a full six months with aunt Eliza.

Little Hal, aunt Eliza said, reminded her strongly of his grandfather,
her brother John. He had the same soft eyes, the same mouth, the same
shy way of stroking a dog or a cat when he did not want people to notice
him, and he would play alone quite happily for hours, as John had done
when he was a little boy.

"Added to which," said aunt Eliza, "he has your own reserve, Katherine, so he won't make his mark in the world unless he can produce
some of Henry's push and go. I must say, I do like a boy to have spirit."

"Hal will have spirit enough if it's directed in the right way," smiled
Katherine. "He needs encouragement, and patience, and someone to
build up his confidence. Talking and walking were an effort for him,
when they were nothing to Molly. She will sail through life gaily, without
any difficulty. Hal is just the opposite, he will need someone to hold his
hand."

And aunt Eliza had sniffed, and snapped her lorgnette back on her
bosom.

"My father would not have had much truck with that sort of talk," she
said. "Nobody ever held our hands as children, and I always pride myself that one of the reasons I have lived longer than any of my brothers
or sisters is because I had plenty of sense, and was practical. My youngest
sister, Henry's aunt Jane, was very sentimental and weak, and I always
used to say John had no backbone. There is a weak strain in the Brodricks, Katherine, and you will have to watch it."

It was good to take the boat at length and cross to Slane, and then
drive down home to Doonhaven by way of Mundy and Andriff, and find
themselves home at Clonmere. Henry, the first morning on waking up,
wondered why they had ever bothered to go away. He leant out of their
bedroom window looking down to the creek, and the familiar prospect
of the day before him filled him with pleasure.

Breakfast in the dining-room, and then going into the library and having the outdoor staff in to report. Old Tim, who was getting rather stiff
in the joints but went scarlet with indignation if it was suggested for one
moment that he should seek honourable retirement, and Sullivan, the
head gardener, nephew to the elderly Baird, now in his grave, Phillips the
keeper, Mahony the cow-man, faces that he had seen upon the place
since boyhood. If there was time before luncheon, a walk round the
grounds, up through the woods and across to the farm, and down
through the park, and so home by the path beside the creek. In the

afternoon up to the mines to see if things were satisfactory. Calling in on dear old Tom at Heathmount on his way home, and asking him and Harriet to Clonmere to dinner, to hear and exchange all the gossip that was going. A very good thing he had stood for Bronsea, even if he had been defeated, because it had been the means of bringing together Tom and his wife, the pretty, bright-eyed friend of Fanny's, and now they had a small daughter Jinny, who came to romp with his own brood at Clonmere. Then home to tea, a roaring fire in the drawing-room, and the children down afterwards, settling themselves about Katherine's knee. Molly, with dark hair flying, usually the most forward with suggestions as to what they should do and what book should be read, while Hal would plead for music, looking as solemn as an owl, until, for the sake of Kitty, the second daughter of the house and the last arrival, Katherine would break into one of the old jigs, lively and gay, and the three children would dance themselves giddy, and Hal, losing his shyness, become the wildest of the pack. Then Katherine would close the piano and go back again to her chair, and read to the children, very slowly, very carefully, with many explanations.

"The trouble is," Henry said to her one day, "you wear yourself out for those children. They never give you a moment's peace."

"The children never tire me," she told him, "I promise you they don't. If they did I should send them back to the nursery."

"I don't believe you," he said, rather sulkily. "You have such a strong sense of duty that if Hal had some imaginary bother and you had a raging headache you would sit by him all day and never look after yourself. And then when I want attention in the evening you are too tired to talk to me."

"Dear one, aren't you being unjust for once? Have I ever been too tired for my Henry?"

He looked down at her, a boyish, disgruntled expression on his face, and then the frown went, he was himself again, and bending down he smiled and kissed her hand.

"Forgive me," he said. "I love you so much."

And he left the room, ashamed of his outburst, and went to discuss with the keeper the shooting-party for the following Saturday, but nagging him, like a maggot in his mind, were the words old uncle Willie Armstrong had said to him last week:

"I hope that the lively young Kitty completes your family. If Katherine had another child I would not answer for the consequences."

Forget it, though. Always forget the unpleasant things in life, the pinpricks, the annoyances. Wasn't that one of his mother's maxims? He would hear from her, now and again, scrappy, disjointed letters about nothing at all, and on the rare occasions when she had visited them it was always to borrow money. . . . He did not ask her again why she wanted it, he simply wrote out a cheque and gave it to her without a word. It was distasteful, a thing that had to be put away in a corner of his mind. It was the one secret he kept from Katherine. He dreaded that this carelessness of hers should become known to people, to the rest of the family, to their friends, and there should be some sort of scandal, as there had been over Johnnie.

Meanwhile, there were great festivities ahead. On the 3rd of March, 1870, the copper mines would be fifty years old, and Henry was determined to celebrate the occasion in style. There would be a sit-down dinner up at the mines for all the miners employed there, and their families, also for the seamen of the vessels that carried the copper across to Bronsea. Toasts would be given, speeches made, and all the paraphernalia that Henry dearly loved. Then, the following night at Clonmere, another dinner for the county, for all those who had been connected, in some way or other, with the original mining agreement. The Lumleys from Duncroom, the Flowers from Andriff, all cousins, of course, and known very well to him, and certain other neighbours who during the course of fifty years had received benefit from the mines on Hungry Hill. Bill Eyre and Fanny would bring their son and daughter down from the parsonage in the north, and Herbert and his wife and boys cross the water from Lletharrog. Edward, returned from abroad, would also join them, and possibly aunt Eliza, if she could be induced to face the crossing during the stormiest period of the year. Of course, Tom and his wife would have a place of honour, and old uncle Willie, who had brought Henry into the world. Molly and Hal and Kitty should sit up for the occasion and have dinner with them. Henry was full of plans, each one succeeding the other with lightning rapidity, until Katherine, laughing, said he made her head dizzy, and anyway she did not know where they were going to put up all the guests. Herbert's boys would have to sleep in the boat-house, and Edward and his bride in an attic. Henry dismissed the matter airily, with a wave of his hand.

"Tom can put up some of them, and uncle Willie one or two; we shall manage all right." And then he smiled, and looked at her slyly. "But in a year's time," he added, "we shall have room for twice as many."

"Why, what do you mean?" she asked.

But he shook his head, he would not be drawn, and she wondered what new project was now in preparation, occupying his energetic mind.

The 1st of March came in, not like the proverbial lion but calmly, serenely, with a soft west wind blowing from Mundy bay, rippling the creek, and the golden and purple crocuses bursting into flower on the bank below the castle. There were no clouds in the sky, and the sun shone fine and strongly upon Hungry Hill. And one by one, during the day, the Brodricks came to Clonmere. Herbert, from Lletharrog, with his wife Cathie and their two eldest boys, Robert and Bertie; Edward, with his bride Winifred; and later in the afternoon Fanny Eyre, her husband Bill, and their son and daughter William and Maria. Aunt Eliza arrived with the Lletharrog party, and in spite of her seventy-two years had stood the journey better than any of them. And how delightful it was, thought Henry, to have the whole family assembled here under his roof, brother shaking hands with brother, sister-in-law greeting sister-in-law, and young cousins standing warily on one foot watching other young cousins out of the corners of their eyes.

Everybody sat down to an enormous tea in the dining-room, with aunt Eliza in the place of honour at the head of it, which pleased her mightily.

"So many times I have sat round this table," she told them, "with your grandfather where you are sitting now, Henry, and Barbara in this place. Your father John was always late for meals; it used to annoy your grandfather considerably, and I must say I dislike unpunctuality almost as much as he did—so very inconsiderate, and careless. Barbara never said very much to John about it, which was weak of her, and of course your aunt Jane could not bear to have him scolded. Poor Jane, she would have been sixty this year, if she had lived."

And Hal, a little uncomfortable in the magnificence of his new Eton jacket and broad white collar, to which he had been promoted in honour of the occasion and his approaching ten years, gazed up at the portrait of his great-aunt above the mantelpiece, and thought how glad he was that she had stayed young and pretty, and had not become old like great-aunt Eliza, who used to come out of her room at Saunby and scold him if he made too much noise on the stairs. Even great-aunt Jane, pretty as she was, would not bear comparison with Mamma, whose portrait also hung in the dining-room, and Hal, glancing from the portrait to the original, caught his mother's eye and smiled. It made a small happiness that she should know he had been looking at her, as though they shared a secret. Someone kicked him under the table. It was Molly, and she was frowning at him. "Don't dream", her lips moved, and he realised with a start that he had paid no attention to the cousin on his right, Robert from Lletharrog, who was asking him, with all the superiority of thirteen years, what sort of fish were obtainable in the creek.

"Killigs and pollock," he said with great politeness. "Perhaps you would like to come with me in a boat tomorrow, if my father will allow it?"

"Oh, sea-fishing," said Robert scornfully; "that's poor sport after catching trout, as we do at home."

"There are brown trout in the lake on Hungry Hill," said Hal swiftly. "They say the fairies put them there, and at night they become little old men and work in the mines."

Thirteen-year-old Robert stared at his young cousin, and then turned away his head. Hal was soft, he decided; how very awkward. And he began to discuss cricket with stolid William Eyre.

The weather held fine for the festivities, and the people of Doonhaven stood at their cottage doors to watch the carriages go through the village up to the mines. The road itself was crowded with the younger and more inquisitive of the inhabitants, all agog at the notion of "the gentry" sitting down to supper side by side with the miners. The full moon shone upon Hungry Hill, and it might have been the light of day as the carriages swung round and came to rest before the great drying-sheds, which, swept and cleared, with three immense tables down the centre, had been turned into a banqueting hall for the occasion. Candles, in their brackets, had been placed at intervals along the walls, and long school forms, borrowed for the night, were to seat the diners. At the far end of the shed, pompous and important, stood the members of the catering firm from Slane, who were to serve the food and wait upon the guests. The miners and their families were all seated in their places when the Brodricks arrived, and as Henry and Katherine entered, the manager, Mr Griffiths, started three cheers for the owner and a general clapping of hands, which was quite unexpected to Henry, and he stood smiling at the entrance to the shed, with Katherine at his side.

"I will thank you for that welcome after supper," he told them when the clapping died away. "Meanwhile, let's get on to the most important business of the evening, and I hope you are all as hungry as I am."

Soup, and roast mutton and beef, followed by apple tart, with ale to drink, put every man in a good temper. The murmur of voices, which had been low and cautious to start with, rose to a roar, and Henry, winking at the manager, who sat on his right hand, observed that the only way to a fellow's heart was to fill his belly first. His speech, when he came to make it, was short, for no one, he told them, wanted to listen to anyone but themselves after nine o'clock at night, and as the next day was to be a full holiday for everyone, in honour of the occasion, the sooner they went home to enjoy it the better. He then announced an increase of pay to every miner, from that day forward, which was received with yells of approval and only one discordant note, from some fellow at the far end of the shed who was moved to shout out "And about time too." Henry, with memories of Bronsea and the heckling he had been faced with then, remained perfectly cool.

"I may say," he added, "that, speaking as one chiefly concerned with my own interests, the idea of this was not my own, but Mrs Brodrick's. It is she you have to thank."

More applause for Katherine, who smiled, and blushed a little, and said nothing.

"Fifty years ago today," continued Henry, "my grandfather John Brodrick signed the original agreement with Mr Robert Lumley of Duncroom, for a mine to be started on Hungry Hill. The original miners were mostly Cornishmen, a few of whom are with us today as pensioners, and whose sons have carried on their work and are settled amongst us. The rest of you, if not all from Doonhaven and the neighbourhood, belong to this country, and know that our granite hills do not yield easily to

pick and shovel like the chalk cliffs of other, easier lands. From the beginning my grandfather had to import gunpowder to do his work, and
blast the copper out of Hungry Hill, and although today machinery and
explosive are modernised, we still have to deal with the same old stubborn
granite. We still have the westerly gales that prevent shipment of the
cargoes to Bronsea during the winter months, and, perhaps most important of all, we still have to contend with that strange fluctuating affair
know as the copper trade itself, the ups and downs of which are beyond
you, and very often beyond me too, and have their origin in the varying
claims and discoveries of other countries. The copper mines of Hungry
Hill have had their difficulties, like every other mining concern. My
grandfather had to contend with riots and floods and many other vicissi-
tudes in his time, which, I am glad to say, have not been my portion.
The troubles today are rather different—the law of supply and demand,
the labour shortage, the more favourable life, on paper if not in actuality,
offered many of you in America, and the fact that the deeper we go in
search of our copper the more reluctant are the old granite bones of
Hungry Hill to give it to us. One day, perhaps not very far distant, we
shall strike for the last time and know that the best of the copper has been
brought to the surface, and that what remains is not worth the cost of
raising it. Until that day, my friends, I wish you good luck and God-
speed, with all the thanks in my heart for your loyalty, your energy and
your courage."

And with these words Henry sat down, wondering, as the applause
rang in his ears, whether his grandfather would have made the same sort
of speech, or whether, in the manner of fifty years ago, he would have
kept his listeners a full hour, and be damned to them if they showed signs
of impatience. Griffiths, the manager, made reply for the miners, and
then there were songs, and talking, and more songs; and finally, about
eleven o'clock, when the air in the drying-shed was becoming thick and
hazy with smoke and the company boisterous and rather over-full of ale,
Henry, and Katherine, and the rest of the family slipped away, and
summoned the carriages, with all the satisfaction of a good deed
done.

"Well," declared aunt Eliza, "I only hope those men are grateful for
all Henry has done for them. But they are all the same; every kindness
is taken for granted, and it was just the same in my father's time. Personally, I consider all these improvements only make them lazy. Great
bits of machinery to bring the stuff up above ground, when I can remember every ounce of copper coming to the surface in a bucket."

"You ought to have been a director," laughed Henry; "hard as nails,
and not a penny extra to the miners. Is it true my grandfather used to
flog 'em in the early days?"

"It would have done them no harm if he had," she replied, "and I
know he quelled the riot they had in '25 by blowing several of them up

with gunpowder, and quite right too. There was never any trouble afterwards."

"It must have left a great deal of bitterness, all the same," said Katherine.

"Stuff and nonsense! They learnt their lesson. My father always used to say that if you once showed weakness to these people they paid you back fourfold in treachery."

"Surely there is a middle way, between extreme hardness and foolish weakness?" said Katherine. "What, for want of a better word, I should call understanding."

"Don't you believe it," said Henry. "The people don't want to be understood, it would spoil their sense of injustice. They revel in their wrongs. My grandfather was perfectly right. Do you think I shall get any more work out of my Doonhaven miners now I have raised their wages? Not a bit of it. Ah, Mr Brodrick's gone easy, they'll say; we'll take an extra half-hour for dinner, and smoke another pipe of 'baccy."

"Did you raise the wages to get more out of them?" asked Katherine. "I thought you did it because we agreed they were too low, and the families were suffering?"

Henry made a penitent face, and felt for her hand.

"Of course I did," he said, "but you know the proverb about killing two birds with one stone. . . . Here, what the devil is Tim up to?"

The carriage lurched suddenly, throwing Henry against his wife. There was a jerk, and a sliding of hoofs as the horses were pulled to a standstill. Tim was shouting to the animals, and the carriage rocked between the wheels. Henry flung open the door and stepped down into the road.

"It wasn't my fault, sir," said Tim, who, white in the face, was climbing down from his seat. "He walked right out into the centre of the road, and was under the horses before I could stop him. . . . He must have been drunk, of course."

He went forward to hold the horses, while Henry bent over the prone figure of the man who had stumbled in front of the carriage. The second carriage had stopped behind them, and Tom and Herbert, realising there had been an accident, came running down the road to assist them.

"What's wrong? Is anyone hurt?" asked Tom.

"Some idiot of a fellow came right out of the hedge and ran straight into us," said Henry. "Not Tim's fault at all. It's a mercy we were not all thrown into the ditch. Hand down the carriage lamp, Herbert, and let's see the damage."

Together he and Tom Callaghan dragged the unfortunate man from under the carriage, and laid him out on his back in the road.

"I'm afraid his back is broken," said Tom quietly. "Let me loosen the collar and turn the head to the light. Henry, I think Katherine and your aunt had best get into the other carriage and drive home to Clonmere. This isn't a sight for their eyes. Herbert, will you look after them?"

"What is it? Who is it?" said Katherine, stepping down from the carriage. "Poor fellow. Let me help, Henry, please."

"No, dear one, I want you to go home. Do what I tell you," said Henry.

Katherine hesitated a moment, and then took aunt Eliza's arm and turned back to the other carriage.

"Drive on," called Henry, waving his hand to the groom; "we shall follow directly."

Edward had now joined them, and Bill Eyre.

"What a wretched business," said Edward. "Is the man dead?"

"I'm afraid so," said Tom; "the wheel seems to have passed right over his head. . . . We had better lift him into the carriage, and take him straight away to the surgery and rouse the doctor. The young fellow, not old Armstrong. Not that he will be able to do anything. I don't recognise the fellow, he's no one I know in Doonhaven. About forty-five, I should say, reddish hair going grey. Give us the light again."

Once more they looked down into the face of the dead man. It was badly marked and disfigured, but even so there was something about the hair, the staring blue eyes, that awoke recognition in Henry and a flood of memories.

"Good God," he said slowly, "it's Jack Donovan."

The brothers stared at one another, and old Tim, coming close to them, bent down in his turn and examined the dead man.

"You're right, sir," he said. "It's him sure enough. I'd heard he was home from America, but I hadn't seen him myself. And what does he do but come home and get drunk and walk straight in under my horse's feet. . . ."

"Is this the man you told me about once?" asked Tom quietly.

"Yes," said Henry. "What a wretched unfortunate business! Why the devil did he have to come back?"

"No use wondering that," said Tom, "we have to get him down to the village. Who's his nearest relative? Hasn't he an aunt, Mrs Kelly? And I suppose that old rogue Denny Donovan, who used to keep a pub, is an uncle?"

"Yes, sir," said Tim, "Denny is his uncle, but the man's never sober, not much use rousing him. Denny's son, Pat Donovan, has a bit of a farm across the hill here; that's where Jack must have been staying."

"Time enough for all that in the morning," said Tom Callaghan. "Let's get the poor fellow to the surgery."

What a damnable end to the evening, thought Henry, as the carriage with its miserable burden rattled down the hill into Doonhaven. And why, of all people, must it have been Jack Donovan, returned from America, who chose to end his life in such a fashion? If only he could

have run into somebody else's carriage. Henry had not the slightest pity
for the fellow, he was a scoundrel in every sense, and the world was well
rid of him, but for anyone to be killed in this way, beneath his horses and
his carriage, and especially after the celebration that had taken place
that evening, was painful and disturbing. It was not his fault, it was not
anyone's fault except Jack Donovan's himself, but that was not the point.
The thing had happened. And it brought back the past and so much
distress that was best forgotten. . . .

It was some time after midnight when Henry and his brothers returned
to Clonmere. The body of Jack Donovan had been taken to the surgery
and the doctor summoned. He must have died instantly, the doctor said,
and certainly Tim could be absolved from all blame, for it was obvious
that the dead man had been drinking. The doctor promised to go himself in the morning and break the news to Jack Donovan's cousin Pat,
and Tom Callaghan also announced his intention of doing the same.

"There's no need for you to concern yourself in the matter, old fellow,"
he said to Henry. "I'm the Rector of this place, and I'm used to this sort
of thing, even if the Donovans don't belong to my church. You have a
big house-party on your hands, and it's your duty to look after them."

The castle was hushed and silent in the mooonlight. Only a pin-prick
of light from their bedroom warned Henry that Katherine was awake and
waiting for them. He was afraid she would be very much grieved at what
had happened. Damn Jack Donovan, he thought angrily, even if he was
dead. His brothers went up to bed, but Henry remained below, wondering whether he should make up some story to Katherine or not. It would
be useless, though; he had never lied to her. He stood by the front door
gazing out across the creek to Hungry Hill. It lay in shadow now, and
the moon, shining high above Doon Island, seemed pale and cold. Fifty
years ago his grandfather must have stood here, with his future before
him and the agreement for the mines in his pocket. And fifty years hence,
what? His own grandson, a son of Hal's perhaps, with this same moon
looking down upon Clonmere, and the creek, and the scarred, blank face
of Hungry Hill?

He turned and went indoors, and climbed the stairs softly to Katherine's room. She was sitting up in bed waiting for him, her long dark
hair in two plaits like a child. She looked pale and anxious.

"I am sure the man is dead," she said at once. "I felt it, directly you
told me to come home."

"Yes," he said, "he is dead."

He told her a little more about it: how they had gone to the surgery,
and roused the doctor, and then, when she asked the man's name, he
hesitated, having some intuition that the name would make her unhappy, as indeed it made him unhappy too.

"It was Jack Donovan," he said at last. "It seems he had returned
from America."

She said very little, and he went and undressed, and when he came back she had blown out the candles and was lying in darkness.

He held her close to him, and when he kissed her eyes he found they were wet with tears.

"Don't think about it," he said; "it was a wretched unfortunate thing to happen, but the doctor said he died instantly. He was a hopeless fellow, you know that, and would only have made trouble in the district if he had settled down here again. Please, dear one, don't think about it any more."

"It's not that," she said. "I'm not crying for Jack Donovan."

"What is it, then?" he said. "Won't you tell me?"

She said nothing for a moment, and then, putting her arms round him, she said:

"I cried just now because I remembered Johnnie, and how lost and unhappy he was. I might have done so much more for him than I did."

"That's absurd," said Henry. "What more could you have possibly done?"

It was Jack Donovan, of course, who had brought back the old tragedy. Johnnie had been dead nearly twelve years, and Katherine had never mentioned him before. And here she was, lying in his arms, with the tears running down her cheeks. He was aware, for the first time in his life, of a queer pang of jealousy. It was disturbing, strange, that Katherine, his beloved wife, so calm always, so patient and reserved, should weep like a little child for his dead brother, after all these years.

"It's that damned accident," he said, "it's been a shock to you. I wish to God it could have been avoided. . . . Katherine, darling, you do love me, don't you? More than anyone else, more than the children, more than Hal?"

The great supper up at the mines, the cheering and the clapping, the celebrations of the day, and the sudden horror of the accident on the way home, were all forgotten in his sudden longing for reassurance. If he doubted Katherine he doubted everything. There was no faith, no hope, no meaning in life at all.

"You do love me?" he said. "Don't you . . . don't you?"

4

Henry decided against taking a house for the season in London that year. For one thing, both doctors, the new man and old uncle Willie, said that it would be too much for Katherine. And the other reason was that Henry wished to superintend the work upon the castle. For his secret, announced to the family during the celebrations in March, was no more than this, that he had been in consultation with a well-known architect, who, at his request, had drawn up plans for an entire new front to the castle.

"How my father and all the aunts ever crammed into the rooms I cannot imagine," he said. "Aunt Eliza has told me that they never could invite people to stay in my grandfather's time."

He smiled down at his wife, unrolling the plan the architect had given him, as excited as a child with a new toy.

"Now admit, dearest," he said, "that this new wing, where you and I and our guests shall live, is really very imposing."

Katherine smiled, and took the plan in her hands.

"It's like a palace," she said. "What are we going to do with all those rooms?"

"Don't you think the idea of a grand entrance hall is rather fine?" he said eagerly. "I've always felt rather ashamed of our small hall, scarcely more than a passage, when I've been to Andriff and other places. What about this staircase? Magnificent, isn't it? Of course, I shall buy some really good pictures for the gallery. We'll go out to Florence and Rome next winter, and really spread ourselves. Now this is what will please you most. Look, the boudoir, all for you, between our bedroom and the spare room on the corner. And the little balcony leading from it, over the big front door. Here is my dressing-room, facing the woods. But tell me that you like the boudoir? It was my idea entirely."

Katherine lifted her hand and touched his cheek.

"Of course I like it," she said. "It's quite true, I've always wanted a little room of my own, where I can write my letters and not be disturbed."

"And you will have such a view," he said excitedly, "the best view in the castle, right away across the creek to Hungry Hill. You see, dear one, if you are not feeling strong your breakfast can be brought to you in the boudoir, and you will only have to walk through from your bedroom. These new rooms will have the sun the whole day long. At the moment we lose it, in winter, almost directly after luncheon. I dare say that is why you often look so pale."

He rolled the parchment back and drew forth another, more technical, showing the construction of the new roof and the chimneys.

"This won't interest you so much," he said, "but I like the way he introduces the little turrets and towers. They are like the pictures of the châteaux on the Loire."

Katherine watched him from her sofa. He was so eager, so impulsive. This rebuilding of the castle would fill his thoughts for the coming months to the exclusion of everything else. She was glad of it, for that reason only. It would mean he would not have the time to worry about her. . . .

"And how long is it all going to take?" she asked.

"Just under a year before everything is finished," he said. "It means workmen about the place for a long time, I'm afraid. You won't mind, will you? Or would you rather we went across and spent the summer with aunt Eliza in Lletharrog? The doctors couldn't object to that."

"No," said Katherine, "no, I don't want to leave Clonmere again."

Then the children came, and the plans had to be brought out once more.

"It will be like a real fairy-tale castle," said Molly, with all her father's enthusiasm. "Look, Kitty, you and I won't have to share a bedroom any more. We shall have mamma's present room as our schoolroom. And Miss Frost has father's dressing-room as a bedroom."

This struck them as highly amusing, and they went into peals of laughter.

"What room do I have?" asked Hal. "Can I have the room in the tower?"

"I was thinking of putting one of the servants there," said Henry, "but you are welcome to it, my lad, if you want it. I believe my father used to sleep there as a boy."

"I like it," said Hal; "it's the nicest room in the house. I shall do my painting up there. Why are we having a new day and night nursery? Now Kitty does lessons with Miss Frost she can eat with us in the school-room, can't she?"

Henry looked across at Katherine. Her head was bent over her needle-work.

"You might have another little sister or brother one day," she said.

"Oh," said Hal.

He was not particularly interested. At any rate, at ten a nurse would have no power over him; that was one good thing. He was too old for any nursery. He leant with his chin in his hands, poring over the new plans. Yes, the old room in the tower would suit him very well. He would find a key and lock himself in, so that Miss Frost could not come and find him. He would make paintings, really large ones, and pin them on the wall, as artists did. . . .

The workmen began on the foundations directly after Easter, and during the long, lovely summer of 1870 there was the ceaseless sound of hammering and knocking at Clonmere. Scaffolding hid the old house, and pillars, and girders. There were ladders everywhere, and heaps of stone and plaster. As the new block of the castle took shape it dwarfed the original building, which before had seemed square and stolid. The rooms lost the sun even sooner than before, because the new block jutted forward, taking all the sun that came.

"You can see," said Henry, "how much better we shall be in the new house. The rooms will be double the size, and so lofty. Already I feel cramped and restless in this old part of the house. I wish they would get on with the work faster."

The children were fascinated by the progress of the building. They chased one another in and out of the rooms that had as yet no ceilings, and only half a wall, while their governess Miss Frost searched for them in vain, only to discover Molly seated at the top of a high ladder, in imminent danger of breaking her neck, or Kitty, with face and hands covered in earth, crawling from the depths of the new cellars. Hal would watch the mixing of the cement, and dabble his hands in the wet mass of clay. And day after day Henry would walk down in the middle of the morning with the architect, who would come to Clonmere perhaps for a fortnight at a time to see how things were going, and the two men would discuss the great chimney that was inclined to spoil the appearance of the new block from the front, or the distance between two windows, or the exact height of the future front door, Henry with his head on one side and his hands in his pockets, the architect scribbling figures on a piece of paper.

Suddenly there would be too many people for Hal, and he would run up through the woods to the old summer-house, where his mother would be resting. She did not walk about much these days, she was always resting. She must have felt that he was there, because she turned her head and smiled at him.

"I rather thought there was a little boy looking at me," she said.

He came forward, and sat down on the chair beside her.

"I've made you a painting," he said, feeling in his pocket. "It's of the creek, on a very rough day."

He presented a grubby piece of paper, watching her eyes for approval with great anxiety.

It was the usual child's drawing, trees and creek all out of proportion, and the waves a nightmare size, while rain, like ink, fell from a thunder-cloud. There was something about it, though, that was not pure childish effort. One tree, bent in the wind, that had life, and the colour of the sky.

"Thank you," said Katherine. "I am very pleased with it."

"Is it good?" said Hal. "If it's not truly good I shall tear it up."

She looked at him, and took hold of his hand.

"It's quite good for your age," she said, "but you've chosen a difficult subject, one that even real artists would not find easy."

Hal bit his nails, and frowned at the picture.

"I like painting more than any other thing," he said, "but if I can't paint better than other people I'd rather not paint at all."

"That's a wrong way to think," said Katherine. "That way of thinking makes a person narrow, and envious, and unhappy. There will always be people in the world who will do things better than you do them. All you have to think about is to do the best you can."

"It's not that I mind what people say," said Hal, "but I want to have the feeling inside me that what I do is good. If I think it's bad it makes me miserable."

Katherine put her arm round him, and held him close.

"Go on making your drawings," she said, "and make them because you are happy to make them, good or bad. And then come and show them to me, darling, and we will discuss them together."

So the summer passed, and autumn came again, and by the New Year, the architect promised, the new wing would be habitable. Already the roof and the walls were built, and the floors were laid. The partitions between the rooms were under construction. The great stairway led from the big hall to the gallery above, and Henry, with Katherine on his arm, would point out the places where they would hang their pictures. The children ran along the corridors, calling to one another, their voices echoing to the lofty ceiling.

"You are going to like it, aren't you?" said Henry anxiously. "The whole thing has been planned for you, you know that, don't you?"

Again and again he would take her through the rooms, pointing out the excellence of the fireplace in the drawing-room, the useful size of the new library, where they could house all the books he had never had room for before. Best of all he liked to show her the boudoir, and the little balcony outside it.

"You can lie in your chair here in the summer," he said. "That is why I purposely ordered the long windows, so that the chair can be moved in and out. And in the winter you can sit here, by your fire. When I want you I shall come and stand below, and throw stones up at the window."

Katherine smiled, and, standing on the balcony, looked out across the creek to Hungry Hill.

"Yes," she said, "it's just what I have always wanted."

He put his arm round her, and they stood together, watching the workmen below.

"In the New Year, when you are up and about again," he said, "we will take three or four months abroad, in Italy and France, and we'll buy everything we fall in love with, furniture and pictures. I want a Botticelli Madonna for the head of the staircase, and there's another fellow, Filippo Lippi, who painted a Madonna exactly like you. It hung above an old altar in a church in Florence, do you remember, we saw it together, the year after Hal was born? We might have nothing but primitives in the gallery, and then, if you fancy them, you shall have your moderns in your boudoir."

"I'm afraid Henry is going to spend a vast amount of money."

"Henry wants his home to be as beautiful as his wife. I must have the best there is of everything, for my wife, for my house, for my children. Perfection or nothing. No middle course."

"Very dangerous," smiled Katherine, "and only leads to disillusion. Hal has the same idea, I'm afraid, and he will suffer many disappointments because of it."

In the middle of December Henry had to be away in Slane for four days, for the Assizes, and on the third day, on returning to his hotel from the court-house, he found Tom Callaghan waiting for him in the lounge.

"What's the Rector of Doonhaven doing in Slane?" he asked, with a laugh. "You've not come to be a witness in the case of assault, have you? Come and have some dinner."

"No, thanks, old fellow. I've come to bring you home."

"What's the matter?" He seized hold of Tom's arm. "Is it Katherine?"

"She had a bit of a chill yesterday morning," said Tom, "and rather foolishly got up, and walked in the garden with the children. By the evening it was worse, and Miss Frost called in the doctor. At any rate, he seems to think the baby is on the way, and asked me to come along and collect you. If you're ready, I suggest we go immediately."

His manner was calm and reassuring. Good old Tom, thought Henry; what a stand-by he was at all times! The best friend in the world. He had got the man at the hotel to collect his luggage; it was waiting strapped in the hall. He scribbled a note making his excuses to his fellow magistrates on the bench, and they left the city.

"The children have been spending the day at Heathmount," said Tom, "helping to make jam in the kitchen. All in a delightful mess and very happy. We've arranged for them to spend the night, or two or three nights, if necessary."

"I don't suppose the business will be long, if you say it has already started," said Henry. "Kitty was not long coming into the world, as far as I can remember."

"It does not always follow, old boy," said Tom; "that was six or seven years ago, and Katherine hasn't been too fit since, has she? Still, this young doctor seems a capable fellow. Old Armstrong insists on being present too, by the way. More from affection for you all than anything else."

"Well, he brought all of us into the world," said Henry. "He probably knows a thing or two about it by this time."

It was nearly eleven o'clock when they arrived home at Clonmere. Uncle Willie Armstrong had heard the sound of the carriage, and was standing waiting for them on the steps.

"Glad to see you, Henry," he said, in his usual gruff, abrupt manner. "Young McKay is with Katherine now. Nothing much happened since you left, Rector. You had both better have a drink. We can't any of us do anything to hurry this child into the world."

He led the way into the dining-room.

"I shall go up and see Katherine," said Henry, but old Armstrong took him by the shoulder.

"Much better not," he said; "she'd far rather see you when it's all over. They've laid some cold supper for you here. You'd better eat it."

Henry found himself surprisingly hungry. Cold beef and pickles. Apricot tart.

"Come on, Tom," he said, "my wife's having this baby, not yours. Don't look so solemn."

He began to tell them an amusing incident that had happened in court during the afternoon. They listened and smiled, not saying much. Old Doctor Armstrong puffed away at his pipe. Presently Doctor McKay came into the room.

"Well?" said Henry, "how is she?"

"Rather tired," said the doctor. "It's being something of an ordeal for her, but she is very patient. I wonder . . ." he glanced across at Armstrong, "I wonder if you would care to come upstairs with me?"

The old doctor rose from his chair without a word and followed him out of the room.

"You would think," said Henry, "that by this time someone would have invented an easier way for these things to happen. Why can't the damn fellows do something? She can't suffer all this pain for hours on end." He began pacing up and down the room. "My mother had all five of us and never winked an eyelid," he said. "She used to sit up and do embroidery five minutes afterwards, and give all the servants notice."

He stopped and listened a moment, and then went on walking again.

"Uncle Willie looks at me all the time with a resigned 'I told you so' expression in his eye," he said impatiently. "I remember his telling me only last year that Katherine should never have any more children. . . . He had an idea she had got something twisted inside. Katherine never said anything. She has seemed quite happy about it all. Women are so strange. . . ." He hesitated on one foot, looking at the door. "Shall I go upstairs?" he said.

"I don't think I would, if I were you," said Tom gently.

"I can't go on standing here," said Henry. "I think I shall go through and walk round the new house."

He lifted a small lamp, and passed through the door in the dining-room that led into the new corridor between the two wings. There was a smell of paint and varnish. The workmen were busy this week on the panelling in the new dining-room. He held the lamp above his head and went through into the great hall. It looked very massive, very bare. The light shone down from the vast skylight in the roof. The place seemed ghostly, grey, and the wide staircase leading to the gallery yawned like a gulf.

"It will be all right," he thought, "when we have it furnished. A big fire in the open hearth, chairs, sofas, tables, and Katherine's piano in the corner here."

He wandered about the empty rooms, his footsteps making a hollow sound. Once he stumbled against a ladder and some pots of paint. There was a little heap of cement in a corner of the drawing-room. The room struck very cold, and air blew in, dank and chill. He turned and went up the great stairs to the gallery above. The children had been playing there. One of them had left a skipping-rope trailing from the top of the stairs. He wandered through his new dressing-room to the bedroom. The paint smell clung about him still. He wished the room could have been finished in time for Katherine to have had her baby there. Then she could have been carried through to the boudoir and spent her days on the sofa, returning to the bedroom at night. He stood on the threshold of the boudoir. Even now, bare and empty, there was something snug about it, a foretaste of the future. Perhaps because they had planned so much of it together. He turned the handle of the long window, and stepped out on to the balcony. A little wind blew towards him from the sea. He could hear the tide ripple in the creek below. His lamp flickered and went out.

He had to grope his way back in the darkness, through the dark, silent rooms, along the gallery, down the great stairs to the hall. There were shadows everywhere, and the caps and overalls of the workmen, hanging just inside an open door, were like the dangling bodies of men. He tried to picture the new wing as it would be, finished and complete, the carpets on the stairs, the pictures on the walls, the fires burning, and for the first time the image forsook him, his imagination failed. He tried to see Katherine sitting in the corner of the hall, pouring out tea, with the children beside her, the dogs lying on the floor, and himself coming in from shooting, with old Tom perhaps, and Herbert, and Edward, and Katherine glancing up smiling. And he could not see her. He could not see any of them. There was nothing but this vast, unfinished, empty hall.

"Henry," said a voice, "Henry. . . ."

Tom came searching for him from the old house, peering through the darkness.

"Armstrong came down for you," he said, "he wants to speak to you."

Henry followed him, blinking in the sudden light. The door between the two wings closed behind him with a clang. He could hear the sound of it echoing through the new wing that had been shut away.

"What's happened?" he said. "Is it over yet?"

Old Armstrong watched him from under shaggy brows. He seemed old and tired.

"A daughter," he said, "not very strong, I'm afraid. She'll need a lot of looking after. Katherine is very weak. You had better go up."

Henry glanced from one to the other, his friend, and the friend of his father.

"Yes," he said, "yes, I'll go to her."

He ran swiftly up the stairs and met the young doctor McKay coming along the passage.

"Don't stay long," the doctor said, "she's very tired. I want her to sleep. . . . I think," he added, "that I shall stay here, and not go home tonight."

Henry looked into his eyes.

"What do you mean?" he said. "Isn't everything going to be all right?"

The young doctor watched him steadily.

"Your wife is not strong, Mr Brodrick," he said. "This has been a very great strain upon her. If she sleeps, all may be well, but I cannot promise. I think it right that you should know this."

Henry did not answer. He went on looking at the doctor's eyes.

"Armstrong told you about the little girl?" the doctor said. "I'm afraid she's malformed, one foot not quite straight, and rather underweight, but otherwise all right. There's no reason why she should not be as healthy as the others in time. Now perhaps you will go in to Mrs Brodrick?"

The familiar new-born baby cry rang in his ear, taking him back to those other times, to the birth of Molly at East Grove. How proud and anxious and excited he had been. And Kitty's in London. The nurse was in a corner, murmuring to the new little one. She brought the baby out of the cot and showed the child to him.

"Such a pity about the foot," she whispered. "We aren't going to say anything about it to Mrs Brodrick."

Henry heard her in a dream. He did not know what she was saying. He went over and knelt beside the bed, taking Katherine's hand and kissing the fingers. She opened her eyes and touched his head. He did not say anything. He went on kissing the fingers. The nurse took the baby out of the room, and the fitful cry disappeared along the passage. Henry tried to pray, but no words came to his lips. There was nothing he could say, nothing he could ask. Her hands were so cold, he wanted to warm them. This seemed to him more important than anything else, that he should warm her hands. He kissed them again and again, and held them against his cheek, and then inside his vest, against his heart.

She smiled then.

"I can feel your heart," she said; "it's throbbing, like an engine in a ship."

"Are you warmer?" he asked.

"Yes," she said. "I would like to leave my hand there always."

He went on kneeling there, and presently, about six in the morning, the workmen came walking along the drive below the castle, whistling and talking, the gravel scrunching under their boots. Somebody went and told them to go away.

<h1 style="text-align:center">5</h1>

It was Tom Callaghan who did everything. He took all responsibility upon his shoulders. He kept the children at Heathmount, out of Henry's way. Then Herbert came over, and took them back with him to Lletharrog, the nurse and the baby as well as the older children and their governess. It was Tom who remembered about Ardmore, and he remembered too the hymns that Katherine had loved best, and her favourite flowers. Henry saw and heard nothing. The only thing for which he gave orders himself was to stop building on the house. He spoke to the men himself. He was quite calm, and knew what to say. He gave every one of them a sum of money, and shook hands with each, and thanked them. And they took away the bricks and the cement, and the ladders, and all the paraphernalia of building, and did not return. The architect went back to England, leaving the roll of plans with Henry. He put them away in his desk and locked it. He never looked at them again. He went down to Heathmount and stayed with Tom, and then, after a few weeks, he became restless. It was no use, he said, every part of Doonhaven held a memory that gave him no peace. He would have to go away. He would let Clonmere, perhaps for a number of years.

"I don't think I should do that," said Tom gently. "You must remember the children. It's their home, and they are devoted to it. Molly is twelve now, Hal ten, and Kitty seven. It's an age when children feel things. Let them keep their home. Memories to children are precious, and not bitter. You must always remember that."

"They will have to come alone then," said Henry. "I can't live there. There's no meaning in anything. Life is finished, that's all there is to it."

"I know, old fellow," said Tom. "But if you would try to accept it, surrender to it, you would find the pain easier to bear. It's only going to add to suffering if you build up resentment against it. And that is what you are doing now, dear boy, it is indeed."

"I build up resentment against nothing and no one," said Henry, "except myself. You see, Tom, I killed her. That is something that I can never forget, or forgive. I killed her."

"No, Henry, you must not think that. Katherine was not strong. I have talked about it all to McKay, and to Armstrong too. She had not been well for years, there were definite signs of internal disorder that could never have been cured."

"You are being kind to me, Tom, but it's no use. This last baby should never have been born. I knew it. And I would not let myself think about it because I loved her so much. . . . Very well. We won't talk about these things again. Anyway, we shan't have the chance. I'm going away."

"Yes, Henry, I think you should go away, for a little while. But don't forget this place is your home, and the home of your children. And we are always here when you want us."

"You're my greatest friend, Tom. Sometimes I think the only true friend I've ever had."

"Where will you go, old fellow? What will you do?"

"I don't know. I have no plans. I want to go somewhere where I shall not be reminded of her every second of the day."

Tom tried to reason with him, but Henry would not listen. No argument, no gentleness, no patience, nothing did any good. Already the harsh lines of sorrow began to show on his face. The warm, care-free smile, that when it came lit up his eyes and the whole of his expression, was a thing of the past. When Henry smiled now it had a twist in it that was bitterness concealed.

"Don't you see," said Tom, in a final attempt to break down the great wall of bitterness, "that every day you are taking yourself farther from Katherine, instead of drawing nearer to her? She will be with you all the time, if you will only forgive yourself and open your heart."

"Of course I see," said Henry, despair in his face, spreading out his hands in futility. "She has been dead now nearly two months; she belongs to the past, the past that can never be recovered. There is no other argument. I can't open my heart. I have none. She took it with her when she died."

"No, Henry."

"Yes, Tom. . . . Yes. . . ."

Henry left Doonhaven in the middle of February, and went to London. He stayed there for a few weeks, and then travelled abroad. He went to Italy and Greece. France was at war with Russia, and he was unable to visit his mother. She preferred to stay in the south, she wrote, and risk the consequences, rather than return at the present time. Conditions were difficult though; she wanted more money. . . . He wrote her a large cheque. It did not seem to matter any more. Her extravagance failed to worry him. If she wanted to take the money and throw it down the nearest sewer she could do it, if it gave her any pleasure. Good luck to her for snatching what trivial happiness she could find. He wished that he could be equally successful. Italy and Greece proved a distraction. He met people he had not met before, and they helped, because they knew nothing of his life. He found that if he lunched or dined with comparative strangers and talked a lot it prevented him from thinking about Katherine. He went back to London in May and bought a house in Lancaster Gate, and when he had settled down, and made some sort of routine for himself, lunching and dining out frequently, and seeing many friends, old and new, he sent for the children. It seemed to him that he could bear them again, and to have them about the house would make another distraction.

The bustle of their arrival made a strange excitement. The two cabs driving to the front-door, and Herbert, bless him, getting out with the usual twinkle in his eye and a broad smile on his face. There was Molly, grown in a few months beyond recognition, and Kitty, very leggy, with two front teeth missing, and Hal, rather white in the face and serious, looking up at him with large eyes. Miss Frost and a pile of luggage, the nurse and the baby Lizette. Molly threw her arms round his neck.

"Father darling, I am so glad to see you."

And Kitty and Hal also thrust themselves against him, eager and anxious. It made a warmth, a queer glow for which he was unprepared, and then everybody was talking at once, and wanting to see the rooms. The house, that had been silent and a little dreary, was enveloped. The children with their youth and vitality took possession. They ran upstairs to see the schoolroom, with all the curiosity of youth, their feet stamping overhead, and Herbert and Henry sat down in the drawing-room to tea.

"They're such dears," said Herbert, "all three of them, and the baby too. We are going to miss them sadly. But how are you? You're looking much better than I expected you would."

"I'm very well," said Henry; "London suits me, you know, always did."

He plunged into an account of his travels and the people he had met, and for the first time in his life Herbert saw in Henry a likeness to their mother. Like her he chatted of trivialities, being amusing for the sake of being amusing, exaggerating often, skimming over the surface of things because it was easier than finding the depths. Herbert wanted to know what was really in his brother's heart, if he suffered less—he had exchanged many letters with Tom Callaghan on the subject—but every time he tried to sound him Henry evaded the issue, and talked about something else. Henry was building a defence about himself that would be hard to penetrate. Perhaps the children would draw him out of this, bring back the old Henry with his true charm, his unselfishness, his unaffected gaiety.

Herbert left after tea, so that Henry could be alone with the children, and they came down about six o'clock, washed and changed, carrying books under their arms as they had always done at Clonmere. It made a pain at once, that they should so instinctively remember their routine, and he began to question them about Lletharrog and all they had done —anything rather than that Molly should sit down, as she used to do, with Hal and Kitty on footstools, and open the book. They chatted for a while politely, like small visitors, and then Molly, leaning against his arm, said:

"Would you read, father? Like mamma used to do. Then it will be just like being at home again."

And she settled herself on the arm of his chair, with easy confidence, while a smile of anticipation lit up the eager, white face of Hal. Henry took up the book and cleared his throat, hardly seeing the print, feeling inadequate, helpless, a sham before his children. The story was one that he remembered Katherine reading to them very often at Clonmere, and as he read, not taking in the words or the meaning, he wondered how it was that the very familiarity of the proceeding, the memory of the words, did not tear their hearts with pain, as it did his. The old ways, the old routine, which to him were now agony and unendurable, were something to which they clung for security. He wanted to lose the memory of that world; they wished to hold it.

He read for two or three pages, and then he could bear it no longer It seemed to him a mockery of the time that was gone. The children might live in the world of what-used-to-be; they must live in it alone.

"I'm afraid I'm not very good at reading aloud," he said, "my throat gets sore. You'll have to do it instead, Molly."

"That won't be the same," said Hal quickly. "Molly is only our sister. She can read to us in the schoolroom."

"Perhaps father would rather play a game," said Kitty. "We have Happy Families. I know where it is, on the top of the toy-trunk."

She ran away upstairs to fetch the cards. Hal busied himself carrying a table into the middle of the room.

"I wish we had a piano," said Molly. "I've been learning while we stayed with uncle Herbert. I shan't be able to practise here without one."

"I'll get you one," said Henry.

"When we go home, Molly can play on mamma's piano," said Hal. "It was so very soft. Uncle Herbert's piano banged a bit. How long are we going to be in this house? Until the summer holidays?"

Henry got up from his chair, and moved restlessly towards the mantelpiece.

"We shall be here indefinitely," he said. "You must all learn to look upon this house as home, now you are getting old. You'll be going to school, Hal, next term. I'm not certain about the holidays. Perhaps we might all go and stay with aunt Eliza in Saunby."

The children stared at him aghast. Kitty, who had returned with the cards, stood on one leg, biting the end of her hair.

"Aren't we ever going home to Clonmere again?" she said.

Henry avoided their eyes. He did not know what to say.

"Yes, of course . . . some time," he said, "but it's let at the moment; I thought perhaps they would have told you at Lletharrog. Some people called Boles, friends of uncle Bill and aunt Fanny, are living there."

The children went on looking at him without understanding.

"Other people?" said Hal. "Living in our home? Using our things? They won't touch mamma's piano, will they?"

"No," said Henry, "no, I'm sure they won't."

"How long are they going to be there?" asked Molly.

Each one of them looked shaken and distressed. He had not realised that they were so fond of their home. He thought that children liked change, enjoyed variety. He began to feel irritated. They were staring at him as though he were in some way to blame.

"I don't know," he said, "it depends upon their plans."

He had not the courage to tell them that Clonmere had been let to the Boles for seven years.

"There are many advantages in London," he said, smiling, and talking rather swiftly. "You two girls will be able to go to dancing classes, and music lessons, and all that sort of thing. And meet other children. Hal must learn to find his level with other boys, before he goes to Eton. All your uncles agreed with me that London was much the best place for education. There will be plenty for you all to do. And I promise you that I'll give you whatever you want." He felt as though he were pleading with them, that they were his judges. Why should he feel this? They were only children, Molly not yet thirteen. "I want to do what is best for all of you," he said. "I think, I'm certain in fact, that this is what mamma would have wished."

The children did not say anything. Kitty slowly shuffled the pack of

Happy Families. Hal drew imaginary lines on the table. Molly reached for the pack of cards from Kitty and handed them to Henry.

"Will you deal, father?" she said.

They drew their chairs to the table, and as he dealt out the cards he could feel the constraint amongst them. The pleasure was gone and they were strangers, being polite to one another for courtesy's sake.

"I've hurt them," thought Henry. "I've broken their faith in some way. And there's no one to tell me what to say, what to do."

He could feel their eyes upon him as he pretended to examine his cards. . . .

"They'll forget all about it," he told himself; "children accustom themselves to everything. That's the blessing of being a child."

And as the months passed Henry felt this to be true, because none of them even mentioned the idea of going home again. They were content, he decided, and because he wanted to believe this, he never questioned them, for fear that they should tell him they were unhappy. The months become one, two years, and except for occasional visits to Saunby and Lletharrog they did not leave the house in London.

The girls attended classes, Hal went to school, the little Lizette learnt to talk and to walk, limping on her poor club foot that could not be straightened. Henry, restless, uncertain, feeling that his children needed a deeper understanding than he could give them, evaded responsibility by giving them presents; while in his heart all the while there was a feeling that what he did and what he gave them brought them no closer to him.

When a letter came to him from his mother in the spring of '74, condoling with him on the death of aunt Eliza at Saunby and asking for a rather larger cheque than usual, Henry determined, quite suddenly, to go out to Nice and stay with her.

He had not seen her for nearly seven years. Perhaps, at last, he would be able to persuade her to return and live with them. The truth was that he was lonely, in mind and body and soul, and Molly at fifteen was still too young to be a true companion. The thought of his mother's gaiety, her wit and her charm, seemed all the more endearing after an absence of seven years. Surely she, more than anyone in the world, would understand this feeling of unbearable loneliness, that became worse, not easier, as the years passed?

He went to France the day after he had seen Hal safely off to his first half at Eton.

The air was brilliant in Nice and the sun shone. He called a porter, and collecting his baggage went in search of a fiacre to drive him to the villa.

No attempt on his mother's part to meet him at the station. She had probably forgotten the day of his arrival. It was pleasant driving along the wide promenade, watching the people. The driver turned away from the sea-front and drove up behind the town, threading his way through a network of little, narrow roads. Once or twice he had to ask his way.

They came at last to the Rue des Lilas (in which there were no lilacs), and stopped in front of a small, shabby villa that badly needed a coat of paint. The gate was half off the hinges. When Henry opened it a bell jangled shrilly, and two dogs set up a chorus of barking from inside the house. No one came to the door, however. The driver put down the luggage on the step, and waited.

Henry went round to the back of the villa. The door was also closed, and the dogs went on barking from inside the house. Henry returned to the front.

"Nobody about," he told the driver.

He became aware that a woman was watching him from a window of the villa next door. He turned his back, and once more wrestled with the handle of the front door. It was the right house, for looking through the glass pane of the door he could see the sitting-room, and a photograph of Johnnie on the mantelpiece. Then a voice called:

"Try under the loose tile—you may find the key there."

The woman from next door was standing on her verandah. She was about forty-six, rather handsome, with steel-grey hair and strikingly blue eyes. She was obviously amused at the situation.

"Thank you," said Henry, taking off his hat. "I don't appear to be expected."

He bent down, and found the key under the tile. He held it up for the woman to see. She laughed, and shrugged her shoulders.

"I thought it would either be there or in the flower-bed," she said. "Mrs Brodrick is usually a bit casual about her hiding-places."

Henry thanked her again, and paying off the driver he took his luggage inside the villa. The dogs came out of the sitting-room, sniffing at his heels. The room smelt of them. It was stuffy, the windows were all shut. There was a saucer of food for them in one corner, and biscuit spilt upon the floor. Dead flowers were stuffed into cracked vases. The chairs and sofas were creased and stained where the dogs had been lying. On a table was a cup that had held coffee, the dregs were in it still. One of his mother's shoes lay beside it, and the other had been kicked under a chair. A wood fire in the grate had not been cleared. Henry left the room and went into the dining-room. This was obviously never used. His mother had her meals on a tray in the sitting-room. The kitchen was full of crockery that had not been washed, and there were vegetables, uncooked, crammed into a coal bucket. He went upstairs and found his mother's bedroom. Her clothes were littered about the room, and the bed had not been made. There was a tray of breakfast things still lying on the end of the bed. Across the passage was a spare-room, intended no doubt for him. There were clean sheets and blankets folded on the bed, but the bed was not made up. He went downstairs and stood looking out on the neglected garden, feeling sick at heart, and filled with depression. Somehow he had not expected it to be like this. He had made a different picture in his mind. The Englishwoman was still on her verandah, watering some flowers in a pot. Her house looked neat and clean, different altogether from this shabby, sordid villa of his mother's. The woman heard his step, and glanced over her shoulder.

"Found everything you want?" she called cheerfully.

Henry suddenly decided to take her into his confidence.

"Look here," he said, walking towards the verandah, "do you know my mother?"

The woman hesitated a moment, and peeled off her gardening gloves.

"We smile and say good-morning, and chat over the hedge," she admitted, "but I've never been inside the villa. Mrs Brodrick is nearly always out, as a matter of fact. I suppose you are her son? You're so exactly like her."

She stared at him with frank curiosity, and smiled again.

"My name is Price," she said, holding down a hand over the hedge, "Adeline Price. You may have heard of my husband, General Price, in the Indian Army. He died three years ago, and I've been living down here. Listen. Can I do anything? Make you some tea or something? It's so very cheerless to arrive at an empty house."

"I wish," said Henry, "that you would just come in and have a look at this place. Yes, I am Henry Brodrick. My mother must know I'm coming, because I found my letter open on her desk."

Mrs Price came down from her verandah and through the front gate.

"There is a maid who comes two or three times a week," she said. "I've seen her go to the back door. A slovenly creature. I wouldn't have her for a servant if you paid me. I suppose this is one of the days that she hasn't come."

They walked through into the villa. Henry watched her face. She was looking at everything with her critical blue eyes, from the dead flowers to the dirty coffee cup.

"H'm," she said, "bit of a pig-sty, isn't it? Reminds me of some of our married quarters out in India. Those women didn't need telling twice, I can tell you. They were more scared of me than they were of my husband. Let's have a look at the rest. You know, Mr Brodrick, the place hasn't been touched for weeks. I've never seen anything so disgraceful, not even out in India, and that's saying plenty. Excuse me for being so downright, but is your mother awfully badly off? Can't she afford to pay a decent servant?"

The steel-blue eyes held his, and would not waver. Henry shrugged his shoulders.

"No," he said shortly, "my mother has everything she wants. I can't understand it. This is all very disturbing."

Mrs Price led the way back into the sitting-room. She glanced at the photograph of Johnnie on the mantelpiece. She ran her finger on the frame, and showed it to Henry, black with dust.

"I suppose," she said, "that Mrs Brodrick is just one of those people who don't care. I'm afraid I just can't understand the attitude. Now listen to me. You're coming next door to have tea with me, and I shall send my little maid over here to give the place a thorough clean. No, don't interrupt, please. She'll be delighted to do it, and I shall be delighted to have a visitor to tea. Come along, and don't think any more about this. I'll make my excuses to Mrs Brodrick when she comes in."

Henry followed her into the villa next door, protesting politely, saying that she must not dream of going to such trouble. Mrs Price waved his protests away. He was not to argue. He was to sit down and have his tea. He laughed.

"I think you ought to have been a General yourself," he said.

"That's what everyone used to tell me," she said. "Now, you relax in this arm-chair, and put your feet on the stool, and try some of my guava jelly. My tea I can recommend, it's packed specially for me and sent from Darjeeling. I always boil the water myself. No servant can ever make tea."

It was very pleasing to sit back and be waited upon in this way, thought Henry, and she was right, the tea was excellent, and so was the guava jelly. The room was clean and tidy. There were papers and magazines from England lying on the table. What a contrast to the villa next door!

He began to talk, telling this Mrs Price about himself, about his children. There was something so sane and encouraging about her brisk, cheerful manner. She was amusing too, her shrewd comments showed her to be no fool.

"Of course you're put upon, all the time," she said; "don't tell me. People always take advantage of a man on his own. And you give way. Anything for a peaceful life, that's a man all over."

"I admit I don't lay down the law very often," he laughed, "and when I do Molly puts up an argument in self-defence. That's the family temperament though. The Brodricks enjoy discussions."

"I wouldn't let a girl of fifteen dictate to me," said Mrs Price. "I've no doubt you've spoilt her, and the others too. A good thing the boy has gone to Eton. They'll soon knock the nonsense out of him there. Pity you go on keeping the governess for the girls. I always think it's a mistake to carry on too long with old retainers. They take advantage so, and have absolutely no control over the children."

"Miss Frost has been with us for years," said Henry. "I think Molly and Kitty could not bear to part with her."

"Because they can do what they like with her, that's why. I believe you're a sentimentalist, and you hide it under that gay, cynical manner of yours."

She looked across at him and smiled. Those blue eyes were certainly very penetrating.

"I've talked too much about myself," he said, glancing at his watch,
"and it's nearly seven o'clock. No sign of my mother. What about dining
with me in Nice, and telling me about yourself instead?"

Mrs Price blushed, and seemed suddenly ten years younger. Henry was
amused. She had probably not dined out since her husband died.

"Please do," he said. "It would give me such pleasure."

She went up to change, and came down in twenty minutes in a black
dress and fur cape that made a fine background to her grey hair. She
looked very well indeed. Henry had also changed, returning to his
mother's villa to do so. The place had been swept and left spotless by
Mrs Price's maid, his room cleaned and the bed made up. He was filled
with gratitude.

"Thank heaven she was looking out of that window," he thought.
"But for her I believe I should have caught the next train home."

They walked to the corner of the avenue and hailed a fiacre, and drove
down to dinner at one of the large hotels on the front.

"This is such a treat," she said. "I live so quietly these days. And in
India there was so much entertaining. I've missed all that more than
anything else."

"You ought to come to London," he said, "not bury yourself down
here."

She rubbed finger and thumb together, and glanced at him expressively

"A soldier's widow's pension isn't a large one, Mr Brodrick." she said.
"My income goes farther here than it would do in England. . . . Look
at that minx over there. Why do French women put so much paint on
their faces?"

"Because they are not naturally so handsome as you Englishwomen,"
said Henry gallantly. "Come on, I'm going to order you the best dinner
that Nice can provide."

It was fun, he decided, to dine opposite this woman, who was undeni
ably attractive and amusing, and enjoyed her food and her wine, and
made such an agreeable companion. The restaurant was filled with
people, and a band played in one corner, light classical stuff he knew
and liked. He had not enjoyed himself so much for years.

"This is a great deal better," he said, "than sitting down to an
egg and some of those vegetables from the coal-bucket at my mother's
villa."

"Don't put me off my food," said Mrs Price, with a mock shudder
"My maid has already told me what she found in the larder, but I shall
spare you."

After they had drunk their coffee, and listened a while to the music
Henry suggested a visit to the casino.

"We may as well be real dogs while we are about it," he said.

The night was warm and still. He hummed a bar from Rigoletto, and
helped Mrs Price into a fiacre.

"You know," he said, "when I stood in front of that villa this afternoon my spirits went down to zero. It really was a miserable moment."

"I know," she said; "you poor thing. I felt so sorry. And how are the spirits now?"

"Higher than they've been for months, for years," he said, "for which my very grateful thanks."

She blushed again, and laughed, turning the subject. There were many people in the casino, and they had to walk slowly amongst the crowd, pushing their way from room to room. The bright unshaded lights made a glare, and there was something monotonous in the flat voice of the croupier, the click of the little ball on the table for roulette. They watched some of the play, peering over the shoulders of the people in front of them. The atmosphere was stifling.

"Couldn't stick very much of this," said Henry to his companion. "What a waste of time, eh, day after day?"

"Appalling," she agreed. "I should have a splitting head in an hour." They moved away into the next room. Two men coming out were laughing together.

"But she's always like that," one of them was saying: "has a flaming row with the croupier whenever she loses. They say she's lived here for years."

"Do they ever throw her out?"

"I believe so, when she gets too excited."

As Henry and Mrs Price drew near to the table they saw that many of the people were laughing, and several at the back were pushing those in front to get a clearer view. The croupier was arguing with someone, talking in broken English, and a woman was trying to shout him down, first in French and then in English.

"But, Madame," the croupier was saying, "do you want me to call a gendarme? I cannot have these constant interruptions."

The woman was talking at the top of her voice.

"It's an outrage, the whole place ought to be broken up," she said. "The management are taking my money through trickery. I've caught you at it, time and time again. In my country they'd shoot you in the back for it, and a damned good riddance too. I'll show you up; I have influence at home, I know people in Parliament, my cousin is the Earl of Mundy. . . ."

There was a shout of laughter as she threw her muff and her gloves at the croupier's head. A man in uniform came to her, and seized her arm.

"Let me go," she cried; "how dare you touch me?"

The shiny velvet cape, the cloud of white hair, the arrogant tilt of the head, all were familiar. As the commissionaire thrust Fanny-Rosa forward she stumbled, scattering her bag, her chips, her few coins, on the ground in front of her.

"You clumsy fool," she shouted. "What the devil do you think you're doing?"

And she came face to face with her son.

For a moment they stood staring at one another. Then Henry turned to the commissionaire.

"This lady is my mother," he said. "I will be responsible for her."

The man let go of Fanny-Rosa's arm. The crowd around the table was whispering and staring. The croupier shrugged his shoulders, and set the ball in action again. "*Faites vos jeux.*" The game went on.

Henry bent down and picked up the bag and the coins from the floor, and gave them to his mother.

"It's all right," he said quietly, "don't worry. Mrs Price and I are going to take you home."

She did not seem to realise what had happened.

"But I don't want to go home yet," she said, glancing from one to the other. "I haven't tried my luck at the other tables. It will be different if we go into another room."

"No," said Henry, "it's getting late. And I've had a long journey today. I want my bed."

He took his mother's arm and began walking towards the door. She kept looking back over her shoulder towards the table.

"I always detest that particular croupier," she said. "I'm sure he has a secret understanding with the management, and they have some means of controlling the ball. I wish you'd write to the papers about it, Henry. You're so clever, you would know what to say."

She never ceased talking all the way to the casino steps, abusing the management, telling Henry and Mrs Price that she was certain the casino staff had been given their orders to prevent her winning. They were so afraid that once her luck was in she would break the bank.

"It's nearly happened several times," she said, as they drove away in the fiacre. "I've had the most amazing run of luck, simply couldn't make a mistake, and then suddenly the whole thing would go against me. O course it's done deliberately. They are terrified of anyone making a big win. But I'm determined to beat them. It's a matter of principle. Henry darling, how lovely to see you! So stupid of me to forget the time of your train. I hope you found everything all right? I hadn't realised you knew Mrs Price. We must all three go to the casino tomorrow and try our luck. Mrs Price has a lucky face, I expect we shall make a fortune."

She rattled on, asking questions and never waiting for a reply.

Henry stared out of the window, holding his mother's hand. Mrs Price did not say anything. He knew now in bitterness and sorrow the story of the last ten years. He could see the life that had been hers, the pretended gaiety, the shabby flag of courage she had flaunted. And day by day, month by month, year by year, this thing taking its hold upon her, so that now she was possessed body and soul, mind and reason gone, nothing remaining but a queer patchwork of memories that served no purpose but to distract her more. Whose fault? Why had it happened? Who was to blame? No answer came to him, and his heart was torn with pity and anguish. The fiacre drew up in front of the villa. Fanny-Rosa fumbled with the gate. The dogs set up their barking from inside the house.

"All right, sweets," called Fanny-Rosa, "mother is coming, and your brother Henry too."

She began to walk up the garden path. Henry turned to Adeline Price.

"I'm so sorry," he began, "so terribly sorry. . . ."

"Oh, please don't apologise," she said; "much more of a shock for you than for me. If there's anything I can do in the morning don't hesitate to come round. Personally, I feel the right thing to do would be to get her into a Home. She'd be well looked after, you know. What I mean to say is, she can't very well go on like this, can she?"

"No," said Henry, "no."

"Well, you'd better go to bed and get a good night's rest, and think it over in the morning. Anyway, I enjoyed our dinner. Goodnight."

She turned away to her own villa. Henry walked slowly up the path. He found Fanny-Rosa kneeling on the floor, playing with the dogs.

"Did the silly boys miss their old mother then?" she was saying. "But mother left a nicey dins for the boys, and the dins has been taken away. That damn-fool of a servant, I suppose. And I always tell her not to tidy the sitting-room. Henry lamb, you look worried. Is anything the matter."

"No, darling, but I want you to go to bed."

"I'm going. I always have to kiss the boys goodnight, though. Did the servant make up your bed? I laid out the clean sheets, but I have a frightful feeling I forgot to air them."

"Yes, everything was all right."

She stood in the doorway of her room. Mrs Price's maid had swept and tidied here, as well as downstairs. The clothes were put away, the bed was turned back neatly. His mother did not seem to notice that any-thing had been done. She was staring in front of her, biting the end of her nail. Henry wondered if some flash of memory had come to disturb her wandering mind, she looked suddenly so lost and strange. He put his arms round her, and held her close.

"Mother darling," he said, "will you tell me what's the matter?"

She smiled up at him, and patted his cheek.

"Dear Henry," she said, "always so thoughtful about everyone. No, I was just thinking what an extraordinary thing it was that not once this evening did the nine come up. But not once. And I backed it every time."

6

He sat in Adeline Price's drawing-room, turning over the pages of a magazine from India. The pictures coveyed nothing and the words even less. He glanced at the clock on the mantelpiece. Surely she should be back by now? The appointment was for three o'clock. He got up and began walking about the room. The maid came in and laid the tea. Fresh-cut bread and butter. Water-cress. Home-made scones. A new pot of guava jelly. And last of all the shining silver kettle. He heard a fiacre drive along the road. He glanced out of the window, and saw Adeline Price step out and pay the driver. The tip she gave him was not enough, apparently, for he began to grumble.

"It's all you're going to have, my good man," she said cheerfully. "Don't you try to work that sort of game on me. You've met your match."

She waved her hand to Henry, and hurried up the garden path.

"They're all the same," she said; "they think we're made of money because we're English. Is tea in?"

"Yes," he said.

She came into the room, peeling off her gloves. She was dressed in grey simple and yet striking. She looked very handsome.

"Well, it's all most satisfactory," she said; "the doctor was an extremely nice man, and understood the situation perfectly. Of course he's had dozens of these cases through his hands. There's no cure, he said. Especially in someone your mother's age. He agreed that you are doing absolutely the right thing."

She lit a match and put it to the wick. The kettle began to simmer. Adelaine Price reached for a piece of bread-and-butter, frowning at the water-cress.

"Why did she bring that?" she said. "She knows I don't touch it. It's never safe in France. You mustn't have any either. These girls need watching all the time."

"Go on about the place. What was it like?" said Henry.

"Oh, very nice. A large garden, with flowers and trees. I saw some of the people sitting about. And I chose a most comfortable room for her, as you said no expense was to be spared. It was twenty francs more than the rest, but I suppose you don't mind that?"

"God, no."

"Of course they won't let her mess it up as she did her room in the villa," said Mrs Price. "They have to have certain rules, and that is one of them. You can't blame them. The place was so beautifully clean and tidy, you could eat your food off the floor. The nurses wear a nice green uniform, which gives a very bright effect. I was introduced to the one who is in charge of your mother's room. A sensible creature, with a nice expression."

"Did she seem to understand—why my mother was going?"

"Oh, yes. And one thing which is rather clever in a way is that she will be allowed to play roulette, if she wants to. They have a room for that sort of thing. Only of course it will all be pretence, no money or anything. She won't know. These modern methods are very ingenious."

Henry got up from his chair, and wandered once more to the window. "Don't you want your tea?" she said.

"How can one tell that she won't know?" he said. "It's not as though she is completely insane. She will know that the thing is a blind. And that she's shut up there, in a glorified prison."

Mrs Price was pouring out the tea.

"She'll be told the place is a hotel," she said, "a kind of annexe of the casino. It's quite all right. I arranged it all with the doctor. He is going to say that you were worried about her being all alone at the villa, and have arranged for her to go there instead. He says she will settle down as happily as anything, after a few days."

Henry picked up a book restlessly, and threw it down again.

"If only I could be certain I'm doing the right thing," he said. "She seemed happy enough in that little villa, even if it was dirty and unattractive. And I don't grudge her the money she lost at the casino. If it kept her happy, if it kept her from thinking. . . ."

Adeline Price blew out the flame from underneath the kettle.

"Of course if that's your attitude, there's no sense in sending her there," she said; "but after what you have been through the last ten days I should have thought you would have learnt reason. Do you want them to throw her out of the casino, as they did five days ago? And then, she's not responsible for what she says. Those awful lies. She told you she was going to bed last Tuesday, and we found she had gone down there again. Of course if you want her to end in the police-court that's your affair. Because that's how it will end, I don't mind telling you."

Henry flung himself down in the chair once more.

"You're right," he said, "I know you're right. And yet it hurts so terribly to do this thing. Oh, God, my mother. She was so lovely, so amusing, such a darling. I can't begin to explain what I feel."

Adeline Price poured out his tea.

"Come on," she said, "have a cup of tea. Nothing like a cup of tea to make a person feel better, man or woman. I can assure you that your mother will be perfectly happy in this place. She'll make friends, and chatter about the past, and you can go home with the knowledge that she s in good hands and that everything possible is being done for her. Oh, they asked me if you wanted her to have a little wine in the evenings? Apparently that's an extra, and so is a fire in the bedroom on cold nights. I said I would let them know. They'll send you an account of course every month, or you can pay direct through your bank. That would save you a lot of bother."

She spread some of the guava jelly on to her bread and butter.

"You've taken so much trouble over all this," said Henry, watching her. "I tell you frankly, I don't know what I should have done without your help. The whole thing has been a nightmare."

Adeline Price smiled.

"Men are helpless creatures in a crisis," she said. "My husband was just the same. Unable to cope with an emergency. Directly I saw you struggling with the front door of the villa the day you arrived I could tell the sort of person you were. I'm glad I happened to be looking out of my window. But it rather beats me how you've struggled along these last few years without anyone to look after you."

"I don't know," said Henry. "I suppose I drifted. All I know is that I felt damned lonely."

"I've been lonely too," she said, "but in a different sort of way. And anyway I always found plenty to do. I've never been one of those people to mope, thank goodness. I always think it shows such a lack of character." She collected the tea-things on the tray, and rang the bell for the maid. "Now I hope you don't think I've taken too much on my shoulders," she said, "but the doctor agreed with me that the sooner we got your mother moved into the Home the better. I quite realise it's a painful business for you to face, so I'm perfectly willing to take her there myself. I'm more or less a stranger, so there will be no emotional complication. So, if you agree, I'll go across to the villa now, help her with the few odds and ends she will want with her there, and take her along in a fiacre. I can explain about the hotel idea, the annexe of the casino, and you will see I shall have no fuss with her at all. I shall say you had to go out, but will go round and see if she's comfortable in the morning. Don't you think that's the best way of arranging it all?"

She smiled at him again, capable, efficient, and he was aware of a sense of helplessness, of utter dependence upon her judgement.

"I don't know," he said in despair; "I seem to have lost grip. I can't make a decision without questioning it five seconds later."

"Don't worry," she said, "leave it to me. And I suggest you go along now and order dinner at the restaurant. I'll join you there after I've taken her to the Home. It will take your mind off this business."

She gave him his hat and his stick and pushed him out of the room.

"You're as bad as a child," she said; "I don't believe you trust me at all."

"I do trust you," he protested, "I have implicit faith in everything you do."

"Go on then," she said, "and don't look so crushed."

He walked along the road mechanically, and down the twisting streets and avenues to the sea-front. It was like a dream, the houses were phantom things, the people were shadows. Nice was a city that he did not know, alien and unfriendly. It seemed to him that this shock of his mother's weakness had shown to him, in ugliness and force, that his own life was also without foundation. There was no security any more. Nothing was sure or solid. Even the children back in London lacked reality. They were like little ghosts who had drifted with him through the years. Nothing had been real or living since he had left Clonmere and turned the key upon the past. As he heard the flat sea break on the dull beach he thought of the swift tide in the creek at home, and the surf running upon Doon Island. He remembered the soft winds and the pale sun, and the white clouds above the top of Hungry Hill. He thought of the little churchyard at Ardmore, and the robin who sang in winter. And all that was finished and done with, he had no part in it, he did not belong there any more.

He went and sat in the lounge in one of the big hotels and waited for Adeline Price. He waited one hour, two hours, and she did not come. Finally he could stand it no longer; he went outside and jumped into a fiacre, and ordered the driver to take him to the Home. It was dark now, and he could not see much, except the endless avenues, and the trees. The sea kept breaking on the shore in the distance. The frogs set up their nightly croaking. The wind was cold.

The fiacre drove past a high wall and came to a great gate. It was shut. The driver rang the bell, and presently a concierge looked through the narrow grille.

"It's prison," thought Henry. "I don't care what they say, it's prison."

After a few minutes the concierge opened the gates. The fiacre drove up a long, winding avenue, closely shut by tall trees. They came at last to the building. Few lights showed. The curtains were drawn for the night. Another fiacre was waiting outside the front door. Henry recognised the driver. He was one of the men who kept his vehicle in the little square near his mother's villa. Henry got out and enquired if Mrs Price and Mrs Brodrick had gone inside the building. The man said they had beem there for over an hour. He said something about extra time, and he hoped he was going to be paid for it. Henry gave him ten francs at once, and the man pocketed them, muttering to himself. Henry went and rang the bell of the front-door. It was opened by a man in a white coat.

"My name is Brodrick," said Henry. "I'm the son of Mrs Brodrick who arrived here this evening."

"Oh, yes, number 34," said the man, in good English. "If you'll come to the reception room, I'll make enquiries for you. Do you want to see your mother?"

"If you please," said Henry. "And there was a lady with her, Mrs Price. Perhaps she could come down and speak to me?"

The man showed Henry into a large room on the right of the entrance. It was comfortably furnished, with chairs, and tables, and books. There was nobody in it. As he waited a loud bell clanged for dinner. Through the half-open door he could hear people file along the corridor to the dining-room. He caught a glimpse of a green uniform, and the white cap of a nurse. A little old man was walking with the aid of crutches.

"Come on, Mr Vines, don't be all day about it," said someone sharply. Other people were talking. Someone laughed in a high, silly way. The footsteps and the voices died away, and a door shut in the distance. Henry went on waiting. Then a man in a grey frock-coat, with a monocle hanging down the front on a black cord, came through the door and held out his hand.

"I am Doctor Wells," he said. "I am afraid my superior is dining in Nice, but I am in charge here for the evening. You are Mrs Brodrick's son, I understand. We've had just a little difficulty, but nothing for you to worry about. Your friend Mrs Price has been so sensible."

"What do you mean, difficulty?" said Henry.

"Mrs Brodrick was a trifle bewildered on arrival. Very natural. They often are, you know. But your friend is with her, and the nurse on duty is an excellent woman. We thought it better she should have her supper upstairs the first evening, and then she will be able to go into the dining-room tomorrow. I think Mrs Price is coming down now."

He turned towards the door as Adeline Price came into the room. She seemed quite unruffled and composed, as though nothing had disturbed her.

"It's all right," she said, "she's quite quiet now. I've left her showing photographs to the nurse. And such a nice dinner has gone up to her on a tray. Well cooked, well served. I must say you look after them well, doctor."

Doctor Wells smiled, and toyed with his monocle.

"The little things are so important," he said.

Adeline Price was staring at Henry.

"Why did you come?" she said reproachfully. "I thought I told you to go and wait for me at the hotel?"

The doctor smiled.

"No doubt Mr Brodrick was anxious," he said smoothly, "and perhaps as he is here it would be more satisfactory if he just popped his head round the door and said goodnight to his mother. He would know then that she was quite comfortable."

"Yes, I should like to do that," said Henry.

Adeline Price frowned.

"Is it wise?" she said. "Wouldn't it upset her?"

"I don't think so," said the doctor; "it might be just the right touch. Of course we shall give her a small sleeping draught, as it's her first evening and everything will seem a little strange."

"I'll wait for you in the fiacre," said Adeline Price abruptly. "No point in my going up there again."

She swung out of the room, a tall, confident figure in her grey coat and gown. Henry followed the doctor upstairs. The corridors were of shiny wood, scrubbed clean, and carpetless. The walls were green, like the uniforms of the nurses. A young nurse at the top of the stairs smiled at him. She looked kindly, sympathetic. Henry clung to this like a straw.

"Are many of the nurses young?" he asked. "That one who passed, will she have much to do for my mother?"

"The matron would tell you that better than I could," said the doctor. "I can make enquiries for you, of course. Number 34. This is your mother's room."

He tapped on the door. It was opened by a stout, middle-aged nurse in glasses.

"What is it?" she said sharply. "Oh, it's you, doctor; I'm sorry. Will you come in?"

Doctor Wells murmured in her ear.

"Mr Brodrick," he said, "just come to say goodnight to his mother. He won't stay more than a few minutes."

"All right," said the nurse, "but I want to get her washed and settled down for the night as soon as possible. We're short-handed this evening."

"It's only eight o'clock," said Henry. "My mother's been used to staying up until midnight or after."

The nurse began to speak, but the doctor cut her short. "It's only for tonight," he said. "Tomorrow she will be with the others, leading quite a normal life."

Henry went into the room. It was green like the corridor, but had a large window, and there were coloured mats upon the floor. The curtains were yellow, with green flowers upon them. The room was smaller than he had imagined. There was one easy chair in the corner. His mother was sitting up in bed, counting some money in her bag. She did not see him come in. She was scattering coins over the bed-clothes, and talking to herself. Her hair hung in a cloud over her shoulders, silver white. Suddenly she saw him, and held out her arms.

"My darling," she said; "they told me you had gone away, that I couldn't see you."

He bent over the bed, and took her hand.

"I thought I would just come along and say goodnight," he said.

She nodded her head, and then winked, pointing to the door.

"Such extraordinary people," she whispered. "I think they're all mad. The maid, I'm sure she's a nurse, insisted on taking my temperature. I suppose it's one of these new hydros I've heard about, but I never heard that the casino had anything to do with one before. Mrs Price says I can go to the roulette rooms in the morning."

"Yes, dear."

"Is it all going to be very expensive? You know what a fool I am about money."

"No, darling. I'm arranging for that."

"Dear boy, so good to me always. But I should have been quite all right at the villa, you know. There was no need for you to fuss." She tumbled her coins back into her bag. "Mrs Price says they have a queer system here," she said. "They give you so many chips, and you don't have to give up your money in exchange. Sounds crazy to me. What about the boys, Henry darling? Will somebody remember to feed the boys?"

"What boys?"

"The dogs, sweetheart. They'll miss me so, they won't understand why I don't come back. A week will seem a long time."

Henry did not say anything. He stood there, holding his mother's hand.

"Put Johnnie's photograph on the mantelpiece," she said suddenly, "so that it faces me. Yes, that's better. He always looked so sulky in uniform, and so lovable. . . . Henry."

"Yes, mother."

"Take care of that boy of yours. I didn't take care of Johnnie." She was staring up at him, her green eyes wide and frightened. "I can't forget it, you know," she said; "that's why I go to the casino. One must do something. John was such a darling—your father, I mean. So gentle, so kind. He understood so much. I've been very lost without him, very lonely. You were all such little boys when he died. Sometimes I think it would have been better if I'd married again." Then she smiled, she ran her fingers through her hair. "What an idiot I am!" she said, "raving on like an old lunatic. I tell you what, Henry. I'm damned if I'm going to let these people get my money, even if their system is a new one. I'll show them how to play roulette. They won't get the better of me here as they did at the casino."

The nurse came in, and stood by the bed.

"Now, Mrs Brodrick," she said, "we've got to think about that big wash, haven't we?"

Fanny-Rosa winked at Henry.

"Such a fool!" she whispered; "treats one like a baby. What does it matter though, if it keeps her amused?"

Henry kissed the top of her head. He knew he would never see her again.

"Goodnight, darling, and sleep well," he said.

For a moment she clung to him, and then she laughed, and let him go.

"Life is so amusing," said Fanny-Rosa; "try not to look serious, Henry boy. Thinking never did anybody any good."

She followed him with her eyes as he went out of the room. . . .

The doctor was still waiting outside the door.

"You see," he said, "she is quite comfortable, quite settled. There is nothing whatever for you to worry about. And I understand Mrs Price has made certain arrangements for her extra comforts."

"Thank you," said Henry, "thank you . . . yes."

He shook hands with the man, he took his hat and stick. He climbed into the waiting fiacre. Adeline Price was sitting in the corner.

"I paid the other one," she said. "It seemed pointless to keep the two. Well, did she seem all right?"

"Yes," he said, "yes, I think so."

The driver whipped up his horse. They drove away down the long dark avenue.

"You must be very tired," said Henry.

"Not a bit. I want my dinner, though. I expect you do too."

The fiacre turned out of the avenue into the road. The heavy gate clanged behind them.

"I was wondering, while I sat waiting," said Adeline Price, "whether there is anything else I can do for you. What are your plans?"

Henry turned to her in the darkness.

"Plans?" he said wearily. "I have none. What plans should I possibly have?"

The horse trotted down the cobbled stones. The driver cracked his whip. In the distance the sea broke upon the shore. He thought of the long train journey, the sea crossing, the house in Lancaster Gate, and Molly, and Kitty, and Hal, and the poor little lame Lizette. He felt very lonely, very tired.

"I suppose," he said slowly, "you wouldn't care to marry me, would you?"

BOOK FIVE

HAL, 1874–1895

I

THE BEST part about Eton, thought Hal, was that they left you alone. You could scrape along through your day, doing a minimum of work, and nobody bothered very much whether you lived or died. There were numberless rules and regulations, of course, and certain hours when you had to be in certain places, but in spite of these things there was a freedom that made for contentment. He could walk about alone, and no one would ask him what he was doing or where he was going. And he had a room to himself. That, perhaps, was the best of all. One or two of his own pictures hung upon the wall, signed with his initials in the corner, H. E. L. B. One of the fellows asked who had painted them, and he lied instantly, saying they had been painted by an uncle who had died. Somehow, he did not feel the paintings were good enough to acknowledge as his own. But when he was in the room alone, at night, he would take his candle and look at them closely with secret pride. They were his creation, the things he had made with his hands, and because he had made them himself he loved them. One day he would make paintings which he could show to everyone, but until that day came it was best to conceal what he did, in case people laughed and did not understand. Mamma had never laughed. She had always understood. And now that she was not with him any more he wanted his father to take her place, so that whatever he achieved might be an offering to him, a pride and a delight. And he would have the certainty of never failing because his father would have faith in him. The trouble was that he felt shy of his father. They might sit in the drawing-room of the London house together and neither speak a word, father reading the *Times*, and Hal staring at his boots. And when his father did speak it would be in a jovial, hearty manner, the manner grown-up people so often assumed to boys in the same way that they did to dogs. It was like the way a person patted a dog's coat and said "Good fellow", and then forgot him the moment afterwards. Sometimes his father would say, "Well, Hal, how's the painting?", making an effort to be interested, but because the effort was obvious and the question a hopeless one to answer, Hal would say, "All right, thank you", and then fall once more to silence, feeling gauche and dull. His father would wait a few minutes, expecting Hal to enlarge upon the subject, and then when nothing happened he would pick up his paper again, or talk about something else to the girls.

The mid-term break, or long leave as they called it, came early in March, and would coincide with his father's return from France. He had been away from England nearly two months.

"Father's coming home tonight," said Molly, who with Miss Frost, and Kitty, and the small Lizette, met Hal at the station, "and he's bringing someone with him, but he won't say who. All very mysterious. Even Miss Frost doesn't know. I think it's Grannie, but Frostie says it can't be, as father said in his last letter that she was ill."

"Whoever it is must be very important," said Kitty, "because he or she is to have the large room next to father's. I wish it could be uncle Tom or aunt Harriet. It's such ages since we saw them last."

"At any rate, I hope the creature won't stay long," said Molly, "as we shall have to make polite conversation at lunch and dinner. Hal, you have grown. You will have to wear tails. And you're thinner than ever."

"It's because I haven't got Frostie to make me swallow apple dumplings," smiled Hal. "No one at Eton bothers whether you eat."

"Perhaps not, but I don't suppose you hide the dumplings in your mouth and spit them out in the passage afterwards, as you do at home," said Miss Frost. "You have to behave yourself at Eton."

"Indeed I don't. I do exactly as I please," said Hal.

When they arrived at Lancaster Gate he paid for the cab in lordly fashion, although Miss Frost had the money ready in her purse.

"Nonsense, Frostie," he said. "I'm not a child any longer."

And he shouldered his suit-case and took it upstairs, aware, now that he was back again, that seven weeks at Eton had changed him in some indescribable fashion. He felt older, more responsible, and the girls too looked at him with new eyes, as though he had become someone of importance. They followed him to his room when he unpacked, little Lizette dragging one foot after the other. He had painted the head of a cat for her, which she seized with shrieks of delight, and there were sketches too for Molly and Kitty, one of his house, and one of the river.

"Have you done anything for father?" asked Molly.

Hal hesitated a moment, and then took a small parcel from the bottom of the suit-case.

"You know the photograph I have of mamma's portrait?" he said. The girls nodded.

"Well, I borrowed a magnifying glass from one of the fellows, and I've made a miniature from the head," he said. "Of course, it's not a patch on the original painting, but it's better than nothing."

He unwrapped the paper and handed a small round frame to his sisters.

"I found the frame in a shop in Eton," he said, "and it just fitted."

Katherine's face looked upon her daughters; the dark hair, with the low knot in the nape of her neck, the grave, quiet eyes.

"You see," said Hal, "I've often thought how dreadful it must be for father having the portrait at Clonmere, and never seeing it. If he has this it might make up for it in a small way."

The girls considered it in silence.

"It's very good," said Molly; "it's better than the photograph you have."

"Do you really think so?" said Hal. "Will he be pleased?"

"I wish it were mine," said Kitty. "I only have a wretched photograph, that I don't like a bit."

"Let me see mamma," said Lizette, and Molly took her on her knee and showed her the miniature.

"It's dreadful that she never knew mamma," said Kitty. "It's like being told about someone in a story that isn't really true. Put it down, Lizette; you mustn't spoil it. Can we show it to Frostie?"

"No," said Hal suddenly, "no, let's shut it up again. I don't know whether I shall give it to father or not."

The miniature, now that he had looked at it again, had become more intimate, more personal, something very precious that he did not want people to touch.

They all had lunch upstairs in the schoolroom, and in the afternoon went to Madame Tussaud's exhibition, going to the Marylebone Road in an omnibus, and returning home in time for tea.

"We'll have tea in the dining-room," said Molly, "and give father a real welcome. It's a nuisance about the visitor, but it can't be helped."

"I think," said Miss Frost, "I will have mine upstairs with nurse and Lizette. Your father will want you to himself."

"Oh, Frostie, you're a coward," laughed Hal, "you don't want to put on company manners before a stranger. Don't be afraid, I'll look after you."

But Miss Frost was firm. And at five o'clock Molly, Hal, and Kitty assembled by themselves in the drawing-room. Hal kept fingering the little parcel in his pocket. He could not make up his mind whether to give it to his father or not. He felt nervous and excited in turn. He wished that he too could be having tea upstairs with Frostie, Lizette, and the nurse. His father would question him about Eton, in front of this visitor, and he knew he would make the wrong sort of answers.

"Here's the brougham," said Kitty, who had been gazing out of the window, "and a cab following as well, simply heaped with trunks. Surely father only took one and his hold-all, when he went to stay with Grannie?"

"They must belong to the visitor," said Molly, looking over her shoulder. "Where on earth shall we put them all? Hal, don't run away. And do try to speak at tea, and don't look as if you have toothache. . . . Father darling."

She flung open the front door and ran down the steps to greet him, followed by Kitty. Hal hung back, his hands in his pockets. He was not sure whether his father would kiss him or not, now that he was at Eton. A smart-looking woman was getting out of the brougham, and shaking hands with the girls. She had a black hat with wings in it. A stranger, no one that they knew. His heart sank a little. Somehow he had hoped that it might have been uncle Tom from Doonhaven. . . . He came forward slowly, smiling at his father, and without thinking held up his face to be kissed.

"Where are your manners?" said Henry, seizing him by the shoulders, and turning him round. "Don't you know the rule ladies first? This is Hal, Adeline. You need a hair-cut, old boy. One of you send the servants to deal with this luggage. We both of us want our tea."

They turned and went up the steps, the visitor talking briskly to his father. She seemed to know him very well. Hal made a face at Kitty behind his back. More than ever he wished he was having tea in the schoolroom. There was much talk and bustle and argument about the luggage. The visitor pointed to the things that she wanted upstairs.

"The rest can go in the box-room," she was saying. "I shan't need the two large trunks, they're full of summer things."

The housemaid, rather red in the face, was bending over a hold-all packed with walking-sticks and umbrellas.

"I'll show you everything after tea," said Henry, "and if there's anything you don't like we'll have it changed. What about you children? Are you having tea upstairs?"

"No," said Molly swiftly, "we've got it in the dining-room, with you. The silver tea-set and everything."

Henry laughed, and glanced across at the visitor.

"Very appropriate welcome," he said. "Come and sit down."

The visitor was glancing at the pictures on the wall in a critical way.

"You didn't tell me you admired the Italian primitives, Henry," she said. "Those languid madonnas. I can't bear 'em. They always look as if they need a plate of roast beef and a jolly good walk, to put some life into them."

Henry laughed. He seemed to laugh at whatever the visitor said. And to the astonishment of all of them the visitor went and sat in Molly's place at the end of the table, in front of the silver tea-set.

Molly went scarlet, and Hal turned away because it hurt him to see his sister distressed. He knew how she had looked forward to pouring out and playing hostess. He sat down and stared hard at his plate. His father did not seem to notice that anything was wrong, and the visitor began to pour out the tea.

"Well, what have you all been doing?" said Henry. "French, German, dancing-classes, music, all the usual things? You wouldn't believe, Adeline, what I spend on these girls' education."

"Let's hope they will make use of it," said the visitor, and turning to Kitty she asked her a question in French.

Now it was Kitty's turn to be embarrassed. She flashed a glance of appeal at Molly.

"I'm sorry," she said, "but I don't understand."

The visitor laughed.

"I thought you told me they were fluent," she said to Henry. "I'm afraid you were boasting. Are you going to pass me a scone, Hal, or do you want to eat them all yourself?"

Her eyes were bright and blue, and she smiled, showing white teeth. Hal mumbled an apology, and pushed the plate across the table.

"Dreaming as usual," said his father. "I tell you what it is, Adeline, the boy is studying your face, in order to paint your portrait. I've told you he was the artistic member of the family."

Hal felt the colour mount into his face. It was coming, the conversation he dreaded, baiting him with questions.

"I had a brother who painted as a small boy," said the visitor, "but he forgot all about it when he went to school. You don't have much time for that sort of thing at Eton, do you, Hal?"

"Yes, he does," said Kitty impulsively; "he's done two lovely pictures for Molly and me, and something very special for father."

"Has he, by gosh?" said Henry. "Come on, Hal, what is it?"

"It's nothing," said Hal, "it's not good enough. I don't think you'd like it."

Nervously he jerked his tea-cup, and the tea spilt over the table-cloth, spreading over the white surface.

"Quick, a plate, Molly," said the visitor, "or it will stain the mahogany. Call one of the servants for a cloth. What a mess! If you want to be an artist, Hal, you'll have to have a steadier hand than that."

Hal stood awkwardly, not knowing what to do, hating her and hating his own clumsiness.

"All right, sit down," said his father impatiently. "Don't stand gaping, like a dazed sheep. Tell me about Eton. Who are your friends?"

"I haven't any," said Hal desperately.

"Oh, come," said Henry, "you must know some of the fellows in the house."

At last Hal admitted that there was someone called Brown he rather liked.

"Brown? What Brown? I don't remember anyone of that name in my time. What does he do? What are his games?"

"I don't think he does anything."

"Sounds an interesting fellow," said Henry. "Come on, tell us some more."

The visitor was laughing, and winking at his father across the table.

Hal dug his nails into his hands. It was no use. He would not answer any more questions.

"I'm afraid my family are not showing off as well as I hoped," said Henry. "Molly looks sulky, Kitty can't speak a word of French, and my son and heir spills his tea all over the table-cloth and can give no account of his first half at Eton except that he admires a boy named Brown who possesses no accomplishments. Adeline, I grovel. I take back all I told you in Nice."

The children stared at their plates. This jocular, joking manner of their father's was embarrassing. Why did he have to be so in with this person called Adeline, who stared at each one of them with critical blue eyes, and did not like the Italian pictures on the walls?

Then the door opened, and Lizette came into the room, changed into a white frock for the occasion, her hair tied with two white bows. She was shy. She stood by the door, a finger in her mouth.

"Well, baby, what's wrong? I shan't bite you," said the visitor.

Lizette looked at Kitty. Nobody in the house ever called her baby.

"She generally has a piece of sugar at tea-time," said Molly. "Come here, darling. Molly will give you one."

The child limped to the table. Hal saw the visitor gaze with curiosity at the heavy foot, in its high boot.

"She ought to do special exercises," she said to Henry. "I knew of someone who was lame from birth, and it worked wonders. But you have to keep at it. Special exercises, for an hour a day, supervised by a trained expert. I'll find out about it."

Lizette stared at the stranger, as she ate her sugar. She knew her foot was being discussed, and she did not like it.

"Will the lady go soon?" she said to Molly.

Everyone pretended not to hear. Molly bent down and whispered in her ear.

Hal, still staring at his plate, wondered if his father was looking at Lizette in the strange, regretful, half-shamefaced fashion that he sometimes did. Hal knew now that if Lizette had not been born his mother would not have died. But this was something that he did not care to think about. People having children was an uncomfortable subject, especially when it was to do with one's own father, one's own mother. . . .

The visitor was getting up, and pushing back her chair.

"Now what about inspecting the house?" she said briskly.

"Where do you want to start?" smiled Henry.

"The most important place of all, the kitchen," she answered.

Molly hesitated, and glanced at her father.

"I don't think they will have finished tea," she said; "we never do invade the basement at this time of day. I'm afraid Mrs Lester might not like it."

"Mrs Lester will have to put up with it," said Henry. "Go ahead,

Adeline, you take command from now on. I wash my hands of everything."

He laughed, as though it were a great joke.

"While you are in the kitchen I had better go and pay my respects to Miss Frost and the nurse, and break the news," he added.

He ran up the stairs whistling, and Molly and the visitor disappeared down the hall to the door leading to the basement. Hal and Kitty looked at each other across the dining-room table.

"What does he mean?" said Kitty. "What is he going to tell nurse and Miss Frost?"

"I don't know," said Hal. "It's queer."

"Perhaps we're all going home to Clonmere, and this person is going to take the house from us. That's why she has to be shown all over it, and to see the kitchen. Oh, Hal, how lovely! Do you think it could be so?"

"Perhaps," said Hal, "it might be. Perhaps we're all going back there for Easter, and the Boles are giving it up."

A wild hope surged in the heart of each of them. Kitty ran upstairs after her father. Hal went into the drawing-room. He pulled the miniature out of his pocket and looked at it once again. If they were going home he would be able to compare it with the original at Clonmere. What a fool he must have seemed at tea, jolting the tea-cup, and talking about that fellow Brown, whom he had gone for a walk with once, on a Sunday. Perhaps if he gave the miniature it would make up for it in some way. His father would know that there was something he could do, and it would show too that he knew his father was often lonely and unhappy without mamma.

He decided to make a secret of it, to put it somewhere where his father would find it at an odd moment. Hal went over to the desk and wrote on a piece of paper "Father—from his loving son, Hal," and taking the miniature out of his pocket he wrapped the paper round it, and put it just inside the desk. Then he went and sat down by the fire, and thought about going back home to Clonmere. Kitty must be right. That was the explanation of the whole business and why the Adeline person had brought so many trunks. Clonmere again, the room in the tower, the horses, the dogs, old Tim, the woods and the creek, uncle Tom and aunt Harriet. Life would fall into pattern again, even if mamma could not be with them. Life would have meaning. He would sail a boat in the creek. He would shoot hares on Doon Island. He would make a painting of Hungry Hill. . . .

Kitty came into the room, round-eyed, mysterious.

"Frostie's upset," she said. "What can father have said to her? And she's gone into the spare room to talk to that woman, with her tight-lipped face on, you know, the one she has when she's worried. Surely Frostie would want to go back home."

She broke off, as her father came into the room, followed by Molly, who was white and strained. Henry shut the door. He went and stood over by the fire-place. He too looked anxious. Perplexed also, as though he did not understand what was the matter with Molly.

"You must be sensible, dear girl," he was saying. "Why, it's for all your sakes, far more than for my own, that I have done this. Do you think it's been easy for me all these years?"

"We were happy as we were," said Molly, "we don't want anyone else."

She began to cry, like a little girl, not like someone of fifteen. Kitty ran over to her and stood beside her. Hal said nothing. He stared at his father.

"She's a wonderful woman," Henry said, "so efficient and so intelligent. The trouble is I've let things go to pieces for too long. You've all been allowed to do as you like—the servants, Miss Frost, and all of you. Now your stepmother will take a hand and put everything to rights. If you have any affection for me at all, you will be glad that this has happened. You'll soon become fond of her, I know you will. I can't tell you what she hasn't done for me already."

Stepmother. . . . Hal went on staring at his father.

"You and Kitty were not in the room when I told Molly," said Henry, feeling his son's eyes upon him. "I married Mrs Price in Nice a fortnight ago. She has been a wonderful friend to me. One day, when you are older, I may tell you all about it. In the meantime I ask you to give her a welcome, and to try to show her some sign of appreciation. Molly seems to have taken it badly, I don't quite know why. It does not mean I love her any the less."

Molly was still crying, biting and twisting the ends of her handkerchief. Her eyes were red and swollen.

"You'd better go upstairs," said Henry in despair. "If Adeline sees you like that she will wonder what on earth is the matter. My God, what a welcome home! I wish to heaven we had stayed out in Nice."

He began pacing up and down the room.

"Will she live here always?" said Kitty. "Is that why she brought all those trunks?"

"Of course she will live with us," said Henry impatiently. "She is Mrs Brodrick now. You can call her Adeline."

Molly ran out of the room. Hal could hear her rush up the stairs and slam her bedroom door. Kitty followed her. Hal felt sick. He did not say anything. He and his father were alone. From the room above came the sound of trunks being dragged across the floor and the low murmur of voices. The little gold clock on the mantelpiece ticked fast and rather shrill.

"It's for your good," repeated Henry, "you must try to realise that. The two girls need a woman of culture and breeding to look after them. Miss Frost is no earthly use. It's not quite the same for you, because you will be at Eton most of the time, but there are always the holidays. Besides, one wants companionship. When you are my age . . ."

He left the rest of his sentence in the air. What was he doing, appealing to his boy of fourteen for sympathy and understanding; who could not possibly know what he had endured these last years? The unprofitable days, the lonely nights, which now could be blotted out and forgotten.

"It's very hard for a parent," he said, "to be left alone with the responsibility of a young family on his shoulders. It happened to my mother. I believe now that she found it a great burden. Your uncles and I could not understand, naturally, and I have no doubt we were a trial to her."

Still Hal said nothing. He went on staring at his father with blank eyes.

Henry walked over to his desk, and opened it, and began looking through the pile of letters that had accumulated during his absence. He tore them open one by one, scarcely reading the contents. He could hear Adeline's brisk, firm tread in the bedroom above as she unpacked her things. There was a constant coming and going on the stairs as the servants carried up the remainder of the luggage. Suddenly a small package and a piece of paper caught his eye: "Father—from his loving son, Hal." He picked it up, and glanced across at the boy.

"Is this your present?" he said, summoning a smile. "Thank you very much, old fellow."

He began to unwrap the paper.

Hal did nothing. He made no effort to stop him. It was as though he could not move, could not speak. He stood in the middle of the room like a dumb thing, powerless to help, his heart aching with a strange anguish but imperfectly understood, his mind mocking, bitter, and a black devil whispering "Go on, open it, open it; damn you."

Henry held the miniature in his hands. The paper wrapping fell to the floor. Hal watched his face, but no change came upon it, save that his lips tightened, making two hard lines at the corners of his mouth. It seemed to Hal that eternity passed as his father looked upon the miniature. The clock went on ticking. A cab passed in the street outside. A piece of coal fell from the fire into the hearth and smouldered there. Then his father spoke, his voice sounding distant, coming from afar.

"It's very good," he said, "very capably done. Thank you." He opened a little drawer in his desk and put the miniature inside. Then he took a key from the bunch on his chain and locked the drawer. "You had better go up to Molly," he said. "See that she does something to her face before dinner. By the way, Adeline likes it punctually at half-past seven, so you must all be ready and changed five minutes before."

"Yes, father," said Hal.

He waited a moment, but Henry did not meet his eyes. He had turned away, and was staring at the fire. Hal left the room and climbed the stairs to the first floor. The spare bedroom door was open. There were

folds of tissue paper on a chair, and silver brushes on the dressing-table.
A strange black evening frock lay on the bed. Someone was drawing the
water in his father's bathroom. . . . Hal climbed slowly to the second
floor.

2

It was worse for the girls, of course. They had to suffer and endure the
changes, while he was at Eton. Molly and Kitty had to see poor Frostie
go, and have that vile Swiss maid take her place. Lizette had five
different nurses in nine months, because no one was supposed to treat her
foot correctly. Letter after letter would come from Molly, furious and
miserable in turn.

"We never see father alone," she would write. "She sticks to him like
glue, and if he gets up and goes out of the room she follows him. And at
meal-times she talks all the time through us to him, and looks daggers if
Kitty or I try to get in a word. And she's changed all the furniture round
in the drawing-room, and had new covers made, which Kitty and I think
are hideous, and I'm sure father does too, but he won't say so. He seems
unable to cope."

Father, who had always been so magnificent a person, so reliable, so
strong, was now, it seemed, a man of no account. The god had fallen
from his pedestal. He had no will, no mind of his own. Whatever
Adeline declared in her brisk, downright way, he echoed, not from
conviction, but because it was less troublesome. Once only did they come
down together to visit Hal at Eton, and the day was a miserable failure.
First of all she criticised his room, found fault with his appearance.

"Don't stoop so," she said, "you're positively round-shouldered.
Henry, this boy ought to have sat with a backboard for an hour every
day. And he's far too pale. He ought to go for a good run. Why don't
you join the beagles?"

"I don't want to," Hal answered.

"In the summer, of course, you'll be made to play cricket. Oh, but
you're a wet bob, aren't you? I suppose you chose that because it meant
less exertion. Boys are all alike. They need driving."

She spoke always in that bright, aggressive manner which was so
characteristic of everything she did, and which made argument impossible. Her blue eyes flitted up and down the walls of his room, seized
upon his pictures. Hal could see her mouth twitch in amusement.

"Studying for the Academy, I suppose?" she said. "That tree is a bit
out of drawing, isn't it? Not that I'm a judge of these things, but I do
know a crooked line when I see one." She laughed over her shoulder at
Henry. "If that's what your old Clonmere looks like, I'm not surprised
you let it," she said. "I'll be bound it was damp too, with all that water
so close. Well, Hal, what else have you got to show us?"

"Nothing," he said, "nothing at all."

"Not very prolific, are you? You'll never make your fortune. What about some lunch in Windsor? I'm starving."

And throughout the day it was the same; mocking, teasing, contrasting his lanky, overgrown figure with that of other boys of his own age.

"You seem to lack ambition," she said, "you have no interest in anything. Wouldn't you like to be Captain of the Cricket Eleven one day, or head of Pop, or whatever they call it?"

"Not particularly," said Hal.

"It's no use, Adeline," said his father. "I'm fated to have a son who is totally undistinguished. It's a pity, but there it is."

He spoke lightly, shrugging his shoulders, but his words stung. . . .

They went away on the five o'clock train, and his father gave him a sovereign.

"Your uncle Herbert has asked you all to Lletharrog in the summer," he said. "Adeline and I will probably go abroad."

He did not kiss him. The train steamed away, and Hal was left with the sovereign in his hand. They never came again.

Holidays at Lletharrog or at Saunby became a method of escape. The girls were so pathetically glad to get away from Lancaster Gate. Now that great-aunt Eliza was dead the house at Saunby belonged to uncle Herbert too. His family would move there from Lletharrog during the summer months.

"I wish we could stay with you always," said Kitty. "I never want to go back to Lancaster Gate again."

"Why, nonsense," smiled uncle Herbert. "I know how fond you are of your father."

"It's different now," said Kitty.

Uncle Herbert did not say anything. But later, when the girls and their brother were walking on the sands, Kitty said:

"I heard uncle Herbert call Adeline that 'damn woman' to aunt Cathie. They were in the study, and the door was open. I heard him say the whole thing was a tragedy. Fancy him saying damn, and he's a clergyman."

"No one likes her," said Molly fiercely. "If only I had the courage I'd run away and be a governess. She told father that poor little Lizette was sly, and that all crippled children had something wrong mentally. Lizette, who is so clever and sweet. It's queer, she dislikes Clonmere, although she has never been there. She's even taken down the picture of it that used to hang in the drawing-room. And whenever anyone talks about the country she makes a laughing, sarcastic remark."

"Just think," said Kitty. "Father has only gone across three times since mamma died, and then he stayed in a hotel in Slane and did his business from there. And when we lived at Clonmere he used to drive up to the mines every day. I don't understand how the mines go on without him."

"A running concern doesn't need the proprietor's supervision," said

Hal. "There's a chap at my tutor's whose father owns a coal mine, and he's never even seen the place. He just sits at home and rakes in the dividends. There's no point in working if you can get money for doing nothing."

"Mamma would have hated to hear you say that, Hal," said Molly. "It goes against all she used to teach us."

"I dare say it does," answered Hal, "but what's the use? No one ever talks to us in the way she did. And the fellows at Eton would think I was pi or a fool if I tried to keep it up. If we'd all been living at home at Clonmere it would be different. I dare say father and I would have gone up to the mines together, and I should have had a feeling for them, as though they were all bound up with the family. Now I don't care twopence. And anyway, there will always be loads of money coming from them, that's the main thing. I shall do myself well when I go up to Oxford, I don't mind telling you."

"Don't forget what uncle Herbert was telling us the other day about the copper trade falling to bits. Several mines in Cornwall have been closed," said Molly.

"Yes, but he also said the more enterprising ones had discovered tin beneath the copper, and would be able to work the tin instead. The price of tin is very high, and the proprietors can go on making fortunes over that."

"It may not be the same at home," said Molly. "Perhaps there isn't any tin on Hungry Hill."

"Tin or copper, what does it matter," said Kitty, "if all the benefit we get from the stuff is living in Lancaster Gate with Adeline, and a Swiss maid spying on us all the time, and father washing his hands of us? I'd rather be poverty-stricken and live in a cabin on the Kileen moors."

"Lancaster Gate and London would be all right if it wasn't for Adeline," said Molly. "We were happy enough when we were alone with father."

"No, we were not," said Hal. "None of us has ever been really happy since we left Clonmere, and you know it. Nothing has been the same since mamma died, and never will be."

His sisters stared at him. He looked white and strained, and there were tears in his eyes.

"Oh, what's the use of anything?" he said. "Sometimes I wish I was dead."

And he ran away from them across the Saunby sands, the dogs leaping and barking at his heels, the wind blowing his hair across his face.

"He's got to the difficult stage," said Molly; "boys always get like that. Aunt Cathie said Bob used to be the same."

"Bob had a home to go to," said Kitty. "Hal only has Lancaster Gate."

The problem of the holidays became more acute as the years passed. Henry's second wife made no secret of the fact that she disliked her stepchildren. There was no question of sharing Henry with his children. She wanted him for herself, and the only way to accomplish this was little by

little to wean him from them, make him believe that they cared nothing
for him, that none of his friends or relatives was worthy of him, and that
she alone understood his needs, his comforts. She had rescued him from
a life of wretched loneliness, and now he must cling to her only for
consolation.

It was exciting, at first, to be wanted with so much passion. It was a
novelty to Henry, who took full advantage of it, thinking he could atone
thus for the wasted years. He was roused and flattered. It was pleasing
to know that Adeline adored him, and while she adored him she was also
able to take all responsibilities upon her shoulders, run his house with
efficiency, deal with his children, tell him all the things that he wanted
to know, and keep from him what was better ignored. Marriage with
Adeline made life easy, he said to himself, made life comfortable and
soothing. If Molly and Kitty and Hal were difficult it was their fault, they
should be more adaptable. Anyway, they must go their own way. He did
not want to be worried about them. Adeline was right, they were an
ungrateful trio, thinking only of themselves. They did not realise what he
had been through. They did not understand that a man needed a wife in
his home, otherwise he went to pieces. If the children did not get on with
Adeline then they must go somewhere else for their holidays, to Herbert
or to Edward. They had nothing to complain of, because he always
insisted that they should have the best of everything. When it was a
question of Molly coming out, parties were arranged and dinners given,
and Edward and his wife came to London to take her about. Adeline
refused, quite rightly too, when Molly had always shown her so little
affection. Henry took Molly out once or twice, but somehow when he did
it seemed to make trouble with Adeline afterwards.

"I wish you would come too," said Henry. "Molly really did look very
charming at the ball the Goschens gave."

"No doubt she did, because I wasn't there," laughed Adeline. "Miss
Molly likes to have all the attention, and always did. I remember the
time she used to make eyes at the music-master."

"Oh, come . . ."

"My dear Henry, I'm not blind. Well, I suppose you are going out
again tonight? You prefer your daughter's company to your wife's."

"Of course I don't. If you'd rather I stayed. . . ."

"It's not a question of what I'd rather. You know I never think about
myself. No, if you enjoy spending a heated evening in a ballroom
watching your eldest daughter doing her best to snaffle a husband, you're
welcome. Personally, I shall go to bed early. I've had a wretched head
all day."

"Well then, I will stay. Edward can take Molly. I don't want to go."

After two or three similar episodes it was simpler to leave Molly in
Edward's hands altogether. The next difficulty was when Hal wrote
asking Henry to come down to the fourth of June. He was rowing stroke

in one of the senior boats, and he wanted his father there on the
occasion.

"Please come alone," he said, "or bring Molly and Kitty with you."
Henry feared that this would go badly with Adeline, and tried to hide
the letter from her on the breakfast-table. Her sharp eyes caught sight of
the Eton post-mark and Hal's writing.

"Well, what's your son got to say for himself?" she said. "Been getting
into trouble with the authorities?"

"He wonders if I'd take the girls down for the fourth. He's stroking
one of the boats."

"Doesn't ask me, I suppose."

"No, not actually. But I'm sure he'd be delighted to see you."

"My dear, don't pretend to me, I can't stand it. I wouldn't go to Eton
if I was asked. As a matter of fact I'd arranged luncheon here with the
Armitages and the Masons. I'd no idea you would want to go streaking
off to Eton. It's going to be very awkward having to entertain them on
my own. After all, they are your friends. But don't let me spoil your
plans, please. I don't know why Hal should suddenly express a wish to
have you down. I suppose he wants someone to show off before, as
rowing seems to be his one accomplishment, besides drinking."

"What the devil do you mean?"

"Oh, I'm sorry. I forgot you didn't see the photograph he sent Kitty.
I happened to see it on her dressing-table. He and some other boy had
a bet, it appears, as to who could drink down the most beer, out of a
monster tankard. Your son distinguished himself by winning, and had his
photograph taken doing it. Of course I always have thought him the
image of that photograph of your brother Johnnie, but never liked to say
so. You'll have to watch out. That sort of thing is hereditary, you know."
She laughed, and got up from the breakfast table. "Poor dear! what it
is to be a parent," she said. "At least I spare you most of it. I'm taking
Lizette to the masseuse this morning, and fetching Kitty from the dancing class this afternoon. If I were you I should write to Hal and congratulate him on his capacity for strong ale."

She swept out of the room for her morning seance with the cook.

Henry did not answer. He collected his letters and went into the
smoking-room. Hal like Johnnie. . . . No one had ever seen a likeness
between them. Or had they? And refrained from saying so because they
had regard for his feelings? Adeline was so often right in her judgement,
shrewd and clear-sighted. That sort of thing was hereditary. Johnnie,
and old grandfather Simon Flower. . . . It was nonsense, of course.
There was no resemblance between Johnnie's years of misery and young
Hal quaffing down tankards of ale for a wager. Henry drummed with his
fingers on the mantelpiece, looking at the picture of Clonmere that
Adeline had moved from the drawing-room to the smoking room. The
Boles did not want to renew their lease. What should he do with the

place? He could not live there again. That part of his life was finished
and done with. It hurt even to receive letters from old Tom these days.
But the mines continued to flourish, now that they had struck tin beneath
the old copper lodes. Hal like Johnnie. . . . He went upstairs to Kitty's
bedroom and the opened door, feeling curiously furtive. The room
was empty. Kitty was away at her morning class. He went over to
the dressing-table and picked up the photograph. Two schoolboys of
eighteen, laughing at one another. One of them holding a monster
tankard, as Adeline had said. What a big fellow Hal had grown! He
had not realised how the years had slipped by. And he saw so little of
him. The boy preferred going to Herbert at Lletharrog in the holidays
rather than coming home. Hal had always been considered like himself.
But that way of standing, one hand in his pocket, careless, rather arrogant,
the other holding the tankard, and the lift of the eyebrow—was not that
Johnnie? A flood of memories came rushing at him, and he put the photograph back upon the dressing-table. He went downstairs to the smoking-
room, and sitting at the desk pulled a piece of paper in front of him.

"My dear Hal, I am sorry I shan't be able to get down for the fourth,
but we have a luncheon arranged here for that day. I shall ask your uncle
Edward to go down instead, and no doubt Molly and Kitty will wish to
accompany him. . . ."

Hal shrugged his shoulders when he read the letter, and tearing it
across, threw it in his waste-paper basket. The woman had prevented
him, of course; he knew how it would be. All right, what the hell? If his
father did not want to see him row there was an end to it. Rowing
happened to be the one thing he could do decently, and he had hoped,
secretly, that his father would be proud of the fact. Apparently not. It
did not interest him. His last half at Eton, and his father had come down
to see him once in four years. The same thing would happen at Oxford.
An occasional letter, a fat cheque, and nothing else. Well, he was used to
it by now. It did not matter any more.

It was during Hal's second year at Oxford that Molly, on a visit to the
Eyres across the water, met and became engaged to Robert O'Brien
Spencer, J.P., a friend of her uncle Bill's.

"He is such a dear," she wrote to Hal, "and loves every inch of the
country, just as I do. And don't think I am doing this to get away from
Adeline, because it isn't true, whatever she may say to father. I am really
fond of Robert. But the glorious thing is this, we shall live only thirty
or forty miles away from Clonmere, and Robert is going to write and ask
father if we may go there for Christmas, home I mean, and give the
darling place an airing. Of course you must join us, and Kitty, and
Lizette."

Home, after ten years. And dear old Molly going and getting herself
engaged, to one of her own countrymen into the bargain. It was the
greatest excitement since he had been up at Oxford—even better than

rowing against Cambridge last spring. He must hold a celebration, give a
dinner-party to all his friends and get gloriously tight. His allowance was
running through his hands like water through a sieve, but it did not
matter a damn. The old mines could stand the racket. And he would
paint Molly's portrait and present it to the happy bridegroom with
compliments. Home for Christmas. . . .

Molly was married in November, and there was a glorious gathering of
the clans that even Adeline could not squash. She arranged the ceremony
of course, and did her best to damp the proceedings by insisting that the
house in Lancaster Gate was too small for the reception, and it must be
held in a hotel, that was big and dreary and lacked all personality. But
she could not take away the radiant look on Molly's face as she stood
receiving her guests in the centre of the room, and she could not stop the
whispered admiration for Kitty, the chief bridesmaid, who at seventeen
had lost her coltish look and was strikingly lovely, like her mother before
her. And though she did all she could to prevent it, she could not drag
Henry away before the stalwart bridegroom had persuaded him to allow
his family the occupation of Clonmere for Christmas.

"We've won," said Hal gleefully, rubbing his hands, "we've trounced
her at last. Don't look so scared, Lizette, she can't hear me. And I don't
care if she does. Kitty and I are going to take you back home, over the
water."

They set forth on the sixteenth of December, crossing to Slane and
going down by train to Mundy, where they found that the little paddle-
steamer was still running in spite of the lateness of the season, and it took
them across the twenty miles of bay to Doonhaven itself. The ten-
year-old Lizette stood by the rail, between her sister and brother, looking
upon it all for the first time, her pinched face losing its haunted expression, and the colour coming into her cheeks. The breeze was soft, from
the south-west, the sky was full of little fleecy clouds, and the hills were
green under the sun.

"There's Andriff Castle, where Grannie was born," said Hal, pointing
to the far distance. "We have cousins there, I expect Molly will ask
them over. They must be grown up by now, and you see that church,
standing in shadow, down by the water's edge—that's Ardmore, where
we used to go every Sunday. Mamma is buried there."

How tiny it looked. How wind-swept and alone. Had she lain there
all these ten years, with no one belonging to her? Did anyone put flowers
on her grave? Hal felt his throat tighten. The past seemed so remote, so
long ago.

There was Hungry Hill, lifting his old granite head to the sky, and the
mine-workings at the base, the chimney-stacks, the sheds, the tracks, and
as the steamer rounded the point the humped back of Doon Island lay
before them, the long line of garrison buildings, and the village of
Doonhaven, nestling in the shadow of the hills.

"Look there, at the head of the creek across the harbour—that's Clonmere," said Hal.

They stared in silence, at the home they had deserted as little children. The sun shone in the windows and upon the grey walls. The new wing had mellowed with the years and had become part of it all, but it was still empty, untouched since the builders had left it in 1871. A flag was flying from the old tower. Boats were anchored in the creek.

The tears were running down Kitty's cheeks.

"I know it's idiotic, but I can't help it," she said, smiling at Hal. "I thought somehow it would be different, but it's not. It's just the same."

"There's a fellow in one of the boats," said Hal. "I wonder if it's a Sullivan or a Baird? He's probably been after killigs."

"The herons still live in the trees below the park," said Kitty. "Look, Lizette, by the other creek, you can see their big, untidy nests. . . . There's the harbour wall. It's low tide, the harbour is dry. We shall have to anchor outside and pull ashore."

"I see Molly and Robert on the quay," said Lizette, "and other people with them. The man is dressed as a clergyman. He has a long grey beard."

"It's uncle Tom," shouted Hal. "He used to be father's best friend. And look, there's aunt Harriet; she's waving a handkerchief."

"That must be Jinny with them," said Kitty. "Good heavens, she was six when we left. And now I suppose she's sixteen."

The paddle-steamer thrashed the water and went astern. The anchor plunged from the bows. And across the dancing water the little boats pulled. Everyone was smiling, and kissing, and shaking hands. Uncle Tom had one hand on Hal's shoulder and the other on Kitty's. Aunt Harriet had picked Lizette up in her arms and was holding her tight. Jinny looked from one to the other with warm brown eyes.

"God bless you all," said uncle Tom, in his deep voice. "We are so very glad to welcome you home, so thankful and so happy."

The familiar cobbled stones, the shingle beach, the boats drawn up above the tide. Old Murphy's shop, the chandler's at the corner, the public-house across the square. It was market-day, and the stalls were being put away. A cowman was driving the cattle up the hill. Men stood about the square with straws in their mouths, staring and doing nothing, as they had always done. A woman was scolding a neighbour from her doorway, and a little slatternly child ran out with his finger in his mouth. The priest stood on the step of Murphy's shop, with a cabbage under his arm. Some half-dozen miners, in their working clothes, came singing down the road from Hungry Hill.

"Why did we ever leave?" said Hal. "Why did father make us go away?"

Uncle Tom smiled, and took his arm.

"Never mind about that," he said. "You're home once more."

How good it was to see uncle Tom again, and kiss aunt Harriet's plump cheek; smell the familiar Rectory smell, of leather chairs, and ferns, and dogs; sit down to an enormous tea, and a fruit cake of aunt Harriet's own baking. And memories, happy ones, tumbling over each other.

"Do you still churn the butter, aunt Harriet, and skim the cream off with a scallop shell?"

"Does uncle Tom still ride out to Ardmore on Sundays?"

"Do you remember how we played charades after tea, and mamma pretended she could not guess the word, and knew all the time?"

"Have you forgotten the picnic on Kileen moors, and Kitty falling into the bog?"

"And the expedition to the Blue Rock?"

"And the party the garrison gave on Doon Island?"

The years in London were as though they had never been. Eton and Oxford existed no longer. Adeline and Lancaster Gate were an evil dream.

Molly had remembered his wish for the Tower room, and Hal looked around it that first evening home, his heart too full to speak. The Boles had never used the room, and a damp, unlived-in smell still clung about the walls. The pictures were faded, and some of them green with mould. On the top of an old cupboard was a case of birds' eggs, thick with dust. He had forgotten whom they belonged to. Was it his grandfather, who had won the silver cup for greyhounds? He took them down and cleared away the dust. There were bits and pieces of an old fishing-rod too. Too broken to be of any use. He was glad the Boles had done nothing with this room. It was intimate, personal, belonging only to the family. Home was the same, unchanged, but a little shabbier, a little more worn. Some of the carpets were threadbare. The curtains in the dining-room were falling to bits. The servants that Molly had brought with her from Robert's home said that the kitchen range was almost useless, and the pump in the stable-yard was broken.

"But what does it matter?" said Molly at dinner. "We're home again, and if the turkey has to be roasted in front of the dining-room fire on Christmas Day it will taste all the better for it."

Once more the lapping of water in the creek. Once more the full moon over Hungry Hill.

There was so much to see, so much to do, and all in a little space of time. It was queer to see none of the old horses in the stables, and the coach-house was empty because the carriage had been sent away to London many years before. Old Tim was dead. The groom that Robert had brought with him lived in Tim's old quarters over the stables. Some of the windows were broken, there was grass growing between the cobbles.

"And it used to be kept so beautifully," sighed Molly to her husband. "I remember the boy washing down the yard every morning, before the horses were groomed, and then Tim bringing the carriage round to the front door, if mamma wanted to go down into Doonhaven. Even if the Boles did not bother about the upkeep, you would think the agent would have seen everything was in order."

"Always the same story when the owner goes away," said Robert. "You can't really blame the agent, or anyone. They feel no interest is taken. What's the use, they think, in looking after a place when the man it belongs to doesn't come near it for ten years? Never mind, Molly, we'll try to get it into some sort of shape while we are here."

Hal and his sister went up to visit the cottages at Oakmount, and they came away silent and disheartened, because after the first flood of conversation they felt tongue-tied and out of place.

"Ah, you're the image of your mother," said Tim's widow to Kitty. "The same sweet eyes, God rest her soul." She ran on in this way for several minutes, making them feel welcomed and remembered, but then she started to bewail the times, the hardness of living, her only son and daughter both gone to America, her eyes fixed all the while on Hal.

He gave her all the loose change in his pocket, which she seized greedily, and when they had said good-bye Hal looked over his shoulder and saw her muttering to herself, her face wrinkled, different, and he knew that she had forgotten them already, his mother's memory was a trick to please them; all that mattered to Tim's widow was the loose change in her hands. They went down to the Rectory, where uncle Tom and aunt Harriet soon restored them to cheerfulness.

"Ten years is a long time," said uncle Tom, "but you must not worry about it. You've come back, and you are going to stay. What do you intend to do with yourself, Hal, when you leave Oxford?"

"Nothing," smiled Hal, "except enjoy myself and paint pictures for my friends."

Aunt Harriet shook her head.

"You've been learning bad ways, I can see that," she said. "Too much money and too little leadership. Come and help me churn the butter. Jinny will show you how to do it."

The white-scrubbed dairy, and aunt Harriet bustling with the pots and pans.

"Come and work for your living," she said, "instead of lounging there on the table, drinking butter-milk. Jinny has twice your energy, for all your size."

"Women shall work, and men shall play," teased Hal, pulling Jinny's hair. "Do you remember when I tipped you out of a wheelbarrow, Jinny, and made you cry?"

"Yes, but you kissed her afterwards and said you were sorry," said aunt Harriet.

Hal dug his finger in the bowl of yellow cream, and looked slyly at

Jinny, who, with sleeves rolled up and hair pinned on top of her head, was working the handle of the churn.

"I suppose you're too old to kiss now, Jinny," he said.

"Much too old," said Jinny gravely.

"And too sensible to fall out of a wheelbarrow?"

"It depends who was wheeling it."

"Would you like me to take you round the garden and see?"

"I would not."

"Then we'll go fishing in the creek instead, if you'll be good enough to trust yourself to me."

"I won't promise anything," said Jinny, "until you take your fingers out of the cream."

Hal laughed, and slipping off the table he took his place beside her and worked the handle of the churn.

"Oh, Jinny," he said, "you've never been away, so you don't know what it is to be home again."

It was no use getting depressed because the years had come between them and the people of Clonmere. The place had not changed. And every moment must be enjoyed. It was a truly happy Christmas. The kitchen range was coaxed into cooking the turkey, and Hal, as master of the house, was persuaded to carve it, which he did in such generous fashion that nothing remained at the end for himself but the carcase. It was a great party, with the Brodricks, the Spencers, the Callaghans, and the Flower cousins from Andriff, Simon and Judith and Frank, and after the Christmas dinner had been eaten they all played hide-and-seek in the new wing, the empty rooms echoing with running feet, and calls, and laughter. Tom Callaghan stood with his wife in the passage leading to the new wing from the old house, listening to the thumps, and bangs, and shouts of triumph.

"What a tragedy!" he said softly. "And it might have been thus all these years. The rooms furnished, instead of bare. The girls and that boy growing up where they belonged. And Henry his old dear, generous self."

"Will he ever come back, do you think?" asked Harriet.

The Rector shook his head.

"You've seen his letters," he said, "you can understand what has happened to him. He's a different man."

"Hal's so like him," said his wife, "the same charm, the same smile, and yet something lacking, not the enthusiasm, not the drive that Henry had. And he sometimes talks so bitterly for a boy not twenty-one."

"Ten years' neglect, and all his mother's teaching thrown away," said Tom. "If Henry would break down the barrier that has grown up between them . . . but even then, I wonder. The foundations have been knocked away."

Kitty ran down the stairs of the great hall, pursued by her cousin Simon Flower. Lizette, her thin face flushed for once, tip-toed into the drawing-room that had never been used. Laughter came from the gallery above, where Robert had caught Molly, and the two waltzed to the head of the stairs. In the little boudoir above the barred front door Hal struggled with the windows to the balcony. They were rusted and damp, and would not open.

"This was to have been my mother's room," he said. "Father planned it for her, next to the bedroom. Do you like it?"

Jinny nodded.

"I've often looked at it from outside," she said. "I used to trespass here, you know, when the Boles were away. It's just as I imagined. In the corner there your mother would have had her writing-table, close to the fire. And there would have been a chair here, and another there."

She smiled at Hal, her eyes warm with understanding.

"Do you remember her?" he said.

Jinny shook her head.

"Only just that there was someone with a very soft voice and dark hair, who used to kiss me when I came to tea," she said.

Hal stared in front of him, his hands in his pockets.

"I know," he said. "The terrible thing is that I can't remember more than that either. And yet she was the person I loved best in the world." Once again he struggled with the windows, but the damp had too great a hold on them. "I can't open them," he said, "they're shut for ever." He turned away, shrugging his shoulders. "Let them stay, then," he said. "No one will ever live in this part of the house now."

She followed him along the gallery to the stairs. The hide-and-seekers had taken themselves off to the old house. The great hall was deserted.

"It's queer," said Hal, "but as a rule you hear of the haunting of old buildings, never new. And yet I feel this wing is full of ghosts."

Jinny put out her hand to him.

"You would not mind if it was your mother, would you, Hal?" she said.

She looked young, and brave, and very confident. She was not too shy to hold his hand there, alone, in the silence.

Hal shook his head.

"It's not my mother who's the ghost," he said, "that's what makes it so queer. It's the ghost of my father still alive, hiding here in the shadows." He looked over his shoulder at the black, gaping doors. "Come away, Jinny," he said. "I don't want to think about him, I want to think about ourselves. It's Christmas, and we've got to be happy, we've got to be gay. . . ."

<h1 style="text-align:center">3</h1>

When the party at Clonmere broke up at the end of January, Molly and her husband took Lizette off to live with them in the neighbouring county, and Kitty went to stay with her cousins the Flowers at Castle

Andriff. Only Hal returned across the water, proposing to spend a night in Lancaster Gate before going back to Oxford.

"Always remember," said uncle Tom, as he shook hands with him on the quay at Doonhaven, "that there is a home for you at the Rectory—not for your dear mother's sake, or for your father's, but for your own. We are all very fond of you. Jinny is going to miss your companionship."

"Thank you," said Hal, "I shan't forget."

There was a great sadness in his heart as the steamer drew away from the harbour into Mundy Bay, and Clonmere, and the village, and Doon Island, became once more grey shadows under the hills. The holiday that had meant so much belonged already to the past. He wondered whether he would ever return, and had a wretched feeling of despair that this was farewell.

When he arrived at Lancaster Gate he found that his father and step-mother were out. He sat alone in the drawing-room, turning over magazines. It seemed to him that the room was full of Adeline. Her books, her knitting, her writing-paper. Everything neat and in order, but somehow lacking comfort, and he sat there in anticipation of her brisk, firm tread, her grating laugh. His old schoolboy dread of conversation engulfed him, and to steady his nerves he went into the dining-room and helped himself to a large whisky-and-soda. It was the only way to get through the evening. Never once had he felt the need of one at Doonhaven. It was only here, in the cold, impersonal atmosphere of Lancaster Gate, that he could not do without it. By the time his father and step-mother arrived he was warm and hazy with false courage. Life did not seem so formidable, and he felt he could stand up against the world.

"I suppose," said Adeline before dinner, "Clonmere was fit for a pigsty, and you picnicked in the dirt without any qualms?"

"On the contrary," said Hal, "Molly fed us like fighting cocks. And no one could go short with uncle Tom and aunt Harriet at the Rectory."

"Is that the Rector whose wife spends all her time in the kitchen?" said Adeline. "I gather he's your only neighbour for miles. How your father ever stood the life beats me."

"The Callaghans are the kindest people I've ever known," said Hal. "Uncle Tom and my father were always together in the old days."

"*Faute de mieux*," laughed Adeline. "I don't think he would find a great deal in common nowadays with a stuffy old parson living at the back of beyond. If it was not for the entail he would sell the place tomorrow. He's told me so, scores of times."

Henry came into the room, and dinner was announced a few minutes later.

Hal ate in silence, burning with indignation. What a liar the woman was, talking light-heartedly about his father selling Clonmere! He would never do such a thing. But during dinner Adeline talked through him all the time, kept making allusions to the absurd expense of hanging on to

places that brought no benefit to anybody, and were only a drag on
capital. Never once did she mention Clonmere by name. She talked of
friends of hers in the north of England who, she said, had been saddled
with an empty house and a derelict estate for years, and had just got rid
of it.

"They sold the land at a wonderful price for building," she said, "and
are thankful to be quit of it. Now they intend spending most of their
time abroad, I believe. Of course there were no children, and there was
none of that absurd entail business."

It was not until she had left the room after dessert that Henry began to
ask questions about Doonhaven and Clonmere. His manner was off-
hand and indifferent, but beneath it lay an anxiety, a strange desire to
hear and to know, which he wished to conceal. How were the Callaghans, he asked? Was old Tom much changed, much older? Had the
Boles taken care of the grounds, or was everything becoming overgrown?
Was the agent civil? Did Hal hear any talk about the change over to tin
in the mines, and the prospects for the future?

"I understand there is plenty of tin there," he told his father, "but it's
easier to work than copper, and not so much labour is needed. Uncle
Tom told me that several of the miners had been turned away. They
don't understand it, when they've been working there for years."

"They'll have to put up with it," said Henry.

"I suppose so, but uncle Tom says it's hard for them, to have their
livelihood snatched away suddenly, almost overnight. There was a lot of
distress last winter. Many of the younger men are talking of emigrating,
and several have gone to America already."

"That doesn't concern me. The ones whom I keep employed I take
good care to pay well. I shall continue to do so, as long as the price of
tin makes it worth my while to work the mines."

"And after that, what?"

Henry shrugged his shoulders.

"Close them down, or sell them beforehand, at the psychological
moment," he said, "whichever strikes me as the wisest thing to do at the
time."

"Uncle Tom said you would do that," said Hal. "I think he was
rather uneasy about it. He said so many people would be thrown out of
work."

"Tom's a parson, it's his job to think about those things," said Henry.
"I don't see that it need concern us. I have a right to do what I like with
my own property, and the mines belong to me."

Hal said nothing. It was not his affair. He remembered suddenly the
visit to his mother's grave at Ardmore, the day before he left. He had
driven out in the Rector's trap, and taken Jinny with him. The grave was
tidy and well-kept, and bulbs were planted round it. Her father and
mother always saw to it, said Jinny; daffodils came every year in spring.

They stood there together, and Jinny swept away the fallen leaves. They read the inscription. "Katherine—beloved wife of Henry Brodrick." Should he tell his father about the visit to the grave? But his father asked nothing. He never spoke of Ardmore. He did not once talk about the empty new wing at Clonmere.

"So Kitty and Lizette have decided to stay out there with Molly?" he said. "They evidently prefer her company to mine."

"I think they would return if they believed you wanted them," said Hal.

Henry did not answer. He was fingering the stem of his glass.

"I suppose," he said, "you would have a great objection to breaking the entail?"

Hal stared at him.

"What do you mean?" he said.

"Your great-grandfather made a long and very detailed will," said Henry. "I have to have my heir's permission to sell the place. It's something I can't do on my own. If you agree, naturally I shall make it up to you when you come of age in a few months' time, and you would have a considerable allowance to live upon. Judging by the rate at which you live up at Oxford you are going to need it too."

Hal flushed.

"I'm sorry, father," he said, "but I can't do it. I don't think you quite understand what Clonmere means to me, and to Molly, and Kitty. We belong over there. It's home to us, whatever you may feel."

"You haven't lived there since you were children," said Henry. "I don't count this Christmas visit, that was only a picnic. Adeline is always saying that it's ridiculous, hanging on to the place, paying out vast sums in wages and repairs and one thing after another, and she's perfectly right. The property is a drain on my income, and gives nothing in return."

"The gospel according to Saint Adeline," said Hal bitterly.

"No need to be impertinent," said Henry. "Your stepmother is a very far-seeing woman, and she talks sound sense. What use is Clonmere to me? Answer me if you can. I haven't been there for ten years."

"That's your fault, isn't it?" said Hal. "The place is there, waiting for you. Just the same, only a little shabbier. You loved it once. You love it still. But you won't go near it because you are afraid."

"What do you mean, afraid?"

"Oh, don't worry. It's not my mother. She won't haunt you. She forgave you long ago. She told me that when I visited her grave, which I suppose you've never seen. You're afraid of yourself, of the man you used to be. You're afraid, if you returned, that he would come out of the shadows and haunt you. That's why you want to sell it, so that he can be buried, once and forever."

Hal rose to his feet, white and trembling. The words had tumbled from him, he scarcely knew what he was saying.

"You've been drinking," said Henry slowly. "I suspected it when we came in to dinner. And it's not the first time either. Adeline warned me about this. She says it's become a habit with you; she has ways and means of finding out, when you are here. She has seen you creep in here to the sideboard and help yourself, when you think nobody is about."

"And if I do," said Hal, "what's the reason? Because I can't face sitting here at dinner between you both, knowing that every day and every night you become more hopeless, more miserable, more utterly dependent upon her for every damned thing. Molly, and Kitty, and I, and poor Lizette mean nothing to you, absolutely nothing. And now she's trying to get you to sell Clonmere. Thank God I can prevent it. I won't break the entail, not if you give me ten thousand quid. . . ."

He broke off excitedly, as Adeline came into the room.

"What on earth is the matter?" she said. "I could hear Hal shouting from the drawing-room. Do you want to call the servants up from the basement?"

"Call the whole world, I don't care," said Hal, "but I'd like you to know you've made a mistake, for once. I'm not going to be bribed into selling my home to please you."

"Leave the room, and go to bed," said Henry curtly. "In the morning you may be able to talk clearly."

"He may," said Adeline, "if he doesn't get down to the whisky decanter first." She pointed scornfully at his trembling hands. "Look at him," she said. "I hope you're proud of your son. A month in that country of yours has done well for him, hasn't it? He can scarcely stand up. He could let himself go over there, and revert to type. Now you can see him at last, Henry, as he really is. And perhaps, since we've got down to it at last, you would like to have a look at some of the bills that have come in for him while he's been away. Oxford tradesmen don't wait for ever, any more than anyone else. Most illuminating, they are, I can tell you. How's this one for a start? Fifty quid for wine, all supplied to the young gentleman last term." She threw the bill on to the table. "And here's another, and another, a whole sheaf of them to keep you busy all to-morrow morning, if you feel that way inclined. And lastly a very pretty little statement from your bank, Master Hal, in which the manager wishes to acquaint you with the fact that you are overdrawn to the sum of two hundred pounds."

Hal saw the two faces. His father's a mask, cold and indifferent, and his stepmother's flushed in triumph.

"How dare you open my letters?" he said. "How dare you?"

"My dear Hal, don't be so theatrical. The initials being the same as your father's, of course I opened them, thinking they were his. And here is a *billet-deux* from across the water, that came by this evening's post. A thousand apologies for having glanced into it. The writing looks like a kitchen-maid's, and whoever it is signs herself Jinny."

She laughed, holding the letter in front of him.

Hal struck out at her, in a blind fury of rage, his blow catching the side of her mouth. She staggered back, her hands to her face, the blood coming from her cut lip in a slow trickle. In a moment Henry was upon Hal, seizing him by his collar, thrusting him against the table.

"You damned drunken young fool," he said, "have you gone mad?" Hal shook him off, and stood staring at his father, white and shaken.

"Good God, you may well look ashamed of yourself," said Henry, "striking a woman, the lowest thing a man can do. Here's my handkerchief, Adeline; you had better go up to your room and call Marcelle to you. But first this boy is going to apologise to you."

"I am not," said Hal.

Henry looked at his son. Hal was pale and dishevelled. The bills lay scattered on the floor. Jinny's letter had been kicked under the table, and lay crumpled and forgotten.

"Either you apologise to Adeline or you get out of my house," said Henry. His eyes were hard and cold and without mercy. "You've always been a trial and an anxiety," he said, "ever since you were born. Your mother spoilt you absurdly, and you've thought yourself God Almighty ever since. In three months' time you will be twenty-one, and so far you've distinguished yourself only by drinking too much, wasting my money, and painting bad pictures. You don't think I'm proud of you, do you?"

Hal walked slowly from the dining-room into the hall. Adeline said nothing. She watched them both, the handkerchief still to her lips.

"Remember," said Henry, "I mean what I say. Either you apologise to Adeline, or you leave this house, finally and for ever."

Hal did not answer. He did not look back over his shoulder. He opened the front door and stood for a moment gazing down into the street. Then he went out hatless in the rain.

<h1 style="text-align:center">4</h1>

Jinny Callaghan decided to have a clearance on her twenty-fifth birthday. Too many things had accumulated in her bedroom at the Rectory. There were her school books, for one thing, which would be of far more use to the priest in Doonhaven, if he liked to have them, than they could be to her. She would take them down the following morning and risk a snubbing. A present from a heretic, bound with red ribbon. At any rate, it would make father and mother laugh. The sentimental love stories of adolescence she would keep for her goddaughter, Molly's child, against the day when she would be old enough to read them. Also her workbasket, her first, given her by her mother when she was ten years old. It was fun to sit down on the floor, with her legs tucked under her skirt, and find the old treasures. Here were the photographs. She could not bring herself to throw them away. Father in his university days, with a group of friends. He looked very dear and wicked, as he probably was. Mr Brodrick stood by his side, and Mr Brodrick's brother Herbert, who also became a clergyman, and sometimes wrote to her father. They all looked very merry. Here was one of herself as a baby, sitting on her mother's knee in a white starched frock. What a little fright, with round eyes like boot-buttons! A picnic-group taken at Glen Begh, with themselves and all the Brodricks as children. Molly had not changed at all, she was still the same laughing, happy person today that she had been at ten years old. But no one would have thought Kitty, the ugly duckling, would have grown into a beauty. Jinny looked for the wedding-group, taken two years ago, of Kitty Brodrick's marriage to her cousin, Simon Flower. They were standing on the steps at Castle Andriff. Kitty was really lovely, and she herself as a bridesmaid seemed such a dowd in comparison. Lizette, poor dear, would never quite lose that pinched, strained expression, but she was tall, nearly as tall as Kitty, and no one could see her foot under the long bridesmaid's dress. It was so like Kitty, sweet and generous, to insist on Lizette living with them at Castle Andriff, and happy-go-lucky Simon did not mind.

When Jinny had cleared out her bedroom cupboard she felt for a box on the shelf. It was fastened, and bound with tape. She hesitated for a moment, and then she took down the box, and sat beside it on the bed. She undid the tape, and lifted the lid. It was full of letters. On top of the letters were some half-dozen paintings. There was one of herself, with her hair down her back, which he had done that Christmas when they had all come to Clonmere. There were two of Clonmere, and a pen-and-ink sketch of Doon Island. The remaining paintings were of mountains, snow-covered, and vast stretches of land that looked bare and unfriendly. Jinny gazed at them slowly, one by one, and then put them aside, and took up Hal's letters. The first wild, miserable ones were from London, and then there was that brave, hopeful letter written in Liverpool, the night before he sailed for Canada.

"I know you believe in me, Jinny," he said, "even if nobody else does. And one day my father will be proud of me too."

The remaining letters all bore the Winnipeg post-mark, and most of them had been written in the early years in Canada. She could see the dates on the envelopes—nearly every month in 1881 and '82. The letters had a light-hearted, schoolboy flavour; everything was new and exciting, he was so glad he had taken the big decision. Oxford, and all that Oxford stood for, seemed another world already.

"I see we lost the Boat Race as usual," he wrote, "so my leaving the boat did not give them any better luck! I thought of the crew on the day, and said a prayer for them, but as I was out on the ranch rounding cattle all day from sunrise to sunset I had not much time to waste thinking of my friends. It's a grand life, and I'm enjoying every minute of it."

They were full of hope, these first letters; he was going to make a success of ranching, he was certain of it.

"Of course the first few years will be the hardest," he said, "and it's difficult living on the allowance I get from great-grandfather's will. But I haven't had to ask my father for a penny, and that is all that matters. Tell Molly I have grown a beard and look strikingly handsome."

There was a smudged snapshot enclosed in one of the letters written about this time. Hal bearded, in his shirt-sleeves, looking a great ruffian. He stood arm-in-arm with two of his fellow ranchers.

"We drive down to Winnipeg once a month," he wrote in '83, "and spend all our money and see the sights and treat the girls. Last month we had a free fight in a saloon, Frank, my partner, getting rather wild in his cups and knocking another fellow over the head. Of course I had to back him up, and we spent a night in jail for our pains. My first experience behind bars. If Adeline got to hear of it she would say 'I told you so'. Thank dear uncle Tom for his most welcome cheque. He mustn't do it again."

And then in '84 and '85 the tone changed, slowly, almost imperceptibly.

"Frank is getting impossible," he said, "and I think we shall have to part company. I am going to try on my own and see if I can't do better. I have enough money saved to buy a small ranch, where I can be my own boss."

Somehow the idea must have come to nothing, for after six months of silence he wrote again, saying that he had been lucky enough to get a position in a bank in Winnipeg, which was a pleasant change after the rough life of the past few years.

"I've come to the conclusion that you have to be born to ranching to make a real success of it," he told Jinny, "and the climate is pretty hard for someone like myself who doesn't belong to the country. I lost about a stone in weight last winter. The early mornings were the worst, getting up in the dark and going out into the snow, and no proper food either. How I longed for one of aunt Harriet's cakes! Now I'm in the town it's much easier, and I have quite comfortable lodgings."

But the bank did not last two months, for the next letter came from Toronto, and was only a few lines.

"I've started painting again," said Hal. "After all, it is the thing I like best, and what I've always wanted to do. No one to give orders, and my time is my own. One or two people here say I've been a damn fool to try anything else. I don't suppose I shall make a fortune at it, but I feel free again, which I haven't done for some time."

There was silence then for a year. The next letter, written in the autumn of '86, was one of quiet despair. The handwriting was changed, shaky, and in places almost impossible to read.

"I've been very ill," he said, "my health has all gone to pieces. Adeline was right about me after all, and you were wrong. I'm useless, a failure, and I would end it all if only I had the courage. I sold one or two pictures, but I haven't done any work now for months. Think about me sometimes, Jinny, and when you do, remember me as I was that Christmas at Clonmere, when I was twenty, and you were sixteen. You wouldn't think much of me now."

This was the last letter he had written to her, three years ago. She had answered the letter, and many months later it had been returned to her, with the words "Gone away" written across the envelope. She remembered going down to the study and telling the whole story to her father, the tears running down her cheeks. He had been so kind and understanding, and had read Hal's last letter sitting beside her, with his arm about her shoulders.

"If only I were a man," Jinny said, between her tears, "I'd go out to Canada and bring him home. I know I should find him."

Tom Callaghan looked at the eager, hopeful eyes, the small, determined chin.

"I believe you would, Jinny," he said, "but God made you a woman, and perhaps one day you will find your Hal, and give him greater comfort."

Three years ago. . . . Jinny put the letters carefully back in the box and the paintings on top, and closed the lid. She would never throw them away, she would read them again and again, until she was an old woman of eighty. Maybe Hal was dead and suffered no longer, but it made no difference. She would always remember the boy who had held her hand in the dark, ghostly wing of Clonmere that Christmas day, and was haunted and alone. He would be nearly thirty now, if he was still alive; a boy no longer. Hal, who had sat on the table in the dairy drinking buttermilk and dipping his finger into the cream when her mother's back was turned. Hal, teasing her, laughing, his hands in his pockets. Hal sailing his boat in the creek. . . . Jinny had many pictures in her mind, all of them dear and sweet. And they would have to last her all her life, for there would never be any more.

She put the box of letters away in the cupboard, and went downstairs to her birthday lunch. Patsy the gardener had killed a chicken in honour of the occasion, and her mother had baked a special pudding. She feigned the surprise proper to the occasion, though the same ceremony was repeated every year, and her parents watched her unwrap her presents and give the usual cry of pleasure and astonishment. It was a year by year routine, delightful to all three.

"Father, dear, a watch! How good of you and how naughty! It's the very one we admired in the shop window in Slane, and now you have slyly bought it."

"No slyness at all," smiled Tom. "Kitty Flower drove into Slane from Andriff and got it for me."

"And a writing-case from you, mother. Why am I so spoilt?" Jinny got up from the table, and kissed both her parents. "Of course, I know what it is," she said. "Father wants to borrow the watch so that he can remember to be in time for church, and mother will write down all the recipes on my new paper. The plot was hatched between you both."

"You see too much," said Tom, "and anyway, what are you going to do with your birthday afternoon? Drive over and see Kitty?"

"No, I think I shall go for a walk, if neither you nor mother need me."

"I intend making jam," said Harriet, "but I'll spare you for once."

It was difficult to believe, thought Jinny, as she walked that afternoon in Clonmere, down by the creek, and looked away across the harbour to Hungry Hill, that beneath that rugged granite face, so white and still under the summer sun, men toiled and sweated and broke themselves and died, and all for the sake of someone who lived far away, in another country, who cared nothing for them or for their families. His house here, beside the water, was like a sepulchre, the windows shuttered and barred. Sometimes it came to life, when Molly and her husband and children spent a fortnight or so beneath its roof, but mostly it would stay closed, as it was today. Henry Brodrick and his wife lived at Brighton now, so Molly said; they had sold the house in Lancaster Gate. And here was Clonmere, waiting for the owner who never came. Jinny stared up at the little balcony in the new wing. It was strange to think that perhaps no one had ever stood there and looked down upon the grass bank and the drive. Once people had done so in their dreams, and the dreams had come to nothing.

Jinny walked away from the castle, and followed the path by the creek to the lodge gates. She could see the paddle-steamer from Mundy thrashing its way across the harbour to Doonhaven. Now it had passed Doon Island, and come to anchor outside the harbour wall. Visitors came these days, since they had built the hotel at Andriff. And there would be some of the miners' wives, back from market-day in Mundy. Soldiers too, bound for the garrison on Doon Island. Now and again the garrison would be strengthened, according to the whims and fears of those in authority. But nobody had much interest in politics in Doonhaven.

Jinny paid a few calls at the cottages in Oakmount, and it was past five o'clock by the time she arrived home at the Rectory. She went in through the garden. Patsy was chopping wood outside the dairy.

"You have a visitor, Miss Jinny," he said, jerking his head towards the house. "Came ashore in the steamer, he did, and I tell you straight I knew him at once, for all he's run to nothing."

"Who is it, Patsy?" asked Jinny.

"No, you go in to the Rector, Miss Jinny. I'll not be telling you."

And Patsy went on with his chopping, shaking his head, and muttering to himself.

Jinny found her mother standing in the hall. She looked anxious, a little sad.

"I thought you were never coming," she said. "Would you go to your father? He's in the study. And Jinny, dear, prepare for a surprise. At least, something between a surprise and a shock. It's so strange that this should have happened on your birthday."

She hesitated, half smiling. Yet there was a tear in the corner of her eye.

Jinny went into the study. Her father was standing by the mantelpiece talking to someone who sat in the long chair by the window, with his back towards her. There was something about the square shoulders, the angle of the head. She took a step forward, unbelieving, yet strangely certain.

"It's Hal, isn't it?" she said.

He rose from the chair, tall, gaunt, a shadow of himself, oddly different from the dream she had made of him all these years. There were lines of suffering and disillusionment on his face, and deep furrows under his eyes. He looked older than his thirty years, older and yet strangely immature. It was Hal with his youth stripped from him, and hope still in his heart. He came towards her and took her hands, and the smile was Hal's smile, the thing that she loved and that she remembered best.

"You see," he said, "I've come back. I'm a failure, I've achieved nothing. But uncle Tom says I can stay. You won't turn me away, will you, Jinny? You do believe in me still?"

5

After Hal and Jinny were married they settled down in what had been Doctor Armstrong's old house in Doonhaven, which had stood empty now since his death some years before. It was only five minutes' walk from the Rectory. The Rector and his wife started them off with furniture and linen, and Jinny was a splendid little manager, she had the doctor's house snug and habitable within a fortnight.

They spent their brief honeymoon by the lakes, bringing back with them a photograph taken of them both the last day in Slane before returning to Doonhaven. They stood side by side, rather stiff, rather self-conscious, Hal with his hat in his hand and a suspicious, proud look on his face, as though he faced an accuser instead of a photographer. Jinny eager, hopeful, her sailor hat on the back of her brown, curly head, her hands clasping a small muff. The photograph was placed with great pride on the mantelpiece of their new home.

It was strange, thought Hal, to be living down in Doonhaven instead of at Clonmere. It gave him a funny sense of inferiority, which he could not quite get over. He hoped Jinny did not realise it. She was so dear to him, so loving and so kind, and took such a pride in their home, which was nothing but a rather bare, ugly house in the middle of the village. Hal would not for the world have her suspect that it worried him to look out of the sitting-room window at the Post Office, and have Doolan the shoe-maker as his next-door neighbour. It was not snobbery that made him resent it, but an unspoken longing for the space and solitude of Clon-mere. It was there that he belonged, not in the village of Doonhaven.

When these thoughts passed through his mind he would hate himself for his ingratitude, taking special care to compliment Jinny on her new curtains, or her arrangement of the flowers, or a cake she had baked for Sunday.

"Sometimes I'm a bear and a brute, sweetheart," he told her, drawing her on his knee, "and I beg of you to be patient with me at those times, and take no notice. I've brought black moods home with me from Canada, as well as rotten health."

"That's what I'm here for, Hal," she answered, running her hand through his hair, "to chase away the black moods and hold your hand."

"You're a darling," he said, "and I am the luckiest man in the world. . . . Now give me the hammer and some nails, and I'll see if I can fit up that shelf you want in the pantry. Canada has done one thing for me if nothing else, it's made me a handy man about the house."

Before they decided to live in the house in the village, the Rector had asked Hal what he felt about returning to Clonmere. Hal had shaken his head at once, an obstinate expression on his face.

"The place is not mine," he said, "it's my father's. He has not written to me since I left London nine years ago. How could I possibly go and live at Clonmere after that?"

"Have you ever written to him, boy, and asked his forgiveness?"

"Yes—when I first got out to Winnipeg. I had no answer. That was enough for me. I shall never write to him again as long as I live."

Tom Callaghan said no more. God alone could heal the breach between father and son, and if he tried to meddle it would only make matters worse. He wrote and told his old friend that Hal had returned to Doonhaven, of his ill-health and failure out in Canada, and the engagement to his daughter. Henry made little comment in his reply.

"I never expected anything else," he said, "but that Hal would make a mess of his life. I am afraid your daughter is throwing herself away on him."

So Clonmere remained shuttered and Hal Brodrick lived in Doon-haven instead, with Jinny doing his cooking and a girl coming in every morning to scrub floors, with himself cleaning the boots and shoes and bringing in the coal.

"I did it all in Canada," he said, "and I can do it here too," and then he would look across the way and see Mike Doolan staring at him with a grin on his face as though he despised him, and if he spoke to him the fellow would be off-hand and indifferent.

"It's funny," said Hal to Jinny, "they don't like it. When we lived at Clonmere and were 'the gentry', and rode past in the carriage, they hated us, no doubt, but they respected us, or at least they respected my father. And now I've come to live amongst them there's resentment, we make an intrusion. Oh, not you: they're used to you. You're the Rector's daughter. But I'm different. I'm a Brodrick, and they expect me to kick them in the pants, even if they hate me while I do it."

"You're too sensitive," said Jinny, "too much on the defensive, and wondering what they are going to say to you. Just be natural, just be yourself. They'll be friendly in time; they are like children."

"Which is myself?" said Hal. "I'm damned if I know. I thought I was a rancher, and I was not. I believed myself a painter, and I could not sell a picture. I can't even call myself Hal Brodrick of Clonmere. I'm a useless rotter with a wife who's too good for me, living on the good-will of my father-in-law. And the people know it, that's the trouble. They've every right to despise me."

"They don't despise you, and you are none of those horrid things. You are my own Hal," said Jinny.

She was just a little worried, all the same.

Hal's first rapture at being back and seeing her again had worn rather thin. He was often silent and depressed, and then would be in despair for fear he had wounded her and was making her miserable.

"I'm a burden to you," he said; "you'll be sick of me before you've been married six months. I'd no right to come home and ask you."

Jinny told some of this to her father, and he nodded his head in understanding.

"The trouble is," he said, "that Hal feels he is dependent on us, and yet he hasn't the strength of mind to try to stand on his own. I'll have a talk with him and see what I can do."

And then, sitting round the fire in the Rectory study, it would be difficult to imagine that Hal was ever anything but charming, light-hearted and gay. He would chaff aunt Harriet on skimming the cream with a scallop shell, and tease uncle Tom on the length of the Sunday sermon, and standing on the hearth with his arm round Jinny's waist it might have been Henry himself, some thirty years before, thought the Rector, with the same amusing chatter about people and places, telling them of wild-cat schemes and pranks he had played in Canada with his partner, the dissolute Frank.

"Are you too proud, Hal," he said, when Jinny and her mother had left the room, "to try to earn your living?"

"Not too proud," said Hal, smiling, "but too lazy. That's why I failed in Canada."

"No," said Tom, "you failed in Canada because you were friendless and alone, and spent all your money in the Winnipeg saloons. That won't happen here."

"What do you suggest, then, uncle Tom? No one will buy my pictures. I hawked three canvasses round Slane last week, and didn't sell one of them. It made me ashamed before Jinny, who still believes I'm a good painter. But after I'd had a couple of drinks I felt better about it."

"Yes, lad, and if you go on like that you'll be ill again, as you were in Canada. No, keep your painting as a hobby, and a very good hobby it is. I want to know if you have the courage to do something else."

"What should I do?"

The Rector looked at him with a twinkle in his eyes. "You know old Griffiths, the manager up at the mine?" he said.

"Yes."

"His head clerk has gone to America. He wants someone to do the books and keep accounts, and the hundred and one odd jobs that he can't see to himself. Office hours, of course, nine till six. Small salary, but not to be despised. What about it?"

Hal thrust his hands in his pockets and made a face at his father-in-law.

"A Brodrick go and earn a few pounds a week in the mine that will one day bring him thousands?" he said. "It's a funny sort of suggestion."

"Never mind about that," answered the Rector. "It's the present you have to think about, not the future. And there would be no question of taking money from your father. The salary is paid to the head clerk, whoever takes the place. The question is, can you pull yourself together and do it? I know someone who would be very proud of you if you did, and that's Jinny."

Hal did not answer for a moment. He stood staring at the fire.

"I want to please Jinny more than anything else on earth," he said, "and yet I know in my heart I shall always let her down. I'm no good, you see, uncle Tom. I shall make a mess of this job as I've done of everything else."

"No, Hal boy, you will not."

"All right then, I'll have a shot at it."

And so on the 25th of February, 1890, Hal Brodrick walked up to his father's mines on Hungry Hill, shoulder to shoulder with the men of Doonhaven, and hanging his hat on the peg in the counting-house sat down on a high stool before a desk, with young Murphy the grocer's son on the other side of him. Old Griffiths sat in state in an inner room. Hal remembered him standing with his hat in his hands before his father in the old days, and now Hal was his clerk, and said "Thank you, sir," for his weekly wage, just like young Murphy and the others.

It was strange to be just another employee in the mine, when twenty years ago he had driven here in state with his father, the men doffing their hats at his approach, and he remembered being taken below to watch the miners working the lodes, and visiting the engine-houses to see the great pumps at work. Now for the first time he became acquainted with the vast inner life of the mine, which seemed to have no connection with the world outside.

At six in the morning, in his house at Doonhaven, Hal would wake to hear clanging from Hungry Hill the great bell that called the miners to work, and allowed the night-shift to come wan and tired-eyed to the surface. The bell had gone day after day for nearly seventy years, calling the men and women and little children to the mines, but the Brodricks lying in their beds at Clonmere had never heard it. There was a line that ran from Doonhaven out to the mines on Hungry Hill, and those miners who lived in the village would ride out in the trucks to their work. Hal would hear the whistle of steam and the clanging of wheels on the rollers, and sometimes the sound of running feet under his window as the men hastened to catch the trucks. It would still be dark outside, with the stars shining.

"Poor devils," whispered Hal to Jinny, feeling in some queer, obscure fashion that he was to blame for their early rising in the bleak raw morning, and then his conscience would prick him as he arrived himself at the counting-house shortly before nine, having ridden out in all probability in the Rector's trap. The women and children in the dressing-sheds who had the work of washing the ore would look up as he drove past, and he would have the feeling that they laughed at him, and resented him too, believing that he had the place by favour and did not need the money.

At the end of each month, when the books had to be made up and the returns sent in, Hal would find himself working overtime to get through with the stuff on his desk, and then he too would catch the six o'clock truck with the miners in the village, Jinny rising bright and early to keep him company and see that he ate his breakfast before leaving. The first time he did this the men stood apart from him in the truck, joking and talking amongst themselves. There was a fellow called Jim Donovan, son of Pat Donovan who kept the farm beneath the hill, and the first of his family, by his talk, to become a miner.

"Sure, it's the truth," he said, "we owned the land for miles around in the old days," looking over his shoulder at Hal as he spoke.

"That's right, Jim," said his mates, "you had it on lease from the devil."

"No devil at all," answered Jim, "my grandfather's grandfather's grandfather, he was nothing less than a Chief, living below there at the Castle, and as for knowing a pig from a sow, I tell you he wouldn't have soiled his hands with either. He had a thousand men to work for him, the King of France was his best friend."

"That's true," said one of the men; "the French were always for helping us, and the Spanish too. I had it from my father."

"Who was it, then," asked another, "who shot a landlord for interfering with the smugglers? That's another true story, and happened in Doonhaven."

"It was one of the Donovans," said Jim, "and small blame to him either. What right had the landlord to spoil the livelihood of innocent men? I'd shoot anyone who did the same to me."

"And be strung up by the redcoats in the garrison," laughed his friend.

"Oh, I care nothing for them," said Jim, waving his hand. "We'll be rid of the lot of them before you can turn round. And then I'll invite you to shoot hares on the island."

If Hal had been in Canada he would have joined in the fun, and chaffed Jim Donovan, as he had done his fellow-ranchers. But back at home it was different. These men could not forget he was a Brodrick, whose father owned Clonmere and the mine also, and they believed him stiff and proud. Should he try to joke with them they would feel awkward and shy, or imagine he did it out of condescension, to stand in well with them for some ulterior design. And so, in spite of smiles and valiant efforts to seem friendly and natural, Hal would achieve no more than a "Good day", and a remark about the weather.

It was part of his work, as clerk to the manager, to supervise the payment of wages every Friday. It was the day he hated most in the week. He would have to sit in the counting-house, beside Mr Griffiths, with a stack of coins in front of him, reading the names out from a sheet of paper, and then handing the required amount to the manager as each man in turn stepped forward to take his pay. The wages seemed so pitifully small, the coins so few in number. Every Friday morning his heart would sink as he heard the tramp of men queueing up outside the door of the counting-house, and then Mr Griffiths would take his place beside him and the names would be called. The skilled miners first, and the engineers, descending in scale to the surface men, and the dressers, and the women and children.

"Pat Torrens," he would call, and a man would step forward, lean and grey, his skin like wrinkled parchment, and a great Adam's apple moving in his throat, big pouches under his eyes. Two pounds. Two pounds for working eight hours at a stretch, on his back perhaps, in the damp, low levels beneath Hungry Hill, and coming to the surface to change his clothes in the draughty shed where the wind whistled through the open doors, home to his cabin or cottage to eat potatoes and salt fish and sleep before the reeking turf fire, and then back again, down to the black rock-face and the wet walls of the mine.

Hal would hand over the little pile of coins, avoiding the man's eye. Surely Pat Torrens must think to himself, "This is one of the men I'm working for. Every ounce of stuff I break out of the rock and bring to the surface, with my sweat and labour, turns into gold when it is sent across the water to Hal Brodrick's father. He lives in a great house and has servants and carriages and sits on his backside all day. He does not even have the running of the mine, like the manager. He just lies back and puts the gold into his pockets." Pat Torrens would shuffle from the counting-house and Hal would call the next name on the list.

And so on and so on for an hour or so, finishing with the women and children. One or two little fellows of not more than nine years of age, coming forward for their two-shilling piece, the reward for standing barefoot on the tin as it was washed in the "buddle", or for breaking large pieces of ore with a hammer outside the dressing-sheds.

One Friday morning, when the last had been paid, Hal turned to the manager in anger and disgust.

"Surely it's not right?" he said. "They ought to get more. Why, when every man, woman and child in the mines has been paid, it's barely a tenth of what goes to my father?"

Mr Griffiths stared at him.

"The pay is good," he said. "I've known it lower in other mines. They don't expect more. Of course your father must make his profit. He's the owner, isn't he? Don't tell me you're a Radical—you'll be preaching revolution next."

"I'm not a Radical, or a revolutionist," said Hal. "I don't care a twopenny damn about politics. But I feel ashamed, that's all."

"Oh, come," said the manager, getting up and reaching for his coat, "that's all false sentiment. You keep the books in order, and forget the moral side of it. Besides, the day will come when you will be the owner yourself. You can give all your profits away then, if you feel like it."

"Yes," said Hal, "but that's just the point. I shan't want to. I'll be thinking of sitting back and taking my ease, the same as my father."

He would drive home in the evening, turning his back on the sight and sound of the mines. The tall chimneys, black against the hill, would point their fingers to the sky, and a glare of fire would come from the open doors of the boiler-houses. He would hear the winding rattle of the drums in the shafts, and the ceaseless throb of the engine pumps. There would be the inevitable pungent smell in the air coming from the dressing-sheds where the ore was cleansed. And once away, along the road, with the chimneys out of sight, and the smoke from the furnaces blown eastward, and the tramping miners gone below on night-shift, there would be no other sound but the steady clop-clop of Tom Callaghan's mare taking Hal back to Doonhaven, and on his left the smooth, untroubled waters of Mundy Bay. Hungry Hill would rise above him, white and silent under the moon, and away yonder the pin-prick lights of Doonhaven danced and flickered.

"Yes," thought Hal, "and for all my brave talk to Griffiths about the hard work and low pay of the miners, all I want really is to be living in comfort in Clonmere, because of them, with Jinny dressed for dinner as my mother used to be, and a butler waiting on her instead of that halfwitted girl. I want to enjoy the mines, as my forbears did, and forget the cost. I don't want to go back to my poky little house in the village street and know that Jinny has cooked my supper for me and is feeling tired and worn."

He would leave the trap with Patsy at the Rectory, and walk through the village to his house. A smell of cooking would greet his nostrils as he entered, a thing he destested and which it was impossible to smother in so small a house, for all the care that Jinny took.

She came, dear girl, running to meet him, with her bright eyes full of love, and her hair a little untidy, her face flushed from bending over the stove."

"Your favourite supper," she said, beaming, "herrings and cauliflower cheese. I've been given a new recipe from mother's precious book. Oh, and the chimney's been smoking in the sitting-room; we'll have to have it swept. Kitty and Simon called from Andriff; they left us a lovely melon and some grapes. So good of them. And Simon wants to buy one of your pictures, the little sketch of Doon Island from the creek."

"He doesn't really," said Hal. "He just does it out of charity."

"No, dear, he does not. You must not be so proud. He thinks you have great talent. Kitty told me so."

"He's the only one that does, then."

"No, Hal, that's naughty. Your wife is proud of your work."

"It's more than I am. I'm a rotten painter, and a rotten husband."

"Don't be so grumpy, love. Come and sit down and rest in your chair, even if the fire is smoking, and I'll bring you your supper on a tray."

Hal flung himself down and stretched out his arms to her.

"Why should you wait on me?" he said, drawing her on to his knee. "It's I who should look after you. I'd like to see you with your hair smoothed back, Jinny girl, and a low-cut frock, instead of that old apron and your little hands all sticky with cooking."

"I'll smooth my hair for you, and I'll wear my wedding-dress, and I'll wash my hands in milk, if you will promise to be a good boy."

"I am a good boy."

"You know what I mean by a good boy."

"You mean I'm not to help myself to the whisky bottle in the cupboard? Don't worry, sweetheart; it's empty."

"Oh, Hal, and I asked you to keep some, in case of chills and colds."

"The winter's over, there won't be any chills and colds. I'm a brute and a swine, and I don't deserve you, Jinny girl. Why should you love me?"

"I don't know, Hal, but there it is."

She smiled, and he did not move, but streched out his legs to the smoky fire, thinking of the great hall at Clonmere and the fire-place there, where no fire had ever been lit. Presently she came back with their supper on a tray, the herrings a little over-cooked, bless her, but he swore they were excellent, and she sat down at his feet afterwards and took her mending, while he stared into the fire and played with her hair.

"It's embroidery you should be doing," he told her, "not my old socks."

"And if I let your socks go undarned," she asked, "who would do them?"

"You ought to have a lady's maid," he said, "and half-a-dozen servants to look after you. And me, dressed in a dinner-jacket, be coming into my drawing-room with a flower in my button-hole, having dined on a saddle of venison and drunk old brandy."

"That means you didn't care for the herrings," she said in distress.

"It means nothing of the sort," he said, kissing the top of her head. "It means that I let my imagination run away with me when I look at that funny little top-knot of yours, pinned out of the way of your cooking. You have a neck that I can encircle with one hand. I wonder Patsy has never run amok and felled it with his axe when killing your mother's chickens."

"Ah, get along with you. Would you take your great hand away? I can't see the hole in your sock."

"Let it alone, darling."

"And you go barefoot?"

"I would have you sit beside me in the chair and watch the pictures in the fire."

She laid the mending aside, and curled up beside him in the old leather chair that had come from the Rectory, and they said little to one another, but listened to the clock in the corner, left by Doctor Armstrong, and heard the soft rain patter against the window, and saw the smoky turf sink lower on the hearth.

Up at the Rectory Tom Callaghan was writing to Herbert Brodrick at Lletharrog.

"DEAREST OLD HERBY," he said,

"You can't think what a real pleasure it was to get a letter once more from one of the family. It is years since I saw you, but I have photographs of you and the brothers as mementos of the past. It was so good to read your kind words about our dear Jinny, and that she has been a blessing to poor Hal. I never now say a word about either of them to Henry when I write, as no matter what I say he always speaks about the hopelessness of Hal's case. . . .I am glad to say Hal is, I think, one of the most charming fellows I ever met—in fact his Daddy over again, only with the one drawback, and he is getting over that too. . . . There are no babies as yet, but I tell Jinny they will come along by-and-by. They are certainly one of the happiest couples it has ever been my good fortune to see. . . ."

6

Hal was not a great newspaper reader. He took little interest in the affairs of the day. On winter evenings when he came back from the mines all he wanted to do was to sit with Jinny in front of the fire, and

listen to her prattle, or laugh with her over the happenings in the counting-house. Therefore when he went one day to Slane, in the early spring
of '94, to make purchases for Jinny and the household, and stood before
the bar in one of the public-houses and turned over the pages of the
Slane and County Advertiser, it was news to him, and something of a shock,
to read a long column in the middle page about the large tin deposits in
Malay, and the companies that had been formed to work them; and
how, in the opinion of the writer, the discoveries would kill the home
markets. Life was so much a matter of routine these days—the day up at
the mines, the keeping of the books, the going home to Jinny and the
baby—that the rise and fall of prices had conveyed nothing to him, and
when old Griffiths shook his head and spoke gloomily about the future
Hal had put it down to the man's natural pessimism, that could see small
hope in mining prospects, for either tin or copper. When Hal had read
the article, he turned to the financial page to see the current price of tin.
It was £84 a ton. It had been £100 six months ago. Yes, old Griffiths
had reason to be gloomy. Hal, content and preoccupied with his own
home life, had neglected to watch the fluctuations of the trade that gave
him his livelihood. He wondered what his father thought about it. That
evening, when he returned home, and found his father-in-law, the
Rector, seated in the living-room nursing the solemn John-Henry, he
asked him if he had read the article in the *Slane Advertiser*.

"Yes, Hal, I have," said Tom Callaghan, "and I think the writer of the
article speaks sound sense. We shall see some changes before very long."

"What do you suppose my father will do?"

"Henry always was a shrewd business man, Hal. You may depend
upon it he has been watching the Malay business and the drop in price
in the last six months. He was one of the first owners to change over from
copper to tin, more than fifteen years ago, and the people in Cornwall
followed suit, at least those who struck lucky and also had the capital
to do so."

The Rector hesitated, and, Jinny coming in at this moment to bear
John-Henry off to bed, he waited until she had left the room, and then
looked up at his son-in-law.

"You haven't heard any rumours, then?"

"No, uncle Tom," said Hal. "I never listen to gossip anyway. Rumours of what?"

"That your father intends selling the mines very shortly?"

Hal shook his head.

"It's the first I've heard of it," he said, "but perhaps Griffiths would
not say anything to me, out of delicacy. As for the men, they fabricate
fresh tales every day. Last week I heard Jim Donovan tell his pal there
was gold at the foot of Hungry Hill, and it all belonged to him."

"Jim Donovan has '*folie de grandeur*', like others of his family. No,
Hal, it's no idle gossip I'm repeating to you. I had a talk with Griffiths

after church on Sunday, and he says letters have been coming from across the water, which presumably you haven't seen, from some director of a London company, also letters from your father and from your father's solicitors, and negotiations are in progress."

Hal lit his pipe, and stirred the fire with his foot.

"After what I have read today I can't blame him," he said. "My father, I mean. If the price of tin falls much further I suppose it will not pay him to continue working the mines. But what fool of a fellow has he induced to buy them off him?"

"Speculators," said uncle Tom, "people who know nothing of the land or the country, and will drive the mine for all they are worth, to get every ounce out of the ground before the crash comes. I'm not a prophet, but that's what will happen, you may depend upon it."

"It will be queer," said Hal, "to think of the mines no longer belonging to the family. My great-grandfather would turn in his grave."

"From all I have heard of him he would do nothing of the sort," said the Rector. "Copper John was no sentimentalist. He would rub his hands in satisfaction to think that his grandson Henry was getting rid of it all, in the nick of time, with his fortune intact. Not like some of the Cornish families, who have gone bankrupt. No, Hal, you Brodricks don't all run to sentiment and dreams. There are some hard-headed fellows amongst you."

"It's a pity I'm not one of them," said Hal. "I'd have done more for myself, and for Jinny as well."

A few days later it was all over Doonhaven that Henry Brodrick had sold the mines to a London company. Mr Griffiths took Hal aside and showed him the letters, and a copy of the agreement.

"Seventy-four years," said Hal, "and now it's finished. All the tears and the sweat and the foresight and the labour. It's funny, I've never had a lot of feeling about the mines, Mr Griffiths. I've considered them a blot on the landscape, spoiling the rugged grandeur of Hungry Hill, but now they're to be handed over to strangers I feel resentful. I wish that it didn't have to happen."

"It won't affect you, Mr Brodrick. The new company will take over the staff, you know."

"Yes. . . . That's not quite what I meant, though."

"Well, your father is a very clever man, that's all I can say," said the manager. "He's made the bargain of a life-time. And you needn't worry. You'll reap the benefit of it all one day."

He doesn't see the point, thought Hal; he doesn't see that the mines were part of the family, like Clonmere. And now one is sold, and the other is barred and shuttered. It's queer. It's the breaking up of things.

A fortnight later the new director came over in person to inspect his property. He was a hard-faced man, with a north-country accent and a

loud, authoritative voice. He walked round the mines, hustling Mr
Griffiths, and rattling questions at him which flustered the old manager.
Hal only caught a glimpse of him as he passed through the counting-house. His visit was followed by others: people he sent down to
give expert advice about the workings; new engineers, new foremen.
Strangers to the country. And for the first time in his life Hal felt one
with the miners, and in a strange way they sensed it too. The men were
more open with him, more friendly, they cursed the intruders as "dour-
faced northern bastards", and laughed when Hal called them something
stronger still. He knew now what it felt like to be employed by a stranger,
working to a stranger's orders, and knowing that the product of the mine
would give him nothing in return but his bare weekly wage.

"You see," he told Jinny, "what a hypocrite I've been. These few
years, going up to the mines every day, I've had it in the back of my mind
all the time that they belonged to the family, and one day they would be
mine. And although it made me shy with the men, it gave me a sort of
satisfaction, deep down. And now they are nothing to do with me any
more. I might be working for the Slane Timber Works or the brick-yard
in Mundy. And I feel sullen and fed-up, just like Jim Donovan or any of
the others."

"I know," said Jinny. "It's sad. Ever since I remember anything, I
saw the trucks going up from the harbour to the mines with 'Brodrick'
written on them. Will they have another name now?"

"I don't know and I don't care," said Hal, "but I can't forgive my
father for it all the same."

The Rector was right when he summed up the purchasers as speculators. The method in the Doonhaven mines, instigated by Copper John
and continued by Henry when he lived at Clonmere, was to explore the
lodes carefully and slowly, never going to too great a depth at a time and
risking the wasting of the ore by excessive flooding. They had planned
for the years ahead, and not for the immediate present. The ore that
might be reached with greater caution and more skill in six or seven
years could be left until that time, and the stuff nearer the surface dealt
with first.

The new company cared for none of these ideas. They wanted immediate value for their money, and the richest lodes tapped and the ore
brought to the surface and away for shipment, all in six months. The
price of tin was dropping all the time, and unless they could make a
quick profit at once their losses would be enormous. The Doonhaven
miners, used to a casual, happy-go-lucky method of working for the
past twenty years, for old Griffiths was no driver, were expected to
work longer hours and to extract double the quantity of stuff, all at
the same time. The only way to achieve this was to raise the men's
wages.

The new owners decided to take the risk, and by announcing a specta-

cular rise in wages all round get the necessary labour out of the men, for
the few months they had set themselves as a working margin.

The news was hailed gleefully by the men, underground and above
the surface. The new owners were no longer "dour-faced bastards" but
"fine go-ahead fellows, who knew their job". A feverish activity spread
over the mining population. The furnaces blazed all night, the trucks
rattled to and fro from Hungry Hill to Doonhaven. Hal, scratching his
head over the books, would come back late in the evening and profess
himself bewildered by the change of speed. His father-in-law looked
grave and shook his head.

"It's a false boom," he said; "the men don't understand. Look at the
price of tin in this morning's paper. £75 a ton. A ten-pound drop in
under two months. The speculators will clear out of it before a very few
months are over, and the mines will close."

"But there's God's quantity of tin still in the ground," protested Hal,
"and copper too, if it was only worked. I heard one of the fellows talking
about it the other day."

"It will be worked just as long as it pays the company to do so," said
the Rector, "and after that it will remain untouched where Nature
planted it in the first place."

April . . . May . . . June . . . July . . . and nearly five months
had passed since the mines had changed hands. The third week in July
the new senior engineer, working under contract to the London company, told Mr Griffiths that he had been sent for by the director to
report.

"If they want me to carry on through the summer," he told the
manager, "I shan't be able to do it without complete new fittings to the
main pumps, and between you and me I don't for a moment think they
will stand the expense. I rather suspect this is the last I see of Doonhaven."

He left two days later, taking his staff of three with him. A new
rumour began to circulate that the present machinery was to be scrapped
and new engines shipped across the water from Bronsea. This was
followed by a further rumour that the wages of the miners were to be
raised again. One or two of the men asked Hal if he had any private
information.

"I'm sorry," said Hal. "I know no more than you do; but with tin at
its present low level I hardly think the company will raise wages any
higher. Have you seen today's paper? Tin's down to £64 a ton."

He was climbing into the trap, preparatory to driving home. One of
the men, Jim Donovan, stood with his hand on the rein.

"Is that why Mr Henry Brodrick sold the mines, then?" he said.

"My father does not write to me," he said, "but I think it's pretty
obvious why he sold them."

"He had the large price for them, I'll be bound," said Donovan, nudging his companion. "He won't suffer from the fall in price, whoever else does."

"That's what they call a sound business sense, Jim, in financial circles," said Hal, driving away.

The men stared after him, muttering amongst themselves. They did not believe a word he told them, of course, thought Hal. They imagined that as the son of the original owner he must know much more than he chose to say.

Old Griffiths began to look preoccupied and worried.

On the twenty-fourth of the month the manager went to Slane, and sent word back by the boy who drove him that business would keep him in the city for two or three days. In the harbour at Doonhaven one of the ships belonging to the company was due to sail with her cargo for Bronsea. Hal had occasion to go on board and give some instructions to the skipper. He knew the man well, he had been master of the vessel since his grandfather's day.

"Is it true, sir, what they were telling me in Bronsea before I left?" asked the skipper.

"What's that, Captain Davis?" said Hal.

"Why, that the 'Lucy-Ann' is the last ship to carry tin back to Bronsea?"

Hal put down the glass of rum that the skipper had poured out for him.

"I think they were pulling your leg in Bronsea," he said quietly.

"I don't know, sir; it wasn't just idle dock-yard chatter. It was one of the agents from the smelting works. 'Next load will be your last, Davis,' he said to me. 'The Doonhaven mines are going to close down.' I haven't heard a word of it this end. The talk here is all for another change of owners again, and a fortune for every man-jack in the place."

"The truth is probably somewhere between the two," said Hal.

"I've been on this trade for fifty years," said the skipper. "Came first as a youngster aboard my father's ship the 'Henrietta', as a lad of twelve. I can remember your great-grandfather—old Copper John, they used to call him—with his shovel hat and his cudgel stick, coming down here to the harbour to inspect the cargo. No Plimsol mark for him. Down to the scuppers with the copper, and the decks awash, and off to Bronsea on the tide, fair wind or foul. Well, that's a long time back now. It will seem strange to come no more to Mundy Bay of an evening, and see the lights of the garrison on Doon Island winking at me across the water."

"Let's try some more of your excellent rum," smiled Hal, "and drink to the past. It never does to think about the future."

Next morning when he drove up to the mine he found the road blocked with men, all standing about talking excitedly, women and children amongst them. Some of the men were grinning, and shouting jokes one to the other, the remainder looked bewildered, and were going from group to group gesticulating, asking questions.

The dressing-shed doors were wide open, no one was at work inside them. One of the firemen leant from the boilder-house, a pipe in his mouth. The biggest crowd was gathered round the shaft, where the shift below had just come above ground, and was being seized upon by the surface-workers.

"What about that three-shilling rise?" yelled someone, and an answering roar came from the crowd of men.

"What's happened?" said Hal, to a group of men gathered at the counting-house door.

"Work's suspended," said one. "Look at the notice there on the door. We're all to be paid off. . . . We don't any of us understand? What's wrong, Mr Brodrick? There's plenty of stuff below ground."

Hal did not answer. He went into the counting-house. Mr Griffiths was standing in the middle of the room. He had not taken off his coat or his hat. He was surrounded by a little group of skilled workers and engineers, who were plying him with questions. His face was white and drawn.

"It's no use asking me," he said. "I can't do anything. I have my orders, just like the rest of you. I shall draw my salary today for the last time. It's not my fault, it's not anyone's fault. The notices came through to the offices in Slane, and were handed on to me. What machinery there is has been bought by a firm in Slane, and will be sold as scrap, I suppose. I tell you I don't know."

"What about the stuff in the lodes," asked one of the men, "where we've been working? There's pounds of it there, not yet brought to the surface."

"It will have to stay," said the manager, "the company aren't paying for any more work. That's what was told me in Slane. Every man employed here is to be paid off today. If the firm who have bought up the machinery care to employ any of you in the clearance, no doubt they will do so. My orders don't give me any authority. I tell you it's nobody's fault. You must blame the fall in the price of tin, that's all."

He withdrew into the inner room. Hal followed him, and found him standing before the desk, turning over papers and documents in a hopeless, resigned fashion.

"What can I do?" he said to Hal. "It's almost as big a shock to me as it is to them. It's true I've put by, my wife is a careful manager, and we've got a small property in the north where we can go and retire. But I didn't expect it so suddenly. And look at all the clearing that has to be done, files going back seventy-five years, all to be checked and sorted, some of them burnt, the rest taken into Slane. But it's the men, and the women and children, who are going to suffer, Mr Brodrick. They don't put aside for a rainy day. And they've been spending more freely of late, ever since they got that rise of pay. If it had come gradually they might have understood, but coming suddenly as it has done, they're going to take it hard."

They were grim hours that followed, when Hal, for the last time, sat beside Mr Griffiths in the counting-house and gave the men their pay. The tramp of feet had never sounded so ominous, so heavy, and each man as he stepped forward to receive his money asked the same question. "Why had it happened?" "What did they close the mine for, when the stuff was as rich as ever underground?" Some were bewildered, some truculent and angry, one or two used threats. "We've been cheated," said one of them, "induced to stay and lost our chances elsewhere. I've a son in South Africa, wanted me to join him two months back, in the mines out there, and I refused. Now it's too late. What am I going to do? Sit in this country and starve?"

"I'm very sorry," said the manager wearily, for the hundredth time. "I can't do anything. Blame the price of tin."

The tramp of feet, the tired, angry faces of men and women—they never stopped coming, one after the other, through the counting-house door.

"The owners don't lose by it," said some man. "They make their pile and retire in comfort. It's we that have to pay for it."

"True for you," said Jim Donovan, who stood behind him, looking at Hal as he received his money. "Here's Mr Brodrick, son of the last owner; he'll not be parting with his shirt, will you, Mr Brodrick? Sure, you can go and live across the water if you have the mind."

He tramped past, sullen and resentful, his usual impudent, cheerful face set in hard lines of anger and disappointment.

They did not understand, once they had been paid, that this was the end, and there was no more to do. They continued to stand about the shafts and the boiler-houses and the dressing-sheds, staring stupidly at the half-loaded trolleys and trucks.

"The waste of it," was heard on every side. "It doesn't make sense. There's something wrong somewhere. There's a mistake been made."

But there was no mistake. The mines on Hungry Hill had ceased to work. The fires went out at last, and the smokeless stacks lifted black faces to the sky. The whine and whirl of machinery was still. A queer silence seemed to fall upon the place, broken only by the restless walking up and down of the bewildered men, who would not disperse. In the counting-house the papers were filed and packed away in bags and boxes. Hal could scarcely see; he had worked up to ten o'clock every evening now for five days. Wherever he went and wherever he walked he would find one of the miners standing idle by the road, that same dazed, resentful look upon his face as Jim Donovan had worn. The women called to one another in shrill voices from their cottages. The children, free and excited, chased each other about the empty dressing-sheds, or made castles in the slack-heaps that had not been cleared away. No one stopped them. They could do as they liked. There was no order any more, no supervision. Four days, five days, six days, and the work of clearing the files and accounts was almost done. The men had begun to drift away, to walk down in bands to the village, coming back drunk and singing from the public-houses. The mine began to wear a deserted air. The door of the engine-house swung backwards and forwards on a broken hinge.

"Desolation reigns supreme," Hal said to Jinny. "I never want to see the mines again. Why the devil didn't I leave when my father sold them five months ago?"

The Rector, and his wife, and Jinny were doing their best to help the miners' families, those who had no money put by for such an emergency. It was difficult for Tom Callaghan, because the most improvident of the families did not attend his church, and came under the care of the priest.

"No time for differences now," said Tom, in consultation with him, a young raw fellow, hardly more than a boy, who had been appointed to Doonhaven only six months before. "We have got to work together, and see what we can do to help the people. It's the greatest mercy of God that this blow has fallen in midsummer, instead of in winter."

The young priest was only too willing to co-operate, and to seek advice from the older man. It was decided to use the parish room belonging to the Rector as a store for food and clothing, and anyone in real need would be able to go there and ask for assistance. The store was put in charge of Jinny and her mother. Meanwhile the Rector and Mr Griffiths were kept busy going backwards and forwards to Slane to see the emigration authorities, for over half the mining population began to clamour now to leave Doonhaven as soon as possible, before the autumn started, and seek a new livelihood in America and Australia and Africa.

It was easiest for those who had saved money and were skilled miners. They would soon fall on their feet again, and it was not difficult to get them a passage. But the odd-job men, the surface workers, the firemen and others, who were trained in nothing in particular and had spent their pay every week as it came along, these constituted the problem of Doonhaven. Many of them were local men, or had come from the neighbouring country, and had worked in the mines from early boyhood. They knew no other trade. The older men, philosophical and more easy-going, shrugged their shoulders and tilled their bit of land. It was pleasant in a way to sit in the sun and do nothing for a change; something would turn up before the winter. The younger men, restless, and dissatisfied, roamed the countryside in bands, bent on mischief which they felt justified in doing. Fences were broken, chicken and pigs stolen, orchards robbed, and a spirit of terrorism began to spread abroad which brought no sympathy for the men themselves, only harsh words from the magistrates and threats to bring the soldiers ashore from the garrison on Doon Island.

"It will blow over," said Simon Flower, Kitty's husband, who had much of the easy-going tolerance of his grandfather and namesake. "In a couple of months' time the fellows will be lifting potatoes and keeping pigs, as peaceful as you or I. Let them have their fling first."

"Yes," said the Rector, "I agree with you. It will blow over, and they will go back to the land. But first they may do a considerable amount of damage, poor fellows, and cause trouble to themselves and to other people."

"Seriously," said Jinny, "there are several people who have become quite nervous of Jim Donovan and his crowd. They flung stones at Mrs Griffiths when she was driving into Mundy last week, and lamed the pony. And you know I am certain it was his lot that broke all the windows in the Post Office."

They none of them really understood, thought Hal, except perhaps his father-in-law, what a shock it had been to the young men of Doonhaven to see the mines go as they had done, almost overnight. The mines of Hungry Hill, which they had known from childhood, and their fathers before them, and to which they instinctively turned for a living, had become dead and lifeless. What irked them most was the fact that the ore was still there underground, waiting to be brought to the surface. They could not understand why a precious mineral should suddenly become valueless.

"The world still needs tin, doesn't it?" Jim Donovan had asked.

How was it possible to explain to him about cheap labour in Malay? No, thought Hal, it was much simpler to give Jim Donovan a drink and tell him to forget his troubles. For himself, he was glad to be free again. Glad that the whistle of the six-o'clock engine and the clanging bells no longer woke him from sleep, and he could lie in bed, if he wanted to, until ten in the morning, and then, leaning out of his bedroom window, sniffing the summer day, decide to take his paint-box and his easel across the harbour to Clonmere, and alone all day, with a sandwich for lunch, paint the still waters of the creek below the house, the low hump of Doon Island, and the great, green shoulder of Hungry Hill.

"It's the best you've ever done," said Jinny, when after three days he brought his picture home to her and put it up in their little sitting-room, the paint still wet on the canvas. "Do you know, I am sure that if you took it to London and sent it up to the Academy, they would accept it, and you would sell it for a hundred guineas?"

"A hundred rejection slips," smiled Hal. "No, Jinny girl, I'd rather not risk the blow to my pride. It's a present for John-Henry's second birthday. He can look at it when he's a man and see the sun, as I have painted it, on the top of Hungry Hill, and think there's the old hill that brought my family good fortune. The grass will be growing out of the chimney-stacks by the time he's turned twenty-one."

They stood together, looking at the picture, and then the door of the sitting-room opened, and the Rector came into the room. He had an open letter in his hand, and he was smiling.

"I've news for you, Hal," he said, "but you'll never guess what it is."

"You've found a new job for me," said Hal, "and I warn you now that I'm not going to take it."

"Nothing of the sort," said Tom. "Here's a letter from your father. He's crossing to Slane, and he will be in Doonhaven the day after tomorrow."

<h1 style="text-align:center">7</h1>

The sun was setting in the west over Mundy bay. Little mackerel clouds had come up against the wind, and now hung motionless in the pale sky, for the breeze had died away with the approach of evening.

Hal stood by the lake on Hungry Hill, looking down on Doonhaven and Clonmere. The village, a small, straggling line by the harbour water, still held the sun, but Clonmere was in shadow. The trees made a tapestry pattern about the castle, and beyond the trees lay the moors and the white road across the moors that led to the Denmare river and Kileen. The world below seemed unreal and remote, like the mist world of a dream at daybreak. Hungry Hill alone had clarity and brightness, the air was full of scent, and the turf under his feet was firm and green. Even the granite rocks were hot where the sun had been all day.

"This is the picture I should have painted," thought Hal, "not how the hill looks from Doonhaven and Clonmere, but how we down there must look from Hungry Hill. . . . Petty and insignificant, little ants running about our business. The Brodricks come and go, the men and women of Doonhaven marry, and give birth, and die, the mines make their song and their clatter for seventy-five years, and then are silent again. It's all one of the fairies and the ghosts of Hungry Hill. One day I'll make a picture of it, or if I'm too lazy perhaps John-Henry will. But whatever happens in this country of ours the hill remains undefeated. He has the laugh on all of us."

He began walking away from the lake, eastward across the shoulder of the mountain, towards the mines. He had lunched early, and had walked all afternoon alone, in a mood of nerviness and strange unrest which he could not explain, even to Jinny.

His father was to be in Doonhaven tomorrow. . . . He would see him, touch his hand, talk to him—his father, whom he had not seen now for fifteen years, not since he had walked out of his house when he was twenty years old. So many letters that had remained unwritten from Canada, conceived during his most lonely moments, but never put down on paper. Letters from Doonhaven too, that had come to his thoughts but not to his pen. Descriptions of the mines, tales of Jinny and the boy. And always the silence between them, always the reserve. It was to be broken at last, and he had a great fear in his heart that the meeting would be a failure. They would stand in front of one another, tongue-tied, awkward, alike in so many ways, different in too much, and then his father would break the silence with that old forced, half-jocular tone that he had used many years ago to his schoolboy son, saying "Well, Hal . . . how are you, and how's the painting, eh?"

The answer would be the same, clumsy and shy, dragged from him reluctantly, "All right, thanks," and then his father, waiting a moment for more and being disappointed, would turn to Tom Callaghan and be relieved because his presence eased the restraint between them.

His father. . . . He would look perhaps with pity on Jinny, who from shyness would show herself too eager, too anxious to please. John-Henry would be produced, and his quiet, silent charm would not be in readiness for the occasion, a baby tantrum at being dressed in his best would have given him a sullen, obstinate air. He would turn away from his grandfather and bury his head in a cushion. The encounter would be a failure from every point of view. As he walked Hal became angry.

Why should his father come suddenly, after all these years, and make a disturbance of the routine? He had business in Slane, he said in his letter to uncle Tom—the sale of property in the city, and some matters to do with shipping and the mining company that needed adjustment.

The mines. . . . Yes, thought Hal, let him come and inspect the mines and see the smokeless stacks and the smashed machinery, the heap of rubble, the general air of desolation. Let him talk to Mrs Connor, who had her fifth baby the week after the mines were closed down, and no money in the house, and poor Tim Connor lying drunk in the street at Doonhaven because they wouldn't give him and his family a passage to America.

There was plenty for his father to see. He did not have to worry, he did not have to put his hand in his pocket. It was not his fault. No, he had got out of the affair like the shrewd, clever business man he was, just before the market struck rock-bottom. He could look at the families, and the stricken mine, and fellows like Jim Donovan who roamed the countryside with murder in his heart; and then go back to his house in Brighton and to Adeline, and live in comfort and security. The tenants would continue to pay their rent to a landlord they never saw, and the mould and the damp would eat the walls of Clonmere. It would not matter to Henry Brodrick. Hal had crossed the shoulder of the hill, and now stood on the ride above the deserted mine. Below him were the dressing-sheds and the tall boiler-house chimney. Someone had lit a fire of the rubble that lay before the boiler-house. The smoke rose in the air, black and foul, and coming down closer, Hal could see a crowd of men laughing and talking through the smoke, throwing bits of refuse and broken timber on to the fire to increase the blaze. One of them bore a great plank on his shoulder, torn from a bench in the counting-house, and hurled it amongst the rubble in the fire.

It was Jim Donovan. Hal climbed down over the heap of slack that lay behind the shaft and joined them.

"Some of that timber would come in handy during the winter, if you saved it," he said. "Why not make a stack of it instead of burning it now? Then you can come down in the colder weather and chop it up for your families."

One or two of the men hung back, looking to Jim Donovan for advice. He stared at Hal aggressively, his cap on the side of his head giving him a knowing, cock-sure expression.

"Good-evening to you, Mr Brodrick," he said. "And you just having a stroll, I presume, round your father's ancient property, to see that no further damage is done to the place, and if it is, why you'll go and report it to the magistrate, no doubt, and have us poor fellows clapped into jail."

"I wouldn't do that, Jim," smiled Hal; "you ought to know me better. You can destroy all that's left of the mine, for all I care. But you might be glad of some of this stuff for fuel a bit later on."

Jim said nothing. His mouth had an ugly, sullen set to it, and he kicked a larger piece of timber into the fire.

"I hear Mr Griffiths is going up north to live," he said. "They say he has a house across the border waiting for him. And then he has the cheek to tell us he knew nothing about the mines being closed. The fellow's a liar."

"Shame to him for it, then," said another, "putting furniture in it as cool as you please, all these past four months, and us poor fellows as ignorant as babies. You'd say there was no justice in the world."

"Nor is there," said Jim Donovan fiercely, "except when you take the law into your own hands. As for Mr Griffiths, he's welcome to his fine house, for all I care. But I tell you I'd like to wring his neck, and all the rest of them that's deceived us."

His voice had risen, and he moved closer to Hal, his fists clenched. His friends murmured in approval, closing in behind him.

Poor devil, thought Hal; he's had a couple down at the pub in Doonhaven, and it's got him on the raw, instead of laying him out quiet and peaceful.

"All right, Jim," he said, "curse old Griffiths if you want to, but he's had no hand in the business, I promise you. He knew no more about it than I did, and that's a fact."

Someone whistled in derision, and another man laughed.

"Ah, laugh away," said Jim Donovan. "Mr Brodrick is like the rest of the gentlemen, smooth-faced and easy-spoken. It's him that is laughing at us all the time. So you didn't know the mines were to be closed, Mr Brodrick? And when your father sold them to the London company, that was news to you too, I'll be bound? We know a bit more than that, I can tell you. We know you were go-between all the while, through from Mr. Griffiths to your father and the London company. Why, didn't you have the letters running through your hands day after day, from Slane and London and Bronsea, besides those that you get at home? I may be the son of a poor man, Mr Brodrick, who has only a few pigs and cows grazing on a piece of ground as big as my hand, when in days gone by we owned all the land hereabouts that your father holds now, but by all the blessed saints in heaven I'm not such a fool as I look."

He turned round on one foot, to survey the effect of his speech upon his companions.

"That's right, Jim," said one of the men, "you have the heart of a lion, I'm always telling you."

Hal shrugged his shoulders. He was suddenly bored by them, and their deliberate misunderstanding of the position. It was useless to argue with a fellow like Jim Donovan anyway. He was tired now after his long tramp on Hungry Hill, and wanted Jinny, and his supper, and his bed before facing his father the following day.

"Goodnight," he said shortly, and turned away, making for the cinder track that led down to the high road. But Jim Donovan and his friends followed close at his heels.

"Not so fast, Mr Brodrick," said Jim. "Maybe the lads and I haven't finished talking with you yet. There's many an account to settle between our families, going back over the years. Wasn't it my own first cousin that was murdered by your father and your mother, travelling home in their carriage after a banquet, the horses whipped on to him by the coachman, and my poor cousin's brains spattering the road, and them driving on with never a care for him? It was common knowledge they were glad to see him dead, for the scandal your uncle brought upon his sister."

Hal looked over his shoulder at the angry man.

"For the Lord's sake, Jim," he said, "go home and get to bed and sleep off your temper. Take him off, some of you fellows, or carry him there, if he can't walk. I'm in no mood to start a quarrel about my uncle or my father or anyone else."

The men stared at him without answer, and Hal moved off down the cinder track. He had walked scarcely half a dozen yards before a stone struck the side of his head. It was a sharp, jagged stone, breaking the skin. Hal turned round to face his assailant, and another stone caught him above the eye.

"You damned fool," he shouted. "What the hell do you think you're doing? If you want to fight, come on, and I'll fight you fair."

He ran up the path towards Jim, his temper thoroughly roused, the blood pouring down his head from the jagged stone. He was met by an avalanche of stones that brought him to his knees, and the moment he was down the men rushed upon him, shouting, excited, one seizing his arm and twisting it behind his back so that he could not hit out at them, one or two of the others throwing themselves upon his body.

"Drag him down to the road and let him lie there, like your cousin," said one, and "Burn him in the fire," shouted Jim, "let him feed the flames."

Someone tied a handkerchief round his eyes, hard and tight, and the blood from the wound in his head began to trickle into his eyes, warm and sickly, and he could see nothing.

The men were shouting and laughing, and now some of them were

seizing his arms, and the rest his legs, and bearing him away up the
cinder track to the fire by the dressing-sheds.

"You bloody idiots," said Hal, weak and faint from the mauling they
had given him. "Do you want the whole country down upon you, and
twenty years apiece at the Mundy Assizes?"

Someone hit him on the mouth—Jim Donovan no doubt—and then he
was thrown face downwards in a heap of rubble, choking, suffocating,
while his hands were bound behind him.

"Ah, leave him there to rot," said one of the men, "and come away
home, Jim. We've had sport enough for one evening, haven't we?"

The sight of Hal lying in the rubble, dazed and half-conscious, made
the men uneasy. Jim had led them into this, and now it was best to get
away, and maybe put several miles between them and Doonhaven. The
sound of their voices grew fainter, and lying there in the rubble Hal could
hear the crunch of their boots as they climbed the heap of slack above
him and made away across the hill. The blood went on trickling into his
eyes behind the bandage, and even found its way to his mouth. He felt
faint, and deadly sick. The bonfire died away beside him, and he could
tell by the stillness and the silence that darkness was falling fast.

"Jinny will be worried," he thought. "She'll go round to the Rectory
and get hold of uncle Tom."

What an idiot he had been ever to talk to Jim Donovan and his friends.
He should have turned back across the hill as soon as he saw them. A fat
lot of use it had been showing sympathy with the silly bastards. Hal
rolled over on to his side, and worked loose the piece of rope that bound
his wrists together. Then he tore off the handkerchief they had placed
across his eyes. He found, to his dismay, that he could not see at all. One
eye was closed up entirely, from the cut above it, and the other was
gummed with the clotted blood. He would have to find water to bathe
his eye before he could make his way home, five miles or more in the
gathering darkness. He struggled to his feet, and peered about him,
trying to gain a sense of direction. There was water hard by, surely, close
to the dressing-sheds, where the tin used to be washed, but with his closed
eyes, and the murky evening light, he could not remember whether the
sheds had been to the right or to the left of the heap of rubble where the
men had thrown him. He moved forward slowly, his arms outstretched,
and as he took step by step, faltering, as helpless as a blind man, he
thought of his father arriving tomorrow morning in the steamer at Slane.
He would come down to Doonhaven and find his son in bed probably,
with his eyes bandaged, and his body black and blue. And he would not
believe the story of a fight on Hungry Hill, for twenty-five years of living
across the water would have made him forgetful of the strange ways and
crazy happenings of his own country, where men drank with one another
one moment and fought the next, all because of something that happened
before they were born. His father would be shown up to the bedroom by

a shy and nervous Jinny, and he would see Hal lying against the pillows with two black eyes, and say to himself "A drunken brawl, of course; the girl is trying to hush it up." The thought of this, so typical and inevitable, made Hal laugh helplessly to himself, and he thought how impossible it was going to be to explain to his father what had happened. It would be simpler to let the matter rest, and for his father to continue thinking him useless, tipsy, and incompetent, staggering home in his cups on a Saturday night, as half the men in Doonhaven had done since the beginning of time.

Hal touched something with his hands, a rough, hard surface, like a brick wall, and he stumbled over a piece of planking at his feet.

God damn it all, he thought wearily. I'm nowhere near the dressing-sheds. This feels like the boiler-house wall—and he went forward, step by step, groping his way in the darkness. He felt himself getting light-headed, and he was aware suddenly of a feeling of sadness, that somehow he had made a mess of his day on Hungry Hill, that should have brought him peace and quiet, and now it was going to end foolishly, like so many things in his life.

Jinny would worry about him, and so would uncle Tom; they were going to be unhappy because of him. Everything was dark, he could see nothing with his damned swollen, bleeding eyes, and surely he was not by the mines at all, not on Hungry Hill, but walking in the shadows of the new wing at Clonmere, a little boy again, trying to find his way to mamma's bedroom? The door to the boudoir was close at hand, and if he opened it and stepped into the room he would go to the shutters and pull them aside, that had stood rusted so long with the damp, and mamma would be waiting for him on the balcony that she had never used.

The moon rose over the shoulder of Hungry Hill, he could feel the light of it, in his blindness, and he thought it was the lamp she had lit for him, and that she stood waiting for him by the open door. He turned to go to her, and the black shaft yawned at him as he went. . . .

8

Jinny dressed her boy with great care, and he did not protest because although he was barely two he understood that sadness had come upon them all, and if he pulled and tugged at his clothes he would make her unhappy. He sat on her lap while she drew on the clean white socks, and the black shoes with the buckles. Then she took out his new suit from its tissue paper. Bottle-green velvet, with lace collar and cuffs. She parted his hair on one side for the first time, brushing away the heavy, dark fringe. She had a tear at the corner of her eye, and this made him sorrowful. There was nothing he could do. He looked away over her shoulder at the beaver hat that had been bought for him from the shops. He knew that it would be uncomfortable, and he did not want to wear it. It was black, like his shoes, and like the dress she wore. Her pretty blue dress was hanging in the cupboard. When Jinny had finished dressing him she stood him up on a chair and looked at him, and he had the feeling that she wanted him to be bigger than he was. Then she smiled at him, although the tear was still in the corner of her eye.

"I'm proud of you, dear," she said, "you look very nice. And I want you to be very good, because we are going to see your grandfather."

He considered this a moment. The word was too long for him, but it had a meaning.

"Granpie?" he said slowly, his expression brightening.

"No, not Granpie," she said, "someone else, that you have not seen before. We are going up to Clonmere to see him."

This could be understood. Clonmere was the house with the balcony and the windows, where they went so often for their walks. And climbing down from the chair he allowed the ugly beaver hat to be placed upon his head, and the elastic snapped tight under his chin.

They went downstairs to the hall, hand in hand, and outside in the road Patsy was waiting, with the pony and trap. John-Henry looked to see if the picnic-basket was to be put in the trap, but there was no sign of it.

"Picnic?" he said, watching his mother's face, but she shook her head.

"No, son," she said, "no picnic today."

He accepted the statement, but it was strange to drive in the trap with Patsy unless food was taken, and Granpie came, with rugs, and sticks, and coats, and parasols. Perhaps the arrival of the trap was a tribute to his velvet suit and the black beaver hat.

As Jinny passed the study she glanced in through the door, and saw that the Rector was sitting at his desk.

"We're going," she said. Her voice was calm and steady.

Tom Callaghan turned round in his chair. His face was grave, but his deep-set eyes were tender as he looked at his daughter and the boy.

"I've told you," he said, "not to expect anything from him. He is hard and cold, Jinny, not the man you remember as a child, who laughed and smiled and was gay, like our dear Hal. The years have been heavy with him."

"I don't want anything from him," said Jinny. "I only think it right that he should see John-Henry."

"Yes," said the Rector, "yes, I understand."

Then she went from the room, with the boy, and they climbed into the trap and drove through the village street up the hill and past the cottages at Oakmount, until they came to the long wall, and the gate-house.

Young Mrs Sullivan was standing at the entrance to the drive, and as the trap drove through she curtseyed to Jinny, who returned the gesture with a solemn little bow. John-Henry sat stiff and straight beside her. People did not curtsey to her as a rule. Another tribute to the velvet suit.

He glanced at her hands. She was wearing gloves, a thing she only did in winter, or when she went to church with Granpie on Sunday morning.

Down the drive bowled the trap, through the rough park-lands and the woods, and there was the creek to the left of them, and the castle standing on the high grass bank above them. There was smoke coming from one of the chimneys, and the windows in the old part of the house had been flung open. There was a carriage drawn up in the turn of the drive before the castle. There was luggage placed on the seat beside the driver. The front door of the great hall, that Jinny had never seen open, was open now.

Jinny hesitated a moment, but custom was too strong for her, and in a low voice she bade Patsy drive to the side door, in the old part of the house. She was a little nervous now. She pulled at the boy's lace collar, and straightened his hat on his head. Something of her feeling communicated itself to the child, and he felt shy and uncomfortable; he wanted to stay in the trap with Patsy.

"No," she said firmly, "you must come with me. And I want you to shake hands very politely when you see your grandfather."

The side door was open, but Jinny rang the bell. It clanged loudly, echoing in a passage far away. A servant came to the door—the valet, she supposed, who had travelled over from London with his master.

"Mrs Brodrick?" he asked, and John-Henry saw his mother bow again. The gesture pleased him. It was so full of dignity. He imitated her, nodding his head up and down, but she frowned, and he supposed it was something that only grown-up people were allowed to do.

The servant opened a door across the hall and showed them into a large room, a dining-room. The cloth had been removed, but there was a long strip of green baize down the centre of the table.

This is where we lunched that Christmas day, thought Jinny, when I was sixteen and Hal was twenty. . . . The servant had kindled a small wood fire in the grate, for although it was August the weather was chill. There were two chairs before the fire. Jinny was uncertain whether she should sit or stand. She had expected that Hal's father would have been in the room, waiting for them. The door at the end of the room was open. She remembered that it gave on a passage leading to the new wing, and she wondered if he had gone through there, to the other part of the house. She went on standing before the fire-place, holding John-Henry by the hand, and the little boy looked about him with interest, and pointed to a picture on the wall. It was a young girl, with soft brown eyes and dark curling hair. She wore a string of pearls round her neck.

"Yes," whispered Jinny, "she's very pretty."

Jinny turned to the other side of the fire-place and gazed at the portrait of Hal's mother. How like him she must have been, that same reserve, that silence for no reason. Then the boy tugged at her hand, and looking over her shoulder, she saw that Hal's father had come into the room. He was not the Henry Brodrick she remembered as a child, not the Henry of the pencil sketch in the study at the Rectory. He was thinner, much thinner, and his face had fallen away, that had been large and firm before. His hair was scarce on top, and nearly white. The mouth was narrow, and the eyes more prominent than she remembered. Then he came forward, holding out his hand.

"You are Jinny," he said, "and I haven't seen you since you were six years old."

She had been ready to stand on her dignity, to speak at once in defence of Hal, of all that had happened, to accuse Henry if need be of neglect, unkindness, hardness of heart, but at his words her antagonism went, her defences were stripped from her, and she saw that he was shy and uncertain, even as she was herself, and lonely too.

"Yes," she said, "I'm Jinny, and this is John-Henry."

The boy put up his hand, as he had been told to do, and looked then around him at the door, wishing they might go.

"Won't you sit down?" said Henry, pointing to the chair, and Jinny held the boy by her side, whispering to him to be still.

For a moment Henry did not speak. He glanced away from the boy to the wood fire in the grate.

"What are your plans?" he said.

"I shall go on living in Doonhaven, with father and mother at the Rectory," she said, "until it is time for John-Henry to go to school. Then, I don't know. It will depend on many things."

"I suppose," said Henry, "that Tom would like him to be a parson?"

"I don't think so," said Jinny. "Once, when I was talking about the future, he said that the Navy would be an excellent thing for John-Henry. But we needn't think about it yet."

There was a moment's pause.

"And Hal?" said his father. "Did he have any ideas on the subject?"

Jinny held the boy's hand, which was fidgeting with the lace collar.

"No," she said gently. "Hal was not interested in education, or professions. He just imagined that—that one day John-Henry would live here at Clonmere."

Henry rose to his feet, and stood with his hands behind his back, looking down on Jinny and his grandson.

"I wanted to sell the place," he said, "many years ago. Hal will have told you that. I would still sell it, but, as you probably know, Clonmere is entailed. When I die, and this boy reaches the age of twenty-one, he can do as he likes. He can break the entail at will."

"Yes," said Jinny.

Henry walked slowly up and down the room.

"Property is a burden these days," he said. "There is not the value in it that there used to be. We're soon going to enter upon a new century too, and things are changing fast. This country may be slower to change than most, I don't know about that. I've lived away too long either to know or to care."

He spoke without bitterness, but his voice was sad, as though, since he had looked upon his home, the past had risen up and closed upon him.
"Will you never come back to live here again?" said Jinny.
"No," he said, "no, that's all finished and done with."
He turned and faced her, his hands behind his back, his head a little on one side. That is how Hal used to stand, she thought. He had been part of him after all, a very great part, he had not belonged entirely to his mother.
"The mines are gone," he said; "they were the great link with this country. They brought good fortune to my family, but I doubt if they brought happiness. That is one of the reasons that I sold them, not to be quit of a bad debt, as most people believe. Now only the house remains, and if you and the boy want to live here, you are welcome to do so. There won't be any money for the upkeep though, not until I die. And I don't propose spending a penny on it in the meantime."
Jinny flushed. This was the Henry her father had warned her about. The business man, who sought first his own interests, or rather those of the wife at his back across the water, and was not likely to put his hand in his pocket for anyone else, not even his own grandson.
"It would be rather too big," said Jinny, "for me and John-Henry alone. Living close by, at the Rectory, we can come here often, and later on, when he is older, he will understand that one day it will belong to him."
It seemed to her that he looked upon her strangely, and with pity, and she held the boy's hand tightly, as though the firmness of his touch gave her strength and consolation.
"This is the third generation of my family," he said, "to be brought up by one parent only. You have lost Hal. I lost my Katherine. And my mother lost her John, when he was only a year or so older than your Hal. You will find it is not easy, for the one who is left. . . ."
"No," said Jinny, "it will not be easy. But I love John-Henry, and I am not afraid."
He looked away from her, up at the portrait of Katherine on the wall. Then, very slowly, he put his hand inside his waistcoat pocket, and drew out a small round leather case. He held it a moment in his hands, and then snapped the clasp. He took from the case a replica of the portrait on the wall, in miniature. The likeness was well done, although the colouring was a little smudged in places, and the hair brighter than in reality.
"I have not shown this to anyone else," said Henry, "and I never shall. Hal did it for me, when he was a lad. . . . He gave it me the night I brought Adeline back to London with me, and I rather think I never thanked him for it. You see, we were both a little shy of one another."
Jinny held the miniature, and then gave it back to Henry. He replaced it carefully in the leather case, and put it in his pocket.
"I've carried it now for twenty-one years," he said, "and Adeline has never discovered it."
A ghost of a smile appeared on his lips, and and in a flash Jinny saw the

gay laughing Henry that once had been, the young man who stood beside her father in the university group.

"You won't give me away to anyone, will you?" he said.

Jinny shook her head.

He turned once more, and looked out of the window at the grass bank sloping to the creek. The sun shone upon a strip of carpet at his feet, and the myriad dust particles danced in a beam of light.

"You are fortunate in having Tom and Harriet for parents," said Henry. "They will take care of you and this boy, and you won't be alone. Hal's allowance will automatically come to you now, of course, you realise that. And when I die, as I told you before, the child has everything."

He glanced down dubiously at the small, solemn figure in the bottle-green velvet suit. "An empty house, and a load of doubts and dreams— notmuch of a legacy," he said.

John-Henry leant against his mother, and tugged at her hand, his signal that he wished to go. He did not care greatly for the strange man who looked down at him with pity, and he wanted to be back at the Rectory, with Granpie, amongst familiar things that he knew and understood.

"He's had enough of me," said Henry, with a smile. "All right, young man, I won't keep you any longer. I am going too."

He walked with them to the hall. The luggage had been put in the carriage, the valet was standing in his hat and coat by the open door.

"It's a mistake," said Henry, "to walk back into the past. Look forward always, if you can."

He gazed up at the house, the barred windows of the new wing, the iron balcony above the door. Then he shook hands with Jinny, and touched the boy lightly on the head. He climbed into the carriage, and the servant slammed the door, taking his seat on the box beside the driver.

"I want you to say goodbye to Tom and your mother for me," said Henry. "I won't see them again. Ask Tom whether he remembers saying to me over thirty years ago, 'I would rather be good like the Eyres than clever like you Brodricks'? The trouble is that goodness dies, and lies buried in the earth. Cleverness passes on and becomes degenerate."

He looked for the last time at the stone walls of the castle, and down across the sloping grass to the creek, and Doon Island, and grey mass of Hungry Hill. Then he smiled once more at Jinny.

"You never knew my mother, did you?" he said. "She died many years ago in Nice. The last words she ever said to me were, 'Don't look serious, Henry boy. Thinking never did anybody any good.' I don't know if she was right or wrong, but thinking always brought me pain. You can tell that story to your son, when he comes into his legacy."

He gave an order to the driver, and lifted his hat, and the carriage bowled away down the drive, and disappeared amongst the belt of trees. As it passed into the woods the herons rose from their nests in the tall branches, and went crying down the creek towards Doon Island.

THE INHERITANCE, 1920

I

As JOHN-HENRY turned into Queen Street a sentry came out of the doorway of a house.

"I wouldn't go any further," he said. "They're shooting down the other end and you might get a bullet in your back from one of our fellows."

As he spoke they heard the rattle of a machine-gun and the squealing brakes of a car. The sentry grinned.

"Trouble for someone," he said.

At the far end of the street a car skidded into the pavement, and from the lowered window they could see the nose of the gun pointing across the square. Three men on the pavement flung themselves on their faces. Someone ran from one of the houses to the car and jumped on the running-board. He had a rifle in his hand. A small party of soldiers appeared at the end of the street by the square, and the car gathered speed and turned sideways, up a back street by the farthest house. The soldiers fired at the retreating car, and then they began to run across the square towards the big post office at the corner. The men who had flung themselves down on the pavement picked themselves up again, and dusted their clothes, as though nothing had happened. A woman called shrilly from one of the upper windows of a house. The church clock struck five o'clock. John-Henry lit a cigarette and smiled at the soldier.

"You'd think," he said, "that after four-and-a-half years of war men would be sick of shooting one another."

The soldier took a fag from behind his ear, and borrowed a match.

"Not in this country," he said; "there's not a man amongst 'em who wouldn't knife his best friend if he had the mind, and then take flowers to his funeral."

John-Henry laughed, and threw away the match.

"That's not fair," he said. "I'm one of them, and I've never wanted to knife anyone."

He went on walking down the street towards the square, where the shooting had been. Many of the windows were broken, not from the incident of five minutes ago, but dating back over the weeks. The square was clear now of troops, but for the guard standing round the police-station. A young man was talking to a woman on the edge of the pavement. His face was lean and bitter. He had his hands deep in his pockets.

"They got Micky Farran," he said to the woman, and then, as John-Henry passed, he stopped talking, and looked down at his feet.

They moved off together, and it seemed to John-Henry that the streets were empty now, and strangely quiet. Across the square, at the far end, were the remains of the barricade. The barbed wire lay in loose strands. A sudden shower of rain came from the bright sky, and was gone again. In the far distance a steamer hooted, deep and low, and was echoed by the high, thin answer of a tug. John-Henry was thinking of the sentry's words, "Not a man amongst them who wouldn't knife his best friend, and then take flowers to his funeral." It was true, he supposed, and yet . . .

Faces of his childhood came into his mind. Dear Granpie, with his great, deep-set eyes, his bent shoulders, his white hair, walking through the market-square at Doonhaven, and one of the old women at the stalls lifting a streaming face to his and calling upon the Saints to bless him. He had found employment for the woman's son, and she had never forgotten it. Gran, small, bright and bustling, skimming the cream off the milk with a scallop shell, boxing his ears because he tickled the kitchen-maid's legs with a feather duster, and she half-way up a ladder at the time. Patsy, gardener on week-days and groom on Sundays, who told him the legends of the fairies who walked on Hungry Hill, and the little pixies who burrowed underground and bewitched the miners in the old days. He would not have known how to handle a knife except to whittle sticks or to cut a pig's throat. Perhaps killing a pig made it easy to kill a man. . . .

The streets looked normal on this side of the city; and as he turned into the terrace where aunt Lizette had her small flat, and saw a child bowling a hoop in the gardens opposite, it seemed ridiculous to remember the skidding car in Queen Street, the machine-gun fire, and the bitter flat voice of that man on the pavement, "They got Micky Farran. . . ."

He rang the bell at No. 5, and climbed the stairs to the little sitting-room, overfull of furniture, where aunt Lizette sat day after day, crocheting lace samplers to be sold for blind babies. Queer passionate hobby, that must have its origin, surely, in subconscious pity of her own childhood, when, lame and neglected, she lived in fear of a resentful stepmother. She rose smiling now, as he came into the room, her sallow complexion a little yellower than usual, her eyes blinking behind the spectacles.

"You dear boy," she said, and he noticed once more, with pleasure, that her voice had the soft, warm lilt belonging to Slane and the south, possessed also by his mother, which brought back to him always, rich and loved, the memories of boyhood.

"Your mother told me you would come, and I didn't believe her," said aunt Lizette, "for surely, I said to myself, a young man has better things to do than to visit an aunt when he comes home."

"Not this young man," said John-Henry. "He can't forget the peppermints you used to keep in your cupboard."

Aunt Lizette smiled, and took off her spectacles, and now he saw that her eyes were fine and handsome, like aunt Kitty's, and he thought of the happily-assorted household they had been out at Castle Andriff, aunt Kitty, aunt Lizette, and uncle Simon, all living together in harmony, with very few servants and too many dogs, until the children grew up and scattered, and aunt Kitty died, and aunt Lizette went on living alone with uncle Simon. These things happened only in this country.

"And your mother, how is she?" asked aunt Lizette.

"Very well, and very happy, and I was to thank you for the lace you sent her, which I believe made a table-centre for her dining-room. I'm to give you the money here and now. She wouldn't trust the post at the present time."

He felt for his wallet and took out a note.

"Ah, she shouldn't have worried," said aunt Lizette. "Time enough when all this shooting is over and everyone behaves like decent human beings. Were they fighting today, tell me, in the streets?"

"They peppered a few shop windows as I came down to see you, but I don't think much damage was done. What's it all about, aunt Lizette? You must be an unprejudiced person."

Aunt Lizette waited until the serving-maid had brought the tea and closed the door behind her.

"You have to be careful," she said softly. "I've had Meggie with me three years, but she has a brother fighting for the rebels. 'I haven't set eyes on him, Miss, not for six months,' she told me yesterday. She was lying, of course. The cigarettes I keep for visitors have been disappearing lately, and where would they be but down the front of Meggie's dress, so that she can slip out after dark and give them to him at the street corner?"

"You'd better be careful," smiled John-Henry. "You'll have the soldiers coming to search your house."

"And they'd find nothing," said aunt Lizette. "I'm a loyal subject of the King, and always have been, like the rest of the family. No Brodrick meddles with politics, although my father tried to stand for Parliament in his hey-days, just before your father was born."

John-Henry munched his buttered toast, and looked round the little room, so filled with furniture from Andriff and Dunmore—where aunt Molly had lived—and bits and pieces from Clonmere also, treasures that aunt Lizette had gathered around her with the years and would never part with now.

"As far as I can discover," he said, "no Brodrick has ever done anything but die young or drink himself to death."

Aunt Lizette frowned, and poured him out another cup of tea.

"The war and the Navy between them have made you a cynic," she said, "and anyway it's not true. The Brodricks were always greatly respected in the country."

"Who respected them, and what were they respected for?" asked her nephew.

His aunt sat back in her chair, and folded her hands. They were long and slender, the hands of a young woman, for all her fifty years.

"They were just landlords, for one thing," she answered, "right from the start. They did their duty to God and the King. They were firm to their tenants, but kindly too. And Clonmere always stood for law and order. The people looked upon it as a symbol of authority, of wise authority."

"Perhaps they did," said John-Henry, smiling over the rim of his cup, "but perhaps also they didn't want authority, or God, or the King—and you see the outcome of it all today. You know their motto, 'Ourselves Alone'?"

Aunt Lizette clucked her tongue impatiently.

"That's all nonsense," she said. "They can't exist that way. And don't tell me you sympathise with them, or I won't have you in my house. You ought to be ashamed of yourself, and you wearing the King's uniform a few months ago."

"I never said I sympathised with them," pleaded John-Henry. "I don't care a damn for one side or the other. It just happens that I have the misfortune to see both sides of a question."

"Don't go and live in Doonhaven, then," said aunt Lizette, "or you'll get rapidly worse. If it's raining there, and you should say how fine a day it is to anybody, they will agree with you, just to please your face, and save themselves trouble."

"But surely," said John-Henry, "that is the ideal way of living? If everybody did that there would be no arguments, no wars, no senseless fighting of one another?"

Aunt Lizette considered this a moment, then shook her head again.

"It wouldn't be moral," she said solemnly.

John-Henry laughed.

"Anyway," he said, "wet or fine, moral or immoral, I propose to go down to Doonhaven within the next day or so, and visit Clonmere. I haven't been down there, you know, since before the war, just before Granpie died. It's probably falling to bits, although the people at the gate-house are supposed to look after it."

"And what will you do?" said aunt Lizette, "when you get there?"

John-Henry smiled, and stretched out his legs under the tea-table.

"I shall live there," he said. "I may telegraph mother to come down and join me. Do you know, all the time I was in the Navy, and the war was going on, it was the only thing that was real to me? The Mediterranean, the Dardanelles, none of it seemed to sink in. I kept thinking, 'This over-grown sub who sweats his guts out in an engine-room and then goes ashore at Malta and overstays his leave, isn't John-Henry at all. The real John-Henry is standing in front of Clonmere, looking across the creek to Hungry Hill. And that's where I belong. That's where my roots are, that's where I was born and bred.' "

Aunt Lizette put on her spectacles and, moving to the window, took up her crochet.

"I was born there too," she said, "but my childhood was spent in London. And then, when I was ten, and your aunt Molly married, we all went home for Christmas. I shall never forget my first sight of the hills, and the colour of the water in Mundy Bay, and the old paddle streamer coming in to Doonhaven." She was silent for a moment, bending over her work. "But it's a great big house for a young man to live in all alone," she said.

"There'll be heaps to do," said John-Henry, "to get it right again. The woods will need clearings, and the gardens put in order. No half-measures for me, aunt Lizette. I'm not a sub in an engine-room any longer. I'm going to be John-Henry Brodrick of Clonmere, and damn all comers! No, not damn all comers, because I like the people, and I want them to like me. And you shall have the best spare-room, aunt Lizette, and when you come to stay we'll have a big turf fire lit in the great hall to welcome you."

"You don't propose living in the new wing, do you?" she said.

"Why not? My grandfather built it to be lived in, didn't he?"

"Yes, fifty years ago, when there were servants by the score, and carriages, and horses, and the mines working night and day on Hungry Hill. Doonhaven is only a sleepy village now, with no one to work for you, and the people shooting one another, as likely as not. Ah, now. . . . Do you hear that?"

As she spoke there was a sound of tramping feet at the end of the terrace, where it opened on to the road. John-Henry leant out of the window beside his aunt. Soldiers were going past in the main street, and in the midst of them two men in civilian clothes, with their hands behind them, their caps pulled down low over their eyes. A little crowd had collected on the pavement to watch them pass. A woman shouted out abuse at the soldiers, and one of them, mounted, rode towards the crowd, pressing them back. The tramp of marching feet passed on. . . .

"Ourselves Alone," whispered John-Henry, "and if you found one of them, your Meggie's brother, let's say, hiding in the kitchen, would you call in the soldiers and give him up?"

"He might have murdered innocent people. It would be my duty to give him up," said aunt Lizette firmly.

"You haven't answered my question," persisted John-Henry. "Would you give him up to the soldiers?"

She looked sideways at him, the dark eyes blinking behind her spectacles.

"I might then," she said softly, "but I'd sign my name to a petition to save him afterwards, all the same."

A shower of rain spattered the windows, and the sky darkened.

"Where are you staying?" she asked him.

"At the Metropole Hotel," he told her.

"Then, dear boy, you'd best be getting back. You don't want to be out in the streets at dusk. How will you get down to Doonhaven when you go? I don't know that the trains are running, or if the steamer goes from Mundy."

"I've got my car, aunt Lizette."

"You be careful, or they'll take it from you, and you trussed up like a fowl in the bottom of it—if you're not lying in a ditch with a bullet in your back."

"Maybe I'll join the rebels," he said, mischief in his eyes.

He kissed her goodbye, and went back through the silent streets to his hotel. There were sentries everywhere now, and he was challenged three times. The people were off the streets. The blinds were drawn across the windows of the houses. John-Henry went into the bar of the hotel. It was empty, except for the bartender and one young fellow of about his own age, or a little older, sitting in the corner, reading a newspaper. He glanced up when John-Henry entered, and then looked hard at him, with that questing stare of recognition which a man wears upon his face when he sees someone after a spate of years and has difficulty in finding a name. John-Henry turned his back, and ordered a whisky and soda.

"There's been a bit of trouble this afternoon, hasn't there?" he said to the bartender.

The fellow wiped a glass with a napkin, and glanced imperceptibly at the man in the corner, who had resumed his reading of the newspaper.

"Three people killed in the square," he said quietly, "or so I am told. I don't know anything about it. I've been in the hotel all day."

He went to the other end of the bar, and pretended to be busy with some glasses.

"Scared," thought John-Henry. "If he says a word more the chap reading a newspaper may inform against him. Where the devil have I seen that man before?"

But the newspaper was up in front of his face.

John-Henry sipped his whisky and soda, and thought about his aunt Lizette living all alone in her flat in the terrace, the youngest and most frail of all her family, and the last survivor—both aunt Kitty and aunt Molly had died during the war, in early middle age. We're a funny family, he thought, we either go quickly, or live to a rude old age. Grandfather Henry Brodrick was getting on for eighty when he died in Brighton. And his wife wouldn't let him be brought across the water and buried at Ardmore, she wanted him in the big white cemetery at Brighton. John-Henry remembered the letter coming from his mother when he was at Dartmouth, telling him that his grandfather had died, and in the holidays they had gone and picnicked at Clonmere and dreamt dreams about the future. The war came so swiftly, spilling the dreams. . . .

The door of the bar swung open, and three officers came in. They were laughing and joking.

"I tell you it's true," said one of them. "A whole party was over in London a year or so ago, and asked to see Casement's grave. They had brought wreaths and flowers and heaven knows what else. And the governor of the place hoodwinked 'em and showed them where Crippen or some chap was buried, and they went down on their knees and crossed themselves, and said 'Hail Mary'. Funniest thing you ever saw, said the governor."

The officers leant against the bar and ordered drinks.

"They're not human," said another. "We ought to have orders to shoot the lot. They're the scum of the earth, and always have been."

The first officer glanced across at John-Henry. He had merry eyes, for all his hard mouth.

"What are you drinking?" he said.

"The spirit of the country," said John-Henry, raising his glass.

"You'd better have one with us, then," said the officer, laughing. "It's the thing we are trying to down."

He put his hat on the bar, and John-Henry looked at it closely. The hated emblem of a hated band. Yet the man seemed harmless enough, and was only doing his duty, and obeying orders.

"Do you belong to this God-forsaken country?" asked the officer.

"I do," said John-Henry, "and what's more I intend to live in it."

"You must be crazy," said the other, "unless you're a sportsman. They know how to breed horses, if nothing else."

"Good woodcock shooting, where I belong," said John-Henry, "and snipe in the bogs, and hares on Doon Island and Hungry Hill. That's the only sort of shooting I care about, not this monkey-business you fellows have to do."

"Doon Island?" said one of them. "I had a friend garrisoned there at one time. It's quiet, I believe, down west of Mundy. The people won't play either way."

"Too idle," said John-Henry, "like myself. They only want to be left alone. And now what about having a drink with me? I don't suppose I'm the first of my countrymen to offer you hospitality."

The bartender came forward, and John-Henry moved up closer to the officers.

"Four whiskies and sodas for these gentlemen and myself," he said.

He listened with half an ear to the stories of the fighting, how the Town Hall, in a city farther north, had been seized by the rebels and set ablaze, and then the fellows had spent all their ammunition and taken to their heels and hidden out in the mountains.

"We went out to look for them," said the officer, "and brought them

all back, two of them dead from lying out there in the cold. We shot the
rest next morning. Oh, we have lively moments. It's not all sitting on
our backsides."

And this, thought John-Henry, has been going on through the ages,
and my family took no part in it. They lived at Clonmere, and built
their mines, and raised their copper, and came in here to Slane to the
shipping-office without caring a damn who bled on the roadside, as long
as they lived in comfort at Clonmere. And all I care about is for this
lunacy to be over so that I can do the same. The officers had swallowed
their drinks, and were fixing their belts.

"And now what?" said John-Henry.

"Patrol," said the first officer, "and maybe a knife under the ribs.
Come and join us."

"Not I," smiled John-Henry.

"We'll come and shoot woodcock with you," said the officer, "when
we've killed enough of your countrymen. Goodnight, and good luck."

"Goodnight," said John-Henry.

The bartender was putting up the shutters and fastening the bolts.

"That's the last of them," he said, "there won't be any more tonight.
You'll go up through the hotel entrance, if you please."

John-Henry glanced round the room. It was empty, except for himself and the bartender.

"There was a man in the corner," he said, "when I first came in. I
seemed to recognise his face. Do you know who he was?"

The bartender shook his head.

"We get all sorts these days," he said.

"He must have slipped away very quietly," said John-Henry. "I'm
sorry about it, because I had a feeling he came from Doonhaven."

The bartender ran a cloth along the side of the bar.

"If he came from your home," he said slowly, "it's a pity he saw you
drinking with the Black and Tans."

John-Henry stared at him.

"What do you mean?" he said. "I don't know those fellows. They're
nothing to me."

"No," said the bartender, "but this is a funny country. . . . Goodnight, sir."

He switched off the light over the bar as a signal of dismissal.

John-Henry walked slowly up the stairs to bed. He drew aside the
curtains of his room, and looked at the sky. The rain had cleared, and
the stars were shining. There was a clean fresh smell in the air of washed
streets, and night itself, and early spring. The church bell tolled out the
hour. Down in the street, below his window, the patrol marched by with
tramping feet.

The rain had all gone by morning, and the sun was shining as John-Henry drove out of Slane along the road to Mundy. His spirits were high, for he was young and in good health, and his car ran well, and he was going home. The dream of boyhood was to come true at last. Gone were the years of war, of stress, and duty, of travelling strange waters, of sweating under tropical skies. He had come back again, to the place where he belonged. And the air had a softness to it, belonging to no other country, the very hills were magic, with the morning mist upon them.

Aunt Lizette had doubted that he could live alone at Clonmere, twenty miles from any railway station. He would not know, she had said, what to do with himself; assuming that because he was war-weary he must be restless too, seeking company, and sport, and entertainment. John-Henry smiled, for restlessness belonged to the days at Salonika, where nothing was certain and nothing was true and fear was present in great measure; a man who trod his own soil and smelt his own land could never be restless, not if he loved it well. As for company, why, he had his own thoughts and dreams to spin at leisure, and the fascinating exploration of the past to make him understand the present. What was John-Henry but the outcome of the years? And looking back into the past he would learn about the future. Maybe a hundred years ago old Copper John had travelled this same road from Slane to Mundy, in confidence and strength, bequeathing to his great-great-grandson no ruggedness of character, no hardness of heart or monetary ambition, nothing but a strange facility for figures; so that lightning sums in the head and absurd mathematical calculations were the easiest thing in the world! Irony of time, that this was the only legacy handed down from the founder of the family fortunes, whose life's work, the copper mines, lay rusted and lichen-covered in the folds of Hungry Hill. Why, thought John-Henry, do I have a sentimentality for very small puppies, and birds that are maimed, and even wounded, blundering bumble bees? Is it because the son of Copper John loved greyhounds better than men, and could not destroy as much as a wasp upon a window-pane, for the good God made all things to live under the sun?

As he drove, bits and pieces of family history came back to him that his mother had gleaned for him from time to time, because she knew he loved the past. The turbulent Fanny-Rosa, who ran stockingless in the dew and broke the hearts of men, and her own as well perhaps, though she told it to no one; and the soft-eyed Jane of the picture, with her hand upon her heart, looking towards Doon Island.

"It was Fanny-Rosa Flower," his mother had said, nodding wisely, "who brought the bad blood into the Brodricks."

Alas, poor Johnnie. . . . His ceremonial swords still hung in the library at Clonmere, crossed, above the mantelpiece. John-Henry would get them down when he reached home, and clean them, and make them bright again, so that Johnnie in his grave would not feel himself forgotten.

"It will take time, son," said his mother, "getting the place to rights again. And you will have to buy furniture, you know, for the new wing."

"Even if it's the work of a life-time, no matter," said John-Henry.

If the floors were unscrubbed and cobwebs clung from the corners, at east it would be his plot of earth, his kingdom. Sport and entertainment; aunt Lizette had wondered about these.

There were woodcock and hares on the island, and snipe in the bogs by Kileen; killigs in the creek, and little brown trout in the lake on Hungry Hill. The people of Doonhaven were all the neighbours he wanted; and if the parson and the priest would sink their differences and take cold pig with him on Sunday, why, he would have done all that was necessary for the future of his country.

The dull miles lay behind him, and in front rose the pass, wild and rocky, with the heather and the gorse amidst the granite, tumbling to the road's edge. This, thought John-Henry, was where Copper John rode in his post-chaise the day he signed the lease for the copper mines with Robert Lumley, and Robert Lumley himself would have travelled down in gloomy state to Castle Andriff, from his solitary mansion at Duncroom, which lies naked to the skies now, razed to the earth by the rebels. The bitter feud—for what fine purpose and to what good end? Once again, John-Henry wondered why men must kill one another and spill blood under God's sky, when the gorse is scented, and the heather blows, and the snipe whistle and tumble in the bogs?

He slowed down the car, for the pass was narrow here, and as he turned the bend he saw, right in front of him, a barricade of torn heather and loose wire lying across the road, and beside it a man standing with a rifle in his hand. John-Henry drove slowly to the barricade and switched off his engine. The man did not move, except to cover him with the rifle, and then, putting two fingers in his mouth, he whistled loud and shrill. Some half-dozen figures crept down from the boulders above the pass. All of them were armed. John-Henry knew none of them. One, he supposed their leader, came to the door of the car and leant upon it.

"What's your name?" he said curtly.

"John-Henry Brodrick."

"Where are you going?"

"To my home, Clonmere, at Doonhaven."

"You served in the Royal Navy in the war, didn't you?"

"I did."

"What are your politics?"

"I have none."

"Were you staying last night in the Hotel Metropole in Slane?"

"I was."

"All right." He jerked his head to a couple of his companions.

"I shall have to ask you to get out of your car."

"What for?"

"That's our business. You'll not be harmed if you go quietly. Try to be funny with us, and we'll put a bullet between your shoulder-blades."

"What are you going to do to my car?"

"You won't see it again. Cars are too precious to us."

The man grinned for the first time. John-Henry shrugged his shoulders.

"I was warned not to take my car on the road. I've only myself to blame. Go ahead then. What do you want me to do?"

"Stand still while we bandage your eyes. I tell you again, we're not going to hurt you. Now put your wrists behind your back. Take his arm, Tim—you know what to do if he plays tricks."

What a damned fool he had been to fall into this trap! They had told him in Slane it was an act of lunacy to take a car out upon the road. And now he would probably be shot in the back and left to die on the hills. It was the loss of his car that angered him most. The old car, the faithful friend, being driven to hell and damaged by these madmen. No hope of ever getting it back again, of course. He cursed and swore uselessly to himself, as he stumbled over the heather and the stones, a man guiding him on either side. They must have walked three miles or more, in heaven knew what direction, before they came to a standstill, and there was a sound of a door being unlocked, and someone saying something in a low voice, and then the bandage was removed from his eyes and the bands from his wrists, and he was standing on the mud floor of an abandoned cabin. There was some loose straw in the corner. The small window was blocked with rags, and the hearth was black with long-burnt sticks and ashes.

"You'll have to stay here awhile," said the man who had unbound him. "I shall be outside on the hill, and my orders are to put lead into you should you run. I'll be bringing you something to eat and to drink."

"How long," said John-Henry, "is this foolery to go on? And what am I supposed to have done?"

"I don't know anything about it," said the man. "I have my orders, that's good enough for me."

And he went out, bolting the door behind him.

Oh, God damn them all, thought John-Henry; what in hell's name do they want with me, and why must I be mixed up in a revolution which means less than nothing to me, and with which I have no concern? He went and sat down upon the straw, for there was no chair or bench, and presently the man was as good as his word and brought him some bread, and some very sour cheese, and a pitcher of water.

"You haven't any ale, I suppose?" asked John-Henry.

"I have not," said the man, "but I have a flask on me with a drop of whisky in it, and you can have a spot of it if you're that way inclined."

John-Henry swallowed the whisky and the man smiled.

"Oh, that's all right," he said. "I can get more when I want it, and you'll be here till the morning, or maybe the day after, I don't mind telling you."

"Look here," said John-Henry, "you can take my wallet—there's twenty pounds in it—if you'll let me out of this place."

"I don't want your money," said the man. "We'd have taken it from you if we'd had the need. Is it robbers you think we are?"

"You stole my car, didn't you?"

"We borrowed it for the cause. When the country is free you can have it back again."

"That's nonsense, and you know it. Why am I kept here?"

"I tell you I don't know, and that's the plain truth, before God. Do you play two-handed whist?"

"I did once. I haven't played it for a long time."

"I have a pack of cards here in my pocket. If you're agreeable we could have a game, and it would help to pass the time. I can't do a thing outside your door but kick my heels and look at the heather. We might as well be company one for another as not."

"All right," said John-Henry, "bring out your cards."

They sat down together in the small, close cabin, with a patch of light coming in at the stuffed-up window, and they played two-handed whist, and finished the whisky in the flask. And this, thought John-Henry, is surely the madness of all time, that my captor and I pledge one another in illicit spirit, and he takes money off me in whist that he is too proud to steal, and we discuss the best method of snaring rabbits. Tomorrow he shoots me in the back, and maybe, as the sentry said in Slane, he will weep with pity and bring flowers to my funeral.

Two days passed, with the fellow Tim leaving him from time to time and coming back with bread, and sometimes cold bacon, or a fowl's leg, and more whisky in the flask to keep body and soul together, and each time John-Henry would ask him, "Well, Tim, when is the execution to be?", and each time Tim shook his head and said, "I've told you before, there's to be no execution."

"Then what am I doing in this confounded cabin?"

"You're having a rest, for the good of your soul," answered Tim, and out would come the greasy pack of cards, and tipple of whisky, and was it fifteen pounds that Tim had won now or seventeen? John-Henry did not remember, but it was fair exchange for the whisky, and maybe if he was warm enough in mind and body he would have no fear when they shot him in the hills.

The third night Tim brought rather more whisky than usual in his flask, and the guttering candle made a sickly light, and the cards stuck, and the few pieces of turf that they had kindled filled the room with smoke, so that John-Henry yawned and stretched and finally flung himself upon the straw and slept soundly, with his head pillowed in his hands. He woke to find a red dawn staring at him through the open door of the cabin, and his captor gone, and the white mist clearing away from the hills. He rose to his feet and rubbed his eyes and stared out upon the day, a lank, untidy figure, with straw in his hair and a three days' growth of beard, and he stood by the open door and felt the sun upon his face, and saw a curlew fly low over the hills and vanish. Then he looked upon the ground, and close to his feet, lying beneath a stone, was a newspaper, with the dew upon it, dated the day before. There was a cross on the front page, and a scrawling writing above it, saying "Turn to page 3." He opened the paper, and there on the centre page was a picture of Clonmere. The caption above the picture, in heavy black type, said "Historic Mansion Destroyed."

John-Henry knelt down and spread the paper on the ground, for his hands were trembling. He placed a stone at each corner of the page so that the morning wind should not blow the curling edges. Underneath the picture, in smaller print, were some half-dozen lines.

"Clonmere castle, at Doonhaven, on Mundy Bay, was last night burnt down by persons unknown. Some of the contents were saved by people in the village who woke and saw the house ablaze, but the building was a shell by morning. The owner, Mr John-Henry Brodrick, is believed to be in the country at the present time."

He knelt upon the ground, looking at the paper, and the first blind rage that filled his heart died suddenly away, leaving him cold, and stupefied, and numb. A lark rose from the ground to greet the day, and the mists rolled back, baring the bright sun. In the far distance shimmered the pale sea. And while the ruins of his home and the wreckage of his dreams stared up at him from the printed page, John-Henry saw once again the eyes of the man in the hotel in Slane, and the blue-eyed, freckled Tim grinning at him over the pack of cards, as, pledging John-Henry's future in a flask of whisky, he whispered, "Ourselves Alone."

3

The anger was spent, and the sorrow too. It seemed to him that he looked upon something that would stand for ever as a symbol in his heart, and could never be destroyed, whatever the fire might have done to the bricks and stones. The past would always cling to him, the unseen, ghostly hands of the people he never knew, but who had so great a part in him. This was no farewell, standing amongst the rubble. In a sense it was a dedication to the future. One day he would understand in full measure what it was that he had lost, and he would return again, because this was where he belonged. Now, being young, rage and grief that have such sharpness in their coming would quickly pass, and even now he felt something of a schoolboy's excitement, bent on treasure-seeking, as he stirred the embers with his feet and looked for the lost treasures.

The people had great delicacy. They stayed away, they did not trample

the grounds and stare at the blackened walls. He had his heritage to himself. And he knew that they had taken already the things they wanted,
for outside one of the cottages in Oakmount was part of a dresser that he
recognised, and a little child at the gate-house was playing with a porce-
lain vase that had stood once on the drawing-room mantelpiece. There
were other things, no doubt, lying snug and secure in the cottages at
Doonhaven, for a fire, like a wreck, is public property until law and
authority walk in. John-Henry was neither law nor authority. He was
someone who must take his chance in a country that was torn in civil war,
and if his possessions were lost to him he must suffer in silence. Little
remained, then, that he could bring away, except that lying on the bank,
untouched and quite unharmed, was the smiling portrait of great-great
aunt Jane, and he was glad of this because he had always loved it, and his
mother should have it in her house. The curious thing was that from a
little distance the walls of his home appeared untouched. The chimneys
stood, and all the windows, and it was only on approaching closely that
he could see that nothing had been left of the inside, and the ceiling was
the sky. Yet the foundations of every room remained. And he could walk
amongst the rubble and recognise each room, although no room remained.
The old part of the house had suffered most. The new wing, always
untenanted, looked as it must have done those fifty years ago when it was
being built and his father had climbed the scaffolding as a little lad. The
iron balcony above the great front door was twisted, but unbroken, and
it clung precariously from the blackened walls like a fairy thing, the
windows bare behind it, and the walls of the boudoir gone for ever. These
were what he valued most, for no known reason, the iron balcony and the
portrait of aunt Jane. With a strange impartiality the fire had spared
them both.

When John-Henry had finished probing amongst the stones, he stood
on the bank below the castle, and he saw coming towards him down the
drive a herd of cattle, which grazed by the wayside as they came, driven
by a leisurely fellow with a cap on the side of his head, who sucked a grass
stem as he walked. The cows took kindly to their new pasture, they
nosed the shrubs, and trod the soft gravel, and the leader of them, seeing
the creek below, led his followers down the bank to the water-garden,
amongst the wild plants that once had been the pride of Jane and
Barbara, and thence to the creek itself, where they drank deeply, raising
their heads now and again to gaze across the water. The cow-man
watched them, swishing the grass with his stick, but averting his eyes
from the ruins of the castle all the while as though from delicacy.

John-Henry walked down the bank to join him, and the man took the
grass stem from his mouth and touched his cap.

John-Henry felt at once that the man, who was young, about his own
age, had a face that was familiar to him, seen surely within the last week,
and in a sudden wave of perception he saw a likeness to the man in the

bar of the hotel in Slane. For a moment he said nothing but "Good-day," and the pair of them stood staring at the cattle which grazed below.

"Were you here when they burnt the house?" said John-Henry at last. The man shook his head, and went on looking at his cattle.

"I was not," he said, "I was in bed up at my house, and I had no knowledge of it until my mother told me." He paused a moment, and then he said, as though in afterthought, "It was nobody in Doonhaven that did it."

John-Henry lit a cigarette, and smoked awhile in silence.

"I'm glad of that," he said. "I've done none of them any harm. I remember your face, but I can't put a name to it."

"Eugene Donovan," said the man, "grandson to Pat Donovan who had the farm up by Hungry Hill when you were a boy. My father was called Jim Donovan. He went to South Africa when they closed the mines here."

"That's right," said John-Henry. "I remember you now. You took over the farm then, when your grandfather died. Didn't you have a brother?"

"I have a brother Michael. He did not care about farming."

"What's happened to him?"

"We've seen nothing of him this long while. He was friendly to Pat O'Connor and some of the boys."

"Ah! I see."

And in the half-veiled admission John-Henry understood that no more would ever be revealed. But he could trace now the story from the beginning, and he could see again the face of Michael Donovan in Slane. He would have gone from the hotel to his friends outside the city, and told them that John-Henry Brodrick of Clonmere gave drinks to the enemies of his country, and was a traitor to his home and to his land. And so they came by night and burnt his house. Not Michael himself, nor any of the men of Doonhaven, because to do so would have brought ill-luck upon them, and the Saints would not have wished it. John-Henry knew this, and Eugene Donovan the cow-man knew it too, but they did not speak of these things. Justice had been done. There was no more to be said.

It was strange, thought John-Henry, that his family had striven now for generations to bring progress to the country, and the country did not want it, and his family would not learn. Nearly two hundred years ago Morty Donovan had shot John Brodrick in the back because he tried to interfere with the ways of the people. Duty, law, discipline, obedience, John Brodrick tried to enforce these rules upon the smugglers of Doonhaven, and they would have none of them. All that remained of John Brodrick today was a stone in a forgotten churchyard, and his life's blood that welled up in the creek year by year, so the legend ran. But the people smuggled still, and took their landlord's cattle, and fished forbidden waters, and the first John Brodrick might have lived longer and died in blessed old age had he the sense to understand the people could not be driven, and the land was theirs. Copper John made the mines, and the mines lay blackened on the hills, covered with gorse and heather and lichen, the ruins of an industry that no one had desired. John-Henry had seen the chimney-stacks like tombstones amidst the granite as he had come down from Mundy to Doonhaven, and he knew too how, when the civil war was over, tourists would stare at the ruins of Clonmere as they had done upon the wasted mines in his own boyhood. Relics that had failed, and would return, as the years passed, to the soil which gave them birth.

"And you," said John-Henry to the cow-man, "have you no ambition to follow your brother Michael and fight battles for your country?"

Eugene Donovan smiled, chewing the grass stem between his teeth, and he pointed with his stick to the cattle, which had left the creek and were grazing now beneath the windows of Clonmere.

"You see those cows now," he said. "Always, since I was a lad, I had a wish to graze them here. No more than a fancy, you see, but it was there, at the back of my mind. And when the fire came the other night and destroyed the castle, I said to myself, 'Now at last I can graze the cattle there.' But I tell you God's truth, I had no hand in it."

"Is that all you want?" asked John-Henry.

Eugene Donovan thought a while, and looked back over his shoulder at the castle.

"There are stables in behind there," he said. "The fire did not touch them, and with a pound or two I could make a cow-house out of them. It's poor grazing up on the hill to what you have here."

John-Henry felt in his wallet, and he found there the three pounds that remained to him. The others had been won off him at whist by the freckled Tim.

"You can have the stables, if they are any use to you," he said, "and the ground for grazing, and these few pounds to put the stables the way they should be."

Eugene Donovan took the notes and counted them. "You're free with your money," he said.

"It's all that's left to me," said John-Henry. "That's where my family went astray, I'm thinking. I have the silver, you have the land. I would prefer it should be the other way round, but they've left me no choice."

"You're a gentleman," said Eugene Donovan; "you can travel and see the world. Sure, you can build yourself a finer house across the water than the one that lies here."

John-Henry did not answer. The rain was falling gently now from a grey wisp of cloud that had come across the sun. He turned up the collar of his coat, and thrust his hands into his pockets. Eugene Donovan pulled his cap over his eyes, and whistled to the mongrel dog that followed him. Through a rift in the clouds there came, for a brief instant, a white shaft of sunlight on the face of Hungry Hill.

3/92 CENTRAL

STAC. 8/95